FOR
JUST KISS ME

FORGET HEAVEN, JUST KISS ME

Jeremy Vine

HODDER AND STOUGHTON
LONDON SYDNEY AUCKLAND

British Library Cataloguing in Publication Data
A Catalogue record for this book is available from the British Library
ISBN 0-340-58985 X

Published by Hodder and Stoughton, a division of Hodder and Stoughton Ltd, Mill Road, Dunton Green, Sevenoaks, Kent TN13 2YA. Editorial Office: 47 Bedford Square, London WC1B 3DP.

Typeset by Phoenix Typesetting, Ilkley, West Yorkshire.

Printed in Great Britain by Cox & Wyman Ltd, Reading.

To my mum and dad.

– 1 –

I'm the sort who'll never marry.

As I pulled back a gear and bounced on the brow of a hill, the football-pitch-sized brown roofing of Saint Peter's reared into view, down among the shops and offices. It looked like some huge pimpled tabletennis bat in the hands of a player about to take a swipe at a ball.

My thoughts – and here I yanked down a hand on the steering wheel, partly to stay in lane, and partly out of a kind of teeth-gritting frustration – were just about as downright unclerical as they could possibly be.

Right foot, as it were, on the threshold of a brand new existence (though in reality pumping a ragged accelerator to take a green Vauxhall Saloon on the inside), I'm telling myself I won't ever find a wife.

A stab of a button on the car cassette machine, Elvis Presley breaking into 'I Just Can't Help Believing', and me braking . . . to join the end of a mile-long jam, tyres squealing in curious harmony with the King.

At the end of the jam: a big, big church. Bigger than I had expected, for sure, when I first saw it on a visit to the Rector to be interviewed about the job as his number two.

Meeting a second time, he had congratulated me on the appointment with handshakes and an inexplicably pained expression, shot through with what looked like embarrassment. I put it down to shyness.

'The post of curate,' the Rector had explained as he watered an obviously dead cactus plant on the windowsill of his office, 'is not easy. Sometimes it can be hard, and sometimes it can be easy. It can be very hard, and there are times when you will find it hard to see it as anything other than very difficult indeed. But we trust that in those times, God will make it easy. Even though that will be hard.'

And so it was that the Reverend Douglas Tredre, fifty-four, came across initially to me, his soon-to-be-new-curate, Reverend Mark Empringham, twenty-eight, as a genial bungler with a wide and vacant smile who might well have played rugby for Cambridge and been in several losing sides. Douglas would repeat adjectives and words *ad nauseam* as though sending them out like dogs to surround whatever point he was trying to make; full stops played little part in his conversation.

I was surprised when he wrote with the news that I had got the job. The hour-long session with him, four members of the Parochial Church Council as well as someone described as Associate Director of Pastoring had not, my sensors suggested, gone well at all. *That was heavy. A grilling,* I had told myself afterwards.

But I was far more surprised by the peculiar sequence of events following my appointment.

Naturally, I had rung the church office instantly to express delight. But the church secretary suddenly became unavailable. 'Praying,' someone had explained. I tried the main number and asked for the Rector. Two calls were cut off. A third was disconnected after several seconds with what sounded like an electronic raspberry.

Finally, I found the ex-directory number of the Tredre flat, and rang it. A woman answered.

'Who's speaking?'

'No, I don't mind waiting at all,' I had piped in an assumed voice that was brisk, female and slightly Cornish.

Then the Rector spoke, and I introduced myself . . . and, amid considerable confusion at the other end, my call was passed to a room he said he would sprint to. Soon he appeared on the line again, breathlessly expressing delight.

At long last, one communication after another did materialise at my small Midlands church, confirming the wish to have me and laboriously distilling the duties of a curate in London – and I concluded Douglas was a better manager of people and things than his blinking, wandering, narrow eyes, erratic grin and Cambridge rugby loser's bluster suggested.

Besides, as he later told me, his sport was fencing at Nottingham Polytechnic. And the team won.

'I'm sorry my suit is crumpled and I'm in a bit of a state.' I uttered the apology as Douglas's padded hand shook mine, his tea-cosy hairstyle wobbling with the motion.

'London traffic,' he said. 'I know. We had a group of missionaries here from South-east Asia last week. They'd been on a trek through jungle territories near Jakarta – they spent three months just cutting creepers and long grasses and swimming across dangerous rivers and hiking for miles across mud and wastelands and jungle. When they got back here two of them were in tears because of the trip.'

'I imagine parts of Indonesia can be rough.'

'Oh – but it wasn't Indonesia that upset them. It was the Hanger Lane Gyratory System.'

The Rector launched into a nightmarish description of a road junction, and, as he did, took me by the arm. Bouncing against the sides of a thin corridor, we passed through a white door with no handle.

We were in the church.

'So this is it – as you know. We think it's beautiful, beautiful, and you're so welcome here, Mark.'

I lost breath. I had forgotten. It was massive.

Row upon row of pews; a balcony, seats ranking right and left; a central section over the entrance; benches rising to the vaulted ceiling. Two thick pillars at the rear; down the sides, white stone arching out from the walls. Big windows, odd panes stained in playgroup-palette purples and greens.

We were on the edge of a jet-black raised crescent of floor, by a skinny pulpit carved in dark wood. Fringed sheeting hung from a rudimentary altar table. Organ pipes stood leaden like soldiers, bolt upright against the wall, huge, dead central and towering.

'We are trying to change with the times and have less organ,' I heard Douglas saying, but I was barely listening. I had glimpsed a picture, a large picture, close to us on the right-hand wall, hanging there, and my heart had snagged on something worse than Hanger Lane traffic.

'We have guitars. A fellow called Philip Harming – um – no, hold on – '

Douglas struggled for the name, and I looked up at spots in the ceiling where small octagons of plaster had fallen.

'Richard Burts. That's him. Charming fellow, lovely man, and plays guitars. Plays guitars and it's sort of a rebirth, when the new music comes in. We love it. Oh yes.'

My heart was still snagged, with black fingers pressing on it, and I felt an urge to disagree with all guitars. I smiled instead.

'It's certainly a change from the West Midlands.'

'We are so lucky – so blessed – with this site. It's so busy. I gather your old place wasn't quite so – '

'No,' I said. It hadn't been 'quite so' anything. 'We were so remote, people set off for services with backpacks.'

'But you had some believers there, people who had – '

'And my old church was only about an eighth – '

' – a relationship – '

' – as big, graveyard included, though of course – '

' – with God?'

Then it seemed for a moment as though time and conversation had stopped for ever. In unison, the two of us quietly breathed the faintly perfumed air of the building.

Stepping forward, Douglas spoke. 'This pulpit – come – '

We were beside the pulpit now, and Douglas rolled the heel of his hand enthusiastically on the bevelled end of its banister. Then he walked easily up its creaking steps as though he had done it a hundred times.

'I've done this a hundred times,' he said. 'At least. I walk up here with my notes and look out. One fellow – his head just lolls, lolls, and before I've taken the clip off my sermon he's slumped and he's asleep. Thirty rows back.'

Looking out at the expanse of pews, Douglas might have been addressing just himself. He was chuckling.

'Someone once gave the chap some sort of resuscitation thing. It was one of the older nurses, off shift of course. I remember the light flashing on the watch on her breast pocket. She had him stripped to the waist before he woke up.'

I laughed. He stretched out his fingers and rolled his palms on the wooden rail of the pulpit. 'This, Mark, is actually the oldest thing in the church. Bought by American friends, who said they would like to remain – er – named.'

It was tempting to ask on cue just how old the pulpit was, but I feared a long answer about the Napoleonic Wars or the era of Pitt. I needed to pull luggage from the Datsun. And only one question begged hard enough to be asked now.

Looking up at Douglas where he stood at the summit of the pulpit, I asked it.

'Incidentally – whose place is it I'm taking here?'

I was stunned by the electric effect of the sentence.

One of the Rector's legs twitched in the manner of a footballer about to shoot for goal, and he ended up leaving it bent only as innocently as a guilty man can, with the toe of his brogue pointing to the floor like a ballet dancer who has abandoned a complicated movement because of poor fitness.

'His name – ' he began wistfully, but then, rather than just saying it, he dropped his shoulders and slid his palms out along the rim of the pulpit, looking away from me.

'It was – was – was – '

Whether or not the Rector was about to say the name may never be known. There was suddenly an ear-shattering and terrifying bang, which ricocheted about the empty hall . . .

. . . and was followed by a loud sound like fingernails scraped down a blackboard.

There was a deafening, booming thump.

Then silence.

My first conscious reaction was to duck my head. But I had already jammed my neck back into my shoulders and dropped the whole of my trunk instinctively – and so I looked up.

Douglas seemed to have ducked not just his head, but his whole body. He had completely disappeared from view.

I moved round the base of the pulpit. There was a small, controlled, groan. 'I am so terribly sorry. Sorry.'

The Rector came into view as I heard his voice and peered round into the pulpit. He appeared to have shot through the pulpit floor. Pieces of broken boards, pointing downwards, hemmed him in at the chest like arrows. His jacket had been caught on the way down, and he now looked like the monster in a science fiction film, who, exposed as a robot or worse, is seen in the final frames reduced to head and shoulders, melting into a puddle of grey.

Fumbling, I asked: 'Do you want me to get some help?'

'I think – I'm not sure – I don't think I'm hurt – at least –' Douglas smiled grimly, and bent, then flexed, his arms. His elbows gave way.

'Mark, I am so terribly sorry. This happened once before, to a woman who was speaking on the Resurrection.'

'I'll get help.'

'I think you might have to. Might have to.' There was a scraping and tearing sound. 'I can't come to any harm. But I think this jacket won't be good for very much else.'

I thought of climbing the rickety steps to try to pull my new employer up from above, but feared the whole contraption might collapse on top of him.

'It's no problem,' Douglas said. 'I don't mind waiting. I can't come to any harm here. The thing's obviously rotten, rotten across the floor here, and we didn't mend it properly last time. A bit of glue and that was all. I'm sorry, Mark.'

'I'm just relieved you're not hurt.' He would have heard the relief in my voice. 'I thought someone was firing a gun.'

'Funny you should say that, but we've never had a gunman in here. We've had an archer, but he was caught before –'

Douglas's sentence trailed off in a kind of sigh, and we both paused. Then he coughed.

'No rush to get me out, Mark. It was obviously rotten through. As long as I'm out by five. I've got a meeting.'

I looked at my watch. It was a quarter to twelve. 'I'll call for help now.'

I bounced from the stage and started down the aisle, catching the painting in my right eye. In full view, the face of Jesus Christ. It seemed quite irritating and unnecessary.

Then there was a high-pitched shout – my name, I thought – from within the pulpit, and, half-running, I looked back.

I could not see Douglas, but I heard his voice.

'Welcome, welcome to Saint Peter's,' he was shouting.

I'm the sort who'll never marry, I was thinking.

— 2 —

Long stretches of that day went by like parts of a dream.

Moonlike, smiling faces floated up to my own, eyes looking deep into mine; my hands were grabbed and shaken like knots in bell ropes. There might have been a million genial and warm encounters with staff and volunteers in the vestry and the domed lobby, out on the steps as I hauled baggage from the car, in the administration office, the tea room, the tiny youth centre annexed above the kitchens.

Question: how many members of the staff at Saint Peter's does it take to change a lightbulb?

Answer: all of them. Except BBF. He hadn't noticed the lightbulb was broken.

The woman running the mission to students told me the joke, blocking my way on the spiral staircase which led up to the church flats. I had been about to see mine.

The man she gently mocked, Dr Barry Bryan-Fryers, PhD, was Stipendiary Parson of Saint Peter's. The origin of the title was unclear. Sixty-eight years old, short, almost bald, and with a brain powerful enough to light six towns during a Cup Final, BBF was a kind of resident academic. Earlier in life he had stunned Oxford with a hundred per cent score in a final-year theology examination; now he wrote books and preached on big occasions – living, with his wife, on a church stipend.

But those around him feared the brilliance was not allied to even a simple grasp of real life. In one example, an anonymous tip-off to a diocesan newspaper had revealed how, on his seventh driving test, BBF had taken the examiner's instruction to 'drive straight ahead unless told to do otherwise' quite literally . . . and, on a corner within sight of the test centre, ploughed straight through a fence and over an embankment.

Luckily, the Stipendiary Parson was better known for his sabre-sharp preaching and meaty books unravelling the intricacies of the Old Testament: *The Spirit of Samuel, The Heart of Ruth, The 'Y' of Deuteronomy, The Eyes of Isaiah*, and, most recent to date, *The Foul Language of Leviticus* . . . which, amid reports of publishers' surprise, had outsold all the others.

So I chuckled at the joke, hoping to please its teller, Vanessa Spicer, who had begun by asking for details of Douglas's accident. She did not get my full attention until she unleashed a form of sonic boom laughter, which I could easily imagine rearranging my hair as it swept around me.

'Thank goodness he's all right and he managed to get out. Through the planks with a crash! That is just so funny.'

She roared again, and I wondered if one of the latest batch of European Community laws might not be enforceable against this level of noise.

'That story will run and run here, Mark, I promise. But thank goodness he's safe. It did happen once before, though – to a woman who was speaking on John twenty.'

'I thought she was speaking on the Resurrection.' I recalled Douglas's account, and wanted to display alertness.

Vanessa looked at me strangely. 'Yes – the Resurrection. The gospel of John, chapter twenty.'

'Of course. In the Bible.'

I returned her glance with a crumbling smirk. The pillar of youth work was tall – in her late twenties – with a hairdo from the cover of a sixties fashion magazine. Her bright blue eyes, like saucers, appeared to me (I was looking closely up at them now, recovering from the jolt of John twenty, almost peering into those eyes) as though tears had just coursed through them.

Hold on, I thought. *This girl has just been crying.*

She was built like an exclamation mark, and had a sharp, pert nose, tight lips, golfball-sized pink circles in her cheeks, those wide eyes that gave her a fixed look of astonishment, and . . . and what was it, anyway, that had made her cry?

Vanessa talked at the speed of Formula One cars.

'If you're wondering about my work, with the students, it's really all to do with mixing – '

'Mixing?'

' – well, mixing this world and the one outside. Mixing students with each other. Yes, of course they fall in love and drink and so on, but we want them to be able to come here and find something refreshing – I'm getting muddled – '

'No, go on, I – comprehend,' I said. I reserved the word 'understand' for counselling.

'They don't want rules and regulations. They want something refreshing.'

I thought of lemonade. 'How do they get that?'

'Just Christ, Mark. We try to put Christ at the centre.'

'Yes,' I said, finding the answer grotesque. 'Yes. I see. And I imagine they're quite a lively group – '

'Lively isn't the word – they really are lively. Some of them played a prank recently – we have a fairly big PCC that runs the church, an elected council, you know – and one of the students, from King's, I think it was, he entered a plant for the Council – a plant, in a pot – and of course, these meetings – the thing got through on a show of hands.'

'What sort of a plant was it?'

'Oh, a cactus, I think. They put it up for a vote – you don't get asked to make a speech or people would have spotted it – they put it up under the name Andrew Prickles.'

She laughed again. I would have to check my hair later.

'I think Douglas keeps it on his windowsill,' she said.

'He does sometimes joke about it having a casting vote.'

'Actually, I think I may have seen it there,' I put in. 'Though I'm worried it might have died.'

More laughter, then: 'I may send my sister up to meet you in our flat – you know you're in the same flat as me, don't you? The only problem is, she's not a Christian. Later on, just to see if you need any help. I think you'll really like her, Mark. Mark – are you all right?'

It's true that I had grown a little dizzy and was now leaning back against the banister. In the distance, I could hear organ music. I trusted it was really there.

'I'm fine,' I said.

'You've gone white.'

'There's still quite a lot for me to do – like buying stamps – ' and now I was thinking of what it would be like to share a flat with this woman. With any woman! I had no idea there was a question of sharing a flat, particularly not with a woman, and had assumed I would have a place to myself. No, I was not fine at all: the thought of it had made alarm escalate in my oesophagus, a bead of hot mercury.

I gulped air.

'You must lie down. You're as white as a notice sheet.'

'It's been a – a day. But I'm fine. Honestly.'

I have no confidence with women. At my last church, one seemed to become attracted. She would touch my arm at coffee and sometimes, as I preached, our eyes would meet. She would hold my stare for a second, as though practising her grip. So I took evasive action, like pulling out of prayer groups at the last minute to stop her following me into them.

But it became more difficult. For I began to desire her. She had a head of brown curls, an intriguing chip in a front tooth, a lovely figure. And then suddenly she had Matthew too, Matthew with the nobbly rings, the job in a Birmingham investment firm and the pitted face. He proposed and she said yes. And then they asked me to take the service.

Oh, it started normally enough. Elephant-hipped women rustled convoluted pleating in the aisle of the little church as husbands, sons and daughters wriggled into pews. Our organist hit the keys so hard that the sound of flesh on chipped ivory was as loud as the notes themselves.

Then Emily came to the front of the aisle, drifting down it, swathed in music, and our eyes met.

Me, smiling, aware of the large and expectant audience.

She, breathtaking in white, radiant like a spotlight.

I went to pieces.

Trembling in my place at the front, I dropped the order of service down an air vent. It was retrieved only after an eleven-year-old on the groom's side produced a screwdriver.

Then there was a disaster with the rings.

Somehow, in those gasping and tragic moments as I realised I was marrying the girl I loved, but marrying her to a pit-faced fund manager, a green-crested ring my grandfather had bequeathed me arrived in the hands of the bridegroom.

Unsure that it was the wrong one, and not wanting to create a disturbance or be the origin of family legend by asking silly questions at a wedding, he put it on. I was then forced to take from the bride the ring she was supposed to give him, and, because slipping it into my jacket pocket would have made the mistake too obvious, fitted it on to my own index finger. The eyebrows of her father, who stood alongside us, rigid, did such a set of acrobatics that I feared one might fly off his face.

The seven-minute nugget of a sermon they had asked of me was also disastrous. My theme was the importance of love. *Hah,* I thought, *Mark, who loves you now?* But the talk became a kind of tombola, with nonsense spluttering out almost at random. My confusion was so severe at one point that I blurted out the word 'Kojak,' as an equally dramatic wedding scene from an American detective series came to mind. Trying to fit the name into my theme, I wound up explaining shakily how those who are not loved, and do not love, could be said – I tentatively suggested it – to suffer a kind of spiritual baldness.

I would never forget the shape and motion of Matthew's back as the two of them moved off, down the aisle, at the end. I felt I had stabbed it with my incompetence.

The wedding was a watershed.

What with holiday and preparations to leave Straithe, the sermon had been my last to date. I became preoccupied with the fact that whatever else being a curate did, it put confidence with women stage centre. A curate's relations with people like Vanessa were spotlit all over. There was no friendship that did not have the talon-like shadow of the pulpit drifting across it. Saint Paul's comment somewhere, that singleness was the best state, gave little comfort in the face of stark reality.

At this precise moment, though, standing on the stairs with Vanessa, stark reality was a toaster.

I caught the end of what she was saying.

' – so if you can remember that, you'll be safe with it. The toaster just takes a bit of practice and an alert mind. On the right of the sink, by the way, are the black bags – '

'Bags for the dustbin – fine,' I said. 'How many floors up am I – are we?'

'Black bags. Yes. Another floor up from here.' That was three storeys. 'And no lift for us, I'm afraid.'

'Great, Vanessa, thank you – nice to bump into you – '

I made a move up one stair, coming closer to her than I would have liked. But she twisted, blocking me again.

'I just wanted to ask, Mark, what your surname was?'

What a peculiar question to ask at the end of a long conversation, I thought.

But as with all questions now, it had been asked genially and warmly. I was tempted to counter by asking her what it was that had made her cry moments before we had met.

'It's Empringham,' I replied instead.

'Oh yes. I remember it now.'

'And yours?'

'Spicer.' She smiled engagingly. 'I don't like repeating it because I don't like it.'

'Of course,' I said, suddenly wanting to complain strongly about everything, and wondering how many lone women liked their surnames.

Now she was pointing.

'Down there – ' I turned and looked out of the window. The street was packed with rush hour traffic. 'That's – I think – yes, look! The white one. BBF's car. Just there – '

'I see. Slowing down now.' It was on the far side of Clemence Road, presumably coming towards the church car park.

'He's about to turn right, I think,' Vanessa said. The car drifted into the centre of the road. 'He's probably been out making a high-powered speech – or just going to talk to the homeless in the parks around Charing Cross, which – '

The car, indicating right, lurched forward a yard as if in an attempt to get between an oncoming truck and taxi.

' – is something he likes to do – '

It lurched forward again, then flew round in an arc and shot across the near lane, into the alley that led down to the parking spaces. A Ford Escort in the near lane stopped dead to avoid hitting it, and – my eyes widened in their sockets – a long, red saloon that had probably been going too fast crashed into the back of the Escort.

We heard the distant smashing of glass against metal, and metal on metal; and then we heard it twice more.

'I don't believe it,' whispered Vanessa.

I was speechless. Down on the road, a taxi and another car had ploughed into the back of the saloon. Horns were sounding. Everything on the far side was at a crawl. Cars on the near side were blocked completely. Drivers got out to inspect the damage.

We watched the scene in silence for a few minutes, and then a third person joined us there on the stairway.

'Mark – can I introduce you – to our Stipendiary Parson.'

I turned to look into those legendary eyes, which I had previously seen only on book covers.

BBF was shorter than expected, with sloping shoulders. He grinned, and the crows' feet went so far back into the side of his head it looked like his scalp might fall off.

'I'm just on my way up to my flat,' he said. 'Mark, Mark – welcome along.' He shook my hand as warmly as it had ever been shaken. 'You ought to see the mess on the road out there. There's been a dreadful smash-up. I saw it on my way up. It's an accident blackspot, that bit down there.'

'We saw it happen,' I said, cautiously.

'Did you? But you know, they happen all the time in London. A hundred a day, I hear. It's mostly youngsters –'

Perhaps I smiled a little too nervously, for Doctor Barry Bryan-Fryers, PhD, Stipendiary Parson, seemed to become a touch self-conscious.

'Well, I must say, it is delightful to have a curate with us at last,' he said, sighing, and turning to Vanessa.

'We've just been getting to know each other,' she said, and I winced as if the words were pincers on a sore tooth.

'I'm delighted to be here. Excited, as well.'

'Remind me, Mark, where are you from? Darlington?'

Darlington? I thought. *Miles away.*

'Straithe – in the West Midlands,' I told him. 'All Saints.'

'Straithe. Yes, I think I know it. Well – I hope you'll be splendidly happy here, and that your first sermon goes magnificently for you. And everything else. And that God is glorified in what you do.'

'Has a date been set for it yet?' I asked.

BBF paused. 'Dates and things I don't really know about, Mark. They tease me about it,' he said, beginning to move past us. 'But check with Douglas – he knows everything.'

'Everything,' Vanessa chuckled.

'Good.' I joined in the chuckling.

Vanessa moved down a stair, and we were alongside each other.

'Just by the way,' I started quietly, aware of a slight quiver in my voice, 'just for my own interest – can you tell me who the last curate was?'

Someone blew a horn in the street below.

– 3 –

I went to the door clutching my right forearm, rapidly thrusting out fingers and then closing them into a fist.

'Hi,' my visitor said.

'Sorry.' We both looked at my hand. 'I've just had a terrible shock. An electric shock.'

'I hope this isn't another one. Vanessa said you were expecting me.'

She walked into the flat. It sounded as though the fact that a high voltage had just banged through the fingers of my right hand was not considered relevant to the visit.

'What's happened to you?'

'I just put some bread in the toaster. It's lucky I didn't touch it with a foot and a hand at the same time.'

'I'll ask my sister. That sounds dangerous.'

'Oh – you must be –'

'Vicki,' she said. 'I must be Vicki and I am Vicki. Vanessa's sister, the black sheep of England, whatever you want to call me. Twenty-two, and pleased to meet you.'

Ah.

I warmed slightly. Somehow naked aggression was less overpowering than a syrupy smile, or creamy purr with milky eyes. Vicki's approach was the social equivalent of an aniseed ball. But at least you knew what you were biting on.

'Well – I twisted the thing up to brown, or deep brown – the brownness control – and I got a shock when it hit eight.'

'Was that the scream I heard as I came up the stairs?'

'It must have been. I jumped back and banged my head.'

'You'll survive,' she said. 'Just about.'

Vicki was lean, serious faced, and short. Unlike her sister's, Vicki's figure was formless and flat. She had hair so close-cropped it might have been the work of an army hairdresser.

And this, it appeared, was a girl who might well be welcomed by the army on grounds other than hairstyle. Her words were driven at me like fixed bayonets.

'If you're going to try and convert me, don't worry yourself. Vanessa's been trying for eight years, and I always just mention the midgets of New Guinea and she shuts up.'

'New Guinea?'

'What happens to the people there who haven't heard of God? The Bible says they're going to hell.'

'No, what it says, in – ah – in Genesis – er – in –'

She held up a bony hand. 'Come on, I did say.'

'I just –'

'No point in saying everything she's said. I'm here to see if you want any help with the flat. Vanessa sent me up here, if you want to know. If that's not rude.'

'Well –' I raised my arms a touch from my sides with a kind of surrendering shrug. 'I'm Mark, anyway.'

'Mark –'

'Empringham, yes. I seem to have everything up here.'

'You don't mind sharing with Vanessa?'

Now I had to be careful. I did not want to mislead; I could not tell the whole truth. 'It's a lovely flat.'

'You sound like a Liberal Democrat. Avoiding the question. Mind you, they don't get asked very many these days.'

Not wanting to veer into politics – shaky ground, since, after a muddle with my licence fee, I had had no television in Straithe – I veered too far in the direction of honesty.

'Well, I suppose it was a bit of a surprise –'

'They didn't tell you? Well, it's so busy here, from what I see of the place, once in a blue moon – '

'What do you do in London?'

'Nothing so far. I work in Coventry. Newspaper sales. Classifieds. But I'm moving down. Up, really. To *The Times*.'

She plumped herself on an armchair pushed against one wall. Office blocks ranged over her head like mountains.

'Nice flat. Good view behind me.'

'Yes.'

Vanessa apart, I was quite pleased with it. Two sizeable bedrooms, a well-stocked kitchen. A good lounge, too, with shelved first reprints of scores of theology books and a sprawling rug bearing a wheel of purples and greens.

'Hand all right?'

'Sorry. I'm being a baby. But it's still tingling.'

'My sister should have told you about the toaster.'

'Never mind.' I laughed, nervously. 'Forgiveness.'

There was a brief silence.

'You unpack,' said Vicki, reading my thoughts.

I did like her directness. Atheists in the West Midlands had never tried to score points using New Guinea midgets. That said, at theology college more arguments had been sparked off over what the Bible said was in store for those who had never heard its message than over anything else. One, at a meal table, had even escalated into a fist-fight which led to a student being stretchered to the local casualty unit after a corn on the cob, thrown across the room in anger, hit him in the eye. Another trainee cleric was expelled from the college altogether, after punching someone during an argument about heaven.

Vicki drank tea and ate biscuits as I moved about the flat, ferrying possessions.

'Do you know people here?' I called from the bedroom.

'Nope. Only one – black guy called Daniel. From a party a year ago. We just clicked, I suppose. Just about. I was in Nigeria when I was little – so was he.'

I appeared in the door frame between my bedroom and the lounge. 'It's just that I asked your sister this afternoon about the last curate. It was most peculiar. She suddenly thought of something she had to discuss with the Stipendiary Parson – it was all done quite politely, but – '

'Yes, I know who you mean.'

'The curate? You're saying you know the – '

'No, the Stipend – the Dipend chap – '

'The Stipendiary Parson.'

'Barry Firefighter, or whatever he's called.'

'Doctor Barry Bryan-Fryers. No, I mean – getting back to the curate – it just struck me – that – that perhaps they didn't want to talk about him, or something – I don't know.'

'Why not? The last curate? Why shouldn't they?'

'I know – it sounds ridiculous. It's not as if I'd say anything to anyone. I don't know anyone here, for a start.'

'You soon will.'

'Did you meet him?' I asked.

'The curate? Funnily enough, I think I may have done. At the party I was going on about. I don't really remember him.'

'Did the two of you talk, then?'

'Not really.'

'What did he look like?'

'I can't really remember. I think he was thin – quite good looking. Maybe he had a suntan. But it was ages ago.'

'It's still interesting. You like to know who you're taking over from. At my last place I met the person.'

'Where was that?'

'Straithe. West Midlands.'

'That's in the area my paper covers, funnily enough. There was a knifing there this week, too, outside a pub.'

'I know. The poor chap was stabbed in the neck. In fact, his wife went to my old church – so I expect the vicar will be helping her. She'd put a lot of starch into her husband's collar, which I think helped. He's going to get better.'

'Aaaaah. Can you imagine – ' Vicki trailed off. 'Life's a slow death, isn't it? Knives, muggings, heart attacks, earthquakes – ' She became conscious of herself, and laughed. 'And, worst of all, new records by the Saint Peter's choir.'

But Vicki was studious as she took a last swig of tea. 'It's good not to think about it. That's where all the people who fill the pews down there – ' she thumbed out of the window, at the roof of the church – ' that's where they've got it so wrong. They think too much, and they sing too much.'

She put her cup down and stared hard at it.

But I was looking in a different direction. The room allowed a view into the upper floors of offices across the road. Glancing where Vicki's thumb pointed, I had seen figures moving in a brightly lit room . . . and one had suddenly caught my attention. My interest was kindled.

'What's that building there – do you know?'

She turned. 'Which? The gigantic one? In the centre? Surely you know *that* one.'

'I've only just arrived. I've no way of knowing.'

She knelt on the armchair and pushed up the window. A distant roar of traffic blew in, like sea sounds in a shell.

''Course you do. The biggest investment firm in London.'

I looked. In a still-bright late afternoon in summer, lights burned behind almost all the office windows. In the one I was staring at, several figures moved around quickly, obvious in plain shirts and braces.

'Marple and Schwartz,' said Vicki. 'They plant your money and make it grow. That's the slogan, at least.'

And there was that figure again . . . catching my eye as it moved, tiny, around the room across the street.

'What are you looking at?'

'I'm not sure.'

'You're screwing up your eyes.'

'I need my glasses. It's just – see over there – '

'Which window? There are hundreds.'
'Two down from the top, three – no, four in – '
'They're making thousands of pounds a minute in that place,' said Vicki. 'When the stock market crashed – our Divinity teacher at school got depression – tons of them over there lost their jobs. But it's normal again now. It's massive. The Saint Peter's of investment firms.'
I stared and stared at the figure shifting around in the room. Despite the urgent sense of recognition, I knew I was a mile from naming the distant shirt and pair of braces.
'They probably earn forty thousand quid per brace,' Vicki said. 'I'm amazed you can recognise anyone from here.'
'I can't. That's the whole point. It was just – '
'Perhaps it was the head boy at your school,' Vicki said, standing up and moving about the lounge. 'Or a failed pop star.' She turned to me. 'You're not married, are you?'
I laughed. 'I think I'm the type who'll never marry.'
'Rubbish. I'm that sort, and we can't both be.'
Twenty minutes later, we were going down the concrete stairs. Vicki wanted to find Daniel Ogumbaye. I could hardly refuse to go along – although it would have been easier to stay lonely, climb into bed and bring down two eyelids on it all.
As we came to a ground-floor junction where three parts of the church intersected, I asked Vicki a question.
'What makes you think that?' she said.
'I'm not saying she's the unhappy type, but I just wondered if your sister might have something on her mind.'
'Yes, she does,' Vicki said.
'I thought so, because when I met her – '
'Don't tell me,' Vicki cut in. 'I bet Vanessa went on and on and you were desperate to get away.'
'Not that. I just noticed she'd been crying.'
Vicki stopped, and touched my arm. 'My sister's a great character, despite this Christian thing. If I tell you – '

'I'm not saying it's right for me to know.'

'I think you ought to,' said Vicki. 'One, because you're new here. And two, she hasn't told anyone.'

'It was only a bit of red around her eyes.' Now I was backing off, adding, 'It might just have been make-up.' I was part of Vanessa's flat; nothing in any contract I could remember signing had bound me to her problems as well.

'I really want to tell you.'

Limply, I protested. 'Look, I don't think – '

She interrupted. 'Vanessa's been accused, unfairly of course, of fare-dodging on the Tube. They're prosecuting.'

I grabbed at a question. 'How do you know?'

Vicki ignored it. 'At Baker Street. She just lost her ticket, some inspectors came down the train, they asked her what station she'd come from, she panicked, gave a silly one somewhere near Leeds, they thought she was lying – and that was it.'

'Didn't they just let her pay on the spot?'

'That was the thing. She found she had no money.'

'Oh, dear.'

'She's out of her mind with panic.'

We started down the stairs again. 'I'm not sure what I can do, but surely it'll be understood by the people here – '

'Surely? I'm not as sure as you are,' said Vicki. Where two stairways ended, we reached an atrium which led into the tea room, whose name came from a rack of urns used to serve the congregation after Sunday services. I caught sight of it, and could think of nothing more to say about Vanessa.

'You seem to know the church quite well, Vicki.'

'Not at all. Just that we had to get into this passage.'

At the kitchen, we searched for the way up to Daniel Ogumbaye's flat. The annexe staircase turned out to be concealed by a door set back from the end of a stainless steel worktop. Climbing, we passed the youth group alcove. The moist wood felt like cardboard underfoot.

The door to Daniel's flat was ajar, and inside we heard a rasping, tinny voice talking in a monotone.

'Hold on,' said Vicki. She knocked.

There was no answer. Behind the door, the voice rattled on, impossible to understand.

Vicki turned to me. 'Sounds like someone's in.'

'Why don't you put your head round the door?'

She did – and then pushed it open, laughing. The voice was coming from an answering machine. As we walked in, a message was ending: but as it did, the final words came into focus, like conversation overheard from a passing car, overtaking with its windows down on a slow road.

' . . . sure that Mark will end up being right, and we just have to pray good comes of it.'

The machine sounded a bleep, then clicked twice, emitted more bleeps and clicked again.

There was silence in the room.

Vicki broke it.

'Daniel?'

There was no answer.

'He's obviously not in,' she said.

'That sounded like the Rector,' I said. 'Douglas.'

'Did it? I couldn't really make out what he was going on about,' said Vicki, looking around the room. A good part of it was taken up by a bright green sofa.

'He mentioned my name, I think.'

'You see? You're famous already,' she said distractedly. 'Only been here half a day and they're talking about you.'

She took a few steps to the centre of the room and peered round the bathroom door. 'Shame,' she said.

It seemed a peculiar phrase to use: *We just have to pray good comes of it*. But I supposed it might have been one of the Rector's favourites.

Vicki turned to me and put a hand on my forearm. 'I'm going to the pub down the road. Wanna come? Or not?'

I was sure I did not. A female, a bar, my first day –
'Mark – Vanessa did send me to keep you company.'
'Still, I'm fine. I don't think I will.' I scuffed the toe of my shoe on the back of a trouser. 'Thanks,' I added.

– 4 –

The pub was grim, but as Vicki brought the third drink of the evening I was pleased I had changed my mind.

'You look happy.'

'As a sandbag,' I said.

'Sandboy, you mean.'

'A bit of both.'

I'd had to get away from the church. It was like being a dwarf, cupped in the palm of a giant. And I had begun to wonder if the collapse of the pulpit might have been some terrifying omen.

'Have you ever been in love?' Vicki's question broke into idle thoughts of whether any neglected Old Testament chapter featured a sign from the heavens in the form of a broken pulpit floor.

'Only once,' I answered. 'With someone called Emily.'

'And what happened?'

'I married her.'

Vicki's eyes widened.

'It's not what you think,' I said. I told her about Straithe, the wedding, Matthew. And then a distant bell tolled, as if calling the story to a close.

'Vanessa was telling me she'd been through it a bit lately,' Vicki said. 'I don't mean the Tube thing now. I'm talking about the students. They're a bit of a handful.'

'I can imagine.'

'I can't see what the point of helping them is. They've got enough parties to go to. And everyone knows students only feel strongly about three things – animal cruelty, Third World famine, and snogging.'

A lengthening sunset shadow stalked our drinks.

'Anyway,' Vicki went on, 'my sister decided to organise a tea run for the homeless. And the students were really keen, though of course half of them found excuses when it came to the crunch of getting up at four in the morning.'

'Did she – did it work out?' I asked haltingly.

'Just about. For a time. But then she rang me in a dreadful state, using all kinds of risky words – "blooming" was about the worst – and told me they'd poisoned half a dozen of these tramps they went to.'

'Poisoned?'

'At least six of them had to be hospitalised. It's the students. The one in charge of cleaning the urns forgot – '

'The tea urns?'

' – yes, he only half-cleaned them.' She swallowed. 'And one went out with a gallon of descaling fluid still in it.'

'No.'

'Yes – the first lot to drink it got angry – livid – and one student was shoved into a fire. His union card got singed. But they say descaler's about the best knockout punch there is, because another tramp was going for a kind of hammer-blow when he just keeled over into his boxes. Then the rest did.'

'How many people know about this?'

'I think just a few nurses. They all had their stomachs pumped. Lucky for Vanessa it wasn't in the papers.'

'Good grief.'

'Are curates supposed to say that?'

'I don't know.'

'You've got to feel sorry for them.'

We put glasses to our lips, and I decided not to ask if she was advising sympathy for curates, tramps, students – or simply anyone involved with any church, anywhere.

Then I said something I regretted, word by honest word.

'I don't think I have anything to offer this place.'

I tipped the glass of lager in my hand a few degrees.

But Vicki missed her cue, or misheard me. She looked up at the sky and spread her palms flat on her cheeks.

'I hope my job on *The Times* comes good,' she said.

We drank in silence, and as we did I played with Vicki's last words, juggling them like steel balls and introducing new ones until a completely different sentence was formed: *We hope it comes good.*

And then, *We pray good comes of it.* I was thinking about the end of the answering machine message that I had heard in Daniel Ogumbaye's flat: *We just have to pray good comes of it.*

Surely, it was about the oddest phrase any rector could use in a reference to a new assistant, a phrase that had come a fraction of a second after my name . . .

Could Douglas Tredre have been talking simply about my appointment? If so, why did there seem to be doubt about it being, as he put it, 'good'? Or was there an unusual complication? Did he have information that someone was going to turn up at a service and lunge at me? Or was the 'it' something in my past?

I found myself anxious. Tried to dismiss it – failed, miserably. It rubbed on a tender spot, like an emotional five-minute appeal at the end of a sermon.

'I often wondered,' Vicki was asking, 'how much a vicar gets paid?'

'I'm not a vicar, of course. I'm here as a kind of –'

'Let me guess. Ten thousand?'

'A bit more,' I said. 'Plus a flat. But not much more.'

'If you were Archbishop of Canterbury, you'd be paid thirty-seven thousand, three hundred pounds a year.'

'I'd have to wear a silly hat.'

Vicki laughed. 'Now, don't be grumpy with me.'

'I'm not. But curates don't talk about money. We get less a year than they earn for a single sermon in America.'

'But those are the televangelists – and they've all been locked up for having air-conditioned dog kennels. Anyway,' she added, 'why did you say you had nothing to offer?'

The question dangled; a monkey from a branch.

'What makes you ask that?'

Vicki looked slightly embarrassed. 'You said it, Mark.'

'Well – I suppose it worries me that after an hour here I've told you nothing at all about Christianity. Zero.'

'You're off duty.'

'I'm not supposed to be.'

'Tell me some other time.' Half her pencil-thin face was in deep shadow. 'I've heard it all, and I'm not impressed.'

The sun had gone. A policeman was trying to fix a ticket to a jeep slewed across the pavement. The thing was straight out of a military factbook, and there was no window for the officer to stick his ticket to; just a glassless frame. He walked off after leaving it on the bonnet, one corner hooked into a grill. But a moment later, a gust carried the ticket away, and a dozen people at the table next to us cheered.

I once went for a job at a large firm of accountants. Miles from the sharpness they wanted, I had walked in and seen a hulking grandfather clock, antique and polished to the point of flawlessness, towering as if in silent judgement on my imperfection. *Mark,* I thought, *they're too good for you.* Interviewing me, a man behind a desk – bearded, pinstriped, and big – had continuously smiled with one side of his face and frowned with the other. Finally, he smiled with both sides and marked the papers before him in one easy motion.

'I think there is probably no point in continuing this conversation,' he had said.

That, gutting, phrase came to mind as I sat there with Vicki. We seemed to have run our course. For now . . .

There is probably no point in continuing this conversation.

'What?'

'I'm sorry,' I said. 'I was years away.'

'Your lips were moving but nothing was coming out.'

'I was thinking – thinking about a lot of things,' I said. And then the answering machine came to mind again.

'I envy you. You'll have loads of time to think here.'

'About what?' I murmured. 'Shall we – our coats – ?'
'Sure.' Vicki grabbed them. 'Listen, Mark. This thing of my sister's – on the Tube – '
'I promise I won't tell a soul.'
'No. It's more than that – please help her.'
The last two words stayed with me as we walked back to Saint Peter's as though scribbled in the sky by a moaning monoplane. We parted at the church, diagonally across from Marple & Schwartz. I looked up for an instant, searching the wall where that familiar figure had appeared at a window. But all lamps on the level had been put out, and the building was being gathered into darkness.
We just have to pray good comes of it.
The line snapped at me. A terrier. I bowed my head at the foot of the church steps, mildly concerned that as I entered the white domed lobby, one of the baggy-trousered individuals browsing through dog-eared books on a stand might stop me for conversation and smell beer.
Suddenly, a lone and dangerous thought took hold – and I began to walk faster . . .
I got through the lobby, walking unnaturally fast, brave with the smack of drink, and trotted down to the tea room.
The tea room was deserted.
And I was out the other side of it now, almost running, bouncing a door open like an American footballer.
I headed down the passage by the tea room, picked up speed, and reached the stable doors of the kitchen.
Calm down, I said to myself, and stopped.
Just calm down.
I leant for a moment in the half-light against the corner of the steel worktop, conscious of the jeopardy.
Calm down. He might be in.
All right. If Daniel Ogumbaye had arrived in the flat above me in the two hours since Vicki and I had left it, I would give him a hearty greeting – as though I had taken the long route to his room just to shake hands.

A small voice begged from the back of my mind, *Think again, think again,* a voice down on its knees with begging; but now it was drowned out by a battery of commands urging me to find out for myself what was on the answering machine.

You're owed an answer, they said. And, for now, they were the only commandments that mattered.

If Daniel Ogumbaye was not in his flat, I would turn on the tape, briefly. That was fair.

In the gloom of the kitchen, I laid out the logic.

First, no clause in heaven or on earth permitted a rector accidentally to upset his curate. And second, a direct approach either to Daniel or Douglas to ask for explanations might get far too intricate and serious. Things might even be written down.

Yes: any curate, anywhere, might take this kind of action, perhaps even in less harrowing circumstances. And having heard the tape I might even, in passing, mention the whole thing to Daniel.

That was certainly possible, if I saw him.

Then I would just forget it, I told myself, climbing the soft staircase.

I passed the youth group alcove, bathing in soft orange from a streetlight by the window.

It was warm up here.

The stairs really did feel very rotten.

Soft, they were, and moist.

At the top, I breathed in sharply. The door of Daniel's flat was ajar, as we had left it, but a light was on now. A fin of yellow was projected through the narrow opening.

So either the light had been on earlier, and we failed to notice it, I reasoned; or Daniel had been in and out.

Or Daniel was in the flat now.

At that moment, notwithstanding the good and complex philosophical arguments against the reality of sin, I became conscious that my position at the top of this flight of stairs might well be coating a part of my soul in something as black and as dense as tar.

Or so the great men of the pulpit might have told me.
But I was not one of them.

I ignored a shudder along my spine, and, to drive away the thought, began singing in a low whisper, bringing out the words of old hymns like dead men on stretchers.

I stepped gingerly towards the door.

> My song is love unknown,
> My saviour's love to me;
> Love to the loveless shown
> That they might lovely be.

I pushed the brass knob. The door swung open.

'Daniel?' I said. 'Mr Ogumbaye?'

The room stared back at me, speechless. The only sound was of cars below on Clemence Road.

I changed hymns

> There is a green hill far away,
> Beside a city wall –

and murmured the words on my way across the creaking floor, towards the answering machine. In the centre of its Bible-sized plastic cover, a red light was glowing

> Where my dear Lord was –

while on its lower edge, a green light flashed

> Crucified –

which I presumed showed that several messages had been left for Daniel throughout the day

> Who died to save us all.

. . . and now my finger hovered over the large grey button at the bottom left-hand corner. On it was one word. *PLAY*.

I had stopped the singing now. I pressed the button.

'Play,' I whispered.

The machine clanked, and I heard voices immediately.

It took no more than a fraction of a second to realise the voices were not coming from the machine. They were coming from behind me.

From behind you.

At least two people were at this moment on their way up the stairs. I looked around wildly.

And then there was a third voice, this one louder than the other two, belting out of the machine like a drill.

'Hello, Daniel,' it rasped. *The first message.* 'It's twenty-five to twelve, roughly, and this is – '

I did not wait to hear the name. I moved swiftly away from the machine, away from the pneumatic drill voice

and the others on the stairs –

– and over –

over the room and on to the sofa, one foot on it –

– and –

a vault . . .

and I was behind the curved elbow of the green sofa, in the space between it and the wall, forcing my head down so that no part of it was visible –

to the people who had just walked into the flat.

There was a loud creak from the door, and then the voice rasping out of the answering machine stopped rasping out.

Someone had pressed a button on it.

'That's strange.' A cultured male voice.

I silently pulled my chin even tighter into my knees, filling with every sort of adrenalin as the fear of being discovered crumpled behind the sofa in Daniel Ogumbaye's flat swept over me for the first time since the pure shock of hearing voices rising on the stairs had collapsed every other emotion.

Daniel Ogumbaye. The voice I could hear had to be his.

'It's never done that before.'

'It was doing it when we came up earlier.'

And that was Vicki, on the other side of the sofa.

Vicki. I pursed my lips as tight as a toolshed clamp. An ache was spreading up my left leg, bent double and pressed hard against the sofa back.

'Earlier?' the man on the other side of the sofa said.

'When Mark and I came up to see you, it was playing.'

'But that might just have been a message coming in. This is old messages. Weird.' The cultured man again.

A moment later Vicki asked to use the bathroom.

There was movement around the room – perhaps Daniel throwing off his jacket – and I heard the tape on the machine spinning. Then it stopped, with more clicks and tones.

Another clunk, and –

'Hello, Daniel. It's twenty to twelve, Tuesday, and this is Davy, the capuccino kid! Just wanted to ask about Leon. Hear he was in an ambulance after the party. Something to do with a police dog and that Mafia costume. Anyway, so far no joy finding out where the hospital is, or even where he was bitten. I'll see you later.'

A piercing bleep, and a sigh from Daniel. A big shadow was thrown across the wall above me. My terror tripled.

'Dan – ' The second message. The shadow shifted. 'Tina. Just wanted to talk about nothing. Never mind. Bye.'

Bleep. I pressed my face harder into my knees.

'Hello, is that Mr – Mr – ' ('Ogumbaye,' Daniel told the machine) ' – Oblong Barney? This is Harry Topping, of the sofa merchants. You weren't in, so we delivered the goods as asked. Hope the colour's all right. Thanks for leaving the door open, Mr – er – as we said, delivery's – um – ten – no, hold on, five per cent – looking at our chit – no, I see you've already paid, so forget it. Much obliged.'

Bleep. The sound of a handset being hung up.

And then: 'Daniel – ' The Rector's voice. 'It's Douglas! I imagine you'll have heard about the pulpit calamity, and we really must decide whether to stick with that old thing or get something new. But anyway, I just wanted to recommend that you meet Mark, our new curate, as soon as you can . . .'

This was the message I had craved hearing. But now every ounce of interest was numbed by the acid threat of discovery. If they saw me behind the sofa, Douglas's words would be nothing. History. I would be out of the church that night, on the very ear I had used to try to listen to the machine.

I was appalled at what three drinks had driven me to. But I became more than appalled as the message spun on.

' . . . because the key, I think, is to involve him now. He went to great pains helping me out of the pulpit thing, calling firemen and so on, and so I think now we need to just forget this terrible muddle, and give him every chance. It's hard not to regret what happened, but it has happened, and now I can't help feeling sure that Mark will end up being right, and we just have to pray good comes of it.'

The machine stopped.

Daniel sighed again, and then I heard Vicki's voice. She was back. I listened to their conversation without ever seeing them, like a radio play that had its audience glued.

VICKI	We heard that sentence when we came in.
DANIEL	Which one?
VICKI	The last one. But we couldn't work it out.
DANIEL	I'm glad you didn't. It's a nightmare. The PCC interviewed half a dozen people for curate. They found the right person, and then there was some sort of misunderstanding between Douglas and the church secretary. She contacted the wrong guy.
VICKI	Mark? The wrong guy?

DANIEL He couldn't be more wrong. There's a story that when he rang up to say he was taking the job, everyone ran away from the phone. No one knew what to do. Douglas just made a snap decision not to reverse it. He thought the best thing was to just go with it – I probably shouldn't be telling you.

VICKI Oh, you should. I think it's shocking. In the real world, the secretary would have been sacked.

DANIEL I don't know, I think they had similar names. The man they wanted was called Luke Bellington. We've ended up with Mark Empringham. Morag just wasn't paying attention when Douglas told her who to contact. Usually she's pretty good.

VICKI Did they tell Luke Bellington? Where was he from?

DANIEL Darlington. He's taken it all right, actually. In fact I think he was relieved about it. But Mark doesn't know. As you say, only in a church would they decide not to say, 'Sorry, mix-up,' and then take the right guy on after all. I told them to. What did you make of him, anyway?

VICKI Mark? Quiet. His mind drifts away from you a bit. He's probably one of these ultra-deep people. Very unconfident about himself. But what I liked about him was that he didn't try to preach at me.

DANIEL That's exactly what they didn't like about him. If he believes anything, he kept it well covered up at the interview, I hear. When they asked him what his main aim would be at the church, he said, 'Not to upset anyone.'

VICKI I can understand that. Just about.

DANIEL But you're supposed to upset people. That's what Christ did.

VICKI He didn't go around at interviews saying his aim was to upset people.

DANIEL Maybe the Rector's right. Mark'll be all right.

VICKI I think he's frustrated.

DANIEL That's one of the qualifications for the Church of England – didn't you know? Along with treating your faith like a state secret.

VICKI Anyway, it's great to see you again. I thought we might have a chat about the old country.

DANIEL We must, soon. And look, if you're going to be in London, you ought to come here on a Sunday.

VICKI Maybe –

– and then the two of them turned their attention to the new green sofa. Daniel said he was upset about the colour, and Vicki giggled at it. Laughing together, they tried to push it closer to the wall, pinning my head tightly into the corner. Every muscle begged to move. I was virtually in panic: wanted to jump up suddenly, shouting my resignation, and sprint away into the night . . . just to empty myself of this soul-convulsing tension . . . and now . . . now, as they guffawed and shoved the sofa into my head . . . now I dreaded discovery more than ever, given what I had just heard. I squeezed my eyes shut, swallowed, and felt sick. I thought of accountancy.

But suddenly they were gone. The voices moved down

the stairs, and were extinguished. I opened my eyes, creaked invalid-like behind the sofa, raised myself criminally in the blinding light of the room, swayed there . . .

And then was out of the flat, almost falling down the stairs.

I saw the Rector for seconds on the way, standing in the tea room with his back to me, arms raised like a bookmaker, tea-cosy hair seemingly tilting at a new angle.

'The pulpit is now helping police with their enquiries,' I heard him call to a colleague.

Back in the flat, I crossed a bedroom floor strewn with shirts which had not yet found their way on to hangers.

Sleepless in bed, I turned my head on the pillow, and thought I detected – what? Vanessa, crying next door? Instead of counting sheep, I counted goats; tried to imagine the taste of descaler, wondered if the sofa man wore a cap to match his Cockney accent, pictured Clemence Road in the seconds after BBF had caused a pile-up in it, studied Vicki's sharp nose and chin in vivid profiles of her, and fumbled with the assumption that as some of those octagons of plaster missing from the vaulted church ceiling fell, they must have hit members of the congregation. The lump on my head where it was banged earlier, courtesy of the toaster's faulty wiring, twinged at the thought. Sitting up in bed, I found the noise of crying, if it had ever been there, had now died.

As sleep came, one of my arms flopped out of bed. My fingertips landed on the leather jacket of a pocket Bible left on the floor.

I recognised what I was touching, and snatched my hand away.

– 5 –

'Right. Go back to the top of the first bit, and Sally – Sal, love – I want you to take the downbeat instead of the off. Okay? And Jim – Jim, mate – for goodness' sake, let's not hit the crash cymbal during that bit about tenderness.'

Behind Sally Halewood, the choir shifted uneasily on the stage. When you sang as well for a church as Ms Halewood, you were allowed to keep your maiden name. Her husband, Francis Bottom – who pronounced his surname 'Boat Home' – was known to have complained to the Rector at the way his wife was introduced during family services, but to no avail. Sally Halewood it stayed.

But perhaps the disagreement had been smothered by musical harmony. For Francis was Saint Peter's Head of Music, and it was he who was now rehearsing his wife, the choir, and a dishevelled band arrayed behind guitars, drums and a keyboard. Tiny under the giant organ pipes, Bottom jabbed a pencil, filling in for a baton, in the air. He wore spiffy black winklepickers. His wife's face seemed to glow with the power of all heaven.

My heart felt pitch black.

In the week since I had overheard Daniel and Vicki, I had suffered all-day blackness. My stomach was an oven, baking pain into a loaf behind a jammed door.

I told myself the lacklustre interview was irrelevant. Now that I was employed by the church, I had my chance. The future was in my hands. I could make them all come round.

But that line of thought worked no magic. Every pair of eyes seemed to glint in the knowledge that I was the dud item who had squeaked past quality control by virtue of a rector's muffed instruction, his secretary's muffled ears.

And if they thought that, I told myself repeatedly with brutal frankness, they would be right. I was indeed dud.

I even prayed. For release and riches. But the tragedy seemed to press down on my flimsy muttering, a boulder rocking on a pod of peas.

And what am I supposed to want, anyway?

Resentment set in, like dry rot. I harboured it towards Douglas – too cowardly to correct the mistake. But I also begrudged Daniel for pressing him to. And I resented Vicki's comments in his flat, which had made me sound about as lively as amateur darts; not to mention Luke Breathington, or whatever his name was, martyred and probably revelling in it.

There was no way of disbelieving Daniel's account. Douglas's inexplicable initial embarrassment, BBF's belief that I was from Darlington, Vanessa's odd enquiry about my surname as though she had been trying to establish exactly which of the candidates for the curacy stood in front of her. That, and the confusion when I rang to accept the post. Well, they all proved the story. It was, as Daniel had said, a nightmare.

And all this distress was being fuelled by the continued saga of the last curate. In seven days, every sort of attempt to find out who he was, what he had done and why he had left were stonewalled. I was not trying to snoop for information; I just wanted to know.

I might have expected Daniel, for one, to offer answers.

He had shown kindness to me. He explained the complex geography of the church, and, to my surprise, spoke positively about my appointment. I came within a whisker of forgiving him for everything. He took me to a friend's house; took me to his own flat. I said I had seen it once already, and then realised I was lying – I had seen it twice. There was no point to the lie, even if I had intended it. The sadness inside reminded me of itself.

One afternoon he offered me lunch, in a crumbling pizza parlour at the end of a stucco sidestreet. Sweeping his hand out from his chest as he enthused about the large numbers of people who, as he saw it, came to Saint Peter's on the lookout for something – an 'X ingredient', he called it – he knocked over a glass of lemonade on the table. It flooded the plastic surface in slow motion, then turned into a minor Niagara that soaked my black trousers at double speed.

As we cleared up the mess, I decided I liked Daniel.

I tried hints about the last curate.

There's not any way of getting to know my duties from someone who's done them, I suppose . . .

Nothing.

I tried mild expressions of interest.

It's intriguing when you begin a new job, wondering what sort of a person did it last . . .

I was afraid of being too direct. But in any case, nothing was forthcoming. Complicated questions were evaded simply, while simple questions – *Did the last curate work hard?* – were evaded with tortuous ingenuity.

'Things have changed since then, Mark, because you now have the day off moved to the Tuesday, and usually the people most in need, and jobs in the church, and so on, are – '

It was like getting encyclopaedias off shelves, putting a million words extracted by razor into a bucket, shaking, and then pouring them out on to my head – and expecting me to nod vigorously at the good sense the deluge made.

I came to accept that this curate's past was being kept away in a kind of Fort Knox. I did not resent Daniel for keeping it secret. Instead, to cut down on grudges, I bore a single one against the church staff as a whole. I could not blame the congregation: I had been called away from the church on my first Sunday to see the

Bishop of London for a formal welcome to the diocese, and so had been unable to mingle after the services and ask the obvious questions.

One morning, I approached Morag.

It was not easy to tell what the elderly church secretary thought of anything or anyone, because of thick locks of grey-black hair which swung in from the sides of her face. The horn-rimmed and thick-lensed spectacles on her nose looked like an alien spacecraft that had somehow managed to make a landing unnoticed.

'Hello, Morag.'

'Pardon?'

'Hello there.'

'Oh – Mark. What are you doing?'

'Setting up a filing cabinet I've just got. It was a bargain, because the thing in it that's supposed to stop it falling over is broken. You know, in case all the drawers are pulled out at the same time. It's a bit unsafe, so I got it cheaply. And I've just found a new toaster for the flat.'

'I'm checking notices for our noticeboard.'

'Really? Do they need checking?'

Morag looked up from a sea of pink paper squares.

'They do now. We had some trouble a month ago. Someone advertised an illegal event on our board, a motor race round the M25 motorway, the London orbital – '

'Is that illegal?'

'I think so – well, I know so, actually,' she said, ducking her head to lay stress on the point with unexpected force. 'Very illegal. It was a cutting from a magazine, and the heading said something like "Cannonball Run". It was put underneath an advertisement for Mission Tuition. The police said it gave junction and time cars were supposed to line up on the motorway for a race around it. They set up roadblocks to stop it, actually. It was all on the news.'

'What did the last curate make of it?'

A pause. 'It's not what *we* make of it, dear, it's the police and the people who use that road – '

And so on. I imagined a jigsaw puzzle in the lobby, with thousands of pieces lying on the floor. I was kneeling, hunched over them, and members of the church staff walked past, laughing, kicking away shapes just as I reached for them. When the jigsaw was done, it was a black silhouette: a man's head, a rectangle of white at his neck. A dog collar. The last curate.

So it was in a state of distraction that I watched Francis Bottom conducting, his wife singing and the choir fidgeting in the big church, brushing up their act for the Sunday service some days in advance of it. And it was in that stage of distraction that I felt the letters in my pocket.

I had written to the Bishop of London to give him notice of my resignation from Saint Peter's church.

– 6 –

At tea-time on Monday, I had taken the decision.

I had begun a letter to an old college friend, Stewart Weeks, who had set up a thatching business in Wales.

'Dear Stew, you old son of a gun – ' I wrote, with little indication of my desperation, on paper headed with the name and address of the church. 'Let's have a weekend break together soon. Fags, beer and skittles! Lots to tell you about the church. Give me a ring whenever you're free and we'll fix up a date.'

I signed it 'Mark' and folded the paper, pushing it to the furthest edge of the dining table. Interlocking the fingers of both hands behind my head, I looked up.

If I told Stewart the truth, what would it be? That I had never been less happy than now? Never felt more threatened?

I could guess the reaction of my old, blunt friend.

'Get out,' he would say. 'Get right out of it now.'

He had jettisoned accountancy after removing his trousers during a finals paper and throwing them at the invigilator's desk . . . and then announcing to the packed hall that he was engaged to a girlfriend of five days.

I imagined telling him the story. The thick lines on his forehead would deepen, his bulbous nose snort with contempt.

Stewart, a committed atheist, had told me in a bar after my ordination that he did not hate God because God was not significant enough. I said he had read too many books by Bertrand Russell, and it was impossible to refer to someone you did not believe in as though they existed.

He retorted, 'But you can prove atheism exists. You can't prove Christianity,' and challenged me to declare whether I was genuinely convinced that a man who had been buried two thousand years before could really be alive 'in any way, shape, or form' today.

I admitted, 'Possibly not – ' but said that Christianity was the art of following the teachings of Christ, and they were alive, even if he was not. Testifying to their life were hundreds of scriptural printing presses.

'But I follow them too. So what's the difference?'

I laughed at his question. 'A white collar – '

And then regretted the joke, because I was the victim.

Doubtless, I reflected, the subject would come up again if Stewart heard how a church had used one hand to dole out a message of peace – and the other to duff up its curate.

So I would act in advance of his advice.

I peeled another sheet of the white, unlined paper from the block, squared it with the blotter, and wrote again.

Rt Revd Tristran Stuart
Bishop of London
80 Barton Street
Westminster
London SW1P 3NE

Dear Bishop,
First of all, may I thank you for seeing me at your estate on Friday. Your welcome and that of your wife Delilah was most warm. I must just add, again, my apologies for the happenings with your dog, but I am afraid I do get into something of a blind panic with them, and I just hope, as you assured me it could, the yukka plant can be repotted.

Right Reverend Stuart, I now write with regret. I have to ask you to agree to my departure from Saint Peter's church. A personal circumstance has cut in, and shortly after the festive –

I crossed out 'the festive' with thick lines –

> the Christmas season I shall need to be clear of my duties. I would be most grateful if you could give me a date, which will be a matter of great regret but there we go.
>
> Yours faithfully, and faithful,
>
> Mark Empringham.

I looked round. The door of the flat was opening.

'Mark! I didn't realise you were in.'

'Vanessa – '

'How are you?' She was busy with a carrier bag, and threw a small book on to an armchair. 'I've just been to the Heights Supermarket. Brilliant place. Are you well?'

'Just fine,' I said, discreetly sliding the letters into two envelopes I had addressed.

My flatmate bent to leaf through the book. The bottom of her jacket rode up over her wide hipline. 'I can't believe it, but I've lost two pages out of my – '

She petered out. Somehow, Vanessa looked different. The teariness was gone. The jagged fringe was more jagged; the pink golf balls pinker. There was a new radiance.

And a new problem.

'It's my address book. Two pages have fallen out.'

'Oh, dear.' I could be sympathetic. The shared flat had not been as frightening as expected. Vanessa had allowed me room to think and breathe, holstered her air-raid laughter, accepted the recluse in me: not even complaining when I brusquely moved her colourful collection of tablets in the bathroom to make way for my steel blades, plasters and aspirin. I pinned up a calendar, and even chose a lampshade.

'You look well, anyway.'

She launched a Derby commentator's gabble in response.

'Mark, I must tell you – well, actually, I can't tell you, but I am just so – today – has been a most – I – well, I'm just so happy – so relieved about – about everything.'

'Oh – good news?'

'Something has happened today – and I can't go into it, Mark, because only Vicky knows – it's been a tricky problem, a sadness – and this – this dreadful burden – has been – '

'Lifted? That's great.' I guessed: that the ordeal on the Tube had somehow abruptly ended, and was now to stay secret. I felt disquiet at the level of my own indifference.

She approached the desk. 'Have you been writing?'

'Not much,' I said, licking the flaps artlessly.

'Letters?' she asked.

'Just a couple.' I pinched the second flap against the envelope edge, and set them face down on the desktop.

'Secret?'

'No, not at all.'

She walked over to the flat door and pushed it shut.

'I can't believe the news from the *Evangelical Times*. There's been a split.'

'What – a banana split?' I could not remember ever hearing of the *Evangelical Times*.

'No, silly! Mark! Your jokes! As I understand it – I think this is it – the editor resigned, with the sports and features editors. You're right in a sense – it has been a bit bananas. They're founding a breakaway magazine, called either *Evangelical Times Magazine* or *Magevangelism*, I hear.'

'That sounds a bit Scandinavian.'

'I can't imagine a church paper without features.'

I was trying to imagine one with sport. Font-diving sprang to mind. 'This is very big news, is it?'

'We all subscribe. Every one of us. A columnist, the Needle, writes a thing called "Eye of the Needle", going around churches anonymously, naming the best preachers – like a kind of Good Sermon Guide! He never had a bad word to say about BBF, but there was terrible trouble recently when he criticised a lay preacher in Brentwood in very strong terms – wrote something like, "He goes so slowly, the sermon could have been simultaneously translated into cave paintings."'

'So will the old paper continue?'

'Well, a lot of people are bound to stick with it. Older readers – or other disorientated people, like students.'

'I'll read it if I see it.'

'What?'

'Oh – I don't know, the Needle, or whatever.'

'By the way, Mark, it's great that you met Vicki. Contact with you is contact with God, in a way, and . . . '

Outside the flat, reflecting that the Right Reverend Stuart was unlikely to view contact with me as a divine incident – although the reaction of Stewart Weeks to his letter would be more positive – I had been drawn by the sound of singing into the main body of the church, and so it was that I had joined Francis Bottom and his musicians.

'Okay? And Jim – Jim, mate – for goodness' sake, let's not hit the crash cymbal during that bit about tenderness.'

Sally Halewood was looking flustered. She let out a piercing note, which sounded like the word 'Thou'.

'All right darling, I know, but we must get it right,' said Francis Bottom. 'And look – the reason has joined us – '

Suddenly he was gesturing at me.

'Hi, Mark. We'll be fuller on Sunday, I promise.'

Help.

I raised a hand, horribly embarrassed.

'Mark's our new curate. This'll be his first service.'

Oh no, I thought. *I wish I hadn't come in.*

'Mark comes from – where is it, Mark?'

All sound was stilled now, barring the noise of the stretching of cheeks as every choir member smiled.

'The West Midlands,' I called out, half-standing. There were at least seventy people in front of me, including the musicians. Surely I would be allowed to leave it at that.

'Where in the West Midlands?'

I'm not ready for this.

'Straithe.' I was standing now, fifty rows back.

'Good,' Francis called. He waved.

I smiled, and looked sheepish. 'Nice to meet you,' I called – and, as my words touched off the faintest echo under the vast ceiling, realised how lame the phrase sounded.

Soon they were singing again. My eyes rested on the framed painting of Jesus Christ, there on the wall. I felt heartless. I would have liked his heart, the heart some of these people claimed to have inside them . . . but life was too grim to be relieved by a dose of salts with a best-before date a couple of thousand years out, and a hand with a nail through it is hardly in a position to tap a shoulder or touch a soul two millennia later. If the man in that painting was alive – more than just having been responsible for some of the world's great moral teachings – well, no, the possibility was too horrendous to contemplate. It would mean that there were some people right at the heart of the Church of England who could not, in the strictest sense of the term, define themselves as Christians.

That afternoon, a dozen men and women gathered around a pine desk, big as a full-size snooker table, for a meeting of the church finance committee.

It was already under way when I crept in, nodding in reply to a wink from Douglas Tredre, who had turned where he sat facing a white square projected on the wall.

I heard the word 'Crisis'.

The square was snapped out by a switch somewhere, and another light came on. A small man with large glasses, who had been standing next to the projector, moved back to the table and sat down. He looked a bit like a garden gnome.

'As you know, I don't use that word lightly.'

Douglas Tredre turned again and gave me another wink. I was unsure how to take it.

'Last year, we met like this, and I used that same overhead projector to show you the figures,' said the little man dramatically. He was sitting on a chair a few inches too low, his fringe looking as though it had been done with a set-square. Leaning back a touch to the left, he looked like a politician on a panel who has been asked an unpleasant question. A badly positioned light threw a shadow the shape of an arrowhead across his face.

'Yes, I showed you very much the same sort of graph, I urged cuts, you didn't make them, and now look where we are.'

There was a rustling. Daniel Ogumbaye was deftly spinning a pen in his hand. Douglas Tredre fidgeted.

'We have done our best – our best, Mr Hendon.'

'I understand that, Reverend. But these shortfalls – '

'We just couldn't – we couldn't act on some of the suggestions, some of the things you put to us last year – '

'But we agreed them,' said Mr Hendon.

'I know that,' the Rector replied, 'but some of the suggestions – some of them – ' and the next phrase came with special weight – 'upset the church.'

'You did say you expected them to, Reverend Tredre.'

'For a start, there is no way we can turn round to the congregation and say, simply, sorry – in the winter months we're not going to have a properly heated church.'

'I thought we'd agreed you could have the heating on up to about halfway through the service. The saving – in that huge place – hundreds – '

'That might be all right, but there's a convector in the floor every fifteen yards, all the way down all the pews.' The Rector seemed at ease with the explanation. 'They make a noise when they're on, and when they go off there's half a minute of rattling because of the backblow from the burners.'

'Couldn't you turn the things off during a hymn?'

'It would need to be a louder hymn, and the louder ones just didn't fit into any of our themes.'

'But that really isn't satisfactory, Mr Tredre, you know. I almost had to ask for the use of your basement so we could project some of the low points of these graphs to scale. We're looking at – we're looking at a crisis here.'

There was a tiny movement beside me, and a profile blocked my view of the accountant, who had now virtually vanished in the smoke that genied from his cigarette.

There was a sandy whisper in my ear. 'Same every year.'

I moved my head an inch to see who had made the comment.

The speaker was fantastically overweight. He scribbled something on a pad in front of him and, with a muffled snort, pushed it over as the accountant continued.

I'm Richard Burts, nice to meet you, Mark, it said, in blotchy biro. I returned a nod.

'The basic problem, of course, is that you're giving too much money away, and frankly, as an accountant – and I stress I'm speaking to you here as an accountant, and not a Christian – I can't bear it.'

More rustling.

'We are very committed to our giving,' Douglas said.

'Yes,' said someone opposite him.

Morag, who was at the table beside the Rector, added, 'Absolutely,' in a small voice directed at the pad she had packed with notes of the meeting.

Mr Hendon coughed, as if to wake dead men, and moved on from the subject of giving. 'You print notices every week now, for every member of the congregation. That's a thousand if your Stipendiary Parson's speaking, I hear. Can't we fix that, Reverend?'

'Well – we've thought of finding the three most, shall we say, gregarious people in the church, telling them the notices on the Friday, and asking them to keep them secret.'

Everyone in the room roared with laughter – bar one.

'You'll forgive me if I don't burst my sides at that, Reverend, with respect, but I did hear it last year.'

'And the year before, I think,' murmured Morag, unhelpfully, thumbing through a sheaf of papers as if to confirm the fact.

'I'm sorry,' said Douglas. 'So – we'll look at the notice sheets – perhaps cut them in two –'

'And you'd be mad not to put off the refurbishment.' Mr Hendon was well into his stride.

There was silence.

Then, 'Mad?' That was a man. 'The refurbishment –'

'The refurbishment of the west side?' A woman.

'Perhaps indefinitely.'

'We'll be able to make do and mend on the west side, I suppose,' said Douglas. 'Or make do and not mend.'

'And possibly charge for the noticeboard,' Morag said, frantically scribbling down her contribution as she spoke.

Richard Burts pointed out that hire of the church halls had stopped after a church worker booked a group called the Disciples, unaware they were not a Christian band, but a heavy metal outfit banned from appearing in four counties.

'Might it be time to rent them again – more carefully? And we could have some sort of appeal, too,' he said.

'Buy cheaper condiments,' remarked one.

'And this idea of scrimping for a new pulpit is out,' said Mr Hendon, raising his voice gradually to override all others. 'Unless you want me to tell you you can't possibly afford to send your missionary to Rwanda this year.'

'We've always done that,' said the Rector.

'In accountancy, the word "always" has no real meaning,' Mr Hendon said, rather mysteriously. 'The only way I can allow you to have a new pulpit, and send someone to Rwanda, is if you make your new pulpit out of old bricks.'

There was a murmur of astonishment.

'Besides all that, you need to get as many people as possible to sign covenants and get the tax back on what they give.' He was moving briskly to avoid confrontation, and now lifted a thick folder. 'I've been looking through these records, and you've got people in here, one man particularly, who are giving hundreds of pounds a year – and you're not getting them to sign a simple form to get the tax back. You could heat the church for a year on all that tax.'

'Some of them won't sign the forms, but we'll try,' said Douglas. 'Actually, the man you mentioned has some sort of phobia about the Inland Revenue – it's really quite serious, really very serious – he's had an awful lot of counselling about it – we only found out when he brought us a whole stack of unopened letters from them, a whole stack, some years and years old, and asked us to perform an exorcism on – '

'Don't let's get bogged down with that,' Mr Hendon interrupted. 'Give me some savings – please – Douglas, soon, or I'll be bringing in receivers and ringing up bishops.'

'I don't believe you know their numbers,' Douglas said, smiling. But I had the impression that mention of his superiors had brought an acidity into the proceedings.

There was silence, and I decided to make a contribution.

I coughed.

'Have you thought – '

'I'm sorry, everyone – ' the interruption was from Douglas – 'this is our new curate, Mark Empringham – '

'Hello,' everyone said. The tension relaxed.

'I was just going to say – have you thought – of perhaps not having a curate?'

During my short life as an ordained part of the Church of England, I had discovered two types of dangerous humour. The first was lewd jokes. The second, more specific area of peril was any pun on a Bible verse.

The list was now adjusted to include a third hazard: any attempt at frivolity during a church finance meeting.

Wan, I spoke into the silence.

'I was just – kidding.'

'I was about to say, we could saw the spire off as well,' Daniel added, and now I knew what salvation felt like. 'Less scaffolding, and we could use the stump as a helipad when the traffic got bad.' Laughter rippled around the table.

'Fine – except that we don't have a spire, actually,' a man bellowed at Daniel.

'I work so hard I never get a chance to get out of the building – that's why I didn't know,' came Daniel's reply, and the room rocked with guffaws.

I said: 'We could have a target amount to raise. It worked at the church I used to be at.'

'How much was the target?' someone asked.

'Three pounds,' I said, risking it, and the laughter rose this time. I felt colour come back to my face.

Now Mr Hendon was standing. 'Good, good. Jokes apart, you've started thinking. Run an appeal, cut the charity, have colder services – it's no good tittering, no one believes nowadays heat and salvation necessarily go together.'

Before the meeting, Vicki had rung, her disembodied voice stirring memories of the agonies behind Daniel's sofa.

'Guess what?'

'What?'

'The thing I told you about. The fares. My sister's got off the charges. They've all been dropped.'

'Terrific,' I said. 'She looked happy today, for sure.'

'The inspector who was going to be a witness or whatever had a stroke. It's made me wonder whether there is a God after all,' she said. 'It certainly seems more probable.'

'The case hasn't been postponed or anything, has it?'

'No. The inspector's dead.'

Later, walking in the park, I felt the week-old feelings of rejection mauling again. If only I was with beautiful, loving Emily, whose gaze I had never really caught full-on . . .

I passed a row of blue benches, and imagined her on them with me, hinting at marriage, winking through a mousy ringlet . . .

I can change, I would have said.

But I don't want you to. I imagined her reply. *I don't want you to change because I love you.*

And then we would have kissed, gently, perhaps twice, as the chill air made us brace in our coats . . . and a park-keeper glanced twice at us as she drew me closer on the bench . . .

Stopping short on the path, I remembered, outrageously, that the woman in my mind was now married.

I tapped a toe on the gravel in irritation.

Tap, tap, tap.

It was icy cold. The sun had turned red as I walked.

I looked up at the branches of a giant oak, and wondered how the church team would react if they knew I was leaving.

Tap, tap. Shreds of white drifted in the darkening sky.

'In the twinkle of an eye, at the sound of the trumpet – '

Tap, tap, tap, tap, tap.

' – we shall all be changed.'

Tap, tap, tap, tap, tap, tap, tap, tap, tap, tap.

'Heaven and earth will pass away, but my words will never pass away.' *Tap, tap, tap.* Bible verses, probably.

Perhaps I would return to Straithe, where there was doubtless still a vacancy. Same pay, less drama.

It was ironic, after all, that I would probably never ascend Saint Peter's pulpit steps to preach the sermon I had dreaded delivering. The relief made me breathe the cold park air much easier. It was not just that Emily's wedding had given me a mental block about preaching. No. My objection was rather more intellectual: by the mere fact of straightening a collar in a vestry, of climbing pulpit steps and breathing lectern air, of opening the Bible to speak and asking others to do the same, and hearing the crinkling of onion-skin pages as they did . . . by the mere fact, above all, of opening one's mouth to preach, one became a hypocrite.

Hypocurate.

That was my view. It might have been over-intellectual. I did not care.

It crossed my mind that the argument with Stewart Weeks after my ordination had been the last argument I had actually been involved in. None had come my way since.

Curates did not appear to argue.

So I argued with pansies on the way out of the park, and I argued with the roses and the chrysanthemums and anything else that looked like it might survive the coming winter.

Yards from a grass border, I posted the two letters without further ado.

When I got back to the flat, feeling light headed, ears aching – *you've just resigned, that's why* – Vanessa had a message for me.

'He's ill, or something.'

She fished a paper square out of her pocket, and held it at arm's length. 'Sorry. I'm having trouble seeing straight, for some reason. Douglas was on the phone. He says – it's here – he says he's unwell, so can you preach on Sunday?'

Then she laughed a bit.

'Preach?' I asked.

– 7 –

'This Sunday. I can't remember the subject,' Vanessa said, putting a hand up to her fringe and smiling in a tired kind of way. 'But don't worry, Mark.'

The assurance failed to knock a single brick out of the wall I had begun to think of as Preacher's Block.

Don't worry? You're asking me to become a hypocrite!

I thought the sentence, but it stayed light years from my lips. To say it would have been to launch a missile.

'Give him a bell and find out the subject,' she said.

'I will. Sure.' *Hypocurate.*

'I hear they're reconstructing the pulpit this week.'

'Really? Well – at least I won't need a safety net.'

'They're sticking bricks under it – surplus from the haulage people in Vail Road – sort of make do and mend –'

The conversation was stilted. I was a galaxy away. A window in Marple & Schwartz caught a final ray from the sun. Vanessa was still talking. I pulled the curtains, agreeing – while declining to take in what she was saying. Flinching, I thought: that was church all over. You agreed, but declined to take in. Those syllable-perfect, soundbite teachings were sent up like flares before gawking nobodies, whose eyes twinkled in their light – but who were more likely to be spirited up by Martians from the portals of their place of worship than love an enemy because the curate in there had told them they should. Tyrants listened and bulldozed; congregations listened and dozed. The classic Straithe gathering was an hour-long exercise in disengagement, and indifference, I had decided, was worse than shooting someone.

There was no doubt about it. Boredom and not listening were the biggest crimes in the world, and church pews were covered in perpetrators' prints. Jesus had left a message and a mystery: respectively, the teachings and the empty tomb. The job of the curate was to make the message interesting, and cover up the mystery. The message, of course, was that you should be good to everyone, and if you were, everything bad you had done would be forgotten by someone. But reporters faced with only that headline might excusably have talked about slow news days. So we curates – well. We were the graphics, the captions, the mastheads and final credits. We were everything to it. We had to make sin sound sufficiently poisonous, and good sufficiently good, to stir the whole world. The very gospel itself had always been no more than one generation of curates from extinction.

But the pay did not match the job description. Ours had turned out to be nothing more glamorous than the Battle of Boredom, the Skirmish of the Drifting Mind. Well, there we go.

All this had come to me while Vanessa talked, and I had left her words behind, exactly as congregations had so often left mine, far behind . . . and now one of those words jarred me to attention.

But it was not a word. It was a gasp.

To hear better, I turned.

I just caught Vanessa falling out of the corner of my eye, slouching against the kitchen doorway on her way down, hitting the floor with the crack of head on lino.

'Vanessa –'

I raced to her side, shocked to see her prostrate, face drained of all colour, head shaking –

'Vanessa –'

Her quivering arms were stretched out at her side and her fingers were pointing towards her feet, and her feet were pointing forwards too. A scream gathered in her throat –

'Vanessa –'

– but the scream did not come, though a cotton-thin line of white marked her lower lip as she flailed about; I crashed to my knees beside her, and pushed down her shoulders; her knees bounced up . . .

God, save this girl, save this girl's life, help her, help her, God, save this girl's life, save her, stop this pain, stop this, save her –

'Vanessa – '

Guessing this was an epileptic fit, I strained for all remembered first aid. I looked for a pencil to shove between her teeth, failed to see one and so, unthinking, tore my white collar, my stiff dog collar, from around my neck and pushed it into her mouth. It flapped, side-on, then went in with a slicing motion as her teeth clamped down, bending it up at the sides so it looked like the smile of a clown . . .

'Vanessa – ' I shouted.

Loosen her clothes. That had to be the first aid I was having trouble remembering. I looked down at the buttons on Vanessa's blouse. She was still kicking, hurting herself because I had not undone the buttons. I reached for the blouse . . . *Loosen her clothes* . . . but – no. I drew back. Might this be something other than epilepsy? Could it be an illness where the clothes needed to be kept tight? I stretched out fingers –

The closest they have ever been to a blouse button

– and withdrew them again.

No.

I would not do it.

Then the dog collar fell out. I looked for a pencil, sprayed everything left and right on the lounge desk, threw a Bible off it, and –

'It's okay.'

I spun round.

Vanessa was sitting up, chin on chest, catching air. She touched the back of her neck.

'Ooooh.'

I was too shocked to speak.

She sighed, the longest sigh imaginable.

'I've broken a heel.'

Then Vanessa cried a little, and I sprang forwards, not even noticing that it was the first time I had hugged someone since theology college, and that had been an accident.

'It's okay.' I had found my voice.

She shook her head. 'Mark – '

'Vanessa, it's okay.'

Now . . . this was intimacy. I helped her sit back against the kitchen cupboards. I found a glass of water.

'So now you know,' she said, at last. 'Epilepsy.'

'It's common.'

'Not for me. I stopped taking my tablets – stupidly. I mislaid them. But I'll be fine. Now – I – what were we talking about when it happened?'

I remembered, and the bottom dropped out of my heart as the toes curled up in my shoes.

The sermon.

'Oh, a message, Vanessa. That's all.'

'Did you get it?'

'Yes. No problem. You gave it to me.'

'What was it?'

'I'm – er – prea – preach – prea – ching. On Sunday.'

She rearranged herself on the floor. 'So now you know,' she said, crying a little more.

'I don't mind. I've done a bit of preaching before.'

'Oh – I didn't mean – I just meant, now you know about the epilepsy,' she said. 'I won't be able to do any driving.'

'Of course you can.'

Vanessa wept. 'Like BBF, maybe.'

'Better than that.'

Then she begged me to leave her alone to recover, thanking me more than was necessary, and, as she saw me pick it up from the floor, apologising for the state of my collar. I bent it several times to restore the shape.

Something moved me. For the first time at the church, my name had been used as the French used 'tu' – with familiarity. I had hugged someone, talked about something other than noticeboards or the provision of biscuits in the tea room; had put a hand on a far shoulder, for goodness' sake! No, I might not have loosened that blouse button, but I had thought about it. Looking at Vanessa, I felt tenderness before I could put on brakes to stop it. The squealing of those same brakes had kept me out of Emily's world. So this was new scenery.

This could be like skidding down an Olympic piste on the seat of smooth trousers, I reflected. Now I feared what was at the foot of the slope. Would this youth worker with the pink golfball cheeks expect something of me now? Secrets? Confidences? Winks across aisles? Hot chocolate after dark – or a preview, perhaps, of my decision to quit? Would she be disappointed if she did not get it?

Will she expect me to hug her again?

I left my flatmate sitting on the sofa. Walking dreamily down the church steps, I resolved to buy her flowers.

Goodness, that girl's life: one minute false charges of fare-dodging, then a fit . . . it swept over me again – a feeling of tenderness, perhaps. A thrill, even. For the first time under the big, brown-felted roof of Saint Peter's, I had had an intimate experience with a member of staff.

I have shared something.

I had never seen another human being writhe on lino, felt their life might depend on remembered first aid . . .

I had lived a sheltered life.

My heart was a rag-bag of different emotions, and I itemised material in it as though opening the bag in court: the resignation letter now sliding deliberately towards the Bishop of London had horror written all over it. Exhibit A. The crazy mix-up over Luke Bellington – Exhibit B – was evidence as to character . . . damning, in my case; and Exhibit C, the framed painting of Christ hanging on the west side wall, made the jury gasp when it was revealed . . . because even they could see the eyes moving, following me around; D was a sample of dust taken from the jacket of my Bible; and, last out of the bag – Exhibit E: a swan, singing.

That was the sermon I was going to have to preach.

Which would, surely, be my first and last in the church.

A swansong.

I passed a hot-chestnut seller and felt the heat of his stove on my exposed hand. Then –

As I approached the flower stall, distractedly, hands in pockets now, I shouted: 'Hey!'

And again: 'Hey! Hey – hey!'

I began to run. I ran towards the back that was disappearing into the crowds, the back I knew and yet did not know, or could not recognise. The last time I had seen it had been with Vicki, glimpsing it on whatever floor it had been of the Marple & Schwartz building and now, yes, that was it, just up ahead. It was maybe a score of people away from me now, and I was gaining on it . . .

When I had first caught sight of that figure, it had been in a plain shirt, with braces. Now it was clad in a deep-blue overcoat.

I heard tuts and sighs as I pushed through the crowds.

'Hey!' I shouted again. Several turned. But not him. Someone swore at me.

But who was it? *Who is it?*

I moved forwards more quickly after stepping on to the road, and soon was only feet from the back . . . crashing shins into the bumper of a parked car.

And then I began to overtake.

'Hi. Hello?'

He stopped and looked over, grimly. I stretched out a hand to shake his and stepped up on to the busy pavement.

'Well – ' The face broke into a smile. 'I know you!'

'Matthew!' I said.

'I recognise the collar! Mark!' He laughed, and swung his right shoulder into the handshake with dramatic force.

Our breath was like smoke in the cold, and the separate streams of it fused before disappearing.

So this was the person I had spotted from miles away, through windows! It was quite extraordinary, but not surprising. For Matthew's was the back I had watched at the end of Emily's wedding, moving off, away, down the aisle with her, after all those catastrophes. I had been sure I would never forget the way that back looked and moved. It had been more memorised than theology college notes.

Flushed at the successful recognition, I could not even feel disconcerted that only a few hours before I had envisioned this man's wife in a public park.

Matthew's face was the same, pitted, but his coat looked new enough to still be in the wrapping, and – yes, through the space between his lapels I could see thick silk – oh, yes, an exotic tie, patterned like an Indian carpet!

People shoved past us. I detected a whiff of alcohol.

'I see you're still in the same job,' he grinned.

'Are you?'

'Yes – fund managing. Doing a bit better for the two –'

'How is your wife?' I was trying to sound casual.

'Oh – there's so much to tell you,' said Matthew.

'Any children?' *Is it all right to ask?*

'Actually – ' He came up closer to me and I thought I saw urgency in his eyes. I felt my forearm touched, gripped, by a leather-gloved hand.

'Actually, I'd love to talk.'

'Well, if you'd like to have a chat now – '

'Oh no,' he said abruptly. 'I must – although, having said that – a quick one – '

'There's a tea bar just down here.'

'No fear,' he said, chummily, and winked. I wanted to shout in his face: *I love your wife*.

'I need to make a phone call,' he said. Someone knocked him in the chest, barging by, and Matthew snapped his head to the left and shouted an uninhibited obscenity.

'Matthew – I'm not – we can meet any time – it doesn't have to be – '

'Oh, go on, Mark.'

'Any time would be fine.'

'But I really would love the two of us to chat now.' And that, I guessed, was the voice fund managers used when they wanted to tell you your stock had sunk, or rocketed, or both.

All right, then. I could not resist it. I could not resist hearing about Emily. It would be like a warm tonic on this dark, cold, epileptic night.

And maybe then I would buy flowers for poor Vanessa. It might even be therapeutic to discuss her with Matthew. I still felt shocked. I thought wildly of her.

Nearly twenty minutes later, Matthew walked in through the doors of the Breaker, a plush cocktail lounge – not the wine bar he had described – where I had been sitting with distinct uneasiness for more than ten minutes. I offered him the slimmest of smiles, and he asked for a drink with a name as long as a Welsh train station. Soon after he started speaking, I abandoned the idea of mentioning Vanessa. And very soon everything that had happened in our flat was out of my mind altogether. The story he told me even made my hands go numb.

– 8 –

'Well – you must be amazed to see me in London, Mark. I remember telling you about all my plans – plans of ours, I should say. Well, demands of Emily's, really – you know, that we should stick at Straithe, build up some kind of – I don't know, "spiritual base", I think she used to say –

'But in the end – and she idiotically said I'd broken a promise here, because I said we would, for a few years – live in Straithe, that is – in the end, we didn't spend a day there. Frankly, I just couldn't bear the idea of living anywhere near her parents. They're complete berks – all lovey-dovey. So we stayed in a hotel, which annoyed them a bit, I think – a real dump, too. Rats and everything. Luckily I was out most evenings for work, so only Em had to put up with them. But as I said to her – you don't have to worry about them now. Not the rats – parents, I mean. That's what the Bible says, isn't it? You cleave, don't you – cleave to your husband, or the milkman, or whatever – that bit always made me think of cleavages!

'And then I chose a house in a lunch break, right the other side of Birmingham, for work, basically – which I think Em came round to understanding –

'Because the only reason she really wanted to be in Straithe was four withered old people she used to visit every day. I don't know what she used to do with them – witness their wills, measure them for coffins, I suppose. I think they were ill. So I said, look, there are old people in this other place, Crimmington, too – they wouldn't take that long to sniff out –

'Anyway, I had to be nearer the line into the city –

'And, I mean, I was doing well in the firm. I got – it's technical – but I got a shifting Quep monopoly quite early on, where I doubled the three basic coupling integers on the units of about seven clients, which made them stacks of loot.

'Despite the Straithe thing, the first few weeks of the marriage went so well for me –

'I was so happy, Mark. I used to rush home after work, and then – I hope this doesn't affect your – ah – vicarly sensitivities – we'd make love to each other, all round the house –

'Sorry, Mark –

'But she'd put me off for ages before we got married –

'It was – is – a wonderful house. A bit box shaped, maybe, a bit Chinky – mauve inside, too, so I asked a few friends round to paint it. She got a bit upset because they were all fooling about – you can imagine – and put a big white splash on some old photo of hers, which was hilarious until she burst into tears – it turned out to be her grandfather – no, grandmother, I think – and, I don't know, she'd died in the war or something, and that was the only photo –

'But it was only a couple of sploshes, you know – a few dots on it –

'The problem was, being in Crimmington made things tricky with her job. She was teaching – and, what with not having her own car, she couldn't get into Straithe. I'd always said we should stick within our own salaries on basics like cars. I think that's good sense, isn't it? Teachers shouldn't have access to unrealistic amounts of money. So, anyway, in a slightly spineless way, she said it had got too tough to travel and she packed her job in.

'We decorated. I remember putting a little computer in the corner of our bedroom with all the exchange rates bleeping. Actually, Em didn't much like that, and we had a wonderful argument about how some types of science could be art, and how the movements of the Yen on a graph could be just as wonderful as Raphael's sketches – I said that, and she said, almost like she didn't care, you know, that Raphael was a painter, and he didn't do sketches – I said all painters did sketches – I won that one hands down –

' – hold on, Mark. I'll just signal here for another –

'Another drink? The same? Okay – yes, thank you, same for both of us – just mark the bill there, please –

'Yes, if you ever get married, Mark, the day will come when you realise you're the breadwinner – especially if you get a teacher, hellfire. I know money isn't everything, but it nearly is. And everything that happens in your marriage is going to register on a bank statement – that's the rule. So if one partner doesn't bother to look hard enough for a job – which, frankly, was Emily's case – she just didn't stir herself properly after she packed the Straithe one in – not until I bucked her up with some home truths, anyway –

'But things in the marriage seemed all right. I'd come home at eight, and she'd have stories to tell me out of the papers and so on. If she was unhappy, she covered it up pretty well, though she used to cry sometimes for no reason. I must say, I thought it was because she was overcome by joy, the joy of being married – you know –

'And we made love a lot – sorry, Mark, I know you're a curate – but making love – the first few Sundays I'd even stop her getting to church –

'Oh – now that's interesting. A bit Freudian. I gave something away there. Straight away after the marriage, as I was walking out of the church – I don't know if you were watching the two of us walk off – anyway, as I got into the sunlight, I knew I'd never go into one of those dumps again.

'Oh, sorry. I don't mean not on Christmas Day, or any big sort of boycott with placards and things – I just meant I wouldn't ever worship in a church again. I felt church had done its job for me – got me Em, I suppose I mean. And then it came to me. I was divorcing the church on my wedding day.

'I'll be really honest with you, Mark, even though I was a sidesman – one of your batmen! – I'll be honest and tell you I don't believe in heaven – and even if there is one, it's got to be a spot of Sunday angling in the Midlands with some cans of beer – which it doesn't take a ton of brain matter to realise church stops you doing, doesn't it?

'So I told Em not to try to make us pray together, which upset her – and I jokingly called her a religious freak, but I could never convince her afterwards it was a joke, and she kept bringing the comment up – and maybe it wasn't so funny, I don't know –

'But I tell you, that place in Straithe – I know we went, Mark, but that church is an invalid home, a place for people who wouldn't know the names of any of the big world banks, who think the ECU's a vegetable –

'And you were way out of their class, Mark, by the way. Miles above it. Furlongs. They probably couldn't even understand most of your sermons. You were stratospheric. I heard one woman – Mary Cribbens, you remember – come out of the church after you'd been speaking, telling her friend the Church of England should stop accepting graduates. Half of them used to walk out scratching their heads –

'And listen. If God is love, he's not going to bung us down the toilet, is he?

'So I just decided to – you'll like this – trust in God for my salvation! Like the Bible says! It's not exactly a loophole, is it? It's there, plain as money! I'm not sure what I'd want to be saved from, unless it's Monday mornings – but if there is such a thing as salvation, I'll leave it in God's hands. It's like the old joke – I used to be agnostic, but now I'm not so sure! And I'm not worrying about hell now. Because that's a joke, too. We have all the technology now, like fireproof clothes, to make it meaningless. If God's there, he'll keep me out of it, and I'll do the worrying when I'm six feet under. Let God take care of heaven and I'll take care of the money – you know what I mean? Yes, and while

I'm at it, there's no such thing as sin, either, which is another nonsense these people in churches get strung out about, hanging around in old buildings where they know every crack in the stained glass, talking about the weather with the sort of people who plonk themselves next to you on long-haul coach trips – sorry, Mark, I'm not knocking your profession, but –

'I've gone down a massive cul-de-sac. Of course Emily takes all that stuff much more – I was going to say seriously, but it's the wrong word –

' – I think we'll have another fizzy one, Mark – hold on a sec – let me just catch this guy's eye –

'No, she prays a lot, sings a lot, seems to read her Bible most days – and, to be honest, because I'm a bit more clued-up on most things, I was really cautious about telling her my wedding-day decision. Some people just need their fairy tales – simple as that. If you look at the lot that voted in women priests, you'll know what I'm saying.

'In any case, I might not have been able to enjoy the honeymoon if I'd started some great controversy, so –

'I've wondered when I might talk to someone like you.

'About a month in – to the marriage, I mean – that'd be about five months ago – I came home late.

'It was about ten in the evening, I suppose – I'd been working on a big portfolio for a South African company –

'I turned the key in the front door.

'Crimmington's about the quietest place in the world, short of Straithe, so I always said, "Hello, darling." It sounds a bit gooey, but there we go.

'But when I opened the door, there was no answer. I thought Em might have gone off praying, as she'd started meeting one or two funny church people on Tuesdays.

'Then I realised it was a Wednesday. It was all a bit unsettling for me – you expect people to be reliable in the first six months. But anyway, there was a salad in the kitchen, and I turned on the radio and listened for about half an hour. I must admit I cursed a bit, because

Emily had this habit of leaving the salad out for ages and not putting any vinaigrette on. Once I'd got so furious I threatened to hit her, and I thought that had stopped it.

'I ate the meal. Then I think sport came on the radio, so I turned it off and walked into the living-room.

'Guess what I found. You're not going to believe it. Emily was sitting there in an armchair, just sort of staring into space!

'I wandered over and put my arm on hers. She half came to life, but in a dopey kind of way. She turned her face towards me and smiled – but not in the way I know you'll remember, where you'd see the top half of her gums – she was just smiling very vaguely –

'Well, I'm not a medical person, though I probably know about as much as an average doctor from the health pages in the quality papers – but I was certain something was wrong. She wouldn't answer anything, and when I said – as a sort of threat, I admit – that I'd call an ambulance – well, she bounced up and started behaving sensibly again, pecked me on the cheek and told me there was a salad in the kitchen. I said I'd eaten it, and when she realised I'd been home for a while, she seemed to get very – very worried – and she went on about vinaigrette for a bit, too – and I got a bit concerned at that point –

'It was all so peculiar. Because over the next few weeks she seemed to get more vague – do you counsel people like this? Where it's clear there's something on their mind, but the something's so big it won't come out? Like an elephant stuck in a fridge?

'I worked harder and harder. What with not having a job, she kept ringing me at work, even trying to get in for lunch. Strangely, we didn't kiss for about a fortnight once, and I started getting livid with her for being so cold. I shouted at her and said she was like Dracula, brooding. She really was, but she had hysterics when I said that. She didn't take criticism very well –

'And I grabbed her wrists in the hall once, and forced her to look at me – and then realised – this is incredible,

Mark – I suddenly realised she didn't want to look into my face. Wouldn't! Her husband's face! I was almost spitting, and she wasn't supporting me in my work or anything –

'Well, I admit I hit her then, slapped her across the face – to jolt her – and it worked for a couple of weeks, actually – which pleased me – she seemed to care a bit more, at long last, about what was wanted –

'Oh, and believe it or not, just then, just after the slap, the postman knocked – and suddenly she was old Emily again – you could tell the slap hadn't really hurt, though I could see the red coming through – but there was our old Em, Em with a red cheek, that's all –

'In the end, she got a job. And then everything seemed to sort of pick up. She got more active, saw quite a few people from her church. Actually, I don't think they liked me. They spent ages in the house, praying, I suppose, or wailing, in anoraks. Em had sort of hardened to my feelings about church – I'd told her. But these Crimmington church types – well, they kept staring at me in their duffelcoats. I got a bit rude. Once they were leaving the house and I shouted, "Go forth and multiply" – you get much coarser things on our trading floor, after all –

'But anyway, the joke made Emily have another of her fits – her turns, I'd started calling them, because I thought if I teased her about them they might go away –

'Believe it or not, she actually tried to hit me with a fist once! It's extraordinary, isn't it?

'But I don't want you to think it was all bad for me. Not at all. Work was soccer on Saturdays, too, and some great people to go out with. I made friends with the boss and his wife – very sexy woman – and got into seeing the odd film on my own, horror, which Em didn't really mind –

'But wait till I say what I've been warming up to. I can't tell what's behind that face of yours, Mark – never could.

'Anyway, Emily realised, I think, that even though she was paid peanuts at work, she wasn't a monkey –

sorry, I love that joke – the number of dinner parties I've used that line at – she's always been very sporting about that –

'Yes, she even got pestered a bit by men, you know, odd ones. But – I don't know, it made me remember how pretty she was, why I'd married her –

'The whole problem was basically her selfishness. Like – we had a do at work. She wouldn't go. No reason. Just, "No."

'And then, I admit, I did something silly – got into a situation.

'I'd rung Em and said I'd be late back from work. No, hold on, I asked her if she minded first. That's vital. She said she didn't. Remember that – she didn't mind.

'Then all the work people went to a club in Birmingham – Mangle's, it's called. Always packed. And the lads were saying, you know, "Go on, she's not here now," and so on – that rubbish. Kids' stuff. But they're a bright lot.

'It got pretty late and we were all talking to a load of women – the sort you see the top half of before they get into the room. Then I suddenly remembered I'd promised to get up early with Emily on the Saturday – we were going to choose a rug or something, some idea of hers, I can't even recall what it was now –

'I offered – I know what you're thinking, Mark, but you understand how you get when it's late and you've had a bit to drink – I offered a lift to a couple of these women who, funnily enough, lived not too far from Crimmington. Actually, they did live quite a long way from it, but I suppose they just wanted a bit of attention.

'After a bit, there I was, taking woman number two home. Even though I was drunk it didn't stop me thinking, "This could be exciting, Matthew, but watch it."

'Having said that, I don't think this girl was very interested. She sort of curved her hips away from me in the car, and crossed her legs in the tight skirt she was wearing. She had a giant couple of brass earrings with what looked like blackbirds hanging on them, and she mainly just looked out of the window in silence. I was just concentrating on getting her home without being stopped, frankly.

'I often think about what happened and blame Emily.

'She'd been behaving to me like a hostile politician for some time, and even though I never imagined that would go on for ever, it seemed to me marriage should end up equalling two people – and I just couldn't work out why Emily was holding the process up and always disagreeing with me.

'But anyway – somehow, when we got to this girl's flat – we got locked in some sort of embrace.

'Totally innocent, of course, Mark. Nothing very sexual. I'm in the clear on that. I didn't keep her address – take a look in my pocket computer if you like. No, it's just that she had to turn at an angle towards me to undo her seat-belt, and I stretched across to open the door –

'I think it was the first thing she said during the whole journey, but she put her hand on my cheek as I leant over, and said: "Aren't you going to kiss me goodnight?" Imagine it! I mumbled something, and gave the door a push so the interior light came on in the car roof –

'I think I mumbled, "No" – though it might have been "Yes" – but anyway, she gave the car door a tug so the light went out again – so we were in darkness – and then she put her other hand on my other cheek –

'And you can guess. The effects of alcohol, obviously. Totally understandable. And it would never have got further, as I say, though, on the spot, it did get pretty – I don't know – passionate, I suppose. Emily's face kept drifting into my mind for some reason, and I was addressing her in my imagination, just thinking – "You'd better pay me more attention from now on."

'Listen, I can't remember all the details. Rightly, I think, I kept it to just kissing, though some hands went somewhere too. I know you understand – this is man to man.

'At long last I got the car door open.

'The light went on and I remember being shocked at how – frankly, how awful this girl was, with bleached hair and fat shoulders. She looked away from me as though she was ashamed, but I held my eyes on her face and said, pretty firmly, "Goodnight." I must have looked contemptuous, because she left pretty rapidly.

'I'll speed up. I drove home, went up to bed and sank into it. Emily was there, lying in the bed, and I reached out and put a hand on her hip and kissed her – on the neck – but she was fast asleep. I ran my fingers down the length of her arm and went to sleep myself.

'When I woke up I looked at the clock, and chuckled – it was after eleven, and Em had obviously given up hope of me waking up. She'd gone out to buy this rug without me.

'I put my clothes on, and walked out of the bedroom.

'No Emily.

'Then I saw this little envelope sitting on the landing carpet at the top of the stairs. It didn't have my name on it, or anyone's – it was just sitting there.

'I picked it up – sorry, I know I'm going slowly. Can you guess what was in the envelope?

'No? Come on, Mark, this is a quiz!

'Well, it was an earring. As soon as I saw it – this sort of brass circle with a blackbird impaled on it – I knew where I'd last seen it. The woman from the nightclub had been wearing it. I knew what had happened straight away – it was obvious. Emily must have found the thing in the car, and left it so I'd feel guilty. She was never usually that petty. Isn't it ludicrous? After, I don't know, a couple of months of marriage, not to be able to trust your partner?

'I mean, a kiss or two – you get that at Christmas from your relatives, and no one starts leaving earrings lying around in envelopes then –

'But I didn't explode about it when she got back, and she didn't mention it either – she was probably ashamed.

The whole thing was like a scene in a cheap suspense film.

'In fact, for ages we didn't have any conversations about our relationship at all. I thought we'd turned the corner and things were steady.

'Then one day she came in and we talked for about eight hours. I'm sounding scientific about it because it's a disciplined way of thinking I've trained myself to have. She reminded me about the salad incident, and then said – very slowly – she said the reason she'd behaved so strangely then was because – because she'd "made a terrible realisation".

'Of course I asked what it was. I thought maybe she'd forgotten to book the weekend in Scotland we were going on.

'Not a bit of it. She just came out with it, Mark, in about as cold a way as you could imagine.

'She said: "I made a mistake marrying you. I realised that day, and I've never doubted it since then."

'I said, "You selfish bitch," obviously. I thought she was quite likely having a nervous breakdown because she hadn't been working hard enough at school. Plus, I said, "If it's that stupid blackbird earring, that was a free gift from the petrol station in Eastcote Street." A little lie like that can save so much time.

'But funnily enough, she didn't even challenge the earring story.

'The situation now – well, I think she realised what she'd lost, frankly, and said she'd give up her teaching for a time and come and work in my firm. But of course I said she couldn't do that because she probably didn't have the qualifications – or qualities, you know – you've got to be honest about things like that.

'Then, about a couple of weeks later, I got headhunted by London – Marple & Schwartz, the best around. They asked me to be an assistant head of their Financial Luring department. I was absolutely over the moon. But Emily seemed almost uninterested, just saying, sort of, "Go if you want." It was almost like she'd given up on the marriage.

'Then I realised she really wouldn't come, and I just felt it was one step down from blackmail – greymail, I accused her of – it's a legal term, I imagine you wouldn't know it – and thought, "Hell, I'm not going to have a ceiling put on my career by someone who doesn't even know what a rolling dividend is." So – here I am. And I thought, of course, that after a few weeks apart Em would be bound to want to move down from Crimmington.

'But – believe it or not, she hasn't, and when I ring, it's always, "How are you?" in this cold, cold voice, and I ask how her teaching is, and she says "Fine" –

'There's lots more detail, but – we could get another drink, Mark, I suppose – though I'm driving later –

'Look. What I was getting round to is this. This is why it's so good that I've seen you – it's your field.

'Essentially – it's about annulment.

'I mean, I was just wondering whether, you know, after such a short time – and this would be in both our best interests, of course – and considering that keeping the marriage going will be tough work for me, and that the breakdown, if you can call it that, has been almost totally her fault –

'I was wondering. Could the marriage be annulled?

'You're looking awfully blank, Mark! You know, annulled on grounds – I don't know, of insanity, or something?

'Of course I imagine that would mean proving something was up before our wedding, but I feel it must have been, or it wouldn't have taken root so quickly, would it?'

Matthew left the most definite question mark at his disposal after the last sentence, and fell silent. He turned slightly and took a long, loud slug from his drink.

Setting the glass down, he cocked his pitted face up at me. He was grinning.

Rising from my seat, I said: 'Thank you for telling me all that. I think you are the most obnoxious person I have met since I was born.'

And then, as quickly as the crowds around the bar would allow, I left the place . . . ignoring a thin whine of protest that rose at my back, begging explanation.

– 9 –

The title of the sermon was handed down, as though from on high. 'Judge not, lest you be judged.'

I had slept soundly on the lumpy mattress, but reality flooded in with the violence of a riverburst on waking.

Swinging cold legs out of bed and into the chill bedroom air, I rested my elbows on naked, pimpled knees as my feet found the carpet.

I meant to pray, but ended up gnashing teeth. Matthew had stayed out of my dreams – but now his grinning face was projected on the insides of my eyelids. Emily's rose beside it, hollowed: a death-mask. She had aged fifty years.

Then a new feeling swept over me, if briefly.

I felt at ease with Saint Peter's.

It was as though I had looked over the top of a stinking, muddy trench and seen the enemy, pure evil, and decided the stink and mud where I was crouching were not so unbearable after all. My rifle might not be loaded, but at least it was pointing in the right direction.

The spindly bedside table rocked when it lost the weight of the Bible. I ran a finger across the cover of the book, clearing a line through a thick film of dust.

I sneezed.

And then began to cry.

I felt the salted water coursing down my cheeks, and wiped my eyes to be able to pick up clothes in the right order. My lips trembled, and thickened. I mourned Emily, Straithe, accountancy interviews, an old man I had shouted a fifteen-year-old's abuse at in a leisure centre. I mourned everything.

Then Douglas rang.
'Bless you,' he said. 'A big sneeze, that one.'
'There's a bit of dust in the room. I'm sorry.'
'Seems awfully strange – ' he went on, coughing. 'I don't – I mean – I just don't feel we've seen enough of each other, Mark, in this first fortnight – '
'Yes,' I said, and noticed a sharp ray of sunlight cutting between the drawn curtains.
'I – well, this call is just to check you're happy with the sermon. You know the title, don't you? "Judge not, lest you be judged" – I think the New American Bible has something like, "Just quit judging, or you'll get yours." But anyway, Mark, basically, choose your own version, and – '
'I'll use the Bibles in the pews.'
'For most of the thing, yes. I mean for goodness' sake if you're going to use a different Bible, for effect or whatever – you know, if it's a different one, do check it with me.'
'I probably won't,' I said.
'Oh, but you must check it, Mark,' Douglas said, misunderstanding. 'We had a novice here, someone from the choir, I think – yes, from the choir, and he was going to give a sermon, you know. He picked up this book from a trusted shop – I think it was called, *The Bible, Holy and Utmost*, you know – an innocent-looking sort of thing – but it turned out to be a Mormon book, and we had all these verses coming up in the sermon about Peru and not driving, and funny types of spectacles – well, no one could follow the thing at all, no one, and I had to step in.'
I restrained a reflex chuckle. 'How long should it be?'
'Tight. I don't want to be too, you know – it wouldn't be right for you to start thinking, "I must finish now," because once when I asked a visiting speaker to keep it very short, he started making his last point after only about two minutes, which was crazy, you know – mad, because the title was "The Importance of Love" – but the main thing for you, Mark, would just be to get to the point quickly and wrap it all up in less than twenty-five – '

There was a spluttering on the other end of the phone.

'I think I'm going to need the attentions of Elijah if this cough gets any worse,' said Douglas.

'It sounds like you'd better stop talking.' I sensed my sustained annoyance at the Rector beginning to lift.

'I'm sure it'll go well, Mark, and what we'll do – what we'll do, when it's over, is have a meal. And I've got a proposition to put to you, too. Something fun. Yes – fun.'

It won't be fun because I'm leaving the church, I thought. *And you won't want to buy me a meal when I tell you.*

For the first time, I felt butterflies. The Bishop of London would surely have received my resignation by now. Perhaps he might even be trying to ring Douglas at this moment, and finding the line engaged. How would they discuss me? Would the Rector's genial and warm face begin to make new and unpleasant expressions – his tea-cosy hair tilt at an aggressive angle? Would his always-smiling mouth twitch in disgust at the inconveniences my departure would warn him of?

After the call, I wandered around the flat. No Vanessa. No surprise: a scratchy note had said she was going to her mother's, and thanked me. 'Vicki might call in for a chat,' it read. 'Hope sermon goes wellsly.'

She was addressing me like a husband! It was exactly what I had feared. I counted on making myself scarce when Vanessa returned, provided she needed no more help. I could go and hide in a vestry or something, I supposed . . . or a tree. Or just pack bags and leave early.

Amazing: as I pulled the curtains to let the morning sun in, I found myself mesmerised by the new associations of the Marple & Schwartz building. I guessed Matthew was in work today. My dramatic exit from the cocktail bar would not have worried him: you could drive tanks over men like that. They only began to notice if their credit cards got bent.

I hated him with all the legendary energy that Christ reportedly used to love his murderers. That shyster, who should never have been christened with a disciple's name, had crucified my love: strapped her to his bed, and rubbed out her spirit as callously as if he was stripping wallpaper. He was a killer. If he tried to come into my church, I would kill him. If I ever came across the keys to death and hell, I would know where to stick him.

A vulture of a thought swooped on my head.

She divorces Matthew – you marry her.

'No, idiot,' I whispered, still staring at Marple & Schwartz. *I'm the sort who'll never marry.*

Anyway, the Emily I loved no longer existed.

Even if she did, and needed to turn to someone – goodness, I could be in over my head.

I'm the sort who'll never marry, I told myself again.

I set about one of my morning duties: checking the church for the trespassers and tramps who, by the week, were finding more and more ingenious ways to spend the night undetected. This Thursday, walking from the bottom of the spiral staircase, every distracting thought was instantly barged out of my head by a foul stench. I put a handkerchief up to my face and made my way through it.

My first suspicions were correct: when I opened the door to the men's lavatory, recently retiled, the smell quadrupled. I leant against the wall, gagging.

'Is anyone in there?'

I was addressing a locked cubicle in a muffled voice.

There was a banging sound and a flush.

'Are you trying to have a shower?'

Silence.

'There are better places to wash,' I said.

Silence, still. Then, from within the cubicle: 'Not many.'

And an aborted attempt at a second flush.

'What is your name, friend?' I asked.

'The Limo under the Lemon Tree.'

I smiled under the handkerchief. 'What's your surname?'

'Lemon Tree.'

I began to lower the cloth, believing I might have got used to the stench.

Not so. In a muffled voice: 'Where are you from?'

'Street,' Lemon Tree said.

'Where's that?'

Silence.

I took the plunge.

'We don't really like people using these toilets to wash in, because they take a lot of cleaning.'

Silence.

I did not want to repeat the sentence – I felt somehow ashamed of it. I changed position slightly. Only the trickling of a cistern disrupted the stillness.

I sorted through a series of possible next lines.

With a mighty crash, the cubicle door suddenly slammed open. The man faced me. He was stooped and dirty, bearded, wrapped in a stained brown coat. His unzipped trousers, soaked below the knees, hung loose at the waist.

'You think I'm nothing but dirt! You stick this stinking loo here in the middle of church, and you only let people in dinner jackets use it!'

I had no answer to that – and so I made a muffled noise, designed to sound like a suppressed truth.

'You frown at people in jeans, you won't let them use your bogs, it's like Vienna! You think I'm dirt! A mate of mine came here to see the service and he got thrown out!'

I was determined to answer the point, but when I took the handkerchief from my face to speak –

'You won't convert people if they can't use your bogs!'

– the stench knocked me sideways again. I replaced it.

'You don't understand us! Never have! You go on about sin but you can't stand bad smells! Some of us don't have great big Alfas like Dug Krugenheit! We need your bogs!'

Dug Krugenheit was a well-known American evangelist.

Lemon Tree took a step towards me and spat a final sentence from lips cracked almost to nothing.

'You're like the Pharisees, you lot!'

I left him, still washing, flush by flush, with the last

sentiment buzzing like a housefly in my clean ears.

It was the wrong day for me to face a charge of hypocrisy. I had enough reservations about stepping up on to whatever kind of health and safety hazard of a pulpit would be provided on Sunday without down-and-outs with strange uses for the Saint Peter's lavatories pouncing on me. King of Hypocrites: yes, maybe I was. I should preach my sermon on why the poor ought to be allowed to wash sodden, stinking clothes in newly decorated church closets, and how no one should ever be rude to fund managers with pitted faces who broke up their wives like Digestive biscuits. Why not? Things could hardly be worse – and that was even without considering the matter of Preacher's –

Don't even think of that phrase, I told myself.

– Block.

Rebelliously, I completed the thought.

Preacher's Block.

If I had believed enough, I might have argued with God. But it would have felt like shouting at the sky in the hope that Noah would hear.

At noon, Morag rang to say there would be spotlights on Sunday: Sally Halewood was due to sing, of course. And a closed-circuit television screen would allow the tea room to be used as an overflow for latecomers.

Terror gripped me. I made half a page of notes about judging, not judging, God's judgement, why courts had wigs . . . and then screwed it into a ball and launched it, badly aimed, at a wicker bin. No. This needed much, much more. You did not ad lib in front of a thousand people.

I would have to go away.

I went into the bathroom and took my bright yellow toothbrush, bristles red with old paste, from a plastic cup; reached round to the mirrored cabinet in the corner of the bathroom –

– and, at that instant, was stung by a thought like a cattle-prod.

Everything seemed to go into slow motion.

I eased the front of the cabinet open, watching my face being gradually abandoned by the mirror.

Behind it: two unused tubes of red toothpaste; my razor blades, plasters, and aspirins; a wad of cotton wool.

And behind them . . .

I reached very slowly towards the cotton wool.

Behind that wad of cotton wool . . .

I pulled it out of the cabinet.

Behind it were two small bottles of tablets.

I mislaid them.

Those had been Vanessa's words. And now I knew what they meant. I, it turned out, had been the cause of her fit; brusquely shoving her pills to the back of the cabinet to make way for my rubbish – a wad of cotton wool for my ears!

And Vanessa thought the disappearance was her fault. Did that mean her epileptic fit was mine?

Good grief.

It seemed almost a theological question, and not one I had enough Bible reference books to answer.

I waited a minute to let my heartbeat slow.

Poor Vanessa, I murmured. *I'm really sorry.*

There was a sharp ringing: the door bell. Vicki. She had fixed up a lunch.

'I only have about forty-five minutes, so let's hit it,' she said. She offered a lean hand, and I shook it. 'Sorry if I'm looking incredibly serious. I've got things on my mind and I'm basically still in work mode.'

'So am I, a bit.'

I asked her how the new job was going, and the answer lasted until we reached the sandwich bar she had chosen.

'I'm glad the work's all right,' I said.

'It's fine. Let's order.' She glanced around the place for a waitress . . . and then at me again, intensely.

'If you don't mind me asking – has someone been chewing your collar?'

'No – '

I touched it. Of course: there was a corner where there should have been a curve, and small dents where Vanessa's teeth had clamped down.

'I'm not sure,' I said. I did not want to start a conversation about Vicki's sister like this.

'So you haven't been having a passionate affair with one of the vergers?' Her thin lips pinched. A newspaper smile.

My breath went shallow, and then I lost it and felt my heart pump all the blood in my body to my cheeks.

'The vergers are male, anyway,' I said.

'So?' Vicki laughed. 'Mark, you look like a lobster!'

When the food came, Vicki held the index fingers of both hands upwards like a fin, then tipped them in an arc until they pointed straight into my face: an arrowhead.

'Vanessa hasn't had a fit for more than two years.'

She knows about the tablets, I thought.

'I think she stopped taking her pills,' said Vicki. She dismantled the weapon her fingers had formed and used them to pick at the sandwiches. We both had hot salt beef on rye.

'That's what I'm hoping, anyway,' she added.

'Well, some medicines don't make that much of a -'

Vicki cut in. 'Mark, I just wanted to say that I'm really grateful for your help – '

'Oh – no – ' I protested, and raised my hands in a way that suggested I had done nothing to deserve thanks.

'But,' Vicki went on, pointedly, 'you really shouldn't have left her afterwards. Her muscles could have locked.'

My heart sank, and so did my hands.

'Gosh.'

'They didn't – I mean – I know I sound so ungrateful – '

'No – '

. . . *Yes.*

'I do, Mark – it's just my concern for her – especially after this thing on the Tube.'

We took mouthfuls of our sandwiches, and I watched cress squeezed out of hers fall on to her plate.

I wondered if this was the moment for me to do my job.

'Have you come any closer to believing in God?'

'Me?' asked Vicki, through salt beef.

'Yes.'

'Not really.'

I carried on eating. I felt I had done my bit for the church. With some people, there was no point.

'I've been getting into something called New Thinking,' Vicki said, slowly, after a while. 'It's not a religion, because it says there's no God, but it's sort of – well, all I've done so far is read some magazine cuttings on it – but it's got a ring of truth, I think. Quite a big ring.'

'What is it?' I asked.

'You concentrate hard on everything you've ever done wrong for about forty-eight hours. You need to take time off work. The end result is you basically don't feel so bad about it. Then you just do whatever you want, as long as it's what – I suppose – what you really want.'

'Does Vanessa know?'

'She's still hoping I'll come over to her side, I think,' said Vicki. 'To – to God, I suppose. But I won't, because it's rubbish. I'm impressed with how she puts up with all the suffering she's had – but all I want is to be happy. Christianity doesn't address that. New Thinking does. Too many of these Christian types treat life like a funeral.'

Treat life like a funeral, I reflected. *Good one.*

'Daniel wouldn't like to hear you say that,' I said.

Her face clouded. 'I do like him. But he's too busy with church lunches. I couldn't meet him today because of one.'

So I was what I was used to being. Second choice.

'What do you think of the beef?' Vicki asked.

'Fine.'

'Mine's a bit too thickly sliced.'

'Yes, I suppose mine is.'

'Have you settled in, then?'

'I think so,' I said. 'It's different.' There was no way I was going to say I knew I was leaving; no way she was going to say she knew I should never have arrived.

Then again, perhaps she felt she was hiding nothing. Women were odd beasts, I decided: wildebeests.

'Have they given you much to do?' she asked.

'They've given me tasks, rather than jobs, if you know what I mean. Douglas – the Rector – hinted about something that was going to be fun. That's what he said. But – oh, I was going to tell you,' I said, betraying as little of the enormous stress as possible, 'I'm doing some preaching.'

'Really?' She sounded nonchalant.

'Sunday.'

'I'll come.'

'Oh – please don't.'

'Last time we met you were going on about the curate who was there before you,' Vicki said.

'Yes. I've thought about it quite a bit.'

'You had a theory he was some sort of a mystery man.'

'No one would tell me anything about him.'

'They're all too busy, that's why,' she said, sensibly. 'Church lunches.'

'No – well – ' I gave up. Protest was futile.

'His name was Brendan,' she said. 'That's all I know.'

I looked up, my teeth clamping down on the meat.

'Brendan?'

This was extraordinary. A door closed for ever to battering rams had swung suddenly ajar in a light breeze.

'Big deal!' she said, laughing. 'That doesn't even tell you the colour of his hair!'

'What was it? Ginger?'

'Mark!' she squealed. 'You've gone mad!'

I returned to the food, but it tasted different now. Brendan. It was something and nothing.

After a while, she broke the silence. 'I'm in love,' she said. 'A guy from work.' She picked at the remains of her sandwich. 'That beef was thicker than the tyres on my car.'

'How's it going?' I asked.

'It's fine. It's just been in for a service. They said the rotor arm was – '

I interrupted. 'The – love, I mean.'

'He doesn't know and he doesn't care,' she said. 'And I probably won't in a week or two.'

'Can you tell him?'

'He's married – '

I had that trench feeling again. The stink and mud in the Saint Peter's trench were beginning to seem comfortable.

' – yes, with four children, funnily enough.'

Much more comfortable.

Momentarily I wondered: had I been right to send the resignation letter? And then I smothered the thought, as if with a pillow. It was done.

It returned, though, on a long-distance train pulling out of King's Cross station.

To prepare my sermon, I needed to think. To think, I needed to be away. And there was only one place to spend the next two days: with Peg Watson, a former parishioner who was eighty-three and lived in the middle of an eyeful of big green fields six miles north of my old church.

The train rocketed out of London as the day died, efficiently setting behind it grim tower blocks and miles of grey homes, squeezed together as though by muscle-men. I eased back in the seat.

God.

I mouthed the word; thought it.

Murmured: 'Onward, Christian soldiers, marching as to war, with the cross of – '

. . . and stopped, as tiredness settled on my eyelids like fat fingers.

Emily.

Matthew.

A pretty face and rotten one.

I opened my eyes, and the fleeting landscape looked darker by degrees. We were far from London now. Out of the window, a white rectangle in the black distance ran parallel to the train, then turned a corner: the last curate's dog collar, I guessed. Brushing the carriage like a phantom.

Brendan.

My resignation – how rash it had been. And how irreversible.

Was this regret?

It couldn't be.

We were guided by God.

I frowned at the irony, and closed my eyes again, thinking I might miss Daniel Ogumbaye when I left. He had switched on friendship like a grill, and I had forgiven his opposition to my appointment. Not just forgiven, in fact, but forgotten: in fact, to be honest, forgotten first, then forgiven, in that order – proving, in an incidental way, that the key to forgiveness was forgetfulness, and the most gracious people in the world were amnesiacs. It was Daniel who had told me, laughingly, how a black bra had been left . . . no one knew how or why . . . on the floor of the tea room: and, when half the church moved down there after a service, 'they fanned out from it like it was an unexploded bomb, or something. People were getting crushed – everyone was trying to move away from it.'

At the time I had been unsure whether curates should laugh at bras: now though, eyes closed, I smiled . . .

And then wondered how Vanessa was . . .

The train wheels pounded the track, my brain pounded with guilt.

I woke suddenly.

'Sorry.' I had kicked a big man who had not been there before, sitting opposite with cans of beer and a T-shirt emblazoned with a trident.

He glanced up.

I looked out of the window, struggling to sit straight.

We were at a station. It was impossible to see the name.

'Excuse me –' I was talking to the drinker – 'I'm just wondering how far it is to Birmingham. I'm changing there.'

The man put down his can of beer, and swore.

'You've gone past it, mate.'

'Oh, no.'

'Where were you going?' He set aside a magazine.

'Todworth – west, sort of.'

'You're a vicar, are you?' he asked, with a burp.

'Curate.'

'Because it looks like a dog's had your collar.' He roared with laughter at the joke, and I automatically reached up again to the dents and grooves in it.

'Mind you,' he went on, 'two more stops and you can change to a bus. Perfect for Todworth.'

'So where are we now?' I asked. The train was hissing.

'Crimmington,' he said.

I looked out of the window, eyes widening.

'Look – just a minute – I've got to –'

'Not here, vicar,' he burped, reaching forward.

Crimmington.

'Can you watch my bag?' I left him gaping, ran down the empty aisle . . . the train began to move, then lurched to a halt, spinning me into a seat corner. The drinker was calling: 'Not here, dog collar! And you've left your bags!'

I did not know what I wanted to do. I just had a sense, suddenly, of the two-thousand-to-one possibility of Emily being there, on the platform . . . waiting for another train, perhaps . . . or looking for a piece of lost property she might have left the week before . . . I did not know. Could not know. But that one chance, that two-thousandth chance of a chance, was enough to propel me down the carriage –

Up to the window of the train door –

Breathless –

I yanked the window down and looked left and right. The train was slowly leaving the platform behind.

Below the window, two men in orange overalls were working under arc lights at the trackside. It was as though I was gliding over them. They were both shovelling a hole in the gravel next to a corrugated-iron barrier. Their lights cast a dark shadow into it – six feet long . . .

The shovels ticked in the gravel: *tick, tick, tick.*

Six long, four deep, I guessed, that hole . . .

The two workmen wore black bobble hats.

Tick, tick, tick. Six feet long, four feet deep.

The train left the hole behind.

We were soon going at a tilt again. 'Told you it wasn't this one, but you wouldn't believe me,' the drinker said when I sat down. In response, I stared out of the window. He flicked a can of beer open with a bang, spraying my ear with froth. I thought of cotton wool wads, then epilepsy pills.

Peg was delighted when I arrived.

'So good to see you, love.'

Her smile was like a fan heater.

'I went the long way,' I said. 'Taxis and everything.'

We hugged on her doorstep, and I felt as though all burdens had been left somewhere between the tracks leading out of London, to be crushed by successive trains. Then, remembering myself, I reminded Peg bluntly why I had come, and shouldered at least one burden again, painfully.

Two words. 'This sermon,' I said.

'You told me, Mark, love, and it's so good to see you, my darling – you can just be all on your own, doing your own thing as much as you like.'

'That's wonderful,' I said, and we hugged again.

I hauled my bags in from the porch of her home.

'One of these is just books.'

'My,' she said, looking down. 'You've brought an awful lot of them.'

— 10 —

We give our praise to you, O God
We give our praise to you
Grateful, hopeful, remembering your cross
We bring our hearts to you

We give our gladness to you, O God
We give our gladness to you
Prayerful, tearful, remembering your grace
We bring our hearts to you

We give our homes to you, O God
We give –

The sound was deafening. A thousand people shouted the words as though calling panicked warnings at drivers reversing blindly towards their parked cars.

Every seat in the church was filled, even the hundreds on the balconies. The five of us with places at a short bench along the stage had a side view of the massed ranks of the choir, belting every note back at the congregation. A vast bank of spotlights, fit for stadium rigging, heated us like food. The giant organ was played frantically, as though to stave off an apocalypse. Scores of heads were flicking in my direction. Yes, the new curate was being spotted.

I might have felt like a pop star, but pop stars' knees did not knock, and pop stars knew tunes and words. I did not this morning. I had expected 'Onward, Christian Soldiers', or at least 'Jerusalem'. Instead there was something called 'Lord, I Recognise Your Famous Name', which boasted some strangely intimate phrases to sing at an omnipotent Creator – 'I want to give you everything I have, And touch you' – and sounded, judging by the vigour of the drums and the speed of guitar-strumming by Richard Burts, like a reserve entry for the Eurovision Song Contest. A woman in the second row was jiggling. I gazed at her, blankly.

Was I more nervous now than at any time in my life?

No. Emily's wedding had been worse.

But today, when I stepped up to the pulpit to preach –

It would be like pressing my face into a tiger's.

On my right, Daniel and Douglas. The latter still had a racking cough. I glanced at him, recalling the words he never knew I had heard: *We just have to pray good comes of it.*

On my left, two of the lay assistants. (There were three in all, spending an unpaid year in the church with the aim of being curates or vicars later – although two former assistants had gone into social services, the last had ended up as a botanist, and another lost his faith and went to work as a press officer for the tobacco industry.) Today, it was Jane Bull and Gregory Runting who had joined us at the rim of the stage. Jane was well built for victory on a rugby pitch. Where she sang at my shoulder, her stocky frame obscured the profile of the other lay assistant.

Gregory Runting's friends called him Grunt. He was a noisy twenty-six-year-old with a shock of white hair and a beaky nose, whom I had been unable to like and thought should not have a place on the staff of any church. Grunt was smart in the worst sense, irritatingly loud rather than witty, and failed to bother to tune in to anyone he had a conversation with. He just blared at them about the environment, mostly, and girls in church who had turned him down.

We give our love to you, O God
We give our love to you

Wishful, thankful, remembering your Son
We bring our hearts to you

We give our trust to you, O God
We give our trust to you
Faithful, mindful, remembering your miracles
We bring our hearts to you.

The song ended in a healthy swirl of clarinet and organ, and then a thousand worshippers closed the book, breathed mightily as one, and took seats in rustles of every material.

Douglas's squeakless dark brown suede shoes moved across the stage. He took his place in the pulpit. Half of it looked to be supported at the back by a neat pile of clay bricks. Someone had done a good repair job.

At the lectern, the Rector of Saint Peter's Church took a sheet of yellow paper from the inside breast pocket of his black jacket and coughed into the microphone. Its shaft flashed a spotlight at me.

Everyone was silent.

'What we are all wanting is to move in the spirit of Jesus Christ.'

It struck me as an extraordinary way to begin giving out notices. The congregation were looking up, expectantly. This was a Douglas I had not seen before: not the genial bungler who had let the misappointment of a curate go uncorrected, not the man who gave a cactus free passage to his Church Council. This was a rector in his element.

Douglas touched quickly on upwards of half a dozen themes. Minny Lury, he said, whom many of you will know as having served coffee and grapefruit juice downstairs in the tea room for more years than most of us have been here, died during the week. Mercifully, it was quick. We thank God for a life given over to serving Jesus Christ.

For the second time of asking for Nayantara Saghal and

Prabhu Ghentali, and for the third for Jock Parry and Beth Cowie, the banns of marriage were published. Many of us knew these lovely couples quite well: Nayan, of course, had been on two local radio phone-in programmes to answer questions on the dangers of prescription drugs. If anyone knew why these four should not be married, they were to declare it now.

Everyone jumped at a thick cough that came from a downstairs seat, somewhere near the centre aisle.

The Rector moved on.

'Those of you who have been praying for Harold Killey will be pleased to know that he can now communicate by blinking.' He moved the paper on the lectern.

'And we're hoping for volunteers for spring cleaning, which will actually be in January – we don't want to use professionals this year.' Now Douglas was coughing, hand on chest. His voice sounded hoarse as he went on. 'Ah – and by the same token, you'll see we have half-size notice sheets today. Cut exactly in half. It's an economy, that's all. Oh, now – I should just point out – that has resulted, I'm afraid, in something misleading in the article about Vanessa Spicer's course for single Christians. You can see the heading – "Singleness, Not Single Mess". Well, underneath it should actually say that the most we can fit on that course is twenty-eight. But because of the cut in the paper, it wrongly says the maximum number is two.'

There was an isolated burst of laughter.

Douglas made one more announcement, about trips to mission sites in Kenya and Indonesia.

Grunt was leaning across. 'I've done that,' he said to me. 'Great. All the boats are falling apart!'

'You may find it brings you closer to Jesus Christ, and what he wants for you,' said Douglas. I winced.

We sung again. My hands were dripping with sweat: my heart beating faster than the drums.

Preacher's Block.

My knees started knocking in a kind of bossanova.

Preacher's Block.

I opened my mouth to sing: it was dry. Unwittingly, I nearly croaked the first words that came to mind –

Preacher's Block.

Had the last curate suffered it, I wondered? Had Brendan, anonymous Brendan, silhouetted Brendan . . . had he sat in the same seat before the same ocean of faces – covered the same songbook in perspiration? Looked at a sheaf of sermon notes as though faced with unscramblable Chinese?

They were singing again.

> Oh can it be that I should gain
> An interest in the Saviour's blood?
> Died he for me, who caused his pain?
> For me, who him to death pursued?
> Amazing love! How can it be
> That you, my God, should die for me!

The night before, Vanessa had walked into the flat.

She looked better: the pink golfballs were glowing.

'I'm embarrassed about your dog collar,' she said.

'My collar?'

'Vicki told me about the state it was in. I remembered you discreetly putting it back on – the – other night.'

I reassured her. 'Actually, I've been away for a couple of days as well. Up in the Midlands. Todworth. I bought a new one up there.' I arched my neck. 'Like it?' The question ended with a slight gurgle: the thing was pinching.

'I hope my sister thanked you,' Vanessa said, vaguely.

'She did.'

Behind the noise, and a tendency to lean towards listeners and tug the clothing around their elbows, was a woman I thought could well be feeling terribly alone. If it were not for the solace she seemed able to draw from her faith in Christian matters, Vanessa might have been a basketcase. But her props were propping her, weren't they? And props they were, were they not? A

Bible, page-ends grey with thumbprints, spine broken through overuse? Periods of three-quarters of an hour when Vanessa would withdraw to pray, turning off the radio in her room and closing the door? The peculiarly husky way she spoke of New Testament figures, especially the central one, whose name I found I was using less and less in any kind of conversation?

Props.

Troubled parts of the world were being named in a voice that echoed. I felt the shiver of tight-buttoned panic again, returning to the present, kneeling now. A rake-thin man was in the pulpit, sniffing, leading the church in prayer.

'. . . Northern Ireland, South Africa, the Baltic States, the Antarctic, Epping,' he sniffed.

'Amen,' the congregation said. Clutching a piece of paper as though life depended on it, the man made his way gingerly down the pulpit steps.

For a moment I thought I was about to faint.

Am I on next?

No. I glanced at Gregory Runting, and the effect of seeing his arrogant profile, perched importantly on the edge of our bench, was like breathing ammonia.

Too late to back out now, I told myself. *Anyway, you're resigning. You have no responsibility for what you're about to preach.*

The thought – a preposterous one – was no help at all. Leaving the church after preaching a bad sermon seemed far worse than leaving it after not preaching at all.

'Brothers and sisters, this is something we've been working on during the week, and we hope you enjoy it.'

It was Francis Bottom. He was dressed as though for dinner with the boss, talking into a hand-held microphone.

And his wife was on the stage . . .

Sally Halewood was wearing a tight slip of a black evening dress with six sequins on the petite hipbone that faced us. Behind her, some members of the choir broke into indulgent smiles.

Francis Bottom said a few words. His wife swayed, grandly, staring into a space somewhere above the scores of faces on the balconies. Then Francis moved a baton through the air in a perfect line, and drums clumped in like mules; notes ticked on a guitar which looked only the size of a medallion on the stomach of Richard Burts; a scale on the piano narrowed and rose – and was joined by double bass; and then Ms Halewood moved forward a minute distance, a tiny distance, less than the breadth of a hair . . .

And sung.

'If ever I should feel/Some hardship done for you/To be too severe/Forgive me, Lord –'

. . . a husky breath; descending beats on tom-toms . . .

'Remind me of that hill/The hill of Calvary/From which they took your broken body/And your loving tenderness to me —

'When you rose again –'

Her crystal voice made musical chandeliers. A second and third verse came like caviar on silver trays. The choir members who had smiled were now intent. Francis, trunk hugged by a tight chequered jacket, stared deep into her eyes as he conducted. The pianist ran through another scale, drummer rattling his stick on a cymbal-ridge . . .

'Because you, you rose again.'

And suddenly it was over.

But there was no applause: just silence, followed by rustling and whispers.

Then my heart fell down in my chest like a sixties tower block.

It's me.

There was nothing else between me and that pulpit.

To my right, Douglas was looking at me, smiling. Jane Bull and Gregory Runting were doing the same to my left.

And now Daniel had a hold of my elbow.

'Go for it,' he said.

'I hope so,' I returned, in a whisper, not thinking.

I stood. Daniel and Douglas made way for me, angling their knees to the right in the cramped space.

Have you got your notes?

The thought that I might have left them at Peg's jolted through my mind.

No: they were in my hand, soaked with perspiration.

Is your throat clear?

Yes. I cleared it as I walked up to the pulpit, feeling the heat of the lights as I came within range of the entire battery. Yards from the bench, the painting of Jesus Christ on the west wall sneaked into the corner of my right eye, staring, aggravatingly. Whose was that black finger that prodded my heart whenever I saw the thing?

I was shaking when I got into the pulpit. Heart pounding, but safe at the summit and level with the lectern, I put the notes down and winced at the typed words in an expression I hoped might be mistaken for a placid smile. Then I raised my head, and breathed deeply.

I pressed my palms on to the pulpit's wooden surround for support.

My audience –

Lord.

It's amazing, this church.

For a second, they must have thought I was shocked.

The lower part of the building looked even bigger, crammed with people.

Some smiled. Other faces looked as bleak as winter. I exchanged winks with a woman in her forties, and then realised she suffered from a nervous tic.

I picked out the first line of my script and read it.

'Judge not, lest ye be judged.'

I heard two different versions of a voice: the small one that came out from between my lips and disappeared inches from my face, and then the booming thing that the big speakers sent rolling round the hall.

The second line.

'That is the title of the sermon, and it's what you've heard our Bible readings today.'

I was thrown slightly as I read that sentence, because there appeared to be a word missing.

After a pause, I added: ' – on.'

I told a brief story about myself. I often misjudged people, I said. A teacher at school had appeared overbearing at first, but had gone on to do more to help me throughout my years there than anyone else, and shown me a bit of the excitement in accountancy.

The sentence seemed to make someone in the congregation convulse with laughter – and the warmth of the reaction gave me the confidence to run through, without overly faltering, the section of my script about the Old Testament book of Judges and the ironies in it; a description of how Israel's system of justice worked; and two passages in Revelation about the Day of Judgement.

We shall all be changed, in the twinkling of an eye.

Suddenly the notes became almost a part of me, and I was reading with growing fluidity. Thank goodness, I thought, for time with Peg. I had taken enough reference books to sink a ship – a couple by BBF, even – and used nearly all of them. I was heartened, glancing up and catching faces in the front row or at the side, not to see BBF there. He might have recognised phrases lifted directly from his own writings.

I showered them with bursts of explanation about any reference to judgement that I had found in the colour-coded index of the Bible, with anecdotes about court cases or the necessity of settling disputes in churches.

'In the book of Corinthians,' I said, 'Paul tells his readers, "One brother goes to law against another – and this in front of unbelievers! Why not rather be cheated?"

'It is better, Paul is saying, to be slighted, than to make negative judgements,' I explained.

And suddenly . . . suddenly, at that instant, at the very moment I read the word 'slighted' . . . at that moment, I realised I was overcoming Preacher's Block.

My heart leapt with excitement at the thought.

Then a dreadful idea struck me.

You have overcome it because Emily is dead to you.

I continued reading my notes.

Dead to me?

Dead.

I carried on with my notes –

And remembered at that moment, up there in the lights, reading pages of typed print as though on automatic, those workmen digging at the trackside as our train had left Crimmington on Thursday. The hole they had been digging . . .

Six feet long, four feet deep.

It was a crazy, obsessive thought . . . a stupid thought . . . but it took hold none the less, up there on the pulpit, where it had no business to: the thought that the hole those workmen had been digging was Emily's . . . that it was a grave . . . that she was dead and buried now, and I would never see her again.

I continued reading my notes to the congregation.

You know, I thought, Mark, as you stand up here, high up, you are burying your dear Emily with this sermon.

You are wiping out the agony of her wedding.

The lights were even hotter than they looked.

Mine was an astonishingly selfish thought, because it counted on the annihilation of Emily for its life: and – look – here I was, right at the top of a pulpit in one of the country's biggest churches, perhaps the biggest, thinking that thought in full view of a thousand Christian worshippers.

But with Emily gone, I began anew. With her life went my love . . . and, when that had fallen from my heart like snow from a rockface, a great burden would go with it.

It was falling now.

And this sermon was proof.

I have overcome.

I simply had to leave Emily dead now, or as good as. To think of going back for her, of looping my life round the tragedy of hers, curling the strings of my existence in the circular saws Matthew had set spinning around hers . . . it would destroy me. I had to leave her for dead.

'In three days he rose, and will come again to judge the living and the dead,' I was telling the congregation. 'God is the judge, according to the Anglican creed. The judgements are thine, God.'

In twenty minutes, three people within view had fallen asleep. The pastor's nightmare is that more than ten per cent of his audience does – the only circumstance, it was said at theology college, when it was acceptable to cut short a sermon. We had been told that shouting certain words from the body of our texts, such as 'fire', if it was there, or 'sword', would often jolt sleepers awake. But this morning – well, three was not even one per cent of my audience, let alone ten.

So, at last, I concluded exactly where I had meant to.

'Feed us with these words, God.'

I stepped down from the pulpit, rinsed with emotion.

Mounting it, I had feared crushing defeat. But now I thought I sensed a victory – no, not a victory, but an easy wave of relief.

I walked past the choir, unable to avoid catching the glances of some of them. They looked engaging. That was all. It was a big choir.

For the first time, as I approached the kindly faces of Douglas, Daniel, Jane and Grunt, I felt a deathly kind of hardness in the place where the agonies over Emily had previously gathered their energies like demons.

What had happened to me up on that pulpit?

A hardman! I became a hardman!

I sat down, and Jane Bull passed the hardman an opened songbook, with a number I was too dazed to decipher staring at me. Organ notes were suddenly thrown like crockery, the drummer woke up – he had been one of the three – and struck up, and now we were singing more of their music:

King of Kings, the great I Am,
Thank you for the morning
Glorious Prince of Peace, giving
us your care;

Glory to God, Glory to God
In the highest
Rule us for ever, Hosanna.

Lord of Lords, the great Creator
Thank you for the afternoon
In glory you came, winning us our
goals in you;

Glory to God, Glory to God
In the highest
Rule us for ever, Hosanna.

God of God, the great Redeemer,
Thank you for the evening
Triumphant in our trust, your
promises are true!

Glory to God, Glory to God
In the highest
Rule us for ever, Hosanna.

Douglas prayed, and then everyone began rustling and moving, standing, or perhaps leaning forwards in their seat to talk to the person in the row in front . . . talking, talking, talking: hundreds, talking! Grunt leant over and gave me a ridiculous thumbs-up sign with a wobbly thumb, and Jane Bull whispered into my ear that I would find it hard to get away, because everyone would want to meet me. But I was not worried about getting away. For as we sung the last song, and the Rector prayed the final prayer, I had been looking at the face and profile of a girl.

She was singing in the choir and winking from time to time at friends. I was able to watch her without being seen.

I had no idea why she had attracted my attention. She looked nothing like Emily, who had been long-legged and slim, with a lazy sense of dress and a head of fair curls. This girl was short, with a full figure, and thick, snarled black hair that hung down over the top edge of wide-rimmed glasses, and was sheared horizontally at the nape of her neck. She was not classically beautiful in any sense, but pretty: yes, pretty; and she looked naturally, effortlessly smart, with a navy blue jacket and glinting brooch. Her lips were made up in scarlet and spread wide in a semi-smile as she sung, though there seemed to be no powder, blusher, or anything else on her face. Just the scarlet lipstick.

The hardman put down his songbook, followed Douglas and Daniel off the stage and down the main aisle towards the domed lobby, registering the dozens of stares at the new curate. He reached the double doors through which everyone passed on their way out of the church, and waited for her there.

– 11 –

Scarlet Lipstick never met the Hardman. She must have slipped by as I waited at the double doors, dozens and dozens from the congregation queuing to grab my hand.

It went on and on. Where had I studied theology? At Oxford? Cambridge?

'At Birkham,' I said.

And where was I born? And what did I think of London?

One stiff-backed man asked if I listened to music.

'A bit of Elvis Presley, maybe,' I said. 'I Got a Lot of Living to Do.'

'You certainly have, if that's all you've –'

'Sorry,' I said. 'That's one of the songs.'

'Oh. I see. Yes.'

Casually working the crowd and asking gentle questions about the last curate – well, it would have been impossible. Douglas stuck at my side, introducing me.

'Empringham,' he would repeat slowly, using a tone that underlined every letter. 'Think of emperor, plus telephone ring, then cheese and ham. Emp-ring-ham.'

'Mark,' I would add. 'As in German.'

Monday came: a bank holiday.

I stayed in London. Seeing my parents in Middlesex did not appeal. I would have to tell them I was leaving the church: how could I avoid it? And they would, of course, not understand. My mother, whom I treasured in the same way as those who never visit the Tate treasure it, would speak gloomily of how much better accountancy would have been for me – she was an atheist – and ask again why I had changed my mind about going into it. I could never bring myself to tell her the reason was a pile of rejection letters.

Saint Peter's was all but deserted. Even BBF, in the habit of using public holidays to write, had left – to take his wife motoring in Devon. In the lobby on Sunday, Gregory Runting had joked loudly that Devon had been evacuated as a result.

Walking through the tea room, I met Daniel. He was wearing a cream cravat flecked with blue diamonds.

'Watch out – the Coppers are locked,' he said.

The Coppers were the imposing pair of copper-coloured doors that opened outwards on to the steps from the lobby.

'I didn't expect you to be here, Daniel.'

'I've got to draw up the schedule for the businessmen's meetings – they've got to get to the printers tomorrow.'

'Why?'

'First one on Thursday. A great chance for high-flyers to hear about God. But my brother's getting married forty-eight hours later in Nigeria, so I won't be there.'

'I thought I'd stay here today,' I said, aware we were just making conversation. 'I had a bit of a bad accident with my filing cabinet last night. I opened the top three drawers, and it toppled over. It made me miss the evening service – it was lucky it didn't fall on me. All my letters fell out, though – everything – ' I made an expansive gesture.

'As long as you didn't work on a Sunday,' Daniel smiled.

I coloured. *I did.*

Now he was laughing. 'Mark – for goodness' sake, I'm only ribbing you! We're not legalists here!'

Sure you're not, I thought, without animosity. When Christians said they weren't legalists, what they meant was they had so many laws they'd lost count of them all, Stewart Weeks had once told me.

'I cleared most of the stuff today,' I said. 'It goes back years – job rejections after university, everything.'

I regretted that, revealing, sentence. But Daniel was gracious enough to ignore it.

'I was interested in your sermon.'

'Oh, thanks.' I took interest as a compliment, though I had been surprised at how few comments there had been.

'Yes – on judgement. A workmanlike bit of preaching.'

Workmanlike? What does he mean?

'It was all right, was it? It didn't ruffle any feathers?'

Daniel smiled; the white teeth shone in the black face.

'There was no danger of that, I can promise you.'

'It was a job to prepare.'

'It sounded like it.'

'Not that I'm unfamiliar with the Bible, you know, Daniel, but just finding everything on a particular topic – '

'Takes time – '

' – takes time – '

' – and you didn't have very much.'

'Only a couple of days.'

'And there was an awful lot of Old Testament in there.'

Was that a criticism? An awful lot of Old Testament? What did 'awful' mean? Was he saying something?

'It generally came up to people's expectations, did you think?' I dreaded a negative reply. The conversation itself was beginning to feel like the Day of Judgement.

He shrugged.

'Mark – it may not have been what they're used to, to be honest – but – I don't know, I suppose – well – maybe it's good to be reminded about – I don't know – eighteenth-century commentators and so on, and bits of Habakkuk – '

'The Habakkuk bit was pretty short – '

'Yes – and, you know – it had its place – '

'Chapter two, it was – "The reckless man will be unsure of himself" – verse four –'

Daniel broke in.

'I suppose, personally, I might have wanted more about Christ, and what he did for us.'

I stared at the dots on the toes of my shoes. Today they seemed to be in the shape of reverse question marks.

'Did a lot of people think that?'

'Oh, I don't know, Mark,' Daniel said, laughing comfortably. He patted me on the shoulder. 'And this, anyway, this was your first sermon for –'

'For six months, yes – the last time I –'

' – for six months, and it's pretty major to go from somewhere like Straithe, I imagine, on to a pulpit that you've only just seen collapse – in front of, well, a huge –'

'I just felt the Old Testament stuff was relevant. I was going to mention Jesus Christ in my next sermon.'

'Yes, absolutely. And I'm only saying this, you know, as a friend – we've got to know each other –'

'I appreciate it, Daniel. Thank you.'

I was hurt. But my relief at having averted a far, far greater disaster on the pulpit smothered most of the effects of Daniel's words.

He brought up the evening service. The worship had been terrific, he said, but a technical problem nearly spoilt it.

'This happens when one has a church so big. Just putting a voice around the building needs whizzy technology. So we've got these new microphones, which transmit sound to receivers at the back, instead of needing wires.'

'Oh yes – I'd wondered about that while I was –

While you were plagiarising commentaries on Habakkuk.

' – while I was – giving my sermon. I saw there weren't any wires, but I could still hear my voice.'

'Anyway – it started picking up the police talking.'

'Police? What – on the same wavelength?'

'Yes, because one of them was in a chase, and he kept breaking in during the prayers – describing another car – and then someone said, "Seen him, Larry" – and there was this bumping sound and a shout – this was while Doris Slattery was leading the evening prayers, and she struggled on – she was praying the church would be shown how many people in London needed the Bible's message, and then one of the police kept shouting, "Four. Four. Four." It was extremely loud.'

'Amazing. The biggest disruption we had in Straithe was hearing a siren in another county.'

Daniel laughed and took a step backwards, fingering the shirt collar around his cravat. 'I must go.' Walking off, he turned back and called: 'Douglas is around too – in bed, though. He just can't seem to shake off this cough thing.'

Half an hour later, I was at Teddy's. The ice-cream shop was a walk away, across a mile of unkempt common.

'Like the Church of England,' Daniel had said once, taking me aback, 'the menu's full of nuts.'

Alone, staring at a Chocolate Fudge Almond Wonder, I wondered which career came after church.

I could be a parson in a public school.

Was it parson or pastor? I would probably be teased.

Actor.

I couldn't act.

Author. I could write a bestseller.

About what? Love? I would be lost for experiences to draw on after the preface.

I could work for a big company.

As what?

As an ethical adviser.

Big companies don't have ethics.

As an accountant, then.

That was better. I had, after all, a training . . . some interview practice . . . an intriguing application form . . .

'But why did you leave Saint Peter's, Mr Empringham?'

True. I would have to explain that.

So join the police.

Policemen sit around making blue jokes.

Curate – again, at another church?

A small church? It had an appeal.

Academic?

That would be all right if I hadn't failed things.

Journalist.

Impossible to get into, and I was no good at creative writing. Plus, the Church would never take me back.

Marketing manager.

Sales executive.

Credit analyst.

No. I did not know what any of them were.

The train of thought appeared incapable of leaving any station, and I dug into the sundae. An array of coloured pellets on the ice-cream made me think of Vanessa's tablets.

She had new ones now. I felt less guilt: partly, for sure, because of whatever purge it was that had happened up on that pulpit . . . Vanessa's fit had gone.

Oh – that reminded me.

The pages.

I fished in my left pocket with one hand, as the spoon in the other scraped fudge from the rim of the glass.

The toppled filing cabinet had emptied a ton of papers on to the lounge floor. To clear them, I had got down on hand and knee. There were dog-eared tax details of a legacy, letters, cartoons drawn at Birkham to pass dark weekend evenings, smeared pages from accountancy magazines with paragraphs ringed in red biro, hardware guarantees . . .

More and more letters . . .

Gathering them from the floor, I split the material into piles: and then found myself with two pieces of paper I knew had never been in the filing cabinet.

I had seen them hidden under the sofa, and pushed my fingers into the inch-wide crack to ease them out.

It took a minute to recognise the pages – Vanessa had complained about losing part of her address book only once. But I knew the handwriting. There were two dozen names and addresses, and I was pleased. Vanessa would be delighted to get them back. My kindness could make up for the pills.

I dropped the spoon into the glass, letting it rattle. The man behind the counter looked up from his book.

'Could I just have a coffee, please? Black?'

'Sure,' he said.

I would have put the pages on Vanessa's pillow the moment they were discovered . . . except that, as I knelt there on the floor of the flat, I had glanced over them.

There was a page and a half of surnames beginning with M, and one side of Ns.

On the first page was an entry with the surname Madill. It had been struck out with strokes of a pencil.

The Christian name was what had caught my eye.

Brendan.

And, in front of that, was a title.

The title was Reverend.

Rev.

Ever since resolving to leave Saint Peter's, the matter of the last curate had become less pressing. It was no longer a challenge to the private detective in me. It was now just another item on my list of Good Reasons to Quit the Church.

But this . . . this was a fact too tantalising to ignore. I had – or appeared to have – it was almost incredible: I had the home address of the last curate. Surely it must be him.

The last curate. The Reverend Brendan Madill.

A young man? Like me?

I stared at the name and the words below it as the coffee came, cup and saucer clinking.

Reverend Brendan Madill (crossed out), *75 Gledhulla Street* (crossed out), *Formby, nr Liverpool* (crossed out).

That did not look like a rectory, either.

I could not face an ethical discussion with myself over black coffee on a bank holiday – so I copied the entry into my diary. Then, at the flat, I gingerly placed the pages on Vanessa's pillow, laying them out in a way that I hoped would suggest they had not been read. I left a two-line note.

I started reading, but fell asleep in the armchair, and dreamt of leaving Saint Peter's ... shaking two thousand hands as I blundered down the concrete steps to the Datsun ... hands pressed into my face, on to my chest: I could see nothing but hands, and I was desperately pushing my way to the Datsun, and then Douglas stepped up, somehow getting through the crowd, and put his hands out too, smiling, coughing, reaching forward ... *No hard feelings, Mark ...*

And I got inside the Datsun and banged the door.

And in the silence in the car the telephone rang.

It must have rung four or five times, over there on the other side of the lounge, before I struggled up, stiff.

I was talking to Stewart Weeks before I knew it.

'Mark!'

He sounded close on the phone.

'We just got back and got this letter!'

'Stewart, hello. Are – are you ringing from Wales?'

'What's this about you leaving the church, you jerk?'

What?

Am I still dreaming?

'I don't –'

'Have we just woken you up? Ducky's here.'

'I –'

'Do you want us to call back?' His voice was loud.

'No, I'm fine. I was just having a nap.'

'You must have a lot of them, you dummy,' said my old friend. 'We've just picked up this letter of yours.'

'Good – I thought it was about time I wrote.' I blinked and looked out. The lights were off in Marple & Schwartz.

'No – Mark, you sent us the wrong letter. The one we've got isn't for us.'

I felt the words echo inside me. For a moment, I thought I must be dreaming; but the hands had gone. My mind cleared.

'What does it say?'

'It says you're resigning from the church, Mark – so thank goodness we got it and not the Bishop of London.'

'You got that letter?'

'Yes – right here – listen, I'll shake it about and you can listen to it moving – '

'I sent you a different one.'

'Well, I suppose that's gone to the Bishop of London. We've got one that's addressed to him – Tristran Stuart, it says, and it says you want to resign after Christmas.'

Oh, no.

'I can't believe – '

'Mark, Ducky and I think it's great! We just got in from France and picked it off the mat! We don't think you should!'

'It's a long story, Stewart.' I sighed. 'You'd understand if I – '

'Rubbish!' he called back. 'All churches are weird! I don't know what's been happening, but don't let it worry you! Don't resign from anywhere, you old dipstick!'

'No, it wasn't – I wasn't worried, it was just that – '

'What shall I do with this letter? Put it in the post to the Isles of Scilly? I'm not sending it to any Bishops!'

'Just throw it away – if you don't mind,' I said.

'That's the best place for it,' the big voice boomed.

Hanging up the telephone, I waited for crushing agonies. But none came. Over the next few minutes, to my surprise, as I looked absently out of the window of the flat, relief crept around my stomach like ivy, and budded.

— 12 —

The front room of the terraced council house was cramped and dark. The yellow curtains were still drawn. A parrot nattered to itself in a corner.

I walked in slowly, and heard the woman. She was sitting on a gnarled sofa. She was wailing.

'Yesterday, her husband had a massive heart attack – I think he died in the street. He was shouting at a parade of Caribbean floats going past his house,' Vanessa had told me. 'Douglas – well – he can't get around to the wife, poor thing. It's this throat of his. So he asked me to ask you – '

'If I could see her?'

'He asked me to remind you of the time he said he had something "fun" for you to do. The proposition he had – '

'Ah – yes, I do remember him talking about fun – '

' – yes, it's quite a big thing. He was going to ask you to take over the counselling in the church. So – following on from that, since he can't see this woman – and she's in the parish, rather than the congregation – she doesn't go to the church – you know – oh, these are such terrible occasions – '

'I'll get the address and go this morning.'

I had imagined myself spending the early part of the day differently: drafting a second letter to the Bishop of London, offering resignation again, addressing it carefully this time. Surely, that ought to be the course . . .

Except that I could not deny an enhanced sense of ease after the call from Stewart Weeks. Somehow, I realised, this resignation, on a kind of principle, had become like grit in me, chafing; an abscess, a sore; worse, maybe, than all the conflicts the act had been designed to resolve.

And perhaps I was not a resigning sort of person. After all, a curate should never do anything on principle. The curate's job was to do things on inspiration, which was the exact opposite, and accounted for the fact that I seemed to spend so much of my professional life waiting for something. As a result, I was prepared to leave the thought of stepping down alone – if it left me alone. I could return to it later in the day, and decide then. For now, there was work to be done.

And however squeamish I might be, this was my work.

'Good morning,' I said to the woman on the sofa, standing uneasily over her. Her son, who had shown me in, hovered behind me.

'I'm very sorry to be here today.'

Those were the words I had used on the few occasions in Straithe when I had visited a home struck by tragedy.

The woman broke into a roar of renewed sobbing.

Her son leant forward. He was greasy and painfully thin, with tufts of moustache in a Mediterranean face. He spoke with the hint of an accent, and in a whisper.

'The floats did it. Coming past the house with the reggae music. He lost his temper and shouted at one. It said "Peace" on the windscreen. Then he fell down.'

It was the most unemotional account of a father's death I ever expected to hear.

The mother looked up.

'I asked for my son to bring you because we must be sure of his father.'

'Please sit down,' the young man said, and virtually pushed me into the armchair facing his mother.

'Yes,' I said to her. 'I'm very sorry your husband is dead.' We had been taught at theology college that distressed people often tried to ignore the cause of their grief – and sometimes the curate's first duty was to remind them of it.

'I –' the woman gasped, and moved a hand in front of her neck. 'Now I – I want to be sure of him.'

'Sure of him?' I repeated.

'Sure – that he is with God.' She cried for a minute.

And now I understood, for I saw that the hand at the front of her neck was gripping a tiny object that hung on a chain. I guessed what it was: a crucifix.

There was silence for a moment. She was staring at the portrait of a man that hung on the wall opposite her. Then she turned to look me in the face, eyes red with crying.

'He never prayed,' she said.

'It doesn't necessarily matter,' I replied.

'Is he in heaven?'

'Was he a good man?' I asked.

'He was –' the sobs threatened to break through again, and her bust ballooned up. 'He was a great man. Good, always faithful, so kind to Lolly.' She motioned to the son, who stood at the door like a security guard.

'Such a good man,' she said again. 'He was never in trouble. He just drove his taxi. The perfect man of honour.'

I felt my heart deeply touched, and turned to look at the curtains.

'Then he will go to heaven,' I said, turning back to the woman. 'God doesn't send good men to hell.'

She sniffed for a moment in my direction, as if in thanks.

'I thought so,' she said. 'But I had to know.'

The woman took her hand from the thing around her neck – and I saw it was not a crucifix at all, but a tiny silver Buddha.

I felt uncomfortable, and ran a finger inside the rim of my shirt. The new dog collar was still pinching. I wanted to redefine the parameters of the conversation. Seeing her neckchain there had made me unsure of myself. But the sobbing had started again.

'Thank you,' she groaned.

The son stepped forwards in the gloom.

'Thank you,' he said, his frame silhouetted against the drawn curtain behind him: a clear-as-day suggestion it was time to leave.

'Is there nothing more I can – '

'My mother will be happy for what you have said.'

I was reluctant to go, but he led me firmly to the door.

'Your mother hasn't been in our church, has she?' I said to him at the threshold. 'Nor have you, I don't think.'

'I went once,' he said. 'Once was enough.'

'But your mother's never been,' I insisted.

'No,' he said. 'She is a Buddhist.'

The wails in the adjoining room rose in pitch. 'Then why did she want to see me?' I asked. 'I'm from the Church of England. Nothing to do with Buddhism.'

'In case she is wrong.' He opened the front door.

'Wrong?' I asked.

'Buddha can be believed with many other religions. Buddha said there was a reincarnation. The Pope might have been reincarnated. As you can see, at this time my mother needs the help of all the religions. You can hear her pain now. It was me who asked the church to send you.'

'Was your father a Buddhist?' I asked.

'He was a hypnotist,' the young man replied. He rocked on the balls of his feet in the front doorway as I faced him, ejected on to the garden path. 'My father offered smoking cures and diets – weight loss, happiness, more money, sex, everything. All by hypnosis. A hobby. Extra to his cab driving. He advertised in the *Bounds Green Gazette*. Got in trouble with the police a bit, too.'

I heard a piece of wood rattle on the gravel behind me. The last rotten slat had fallen from the front gate.

A man walked eagerly through it, head nodding, grinning through a neat black beard. He wore an ochre skull-cap.

'Danny Olmert,' he shot at us nasally, chin weaving left and right like a puppet's. I was all but ignored. 'From the synagogue on the green. I'm sorry we're having to meet like this. Thank you for ringing us, Mr – er –'

'Thank you for coming,' the young man said. The rabbi gave me a football-flick of a nod and a wink before sliding into the house with the son. 'Is she through there? How's she been? I am so sorry to be here today –'

The twittering voice faded, front door banged shut. I was left to the garden path and my own thoughts.

The sky was cloudless, but a late November freeze was in the wind, a blue chill. Even the sun looked cold, bracing itself for the shallowest of arcs. This street was treeless and bleak, I reflected, shoes padding on the pavement.

Who wants to work the winter out in that bleak church?

Not me.

Hands in pockets, I wondered if hell might be a state of being permanently caught out by Mediterranean Buddhists. The dirty had been done on me, that was for sure. There was only one thing worse than not believing anything, and that was not knowing what you believed. Worse than that, was having the whole business exposed by an uninvolved third party, a party ignorant of the complexities of theology. If I genuinely thought a cab-driving atheist who got into trouble with the law hypnotising overweight smokers into better sex was now in a Christian heaven, then I must have a very odd set of beliefs indeed. Even I knew that.

That was no belief at all. Yes, even I knew that.

I was strafing faith now, a fighter pilot.

It seemed to me that before I took my leave of Saint Peter's, I ought to decide exactly which religious standpoint I was operating from, if any. I did not rule out deciding for atheism. *Better that than Buddhism, at least*

– although I sensed that while I might have enough faith to believe something, I did not have sufficient conviction to disbelieve everything.

There were several standpoints to choose from. They were known to all curates. Turning left to walk alongside the flaking railings of Bounds Green park, I listed them in my mind.

It was obvious what the first was. I called it Left-wing Religion.

Left-wing Religion was a state of belief that focused exclusively on love. The gates of heaven flapped open, unpatrolled, with sloppier ticket inspectors than British Rail. Anyone could amble in through a side door if Saint Peter booted them out of the front. God was love. Lesbian weddings and the winks Stalin gave his mistress were manifestations of love and therefore of God. And the great Creator would never, when push came to shove, reject any man or woman. The world was flooded with mercy and smiles through every available sluice.

Left-wing Religion was tremendously appealing to almost everyone. But there was one problem. It tended to make the believer lazy. It required no effort, no prayer, no discipleship, no fear, no concentration, no thought. It very nearly required no God, and certainly no Son of God. It was therefore hard to maintain, precisely because it required no maintenance. Left-wing Religion created a world where a distant, dumb God spent all his time downplaying the significance of evil with a doctrine that had forgiveness oozing out of every mousehole. But all too often, when you turned round, Left-wing Religion had changed; slipped into Atheism With A Duty To Love. And when that point was reached, any God there had ever been had disappeared . . . drowned, most likely, in a love flood.

Having coined the definition, I bent the coin. Left-wing Religion was garbage. I pondered the second option.

Naming it was easy. Not love now, but judgement, judgement and more judgement: Right-wing Religion.

The Right-wing Religious had tended not to stay long at Straithe. Their faith demanded total enslavement to a gospel of pure condemnation, and the reward seemed to be to feel so bad about yourself and the world around you that it was quite impossible to believe an afterlife could be any worse. No one escaped their piercing, eagle stare, not even themselves. So many fell under its awesome burden that it was incredible the most virulent strains had survived.

Survive they had, though. They bred off tough phrases from nineteenth-century hymnwriters and hypocrites, and Old and New Testament figures alike. John, in Revelation, saying God would spit out 'lukewarm' believers. Paul, in one of the letters, telling women to wear hats. Bianco Da Siena, whose 'Come Down, O Love Divine' extolled 'true lowliness of heart, which o'er its own shortcomings weeps with loathing' – as though faith was a state of occupational misery –

I stopped in my tracks for a moment, debating which way to turn to reach the Ferndown Highway. I went left.

Padding down the pavement again, I smiled into the raised lapel of my coat. Right-wing Religion might feel more real than its counterpart, but it was so grim . . . yes, it might have been a brave attempt to grasp nettles, but if your hands were stung into non-existence . . . and how could you smile, anyway, if the God in your mind was always wailing?

Left-wing Religion dispensed love. Right-wing Religion dispensed six-inch nails, in sets of four.

But there were others, too. I stopped for a second, hands on hips, turning to look back at the way I had come.

I wonder what sort of religion the last curate had.

Somehow I could not remember seeing the same pattern of branches on my way to the woman's home. Never mind. I snapped round on a heel, sure there was a junction up ahead.

Yes – there were other paths of belief, too.

There was Dead Letterbox Religion, for a start.

This was the kind that gave evangelists nervous breakdowns. The mark of the Dead Letterbox Religious was, simply, that at some time they had allowed the existence of God to become a fact they accepted. That fact had been slipped into them, without drama, like a sealed package into an inoperative pillar box. It just sat there: the belief never touched a single operating cog of life. None the less, at the smallest stimulus the Dead Letterbox Religious would produce the package with a flourish and admit to any kind of faith. They would beat you to your own beliefs even, agreeing fiercely before you had finished the most careful description of them. The Dead Letterbox Religious, who had a particularly visible presence in homes for the elderly and the armed forces, gave the impression of having already taken delivery of every belief. They were the nodding dogs of religion.

Strolling towards a junction now, I wondered how many in all . . . how many different . . .

Of course: there was Pass-the-Port Religion.

Unlike the malleable mass that was Dead Letterbox, Pass-the-Port Religion usually generated very specific articles of faith. Like membership of the National Delphinium Society or views on shoving Ulster out to sea, its main feature was that it only came out at dinner parties. Pass-the-Port Religion existed purely to surprise, and was held with conviction only as thick as cigar-wrapping. It was hardly a belief at all. Its principle was simply that it was possible to believe in nearly anything after two or three glasses of wine, and essential to believe in absolutely anything after four. The Pass-the-Port Religious constructed lavish, instant defences, laughed off offence, hogged spotlights, and shunted any more substantial belief at their table into oblivion. Pass-the-Port Religion usually came complete with cigarette, guttural laugh, and reclining posture. I thought of the college acquaintance who once said he was convinced the Second Coming had already happened, and it was Cliff Richard. For the believer, Pass-the-Port was nothing more than a giant hoot. For everyone else, it was nothing at all.

Then – well, what should it be called?

Toothbrush Religion, I supposed: a commoner faith, of course – perhaps the commonest; perhaps mine for a time, too. The Toothbrush Religious prayed each morning for the same length of time as they brushed their teeth in the bathroom mirror . . . and in the same way. Prayer was a formal cleansing of visible parts, done from habit out of a long-remembered something or other . . . something taught by a father, perhaps, who offered five pounds for no fillings at fifteen. The prayers were simply routine cleaning.

'God forgive me for this and that, help me today, please forgive me for anything I might have missed out, help The Queen and my gums, please make that promotion happen soon –'

Then a clink as the toothbrush was put back in the glass on the bathroom basin shelf: the prayer was over, teeth were clean. Real life could resume.

And I had forgotten now which way I had been intending to go. *Darn,* I thought. The street had curved and turned into a thin alley, proving I had not been here before.

I retraced my steps, finding a larger road and crossing it, stopping to wonder at the centre island how many other so-called Christian beliefs there were – and where I stood on the sail-sized map of it all. Doing sixty, a string of cars shot past.

And then – wondering, *How could I have left it until now?* – I remembered Christianity's most famous brand.

Fruit-and-Nut Religion was legendary because of high profile in the market and the secrecy surrounding its ingredients. To many, it was simply bizarre. Its holders were sometimes called charismatics – but that might have been unfair on people with charisma. They clapped a lot, and cried. They were, like the chocolate bar, part crunchy and part chewy; one minute speaking with the soft voice of a late-night disc-jockey, the next setting their faces hard, like flint, against all comers. They made much of forgiveness, but would never forgive a dirty joke. The whole world was a hard-porn magazine, and the Fruit-and-Nut Religious wanted dog collars confined to kennels, robes to bathrooms, candles to caves. If a window was stained, it needed wiping.

There was Stop-Press Religion too, among more minor –

(I raced across to a road I thought I knew, then realised I did not, and turned round, wishing there was a sign, or something, to point me back to the highway)

– among more minor varieties. Now that, I decided, might be the saddest faith of all. Every one of the Stop-Press Religious had a Road to Damascus, but there all consciousness had withered. The moment of conversion was the amphitheatre of all proof and all belief, and no other moment mattered. The story would be told again and again. A blinding flash had set them sprawling in a second. But, though they would never admit it, it had never been followed by the simple dawn of new day. The special tragedy of it was . . . ah . . . now – hold on, I had to think again about which way to go.

I was moving down another lane that branched off the main road. It should have led directly to the church from the north-east side – but the church was nowhere to be seen.

There was no clue where it was. And all this was making me late. All right, I was grappling with the very soul of my profession, but I did need to get back to work some time . . .

And now, where am I – where am I in all this religion?

Where the heck am I?

I glanced up at the sky, tripping slightly like a wino, one toe on the pavement, a heel pivoting on paving stones.

There was no one to see me wheeling, mouth gaping wide enough to net a meteorite. I turned my head up to the clear sky, raised my arms above shoulders, clenched fists . . .

I called upwards: 'I know exactly where I am!'

Then exploded at the blue silence that bore down on me.

'I'm lost!'

– 13 –

From the Bishop of London

Revd Mark Empringham
St Peter's Church
Diocese of London

Dear Reverend Empringham,
The Bishop of London asks me to thank you for your suggestion that you and he should go on holiday together.

You will obviously know that his diary tends to be fairly full, and he has asked me to say that he would unfortunately not be able to fulfil such an engagement.

He notes that you say you have comments to make about Saint Peter's Church. His main point of reference would usually be the Rector, but if you wish a further meeting with the Bishop you are of course welcome to ring this office.

Ruth Gore, PA to the Bishop of London.

I had picked the letter out of the box in the church lobby. It took a second to register the contents.

I had not made the obvious deduction, though I supposed it had been in my mind, that if Stewart Weeks, in Wales, had got the Bishop's letter – his would end up with the Bishop.

The Right Reverend Tristran Stuart.

And that letter – yes, I recalled it now. The Bishop might not even have known it was misaddressed, because it began, 'Dear Stew' . . . and suggested –

what was it? 'Fags, beer and skittles?' And hadn't it contained some awful term of familiarity – 'you old son of a gun', or something?

The last line came to me, clearly: *Give me a ring whenever you're free and we'll fix up a date.*

And I imagined that all this had gone through official channels, been taken from the Bishop's postbag and put on his secretary's in-tray; then shown around, perhaps, a suitable reply talked over, the original photocopied, both filed . . .

Dear Stew.

Dear me. A moody contempt swung overhead in an arc as I reread the secretary's delicate phrasing. 'His diary tends to be fairly full.' What hypocrisy. She knew, and she knew I knew, that bishops did not holiday with curates, period. It had nothing to do with full diaries.

Bishop's-Letter Religion: what was that, I wondered? Preaching hard, acting soft? Saying one thing, meaning another? Talking double declutch, let alone double Dutch?

Or just Left-wing Religion in a silly hat?

The thought brought a smile to my face – a smile that Morag saw and returned. She was walking across the lobby.

'Hello, Mark.'

'Hi.' I let the hand holding the letter fall, casually.

'The Parson – BBF – just rang us to say he was stopped by the Devon police,' Morag ventured, unusually forthcoming.

'Why?'

'Oh, they say he was going below the minimum speed limit. I think he got an on-the-spot fine.' Morag chuckled. She really was in a remarkably available mood.

'Now – ' she looked at her watch, and then asked a question as a statement: 'Would you be able to pop in to see Douglas today. It's quite important.'

'Of course I would.'

'When is the best time for you?'

'One-thirty?'

'He's still not too keen on going out, so if you go to the rectory he'll see you there.'

I headed back to my own flat with the letter. I thought of the alternative: Stewart Weeks getting a weekend invitation, and the Bishop of London a request to accept the resignation of his newest curate. It was hardly preferable.

Reaching the top of the stairs, unable to stop myself, I broke into the widest of smiles.

I opened the flat door. No Vanessa.

I walked over to the window, looked out at the Marple & Schwartz building and beyond.

In terms of Christianity, I had found precisely where it was I stood: I was lost.

But I had preached a competent sermon, helped a widowed woman, been no embarrassment, perhaps even learnt something about myself; lost the burden that was Emily . . .

I looked over at Marple & Schwartz again.

And, yes, I feel more at home here, on this side . . .

I plucked the Bishop's letter from my pocket again, read it, saw the joke of it all, the hand of fate, the biblical appropriateness of it – and, as only a solitary person can, burst out laughing as I imagined the esteemed Bishop of London, the Right Reverend Tristran Stuart, getting a letter that started, 'Dear Stew'.

The laughter rattled off the windowpane.

I guessed I was now creeping towards the surest decision of my life. For perhaps being a curate did not necessarily mean believing in anything. It just meant being sure. And I was sure, very sure, sure that I was lost . . . and that was enough.

I beamed at the irony. I probably had more conviction than the Bishop of London.

So I would stay at the church.

I would not resign.

In the twinkle of an eye, at the sound of the trumpet, we shall all be changed.

It was the will of God.

Three Months Later

– 14 –

When I knew that she was rehearsing for choir, I would walk nonchalantly to the first-floor committee room on the spiral staircase. It was nearly always empty.

There I would spread some papers on the small table at the window, draw a pen from my jacket, and begin ticking, doodling, underlining, squiggling or shading . . . any meaningless movement of the pen that meant I would be ready to look down when she passed and, *yes*, there she was, just one floor below, walking down the street, balancing a songbook on bare forearms.

Always wearing scarlet lipstick.

My Scarlet Lipstick.

In the mirror, I looked at myself. Black shirt, jacket, dog collar (the third in as many months!), glasses, black acrylic trousers. I looked like some Gestapo agent, except that my face was too pallid and anxious to be evil – and, surely, Gestapo agents did not wear acrylic trousers.

Has it grown more pallid since I arrived at Saint Peter's, or less?

Or does the anxiety come from my new duties?

Winter had locked in. Today was New Year's Eve.

Freezing, I went into the main body of the church.

There it was again: the picture of Jesus Christ.

Bearded, English looking, purposefully nosed.

For minutes, I gazed at it.

'It's not the greatest, is it?'

I jumped. 'Oh – Richard.'

The plump guitarist had become something of a friend. The swollen frame of Richard Burts, which had seen him consigned to the margins of church social life, exuded an engaging air of self-doubt, yet his genuineness was apparent. He was kind. He was lonely, but never complained.

There are a lot of lonely people in churches, I thought.

I had told Richard almost everything: told him about Luke Bellington, about the hunt for the last curate, told him I was lost – that not only was there nothing I believed in, but that I did not even know what it was I disbelieved.

'As long as you care about it,' Richard had said.

'I don't know if I do,' I replied.

And Richard had swept back oily strands of hair.

'You've had quite a hard time here.'

I said: 'One morning I even woke up in tears.'

'But that was about Emily, wasn't it?'

I really had told him everything.

Looking at the painting, I said: 'I just wonder if I should swap it for – something a bit classical, maybe?'

'There'd probably be an outcry. But it doesn't mean much to me, so go ahead. You could probably redesign the whole church interior if you wanted to. You've got the power now.'

Richard looked, with me, at the picture. 'Anyway, it isn't Christ, and he probably didn't have that sort of face at all. He was Jewish,' he added.

'So what does it mean to people, having it there?'

'People who really believe – I think they feel they've got a relationship with God, not a painting.'

'It's so strange.'

'The painting?'

'No – sorry – ' I shrugged. 'I was just thinking – my clothes aren't different – I've had no change of heart – '

'I can guess what you were thinking.'

'I've got the same marital status – '

'Same as me, anyway.'

' – so how can I be vicar of this place?'

We gazed on at the picture.

'If I could just have some sort of proof about this bloke. A – a signed letter, or a fingerprint or something – '

'Do you think it would help?' Richard asked.

'Of course,' I said.

The morning I got Morag's call, even on waking, I had detected unusualness in the air.

The internal telephone system in the church was in a bad way, and the first thing I had thought, hearing a volley of crackling as I raised the handset to my ear, was that the vicar ought to do something about it.

The second thing was that I became the vicar.

'We have a major crisis, Mark.'

Morag's voice had a panic-stricken undertone. I knew she was going to mention Douglas. For two months, he had been unable to preach.

A day after the first bank holiday weekend at the church, he had asked Morag to summon me to his flat. We sat facing each other in flowered armchairs, at one-thirty. Coughing, Douglas had pushed a piece of paper towards me.

Mark – won't be able to speak. Voice has gone. Doctor says it needs total rest. Need you to do a few things . . . ?

'Of course,' I had said, pushing the paper back.

And a list slid over. Check choir weekend and report back, it said. Make sure Daniel happy with business meeting keys. Find out if both chefs okay for diplomats' dinner.

Nothing a curate could not do. And nothing, I noted, that was anything to do with preaching.

'Fine, yes – yup – diplomats – okay,' I had said, reassuring him. 'Are you very unwell, Douglas?'

Silently, he had shrugged in the chair, firelight catching the side of his face. He turned his palms up.

'I understand,' I said. 'You'll have to wait and see.'

The Rector nodded, and uttered five hoarse words.

'I – trust – in – my – Lord.'

But he did not get better.

Suddenly Morag was saying on the telephone, 'He's got cysts. He's going to have to stop public speaking if he wants to carry on speaking at all.'

'Cysts? Who?' I asked.

'Douglas. On his throat. Non-malignant. He can apparently do broadcasting if they turn everything up, but that's about all. It's medical,' Morag added, confidentially.

Then she broke the news. 'He's going to have to leave.'

For a moment, all I heard was spitting on the line.

I rallied. 'So who'll be taking over, then?'

'You, for now.'

. . . *You, for now.*

The meaning of the three words, strung together, was not recognised by whatever part of my brain they appeared in.

'But what does a church do without a vicar?' I asked.

'You take over.'

I remained silent, registering.

'That's what happens in every other church in the country, Mark, and we're no different.'

'But this is one of the biggest. It needs someone –'

'Finding him takes time, though. So the curate has to become acting vicar. Or acting rector, in this case.'

'Me? Vicar?'

'Rector.'

She said it almost angrily.

I had achieved a certain kudos at the church by being stabbed with a snooker cue during a semi-official visit to a South London club used mainly by former punk rockers, and my occasional sermons, in which I stuck rigidly to sentences lifted from nineteenth-century commentaries, did not seem to have wiped out my stock with fellow staff members.

I was aware of only one who voiced reservations.

Richard Burts came gently to the point. 'I just feel, Mark, you know, the way you've been talking to me about God, that it's perhaps not – not the right time for this.'

'I know, Rich,' I said, 'but I just don't seem to have any choice. Remember, I'm only in this job because I couldn't get into accountancy. I'll do my best.'

But one unfortunate aspect of taking charge struck almost immediately, winding me.

I had, undoubtedly, developed something like love for Scarlet Lipstick.

It had come out like a rash in my heart; like blue perfume hanging over poor Emily's green grave. It felt as visible as a stack of Bibles at a Communist checkpoint.

The choir member's real name was Gillian Mitchell, though friends all called her Gilly. I thought she was beautiful, but it was impossible to approach her carelessly.

Even moving ten yards across the crowded floor of the church, I would be stopped and greeted by one, two ... maybe ten or twelve ... of the faces who made up the congregation.

I now knew some of them: knew the Faulkeses, the Wells family. Knew Buck and Abby Peterson, the Gibbons, Joneses, Joneses, Joneses, Knudsons, Byes, Crotty-Matthewses and Hittites; the Frett cousins and Muntz brothers, together with Shannon and Summer, American sisters whose first names were so memorable I could never bring their last one to mind; I had met Jack Petherick, Shirley Logue's prayer group, Hugh Nelson, 'Cook' Wookey-Hobbs, Alan Jenks and Heather Tinsley, as well as Jayne Bottom, the youngest daughter of Francis and Sally; shaken hands, at least, with Drinilee Crouton and Amanda Fennish (engaged), Lynn Winchester and Richard Morgan (likely to become engaged), Guy Stonnet and Grace Bailes (likely to break up), Shenzhal Bhutto, Jon Shepherd, Gillian Mitchell ...

Oh – Gilly, Gilly, Gilly.

On the first Sunday in December, I had been in a group of people which she was in, too. We shook hands.

Hers was cool.

I looked at the hand, not her face, as I touched it, trying to work out the meaning of a solitary ring.

She was Northern Irish. Full faced, with the most beautiful ever of mouths agitating parallel crescents in her cheeks – a thin mouth; and eyes like dreaming moons; she was short, too, though it made no difference; her face was a pure white circle in chalk, a splash of blood for lips.

Her smile could bring down aircraft.

Thick black hair hung in any shape she chose, and mainly she just left it, and it didn't matter . . . in any style, I decided, her hair looked just like the gospels. Unbelievable.

She was young. Twenty-three.

I would often see her with small hands on hips, one leg straight, one bent, shoulders braced . . .

As though uttering strong, soft-voiced views.

You will lose your job if you make these feelings known, I told myself – and might even have been right.

For a curate, no friendship did not have the pulpit, in cloud form, hanging overhead. But for a vicar, the cloud was fog and covered everything.

So the thing was finished the minute Morag called me, even though it had never begun. My second thought was – well, at least I would be able to watch her from the pulpit.

As vicar of one of the biggest churches in the country.

Acting vicar.

Of course: acting vicar.

In more ways than one.

'This picture,' I told Richard, 'ought not to be here. Especially if it means nothing to the switched-on types.'

'You sound a bit irritable,' Richard said.

'It's New Year's Eve, and I suppose I'm a bit nervous about tonight. I don't want to go.'

'What a hermit! It's only a party – Francis does it every year.'

'I'm going to lean against something in a shadow. Anyone who pronounces their name "Boat Home" when it's obviously "Bottom" ought not to be allowed to throw their voice, let alone a party.'

'Don't be like that. I'd come with you, but Mum's ill.'

I yawned. A twenty-nine-year-old's yawn. My birthday had been in November.

An acting-vicar-in-more-ways-than-one's yawn.

A lost yawn. The picture stabbed me again: that black finger I had felt, oh, moons ago, on my first day . . .

The finger relented only at Francis Bottom and Sally Halewood's front door. Anxiety took its place. Violin music was pulsing out of the letterbox. I hit the knocker.

'Knock, and the door shall be opened.' It was Sally.

'There's a Bible verse exactly like that,' I said, looking down at the carpet. 'Do you do this every year?'

But she was off, filling the hallway with a tra-la-la voice. 'Francis, our vicar has arrived! Can you make sure . . . '

I waded through shoulders and faces, fending off all questions – for now they were not about Birkham or my parents, but about the church I had taken control of, their church. And I was supposed to have all the answers.

'Where do you think we're heading?'

Or, 'Are we being strong enough on street evangelism?'

'Could we do a series on the minor prophets?'

I asked: 'Isaiah, you mean?'

'No – the minor prophets – he wasn't minor – I meant – '

One man shook cider over my shirt with the vigour of his question: 'Could we not extend the services, make them more like two hours long?'

Two hours!

'I thought they were already,' I said, checking the joke, too late, for indecency. Making a note not to drink in excess, I moved on.

The flat filled up. At every turn, I came to a new room. It was not that hard to move around. So many people wanted my attention that I had an excuse to end any conversation. To my surprise, I caught myself finding the whole thing enjoyable.

I spoke with Francis.

'Plans for the New Year?'

'There's a lot to do here,' I said.

'Such as?' He spoke staccato – swung his chin at you like a fist, eyes twinkling, hair bouncing.

'Services. I've got to plan a lot of titles.'

'Could we do – ' Francis squinted up at the ceiling. 'Could we do a sermon on why a church needs good music?'

'Yes,' I said. *Except I wouldn't know the answer.*

'How's Vanessa?' he asked. 'She's not here tonight.'

'I just don't know. Ever since she changed flats – '

'You're coping, are you?' Francis asked.

Coping.

'There's not that much extra – it's such a big place, everyone – ' I was shouting above the music: flutes, now.

'What about money? Are we in the red, the black, the green, the orange – the pink with purple spots?'

The question stumped me.

'I trained as an accountant,' I said.

Moving around the guests, I thought of my predecessor.

Not Douglas Tredre, but Brendan Madill. I had been about to write to the last curate, to ask him directly why he had left the church and why no one would say a word about it . . . when suddenly, someone did. Casually, too.

'We got on quite well,' Richard had said.

And then he told me why it was no one spoke about him.

'He left in a flash. He was just gone one morning. He didn't have many friends, and Douglas was pretty upset.'

Richard could see I wanted to hear more. 'One morning, someone came into his flat – I think it was Vanessa – and he was gone. He had even taken a book or two that weren't his. It was like a slap. An insult to all of us. We'd helped him.'

'Was he miserable, then? Was he discontented?'

'That was the strangest thing about it,' Richard said. 'Not at all. He was a magnetic figure. He was quite dynamic.'

'Was he married?' *I'm the sort who'll never marry.*

'No, not married. But he – he was a tremendous guy – I suppose it's painful for people. It was weird.'

'He just upped and left.'

'That's right. You won't find anyone talking about it.'

A crash of bottles in the flat.

One of the choir members, Denise, had bounced through a doorway, kicking over the bottles, half-calling, half-singing.

'I'll be going all over the world/Shouting loud songs and getting drunk/Shouting "I love vicars" and things like that – '

She tailed off. Everyone in the room was staring at her.

Denise had fixed her gaze on me. Then she began giggling. Some of her friends giggled too. I noticed one or two looking at me, and felt my cheeks flush beetroot red.

'Some people are having a good time – '

I faintly recognised the female voice at my shoulder, and agreed without turning. Instead, I watched Denise flop on to the arm of a sofa, drooping across a man in spectacles I did not recognise to scoop peanuts off the coffee table.

Then I turned, turned to see –

Scarlet Lipstick! And fought to keep my breath even.

'Yes, Denise seems to be enjoying herself, Mark.'

She is saying my name for the first time.

'She does,' I said.

'I think she's had a bit too much to – well, you know.'

'I do,' I said.

'It must be funny – everyone here knowing you.'

'They don't. Not really. But – yes, it is funny.'

She looked up at me, confirming her beauty. One lens in her wide, thin-framed glasses caught a yellow bulb somewhere. I could almost feel her moving in that red dress . . .

'I'm just trying to remember – have we – '

'Met?' she asked. 'Well, you won't remember, but we did just briefly shake hands once in the church hall – '

'Oh – right.'

'Anyway, you won't know my name because – heavens – you have to meet so many people.'

Forget heaven, I thought. *Just kiss me.*

'I'm trying to remember.' I sensed an eyebrow tremble.

'Gillian Mitchell.'

'I'm Mark.' We both laughed.

'Everyone knows that,' she said.

I love you, I thought, stupidly. I did not care who was watching.

'Where do you work – during the days, I mean?'

'In a supermarket,' she said. She looked so beautiful to me. The curve on her hips was more beautiful than anything. And those heavy Irish curls that came down diagonally across her face, masking an eye and a triangle of white forehead above it . . . oh, and always that lipstick.

I wonder if she loves someone.

'Do you go to parties often?'

What a pathetic question. And she must have heard the tremor. Gillian laughed, easily. She moved her head, flicking back hair. 'A few.' Her voice was soft, and the diamond-edged accent was draped over the words like a rug.

Then she threw a hand grenade at me.

'How did you become a Christian, Mark?'

I inhaled and looked away from her for a moment. I played, like a fast juggler, with different, dishonest, answers; thought about the time-proven honesty: *I am lost;* then took the middle ground, abandoning deceit – or at least scaling it down . . . throwing myself, in any case, on her mercy and pity.

'Sometimes I wonder if I am one.'

The magnitude of the mistake was instantly obvious. She smiled, but weakly and with glassy eyes. I wanted her to hold me, to say she had seen me studying her from the first-floor room and knew why I was watching, and that she felt the same; that she knew all about my lost, cold heart . . . but instead I had embarrassed her.

A parishioner had just been told that the big church she worshipped in was leaderless, its leader helpless. Sympathy for me was out of the question.

The conversation went on for a few minutes more. But when, at the stroke of midnight, I was alone and looked for Gilly, I saw her close to another man. I felt broken.

Back at the flat, it was hard to sleep.

Later . . . later in the night, I had myself walking, alone, into the deep darkness of the church.

My footsteps sounded like mallet-blows. A rattle of the keychain in my hand leapt from wall to wall.

The small hours, New Year's Day.

I'm getting married in the morning.

The line sang itself around my head.

My eyes adjusted to the gloom. Why was I here?

I was trying to think.

Because I just have to look at the painting again.

Diffracted streetlight beams filtered through the windows, high up. I was in the belly of a whale.

Going down the dark aisle, I saw veils and smiles . . . heard well-known organ notes ripple through a ready audience, the creasing of pages as the first hymn number is called, hands touching; a bride walking down with a torn look at father, too ill with cancer to give her away . . .

I longed for it. Longed for the love in a wedding.

At the picture, I was methodical. I was going to take the thing off the wall.

'You have caused too much trouble,' I told the big yellow face. The top of it was slashed by two pale lines of light, crossing on the forehead.

Unhooking it, I added: 'Far too much trouble.'

I coughed in an officious, tax collector's way. My heart leapt in the rightness of what I was doing. I was taking action in the church I now ran. There could be nothing wrong with that. Most morality was approximate on New Year's Day.

All authority is mine.

With a tiny clatter, the thing came off the wall. It was heavy, too. The picture pressed into my face and chest as I tried to jostle it into the best carrying-position.

Suddenly, there was a noise. Soft talking, and some movement in the gloom at the back.

Young lovers.

It amazed me that they could have found a way in – but a curt giggle at the rear of the church confirmed it.

I believed I was almost invisible, standing alongside the shaded wall and untouched by direct light. But now, for sure, I had to put the picture back. I lifted its base shoulder-high, silently, and tried to catch it on the hook.

A corner slipped in my fist and I lost control. The picture banged against the wall. The impact echoed.

There was a sound from the other end of the church – *a shout?* – and I guessed whoever was there had stood up to run towards me. I panicked, snagging the brass triangle in the back of the painting on the hook in the wall.

I flailed, losing my grip on the picture, sensing the figure coming at me, letting go of the painting altogether and gasping in horror as it crashed to the floor . . .

I pick up the thing and run with it. Run straight across the church, along the front of the raised platform, past the pulpit – hear another shout, quick footsteps in broken glass behind me. Then, an open door; an empty street; a corner, pressure on ankle in fast turn, two hundred yards at speed, another junction; another turn; and then silence.

In the shadows of a side alley, I hug the picture to my chest, dreading a rip in the canvas, fearful of being found with it – dreading even more being caught disposing of it; wondering, under the clear and starry night sky, how safe returning to the flat would be . . .

I might have to sleep on the street with this thing.

And then the pillow reared up in my face as I rolled

over in bed, blinking back the nightmare, running a hand over my chest to confirm the painting was nowhere near it and never had been. I gazed at the small numbers burning in the digital clock on the table, and wondered why the dream that had already troubled me a dozen times had chosen the first day of a new year to trouble me again.

– 15 –

Inverted, I dangled the pen over the name of Dr Barry Bryan-Fryers, dazzled at the power. By putting a line through it, I would be removing one of the foremost Anglican thinkers from the list of approved preachers in the church.

All authority is mine.

In reality, I had asked BBF: 'Could you do a series?'

'What on?' he glittered back at me.

'I hadn't thought.'

'I think we need a title, probably.'

'What about, "Aspects of Faith"?'

He paused, looking down at a sheaf of documents.

'I'll ask my wife. She usually has several ideas.'

I did not take offence. 'It would be three months long.'

'The first sermon?'

'The series. Four, let's say. Two or three a month.'

'That's a sizeable deal.' The Stipendiary Parson's words often gave an impression of near-scientific precision. 'I'm writing a study on Joel – the prophet Joel – at the moment. A pamphlet, between forty-five and forty-eight pages long.'

'The Janglings of Joel?' I suggested, and he laughed.

'I will remove the northern peril,' he said.

'I beg your – '

'That's one of the verses.' The puzzlement on my face cleared. 'I was contemplating that as a title. It would be several mites better than, "Joel, Book of Hope", I think.'

I will remove the northern peril. I thought suddenly of the last curate, up there in Liverpool, or wherever he was . . .

thought of his swift exit, of dust kicked up in faces.

Interesting, how familiarity always rubbed out respect. I recalled the shock of first seeing BBF on the staircase: the Roman nose, tight lips and crow's feet; the rock-hewn preaching that followed. The driving was soon discounted. I was awed by his public standing and book sales.

But how much respect can lost sheep have for a shepherd?

In any case, I had found it enthralling, in a way that was probably perverse, to monitor what my colleagues would have called sin – sin, around the church. Recently, I had discovered BBF's. Looking down at the brilliant man, I brought it to mind – and the others, too.

Douglas's sin had been failing to correct the mistake over the curates. And, it transpired, to be a touch lazy. He would rather walk than work. He once told me, unaware of the insight the remark offered, that he began a five-year diary on being appointed, but, six days into the first month, made his last entry. 'There just was – ah, well, it was sort of a matter of there not being the will there, no will in it. It petered.' For that, I marked his copybook.

Daniel's sin, with his over-cultured accent and tiny-triangled cravats, his highblown sense of what a church could and should do . . . Daniel's sin was pride and gratuitous slickness. He thought he had copyrights on truth, but was more like a cartographer who does every map by guessing. I found it offensive.

Vanessa's sin came to me by way of confession.

'The Tube fare thing,' she said.

'Yes. Actually, Vicki told me before you did,' I said.

'What did she say?'

'They tried to charge you because you lost a ticket.'

Vanessa smiled, and a lower eyelid brimmed with tears.

'Mark, can I tell you something?'

'Of course.'

'I – '

She looked down at her shoes.

'Don't, for goodness' sake, if you don't want to.'

'Who else can I tell?' she asked. 'You're the only one.'

The only what? The only hypocurate?

She took a deep breath.

'I did dodge the fare, I did dodge it, I didn't pay, I didn't pay – and then I lied – I lied –'

And then she broke down, sobbing, falling into my stiff arms, putting her head on my shoulder . . .

I could not provide an embrace of the tightness or tenderness she required.

And when the moment had gone, and so had Vanessa, I wondered if two recent fits she had suffered, one after the other, were the punishment of God. *It is easier to believe in God's punishment than in God himself,* I thought in consequence. Vanessa's sin was fare evasion.

She appeared to believe her credibility with me had sunk. We drifted apart. Then she changed flats, and her mother was often seen in the church. A punchy Australian named Di saved the youth work from collapse.

After Vanessa, Morag struck me as being guilty of taking sides, of criticising people, of prejudging them. I didn't know. Morag's sin was not combing the knots out of her hair.

Francis Bottom's sin was a tendency towards champagne socialism, Sally's was being too beautiful and enjoying singing in public too much, Richard's was befriending me . . .

And that wretched guitar . . .

The whole place was full of sinners, in fact. It lent weight to the notion that even worse than being lost was believing you were found, and being wrong.

Knowing the answers were confidential, I wrote on a census form, under the heading 'Profession': 'Vicar, sort of.'

And in a column headed, 'What type of duties does your occupation involve?': 'Hypocrisy on a large scale.'

I was overly harsh on BBF, perhaps. Or perhaps not. Watching him through the window of a tea shop on Izard Street confirmed my suspicion. Prior evidence had been from the dinner for diplomats and a buffet for the leaders of local scout troupes: yes, it was proven. Even the author of *Finding Christianity, Becoming a Christian, Loving in a Christian Way, Ten Things That Will Happen to You If You Are Not a Christian, Staying a Christian,* and goodness knew how many others, was himself in the grip of sin.

BBF's was chocolate fudge cake, in dollops of cream.

Sin. Great big spoonfuls of it. Gorging himself.

Now although it was stirring to dangle a pen over his name, and, as vicar-by-a-stroke-of-fate, vicar-by-a-stroke-of-the-pen, as acting-vicar-in-more-ways-than-one, to consider lowering the nib and removing the country's top Anglican from the pulpit of Saint Peter's – despite that, I needed BBF to do extra preaching.

For I wanted to stay out of that very same pulpit.

So he kindly agreed to the idea of a series, and put forward a title. I scratched crosses into calendar squares.

January . . . February . . . March . . .

April?

No. Not April. The PCC would surely have found its new rector by then.

I wanted to stay out of the pulpit partly because I was unable to give a sermon that was any distance towards being half-decent; but also because I found I felt more at ease spending my time counselling.

Douglas, in healthier days, had asked me to start. 'Fun,' he had called it. And in a way, he was right.

But there was art to it too.

I began by reversing all the rules and maxims I had been taught at theology college. I offered no spiritual element, just a cursory prayer. Instead, as with the bee-hived and fur-coated Mrs Styla Andreanoupolkis, I just listened.

'First – my real name is Eileen. Second, I've been drinking. I fell over in church.'

I cut in, feeling like a scientist bent over a microscope. 'What sort of faith do you believe you have?'

That was the razor.

'I was worried about seeing you.'

'Why were you worried about seeing me?'

That's it. Make an incision.

'Oh, I don't know. I need some less normal problems, like having evidence and not knowing whether to give it to the police. At first I tried to spend all my time praying, like Wesley – and I thought that five hours of prayer, plus an hour and a half for lunch and the same for supper – that's an eight-hour day, so I thought it could be like a Christian working day – but then it went down to four, then three . . .'

There was not much I could do for Mrs Andreanoupolkis. I recommended a course to talk about the vodka, and some contact with Daniel after services.

One parishioner, the quiet and grey Clive Souter, had a problem he was less forthright about.

'Up there on the top shelves, and I'm always staring down at the floor, but somehow they drift up.'

'What drift up?'

'My eyes. And suddenly I'm – I'm looking at them.'

For Clive's difficulties with pornographic magazines in newsagents, I suggested he have his papers delivered.

'Thank you,' he said, 'for such a practical answer.'

Waldock Baker, a computer specialist, told me: 'A guy at work kept swearing all the time. I was fed up with it. Then I just prayed about it. Next day he was sacked. Made redundant. I know God works, but I feel guilty about this one.'

I told him he ought to feel guilt for about three weeks, and to come back if it was still there in a month.

Others wanted to talk about their beliefs. I could do nothing for them, of course – but they did something for me: reinforcing my titling and subtitling and subsectioning of Christianity, the hanging and drawing and quartering of Anglicanism and everything else; the highlighting of the drawbacks of ever getting involved in the first place.

'It all seems to have faded,' said Bobby Gliff, uttering a typical concern. His was a bad case of Stop-Press Religion.

'It was about five years ago, and I was travelling in Norway I became so conscious of the love of God, and I just found myself asking him to forgive my sins, by a fjord,' said Bobby. 'It was amazing – like a rainbow in my heart – '

He drew breath. 'Now here I am, stuck in this job as a fridge fitter, and I don't know where I'm going or what I am or who I am. It all seems to have faded away.'

And what could I say to him? Shoplifting and murder were easier to deal with. I just listened – as speaker after speaker played themselves out, tantalising me with each different fingerprint of faith (I was like a detective inspector, checking marks in talcum powder against computer files). Rising from the chair, they thanked me. I replied: 'I understand.' In my poverty, I could offer little else.

Plunging into counselling, I tried to put the fiasco with Scarlet Lipstick behind me. In January, my heart thumped at the sight of her in church, my head thumping with the question: *Why did you speak to her like that – tell her the rector of her church was as lost as the most lost of sheep?*

Thumping, thumping.

I became my own counsellor. *Forget her, Mark.*

Tried going softly on myself. *You need to rest after Preacher's Block, and Emily . . . becoming vicar . . .*

It's not right, dragging something else into the picture when you still need to paint Emily out of it.

But it was unconvincing. I had not even been thinking of Emily. I was besotted, infatuated, with Scarlet Lipstick. Could I not have avoided ruining it with her?

I would just have to hope that the burst main in my heart, from which love shot, fountain-like, would slow to a trickle before I lost the energy even to sleep. I banged the wall of the flat with a fist. With pain like skin at a sliding scalpel, I sank myself in the counselling.

It surprised me when Ben rang, requesting time.

I asked: 'Do you want to tell me what – '

'No way,' interrupted the voice.

Ben Jivvard had the ruddy look of a farmer: tall, thickset, with glossy ginger hair. He was also a Conservative who had lost battles for parliamentary seats. He harped on about God and morals too much during the campaigns, and the Press had got him on it. After elections, Ben returned to his small firm. It made a patent watertight plug for boats.

As he walked in, I remembered a talk for businessmen I had watched him do, when he spent more than twenty minutes trying to glide logically from the shape of one of the plugs to the theological concept of substitution.

But I was now looking at a different man.

'You know me.' He agitatedly rubbed bristle on his chin.

'Not that well,' I replied. 'No, not that well, Ben. I suppose we've bumped into each other twice down in the tea room – that was before I became vicar – and then – '

'Forget that,' he cut in. He leant back and breathed through his nose, with a whistle that sounded like a kettle.

True to rule, I was silent.

'No,' he said, as his breath steadied. 'Don't forget it. She's committing adultery, vicar.'

'Acting vicar,' I murmured, thoughtlessly.

It was ignored. 'My wife's committing adultery.'

He looked up at me, nostrils flaring. Fist cracked against palm. He rubbed the bristles again.

Now I had to ask a question. 'How do you know?'

'That's why I'm here, isn't it? If I was sure, well – it would be easy. But I'm not. So I'm here.'

He seemed about to cry; I had not seen a Conservative cry before. Then the tears went away and anger returned.

'Whoever it is – if I find him – he's going to have his head cracked against a wall like a small nut –'

'All right,' I said. 'All right, Ben.' I waved a hand gently, to calm him. The chin-rubbing was no aid to concentration. I had a sudden sense of doom.

'It's not all right,' said Ben.

'How do you know this is true?' I asked.

'I don't. She comes in late, tells me she's been in the office when she hasn't, because I've checked.'

'Maureen, isn't it?' I asked.

'Mandy. Ben and Mandy, people used to call us. They still do. I check at work – they say she's gone. I get in from a business trip unexpectedly, she's lying there with the bed covers everywhere –'

'Well, lots of people lie in. It's quite normal.'

'At three in the afternoon? Come on! It's murder! That's what it is! I'm being murdered. It's like electrocution, but the shock's worse. I found a miniature bottle of aftershave in one of her pockets – and she won't have sex any more –'

Colouring, I raised a hand. 'All right. I don't think the fine detail is probably that important, unless there's –'

'A hair on a dress.'

'Right.'

'Because there's been one of them, as well.'

'Not one of hers, Ben?'

'Of course it wasn't! You think I don't know what colour her hair is?' He started rubbing his bristles furiously.

'Look – sorry – I'd be really grateful if you could stop rubbing your chin. I am having trouble counselling you.'

He blearily pulled the hand away from his face.

But the ranting went on for twenty minutes. Ben would make wild-sounding accusations, then speak dramatically of his own anguish. 'I'm not beyond suicide,' he bellowed.

Meanwhile, my life at Saint Peter's was flashing before me. *Adultery*. What would people say? That the two of them had missed out on the right preaching? That the church was falling apart since Douglas had left? Crumbling?

'Believe it or not, Mandy's been coming here still, too. She won't pray with me any more at home, and she never opens her Bible, but she's carried on coming here,' he said.

That's great. I'm running a church where adulterers feel at home.

'She likes your preaching,' he said, tonelessly.

That's great.

He cried some more. True to my art, I said nothing.

Suddenly, Ben looked up.

'The diary,' he said.

The diary? What is he talking about now?

Soon he explained: Mandy, he said, wrote every detail of her life into a series of big diaries. Everything. She had never let him look at them. All secrets, she said. Some of them about her feelings towards God.

'Her creator,' he hissed, distractedly. 'Whoever created her needs to have a read of the Trade Descriptions Act.'

There was a pause. He composed himself.

'I'm here for a reason,' Ben murmured.

I felt my spirits sink. 'Um – yes?'

His clear blue eyes, red around the rims, caught mine.

'Can I look at the diary? Morally?'

Don't get drawn, I told myself. *Don't let him draw you.*

'I'm surprised you haven't already,' I said.

'I need you to tell me it's all right,' he went on. 'If I find anything – it'll be the end of her marriage.'

Her marriage. The conversation had grown more and more ominous. I was being asked to end a marriage.

'You would look at it whatever I said, wouldn't you?'

'I'm scared to,' Ben answered, looking more farmer than Conservative as he leant forward. 'She's a smart tart. I'm scared. It's in a locked drawer, with binding around it.'

His head dropped. I pondered.

I was furious for getting involved. It was too late to pretend I was not. All those rules on counselling – shut up, nod, use shrugs when possible, don't have views, never ask for details, don't mention God – they had all gone missing.

The easy life had jumped out of the window.

There was no question of praying with the man. This was much more serious than that.

I thought long and hard; then longer and harder.

You could not ask a woman directly about adultery, I reflected – so I supposed looking at the diary would be better than asking. Finally, I told Ben Jivvard so.

'Really?' he said, looking up; looking a mess.

'I don't know.'

'It sounded as though you were pretty sure.'

'I think I am,' I replied.

'You think you're sure?'

'I don't know.'

'When?' Now there was a victorious certainty creeping into his voice, as though he had official sanction.

This was new ground. It felt like safe-cracking. We were looking for the combination, and I was already in a mask . . .

I heard myself sigh. 'As soon as possible, I suppose.' That was the cosh. I sounded weary in the criminality of it.

'Can you ring me when you've read it?' I asked, urgently. 'Don't do anything until you ring me.' Someone would have to try to control this, to put a lid on the thing.

'I'll read it tonight.'

'Oh.'

'My wife's out all evening. I'm pretty sure about it.'

'Can't you open it without your wife finding out?'

What are you saying?

'I've never seen the key to the drawer, or the diary.'

'You don't know where it is?' *Haywire. My counselling technique has gone haywire.*

'I could look.'

'If you prise open the drawer, I suppose – '

'I'm not going to fake a burglary, if that's what you're about to suggest,' he said.

'No, no, I wasn't going to say that at all – '

What's happening? Everything's falling apart!

'Maybe it doesn't matter. If it's true – '

I said: 'Don't be hasty, now, about – '

' – the marriage is finished, but if it's not, I just say, "Look, darling, I just suddenly got very keen to read your diary," which – '

'I don't – '

' – yes, which I agree won't be the best way, but at least we'll be relieved of all this.'

Now that's true. If the diary is empty, we're safe.

'What time is it now?' he asked.

'We've been talking for nearly an hour and a half.'

'Okay. Now let's see. I'll go right back there,' Ben said, bouncing up with vigour as though I had opened new avenues to him. His face was aglow too. There was a disturbing, deadly sense of mission in it.

'I'll ring you – at – let me see – '

'It's five-fifteen now,' I murmured, lost in thought.

'I'll ring you at seven.'

The words came out in a rush.

'On the dot, no matter what. Seven, Mark. Don't forget.'

And he was gone.

Almost as soon as the latch on the door clicked, fright and dread swamped me – numbing, momentarily, even those parts of my heart which were dedicated to Gillian Mitchell.

The papers would find out, wouldn't they?

Yes, the newspapers would uncover the adultery for sure if it had happened – and perhaps even if it had not. In their terms it was a super, scoop of a story: the churchgoer whose electoral campaign got bogged down in morals and God now found his marriage bogged down in adultery.

As long as I had been in the Church of England, I had feared newspapers. We all did. They once made a huge issue of a mistake by the vicar in Straithe. One year, he simply forgot to celebrate Remembrance Sunday. After a predictably large number of local people appeared for their six-monthly visit to the church and the service failed to happen, a disgruntled parishioner must have telephoned one of the national tabloids with the details . . .

For the following day it dedicated a full quarter-page to the story, under the headline, WORLD WARS 'JUST SLIPPED MY MIND' SAYS DIZZY VICAR.

It listed questions candidates for the clergy ought to face in future, including: 'Who did we fight in the last war?' 'Which side was Montgomery on?' and 'Which harbour in the United States was bombed by the Japanese: was it (a) Rhinestone, (b) Amethyst, or (c) Pearl?'

On the day he read them in Straithe, the Rector was inconsolable. On another occasion, involving a different newspaper and a different story, it was I who was the victim.

The same inconsolability gripped me when Ben was gone.

I had done nothing to deserve this. It could almost be said that I had done nothing. I had held the church – this giant liner of a church – on an even keel since becoming vicar. It had been steady-as-she-goes.

Now, I considered, *it could be steady-as-she-sinks.*

Never, ever, should I have given an indication that it was all right to read the diary. But he had wheedled it out of me, with his tears and chin-rubbing. My uncertainty had translated into his certainty, and now I was in trouble. I dreaded seven o'clock. What news would Ben's call bring?

There were items on my desk, and I turned on them.

One needed careful handling: a list of damage done to a school in Hove during a visit by children from Saint Peter's and two other churches. Despite supervision, seven fire extinguishers had been let off – two jetting foam on to the head of a town councillor, walking below a library window. Then a false ceiling above the girls' dormitory had given way after one of the spottier youths tried to crawl to a vantage point; a small boy playing with a mallet and pistol rounds had taken a bad cheek wound; the over-zealous worship leader woke one night to find his hair on fire. It was now the duty of the churches involved to apportion costs, but since the congregation of Saint Peter's was somewhat more well-to-do than the others, I was under pressure (mainly from Morag, who had been listening to the parents) to refuse to contribute.

Strange . . . it was at these most ridiculous moments of my Anglican career that, far from being unconvinced about the reality of God, I was most taken with the idea.

I speculated: *How could there be all this junk, and no jewellery?*

How this much chaos – and no Calvary?

I wanted to live life in a darkroom. Bowed by new worries about Ben Jivvard, who was probably going to bring the whole church crashing down around my ears in an explosion of tombstone headlines, I walked dozily out of the flat and down the stairs.

Shock cleared my mind rapidly at the foot of them.

– 16 –

A shoulder was visible through the doorway, and I recognised its owner just at the moment that I walked into the tea room. Too late to change direction.

I bridged the threshold as though in slow motion, seeing the shoulder extend into side and neck – and then, touching the floor of the room with my rubber-soled shoes like a moon-walking astronaut, watched the side and neck spring into hip, skirt, stockinged calves; a curve somewhere; a head of hair.

I was shocked to see her.

Scarlet Lipstick turned. Goodness knows what she was doing here on a weekday.

Her small haversack was imprinted with blue and red flowers, and she was wearing a thick wool wrap.

Beautiful as she smiled at me, she flushed slightly, stiffening her back and reassigning the haversack strap to its home in a nook of her shoulder. She cleared her throat and reached a hand out to shake mine as the smile etched those whisker-thin, concentric lines into her cheeks, and her eyes flashed and the wide-rimmed spectacles she wore flashed too.

Beneath her long coat, lower buttons undone, I noticed she was wearing a tight-fitting skirt.

She is also one of your parishioners.

'Hello.' I recognised my voice as though it had been pointed out to me long-distance, through binoculars.

'Hi.' She looked flustered.

So we were alone for the first time! The tea room was empty. Mittens hung from her wrist on a string. Our hands, as they shook, would have bent the needle on a Richter scale.

She said: 'My father has the words "Kevin McGlinlick" tattooed on his leg.'

I opened my mouth slowly, gathering a response.

'Sorry. I was just thinking about it,' she blurted. 'About how permanent it was. Just above his sock. He's a Northern Irish folk singer who has a place at Portadown.'

'Portable what, sorry?'

'Down.' She made it sound like 'Dine'.

'Dining where?'

'What?'

'I didn't hear what you said. Your accent –'

'Portadown.' *Pawrder-dine.* 'Portadown, Mark,' she said magnetically, in that foxy voice, and smiled up at me, giggling, with more intimacy than I could ever have wished for on a second meeting. 'Where the singer lives! Portadown!'

I laughed too, repeating: 'Pawrder-dine!'

And then looked for my watch-face, thinking: *Ben.*

Finding hers first, she said it was a little past six. We both hesitated for a moment, and the pause made me panic for conversation. 'I once saw a gardener with a Rod Stewart tattoo on his knee,' I stuttered.

'Sorry,' she replied. 'It was a silly thing to say.'

'No – it just took me by surprise, that's all.'

How strange to be speaking like this to Scarlet Lipstick, after so much silence! I imagined my small talk translated into a headphone at her ear by a United Nations linguist: 'Mark Empringham loves you. Your acting vicar loves you. The man in front of you is in love with you.'

Then she asked what I had been doing, and I told her. Yes, I said, helping people was something I enjoyed. Was her job going all right? That's good, I said when she told me so. Remembering the ghastly indiscretion at New Year, I moved as though to head for the exit – but she stopped me with more questions about the counselling.

'Oh, obviously I can't say exactly who I was talking to,' I replied. 'It was a tall man needing some advice.'

There was another pause.

'So what brings you here, um – '

'Gilly.'

'Gilly.' I had nearly called her Scarlet. 'Not many come to the tea room midweek – the urns are switched off.'

'There was a reason,' she said, fumbling with a stray thread of cotton at the hem of her blouse.

'To be here in the tea room?'

'Yes.' Always that wonderful, glue-thick Northern Irish. I still could not believe she was so close to me.

'Well, I hope you don't have to wait for – ' I paused, looking into her round face, framed by the thick black curls, always revolving around that smile or the hope of it, binning all maxims about avoiding eye contact . . . seeing something there, in that instant, which might have been personal between us. And hearing, perhaps, the answer to the question before she even said it.

And then it came, prefaced by an unsteady breath.

'Actually, I was sort of wondering if we might meet.'

When I realised what she was saying – when I realised that Gilly Mitchell, my Scarlet Lipstick . . .

That she was saying she had been waiting in the tea room in order to catch me as I walked past –

Me! Waiting to catch me!

. . . I suffered a bout of coughing.

No rescue came. So she was not in love with her acting vicar, or she would have touched his arm as he spluttered into a fist.

Instead she just looked on, kindly. And then explained.

'It was to do with New Year.'

'New Year?' I mumbled the question.

'Yes. The party, Mark. You must remember – we met there. Francis and Sally's.' Her face was reddening.

My heart began to sink. In churches, intimacy with rectors and curates was a right, not a privilege; and today, without warning, Gillian was claiming what was hers.

'I think we met once before, actually, after the – '

She interrupted with sudden fierceness.

'No, but I wanted to talk to you – I mean, I thought you might want to – to talk about the – the party – about the party, because you said something, and it's been on my mind.'

I said: 'Oh, you know what parties are like.' She was very close to the bone now. 'A lot of joking – japing and so on. Tomfoolery,' I added.

But my Scarlet was not to be disarmed.

'It's just that you said something to me – you said you sometimes wondered if you were a Christian, Mark – and I wondered – I suppose I wondered if you'd told anyone else.'

'Oh, yes – I think I remember the party now – '

'I asked you how you became a Christian, and you said you sometimes wondered if you were one.'

I maintained a queasy smile.

'Well,' I said briskly, 'as you can see, I'm vicar now, so there's not much to wonder about any more.'

But the sentence came out on crutches, not stilts.

She said: 'Being vicar has nothing to do with – '

'I know,' I broke in. 'I know, I know, I know.'

I had always reckoned that at some point after my arrival at the church, this challenge would come: an unwanted attempt to excavate my system of belief. But I never expected the challenger to be the only person in the world I loved.

'I'm sorry, Mark – you must think me terribly rude.'

'Not at all,' I said, reeling.

Her nostrils, built into a definite, stone-sculpted, chalk-white nose, were flaring slightly. She was so pretty.

Please, I thought, *leave it there*.

'It's – I was talking to you, if you remember, and – '

'Yes, that's right – just before midnight,' I said. 'I do remember chatting to you. I don't know what you think about him, but I was talking to Francis, for the first time really, and – do you agree – he's a terrific – '

'Yes, he is,' she interrupted. 'But it's this comment of yours, Mark – it's just been worrying me.'

'Which comment, again?'

'When I asked you – I said, "How did you become a Christian?" And you said you didn't know if you were one.'

There was a lot riding on how I answered. I could not walk away from Gilly without proving her worst fears. How many people would she tell? *How many has she told already?*

But it was odd that I could even consider walking away. I loved my Scarlet Lipstick. Now that she was in front of me, curved like suspension bridges, haversacked, sets of fingers intertwined thoughtlessly, I was used to the feeling of having her there. And now I never wanted her to go.

We sat down on two orange chairs by the tea urns, and I went for mercy.

'Please don't be hard on me,' I said. 'Not just on one comment at a party.'

'I'm not trying to be hard!' Scarlet seemed genuinely astonished. 'I thought – just that you might want to talk.'

'It's nice to talk.'

'No, but – about the comment you made – did you really mean it? Do you really think you're not – not there, as it were? Not a Christian?'

I stared at her. At least we were sitting now.

'Did you mean it, Mark?'

There was the rub.

It was peculiar hearing it. Faith and Irishness and beauty were trained on me like a cannon.

It was obvious what would happen if I told her I was lost. If I ran through all the different modes of belief, from Left-wing to Right-wing and all the rest, and then listed all the good reasons for ditching every one of them, reasons Scarlet could not but agree with because they were so clever and complicated and she was probably not, and told her about Emily, and how Matthew – a sidesman, for Pete's sake – had turned out to be a greedy wife-basher, and asked her where the midgets of New Guinea would go when they died . . .

And why, then, if she told me the best-behaved midgets were going to heaven, it had been necessary to have a Son of God, and all that pain, in the first place . . .

And then asked her whom exactly Cain had married, since he was supposed to have fathered the entire human race, from China to Chingford, with only his mum and dad for company . . .

And questioned her on how you could trust a church which had scooped up the lost sheep she was sitting with, and made him a shepherd . . . scooped up this sheep in vicar's clothing . . .

But no. All those questions – all that sophistication and thought – would amount to a single word only four letters long, so far as my Scarlet was concerned.

Lost, she would think.

And I would be allowed to love my Scarlet no longer.

If word got around – well, I might even have to resign.

On second thoughts, I might be promoted to Bishop.

I thought very carefully before speaking.

And, when I opened my mouth . . . all time seemed to stop.

'That comment at the party, Gillian – it was a joke.'

She tensed slightly, and leant forward.

'A joke?'

Doesn't she believe me?

'A pun.'

'Pun? What – in answer to the question?'

'I don't mean a pun, I mean I was trading on the point of what you were saying. I was heightening the – the emphasis of the choice.'

'The choice?'

'Of whether or not to be a Christian. The choice – ah –

we've all made, to – er – to be one. To be a Christian. What I was saying was that it's important to keep reviewing it.'

'Oh, and checking you're still –'

'Still reviewing, exactly. I mean, still following the right thing. You know, the importance of watching yourself and watching the road you're on, of – er – asking yourself whether you're still being true. To it. The – um – importance of – just, of wondering about the whole thing.'

'Oh, I see –' She laughed, relaxed, and leant back. Then her brow creased. 'So it – it wasn't really a joke.'

'It was serious, but it had the elements of a joke.'

She breathed deeply.

'So you have put your trust in God – in Christ.'

'Yes.'

Looking past her crossed, skirted legs to the floor, she said: 'I'm really sorry. I suppose I thought you were telling me you weren't really a believer, and I admit –'

'Oh, no –'

I do believe. In fish and chips.

' – that I thought, well, you know, it wouldn't be that amazing – to have a curate, you know, who didn't –'

'Oh, no –'

' – yes, I know you think I'm crazy – and then I sort of thought perhaps you might want to talk with someone.'

'Oh, no,' I said breezily. She ignored the hollow ring in my laughter, which ended in a cough. 'But thanks – Gilly.'

'That's okay,' she said . . . so sweetly.

I was sweating. My face must have been glistening.

'Are you enjoying it? It's an awful lot, isn't it?'

'What?'

'Being vicar here.' She gestured, as though indicating points of scenic interest in the tea room.

'Acting vicar,' I said, adding: 'Rector, strictly. I'm not doing what Douglas did. He was a real vicar, you know –'

'But you're a real vicar too.'

'Acting.'

There was another silence.

'Where do you live?' I asked.

'Oh, miles out. Past Wembley – in Pinner. I'm renting the last house on a council estate. It's cheap, but it's a bit cut off. You have to go across a field in the morning.'

'Are you on your own there?'

'No. Well – actually, I am at the moment. My flatmate, Brinny, is on holiday in America.'

'Which part?'

'She's in Montana.' *Maen-tanner*.

'What's the crime like there – in Maen-tanner?'

'There's a lot of rustling, I think,' she said, soberly.

There was a gap, as though to let gangs of horse thieves get away.

'I did some rustling yesterday,' I said. 'I can remember it. I rustled some of the papers on my desk.'

To my surprise, Scarlet laughed . . . a beautiful laugh, naturally, tailing off in livid giggles that sounded like a stream running over secret gold.

'I know Daniel. And Vanessa,' she offered.

'Yes, Vanessa's another one who helps look after lots here – though she's been a bit ill recently. Having said that, she's always done a great job with the youth work, and I think they've sorted her medicines out now – though I get most of the news now from Vicki, her sister, funnily enough – '

Now I was small-talking with my Lipstick!

'I didn't know Vanessa had a sister.'

'Vicki? The last I heard from her, just after Christmas, was that she was going to this thing called New Thinking.'

'A concert, is that?' Scarlet asked.

'No – some sort of religion. Vanessa was very upset – she calls it "Christianity with perks". But I suppose she's free to go her own way.'

The last sentence knocked a spark off Gillian.

'Oh, but – she's missing out. On Jesus Christ.'

I curled all five toes on one foot hard round in excruciating embarrassment.

'She's missing – the love of God, forgiveness –'

'I think the idea of New Religion is that you try to forget your shortcomings, so the sin – ah – just vanishes.'

'It's crap,' said Scarlet, shocking me into even greater adoration of her.

I had sold my soul now. Telling young, Irish Gillian Mitchell, twenty-three, that I, twenty-nine, believed what I did not . . .

And how could I regret it? She was so silken . . .

Me? I stood for nothing: I was nothing.

Her mouth was red as strawberries . . .

I had sold my soul to kiss it. Like Judas, I betrayed my calling for a kiss – it was as simple as that, and so similar to the Bible story that, doubtless, someone's ear would soon be cut off with a Roman sword, right in the middle of the domed lobby of Saint Peter's, and replaced; pieces of silver would be found near the noticeboard; there would be a burial, a rock rolled back from a tomb entrance, racing disciples, discarded funeral sheets in the gloom . . .

But I do not believe in all that.

Surely, I had betrayed nothing – barring my own disbelief. Besides that, there was nothing.

In any case, I thought, *I'm the sort who'll never marry.*

But we were still talking, here in the tea room, and while we talked I still had hope, even of eternal life.

She was telling me about her mother's death.

'Mam got ill so quickly after the conversation,' she said. 'We had talked about her faith in Jesus Christ.'

'That's terribly sad.'

'No, it's not. She's gone to be with her Saviour.'

'Of course. It's very exciting.'

'It is.' Her eyes misted. A scarlet lip trembled.

I must have had the courage of seven thousand men, for I reached over then, and touched her hand – the one the mittens hung from. I just could not bear to see my love so sad.

A voltage passed through me. Before I had any idea what was happening, Gillian's other hand was on top of mine.

'Thank you,' she said. 'It's been hard, and people have asked me out to parties, and for dinner and things, and I haven't really been able to say yes.'

She is single.

I wondered who I was: her suitor, counsellor, rector, or resident devil?

Or just an hour-long cuppa in the tea room?

She asked me routine questions, and, succumbing to a Kamikaze instinct, I put in: 'Yes, I was on the verge of leaving the church soon after I got here.'

'Why would you – '

'Oh, I just didn't know if it was me,' I said. 'I guess the last curate was the same, judging by the way he left.'

'I don't know why he did that. He seemed so happy here. But someone told me he'd been got rid of.'

'Really? For what?' I asked.

'No idea. He seemed very much into his job, and he was really great with old people – like when my father, when he came over soon after the funeral – '

I cut in. 'Where is he now?'

'Oh, back in Northern Ireland, of course, in – '

'No, I mean the curate – Brendan.'

The answer never came. We were suddenly interrupted by the sound of steps on the stairs leading down from the lobby.

'I think I'd better be off,' she said. As I struggled for a way of keeping her or going with her, Richard Burts came into the tea room, apparently propelled by a trip on the last stair.

'Mark – ' he called, out of breath, and broke into as fast a jog as he could manage across the carpet towards us.

'Oh – sorry,' he said next, slowing as he saw us, grossly out of breath now, running a gloved hand over long hair.

There were heaps of melting snow on his shoulders.

'Do you know Scarl— ah – Gillian – Mitchell?' I rose reluctantly, and blushed. I felt like some sort of gigolo.

'Yes, I think –' Richard began.

'We've seen each other around a bit,' cut in the beautiful Irish accent without a trace of shame. *Arind,* she had said, enunciating the word as though it had eight or nine vowels in. Richard nodded briskly in agreement.

Then he flicked his head to me, breathlessly.

'Mark, please come with me.' He lapsed into wheezing. 'Something's happened, and you've got to do something.'

The urgency pumped me with glamour. Leaving my love behind with a brisk wave and roll of my eyes – as if to say, 'Well, this is what it's like to run the biggest church in the country' – I walked briskly towards the tea-room door with Richard.

As I walked away, she said: 'Thanks again, Mark. Thanks for telling me all that.'

Going up the stairs to the domed lobby, Richard asked: 'What did you tell her? I didn't know you knew her.'

I replied, 'I don't, really.'

When we came out on to the steps of the church, Richard grabbed my elbow as we stood in the freezing winter air.

'I'm not dressed for –' I began, shivering already.

But Richard spoke across the sentence.

'Look.'

I could not see whatever it was that he was expecting me to see, staring left and right over hundreds of yards of new snow. 'Sorry, Richard – what am I looking at?'

'All around!' he said. 'Look!'

But all I could see through the freezing air were the snow-covered streets, seeming orange under the lighting; and cars, moving slowly, their beams picking out drifting flakes.

'Look, Mark! Snow!'

'Yes, I can see it.' *Snow?*

'But you know what it means?'

Poor, duffel-coated Richard, so overweight, was still breathless.

'It's a chemical reaction, isn't it?' I asked.

Richard moved carefully in a diagonal line down the church steps. As he reached the street, he stepped into the snow. It went a quarter of the way up his shins.

'Look how deep it is, Mark.'

'I can see. It is deep,' I called back.

'That's why I had to get you.'

'Of course.' I still did not understand.

'I'm talking about the old people.' Richard was calling up to me now, over the roar of a truck that ground its way past the front of the church, its wheels spitting slush.

'I've just come from work,' he shouted. He was transport officer with a council, responsible for riding around the area on a motorbike to decide which roads had the strongest call on local money. 'They just can't get out to them.'

'To the old people?'

'Exactly! They won't be able to bring their meals out to them, and the volunteers can't get out in this. No way.'

'What about the army?'

'What about us, Mark? What can we do? For Doris Slattery? And Peter Mayre, the retired gardener who always takes twenty minutes to get down the aisle? What about Vera – and Mabel – Edith – Sandy – and Fred Coombes? What do we do?'

I felt snowflakes drift on to my head, and resentment drift into my heart. The list of church pensioners Richard Burts was so ready with – had they not already survived more harsh winters than any of their fellow-worshippers? What did they need so badly that it was worth us half-dying to get it to them? And why was a vicar taking orders from a guitarist?

Richard answered the question without even hearing it.

Moving back up the steps, towards me, he said: 'If they get cold, that's going to be really dangerous.'

I said: 'You're right.'

'I know they have wigs and things, but you need an awful lot of insulation in weather like this.'

'They have blankets, I suppose.'

'But if the council can't bring their meals round – '

'Yes, Richard, absolutely – '

' – and if the phone lines go down in this, or chimneys start collapsing – '

' – and their pipes freeze – ' I was getting into the swing of it – 'or their foundations crack, or – '

'Exactly, Mark. This is – ' Richard made claws out of his gloved hands, as if grappling with the neck of an impossible idea. 'It's massive. We need a plan.'

'A crisis plan,' I said.

'And we need to have a meeting.'

'Yes – a crisis meeting,' I said.

I assured Richard I would organise one for the following day. He admitted he would not be able to attend, and my resentment rose inches. We did not discuss a time.

'Great,' he said. 'What about the plan? We've got to be really organised – we've got to really help these people.'

'I'll draw up the plan now, in my flat,' I replied. It was certainly a heavy fall of snow. Everything was submerged.

When I got back to the flat, I unlaced my damp shoes and set them upside-down on top of the radiator.

Then I peeled a piece of lined foolscap from a pad.

But when I began to write, there was nothing about snow, chimneys, emergencies or hot meals; nothing about any of the church elderly; nothing about hot drinks, warm blankets, camping stoves, heaters, shovels . . .

Just the words, 'Scarlet Lipstick'.

Then I wrote them again; doodled around them, adding a G-I-L-L-I-A-N, skirted stick figures with mittens hanging from wrists; crosses for kisses; *Mitchell*, and every possible anagram of it: *Chime. Hill. Mile. Chit. Met. Mite. Millet. Lime. Letch. Mill. Chill. Ill. Lice. Lithe. Mice.*

. . . and, last: *Hell.*

The page was full when I put down the pen. And even when I looked at the clock on my desk and saw it was ten-thirty, and remembered the vital call from Ben Jivvard that had seemed a matter of life and death but which I had long since missed . . .

Well, it hardly seemed to matter at all.

– 17 –

'So what do we start with? What's on the agenda?'

'The snow.'

'The snow? Not the accounts? I thought Hendon was – '

'No, there's no Hendon – it's simply – snow,' I told Daniel, feeling silly. He had just arrived, briskly, in response to a note pushed under his door late the previous night. That had been the sum total of my efforts to organise the rescue of the Saint Peter's elderly: one note. No plan.

In fact, there would have been no action at all had it not been for a vivid prompt my memory gave me as I sat at my desk, swimming in late-night love for Gillian Mitchell.

I remembered her words in a flash: 'I live miles out. It's a bit cut off. You have to go across a field.'

. . . And was suddenly panicking for her safety, recalling too that her flatmate was abroad, shoving my pad to one side, grabbing for the plastic-coated list of internal telephone numbers. *There has to be a crisis meeting: my Scarlet might be in danger*. The fear rose in my throat, energising me.

Present too at the meeting was Kennett, the church janitor, a burly, forest-eyebrowed handyman, never seen minus his boiler-suit, whose voice had been strangely warped by a lung infection from a sewer under the church; and Hugh Nelson, a parishioner with a florid birthmark on his forehead. As he had arrived to offer his services, I was swept with great glee. Succumbing to a delightful sense of professionalism, with an associated whiff of accountancy, I told him that – well, as it happened, a snow-crisis meeting was about to begin and he was most welcome to join us.

Yes: arrangements were already under way to save the lives of all the old people in the parish.

And my Scarlet Lipstick.

'You're the vicar,' said Daniel, as we sat down. 'I guess it's a good decision. My windows look like those Yule scenes on cards. I saw a car skid into a lottery kiosk.'

Vanessa, sitting opposite, spoke at speed. 'Not good luck for the kiosk. I heard this is the most sustained – I don't know – something was sustained, and now it's the first of Feb, and the whole of London is a fridge. But God works.'

I noted that my former flatmate had changed her hairstyle, a decision that was easier to understand than her commentary on the weather.

Kennett had just croaked: 'I don't know why I'm here.'

I took it as a cue.

'We need to organise cars and people to go to see the old people.'

It was hardly an heroic address.

Kennett mumbled again: 'I don't know why I'm here.'

But soon the janitor was in a minority of one. The others responded with enthusiasm, listing cars they thought might be free. (My Datsun was ruled out, because it was the same model and had almost the same number-plate as a car used in an off-licence robbery, whose details had been on television; and after being stopped by a would-be hero who dived through the open window of the passenger door and jammed on the handbrake, I was advised by the police to keep it stowed in a garage for at least a month.) Then, with a gusto which even touched Kennett, who leant his bulky torso and spanner-fat suit across the tabletop as he offered nigh-on inaudible suggestions, the group ran through the names of those in the church who might be in danger.

Morag poked her head around the door.

'Mark – there's a phone call.'

I looked up, losing track of a count of names.

'What?'

'A call. It sounds like Ben Jivvard.'

'I don't think I'd better take it now,' I said.

'He says it's urgent. He can't leave a message.'

'I think we'd better get on with this, even so.'

Morag disappeared as I thanked her, my heart drooping.

But we got on with it. Vanessa and Daniel had five cars within half an hour; Hugh talked a neighbour into bringing his jeep. I was amazed at the readiness to help. Three young sons in the ultra-successful Dibble family arrived in a chauffeured Mercedes. BBF sent down his car keys. By the end, after forty or fifty calls, we were standing in the snow with easily as many vehicles as we had hoped for.

We all stood there, shivering.

Cars, parked jaggedly, fanned out from the steps as the snow fell. Someone had even brought a Canadian saloon, wheels criss-crossed with snow-chains.

Extraordinary, I thought. *This is Christian. I am doing something Christian.* And despite the holy aura of my colleagues . . . despite that, compared to my lostness, I felt a part of something here. Perhaps it made me a Christian now: now, as I looked down on to these cars and drivers, in generosity?

Perhaps not, I concluded. *I am lost*.

Fewer lights than usual burnt in Marple & Schwartz.

An old face presented itself.

'Vicki,' I said, stretching out a gloved hand.

'Vanessa told me what you were doing.'

'Are you off work today, then?'

'I am, actually. I get this off instead of Sunday. It's a bizarre rota system we're on.'

Vicki looked as though she was wrapped in skintight fur. Her face, like her sister's, was as white as the scenery.

She said: 'What can I do – vicar?'

'I'm not sure.' I laughed at the title. 'I'll be taking a car out to a couple of places. I think we have enough drivers. Mind you, people will go in the cars – '

'That's novel.'

' – as extra passengers, then get off at the home of an old person and try to work out how they can be helped.'

There was a strange sound, like a vat of syrup coming to the boil. Kennett was shouting at a reversing car.

'So why don't I come in yours?' said Vicki.

'Mine? Well, I really don't think my strike rate is going to be – er – as high as the others – or – um – '

There was simply no way I could have Vicki with me on the journey to Scarlet's home on that council estate. I would have to be alone.

'But where are you going, exactly, Mark?' she persisted. 'Can't I come? We haven't seen each other for ages.'

I raised my voice slightly: 'No.'

Someone turned to look, then turned away again.

'I'm sorry, Vicki. Let's meet later on.'

She looked hurt. 'Anyway – all's well with me, Mark, if you're interested. If we don't see each other later.'

'I am, I am. I'm really sorry, Vicki. I didn't mean to be rude. How's the New Thinking going, then?'

'Very well.' Vapour blew from between Vicki's thin lips as she spoke. 'We've been concentrating on what they call "fruitening" our emotions.'

'It sounds interesting.' *It is probably as much fruit-and-nut as the nuttiest fruitcake in any Anglican church.*

'Yes. And this – this is part of it. Helping people.'

'Oh,' I said. 'So it's like Christianity.'

My voice was sounding stiff as a board in the cold. Someone shouted that drivers ought to get in their vehicles.

'And make sure you've got your lists!' I recognised the piercing voice: Morag. Her duffel-coated outline, a tuft of seal-coloured hair protruding from under the green hood, was in the centre of everything. *That woman is really in charge,* I thought. *She's the one who wears the dog collar around here.* But I was happy to hand the leash of power to anyone.

I somehow ended up with BBF's keys, and managed to open his car door and climb in, alone and unnoticed.

Almost unnoticed.

'Where are you going, Mark?' asked Morag, approaching the driver's-side window at speed.

I wound it down. 'I've got a couple of names.'

'Whose names?'

This is like secret police. 'Sheila and Derek Cryer, and Peter Mayre,' I answered. 'Three names.'

'You don't want someone with you?'

Is she going to shine a spotlight in my face next?

'I think I'll be fine.'

Convinced, she waved me on.

Moving slowly down the Ferndown Highway, I marvelled that I was in the car of the Stipendiary Parson. The position seemed peculiarly intimate. It was an old model, and an air-freshener hung from the rear-view mirror. Snow whipped the windscreen as I flicked a knob on the cassette player.

There was a powerful organ-blast.

I switched the player off, turning a corner and feeling the wheels slip on the road below.

Pulling in, I scanned a map for the route.

Sheila and Derek Cryer turned out to live on the way, near a large intersection. Seeing them did not take long.

'It's so kind of you to come,' said Sheila in a wrinkled voice, after serving a cup of tea.

'Hot tea,' I said.

'It's keeping us alive,' Sheila remarked, and Derek laughed. 'Hot tea, and our Lord watching over us.'

Derek's comment reminded me I had not opened the Bible in my flat for weeks, apart from a single occasion when I mistook it for a telephone directory.

'Always watching,' I said.

They waved me off: their waves were firmer than my legs. I was thinking about seeing my Scarlet again.

Slowly, endless curves and corners presented themselves on the way to her home, another seven or eight miles away.

As I drew closer, a thought chilled me: of Matthew divorcing Emily and marrying my Scarlet.

I would kill him.

Earlier, with the elderly Cryers, the fear for Gillian had swelled. But when her estate came into view at last, plastered with snow, it was obvious she must be safe. At the very worst, she would be stuck at home and bored. Letting the car drift lazily, down street and past street-corner, I wondered: *Should I bother, after all?*

And then there was a sign to her road.

No. There was no choice. Turning, I saw odd numbers.

My heartbeat was just as uneven. The car slid on, engine whining. It had stopped snowing now. Sun was breaking out from behind a corrugated cloud in a giant patch of blue, and the scene was confirmed as one more of elegance than peril.

I am a fool.

The brakes moaned slightly as they were applied, and the car edged, semi-spiritually, into a space just yards from Scarlet's home. Somehow, its brown-bricked front stood out.

Climbing from the car, I shivered. Its heater had been blasting insulation against the cold outside.

I knocked on the door. Nothing happened for at least a minute. I stamped my right foot on the snow-covered drive.

What a fool I am.

Suddenly, with a click that sounded like a tick placed at the end of the thought, a latch snapped from the inside.

My stomach banged like a drum when she appeared.

After the moment it took Gillian Mitchell to register my face and recognise it, she stepped forwards, grinning.

'Mark!'

'Hi,' I said, weakly. 'Are you all right?'

'Fine.' A puzzled expression began to emerge on her face. 'The house is warm. But as for work – well, forget it.'

'Oh.' I hoped I did not sound disappointed. 'Right, well – I suppose – '

Her expression found utterance in a question. 'Did you come all the way out here for – '

'Yes,' I answered. 'Well – no, really – we're doing a fast run to all the old people in the church, and – '

'But I'm only twenty-three, Mark!'

' – and – yes, but it was such a heavy fall, and I remembered what you said about your flatmate – '

'Brinny – '

' – about Brandy being away – '

'Brinny.'

' – yes, Branny – '

'And I am pretty far out – there's no doubt about that.'

'Yes,' I said, triumphantly. 'I was visiting a couple of the elderly people. So I thought I'd see you on the way.'

'Oh – which ones? Which old people?'

Without thinking, I said the names.

She said: 'But the Cryers, and Peter – I don't know the Cryers, but I thought they all lived quite near the church.'

We had moved into her cramped hallway now. There was a painful silence. She pressed it home. 'I mean, the Cryers, they live on the Gladway intersection, don't they, so – '

'Yes,' I said. 'On this side of it, anyway.'

'So – I don't understand,' she said. For a moment, I thought I was about to weep in front of her and confess.

'You came all the way out here,' she said in a low tone.

There was a hush in the house. And then I knew that it had all fallen into place for her in an instant, perhaps even my indiscreet comment at New Year, perhaps even the shadowy form at the first-floor window . . . perhaps all of that, and more, and things I had not even been aware of, too . . .

It was like turning a television on. A picture flickered, and then unfolded vividly in her dark eyes.

'You came all this way out here?'

'Yes.' Not denying it was the most courageous kind of statement that had ever been made or could ever be made.

Blood zoomed to my head. Her cheeks flushed red. *Vicar and parishioner*, I told myself: *remember*. We sat down a few minutes later for tea, me twittering about the effort to help the old people and Scarlet saying how the engine of her car had failed.

I wondered if I could help. I knew a bit about cars. What was wrong with it?

The hinged gangle pin had been displaced, she said.

I told her I had not heard of hinged gangle pins, and she poured more tea and said it was a foreign part.

And talking of foreign parts, she said, she had got news from Brinny: a romance had started, somewhere near Boston. I asked who was the lucky man, and she said a lawyer who specialised in oil-rig contracts, and that Brinny was very excited about it, and praise God because she'd needed a romance to lift her spirits and she was interested in oil.

And then her acting vicar grabbed at nettles.

'Have you had any romance, at all?'

'Mark,' she said softly, 'I don't think I should say.'

We went on drinking tea. I felt as if some sort of masculine autopilot had taken over the controls of my mouth.

'It was nice to see you yesterday,' she remarked.

'It was good to see you,' I said. 'To be honest, I had been really looking forward to meeting you properly.'

That was the autopilot operating again.

My Scarlet was dressed in thick sweaters, with slippers. There was no lipstick today, but the round face was as expressive as ever . . . and when she closed her mouth, her lips grew thin and the perfect cheeks seemed cast in marble.

And now she caught my eyes, and flashed back the reflection of the obvious, objective fact that I loved her.

'What are you doing, Mark?' she asked.

'Putting another sugar in my tea,' I said. I felt the controls slipping from me completely now.

'Why are you here, though? That's what I mean.'

'I don't – I wish I knew.'

'You said it was the snow.'

'It was.'

'But why? You must have known there'd be no –' she laughed, bewildered – 'no danger to me.'

'I don't know,' I said.

'I want to tell you something,' she said.

After a sip of her tea, she went on: 'I don't like living here, and I'm not very happy in London. About eight months ago, a bit before you arrived at the church – a bit after my mother died, actually –'

She caught her voice slightly, controlling it.

'I was in a different home, taking some time off from work – I was very upset about Mam, and I needed some rest –'

'I can comprehend that.'

'And then there was this noise downstairs – I was in bed – and I realised someone must have broken into the house.'

Hise, she had said, beautifully.

She shifted on the sofa, staring down at her mug.

'I just had to listen to this moving about, downstairs – you know – for about half an hour. I just lay there with the blankets over my face – and I heard all this noise –'

'A burglar?'

'Yes – going right through the house, and then he started coming up the stairs.'

'Goodness.'

'Well, thank goodness, he went away again – I heard the door slam – but he took quite a lot, and somehow a photo of Mam went too. But it really affected me, and I didn't realise quite how much until today, now that I'm on my own here –'

She had tailed off. We looked at each other. It was not possible to say how we looked. I leant towards her at that moment, with courage from heaven-knows-where, never evaluating the hugeness of what I was doing, just doing it on four months of emotion, putting my arms around her . . .

Putting arms around her, saying just: 'My – my –' and never managing to get any other word out . . .

And suddenly my right cheek was sliding across her right cheek, and my palms had found her shoulder-blades, and my front was touching hers, and I realised what I had done.

I drew back, looking at the perfect face.

As though a camera in the room had moved to her, she blinked firmly and smiled in a way that etched those fine troughs again in her cheeks, white as the snow outside.

Her jaw clenched slightly as she looked down, two ridges of muscle standing out on the bone, the expression on her raw lips going from nothing to something like irony.

In Northern Irish sharp enough to have sliced a sheet of glass, she said: 'I'm sorry.'

My eyes sunk to her slippers.

I put my left hand up, spreading the fingers, as though to stop the remnants of the act escaping my spirit. 'No – I'm really sorry. I've been doing a lot of counselling – and – I think I confused some of that with – with – this. With you.'

'It's not the same,' she said.

'I don't hug people. Not professionally.'

'But this shouldn't be –'

Oh, I know, I told her, vigorously, and in a flood of words, it shouldn't be because I'm your vicar, and you're one of my thousands of parishioners, and it's one of the biggest churches in the country, too. But, I said, I am just acting vicar, remember, and I could go at any time, and there's no rule about us loving people, and I've wanted to say ever since I saw you that I know this is real, ever since I saw you in the choir as I walked up to preach my first sermon –

'Oh yes, I remember that sermon,' she said.

I blurted out four words that sang like birds in the gloomy room, echoing off all walls and coming back to roost in my memory for ever.

'I love you, Gilly.'

What did she see in front of her as I said it?

Her vicar, in one sense. In another, just a man in a jet-black jacket, a man still looking moderately young, a man wearing a thick white strip of plastic around his thin neck; I could not imagine anyone falling in love with what she saw. People always say I look too earnest, and so I do; and I was looking mightily earnest as Gillian heard the words, took them in, and looked back, wide eyed. She looked into two blue acting-vicar's eyes, which blink a sight too often . . . and, as they met hers, I stirred in my suit, sensing a revolution. It was not just Preacher's Block that had taken a tumble. Every sort of block now seemed gone; it all flowed out of me . . . all flowed out . . . wordlessly, everything.

'I don't know what to say,' she said.

'You're too good for me, Gilly. I'm a selfish person.'

'I never thought – '

'I'm really sorry for that hug.'

'Would you like some more tea?'

'Yes, please.'

When she came back to the lounge with it, she said: 'I feel I'm going a bit mad.'

'You're not. I am.'

'No – I just wonder if maybe in my faith, my life with Jesus Christ, I'm not open enough to these things.'

'Yes – yes, good point.'

Her face hardened. 'Well, I don't think – I'm really sorry, but this thing isn't right for me, I don't think.'

I don't think. The phrase bounced around my head like a roulette ball, elating me, bouncing off blacks and reds: *She doesn't think. So it's conceivable – there is a chance.*

'No,' she went on, 'I mean – you're my vicar – you're here to do counselling and things like that – not –'

'I know, it's –'

'Not fall in love with people.'

I felt reprimanded, and sunk back for a second; then tried to rally.

'I think a lot about things. I don't go around hugging indiscriminately, Gilly. And I haven't really spoken to anyone properly since I arrived at the church.'

She looked at me, and blinked.

I went on: 'I'm sorry. I don't have all that much confidence – I'm not used to this. I'm only acting vicar.'

I had blown it. Language, the preacher's tool, had failed me.

We talked for a while, leaving the declaration of love behind us only in time; I wanted to go back to it at every moment, desperate to restate my feelings, clarify things, wave my hands like a politician and be specific and strong about it all. But instead, limply, I resisted the temptation, and went along with her obvious desire to chatter.

'I wish I could do something else in life, rather than working in this supermarket.'

'What like?' *Be a churchman's wife?*

'Something where I felt I was serving God.'

'Instead of customers.'

'Oh, no – I'm not at a till. I'm in the head office, testing products with surveys and so on.'

'You sound as though you're doing quite well.'

'Not really. Unless you count moving in one year from flans to yoghurt.'

'If you want, I'm driving back in to the centre –'

'Oh, don't worry. I'll leave it till tomorrow.'

'Are you on – on yoghurt tomorrow?'

'Ready-washed salads.'

Leaving her home, I watched a rectangle of snow slide from a roof opposite, break up on guttering, and descend as dust to the ground. I empathised with the disintegration.

When we all met on the steps, two hours later, the setting sun gave us haloes.

'Did you see Peter Mayre?' Morag asked me.

'Yes, eventually.'

'He rang us, and we told him you were on your way.'

'He was fine.' I dreaded a question aimed at finding out how I had taken five hours to visit two addresses.

Vicki grinned at me, chisel nosed: 'We'll meet soon, will we, vicar?'

'Oh, yes.' For some reason, I was offended by her. I was miles away. By the time I returned to the church, my head and thoughts and soul were in delayed shock over Gillian.

I told her I loved her.

I kept replaying the conversation, thinking I must have said something else. Did I mishear myself? Or had I talked all the time about supermarkets, but thought all the time about love . . . and, on leaving the house, mistakenly believed I had spoken about it?

But there was no mistaking the look of the hands and forearms that were mine; no mistaking that they had touched my Goddess. There was a new sheen on my jacket-sleeves.

If a Bible were written about Gillian Mitchell, I would study it every day, even the minor prophets.

I never expected her to love me, and she did not. So I was not disappointed. Where disappointment did arise was in the hug, the heady declaration of love – and then the attempt to explain them. In the Church of England, we were all so unused to the idea of having to explain things.

On my knees, in my first prayer for weeks, I mouthed: *Give me Gillian Mitchell, and I will swear everything over to you: my clothes, my Presley tapes, even my thoughts. I will think better things, be a better person, walk in the way . . .*

What way, though? And saying it felt to me like talking into the mouthpiece of a telephone that was entirely dead. There was no power on the line, none whatsoever.

I tried to put my arms around her.

It was unbelievable.

The recollections were ringed with regret.

'Are you okay?'

That was Richard Burts, outside the church.

'Oh – I was elsewhere, Richard.'

'Whereabouts?' He was laughing.

'I don't know.'

'Faith?'

'Conviction,' I mumbled.

But he was not really listening. 'It went really well,' he said shrilly. 'We saw everyone. And Hugh organised an ambulance for Marna Fairhurst, who was very cold. She was just sitting there, staring – her son had skidded into a fence on the way to her house, so she was completely alone.'

'Fantastic,' I said.

'It was a really good idea,' Richard said.

'Thank you,' I said, thoughtlessly.

'God is so good.'

'Yes,' I said.

The sun set. More snow fell, but thinly now.

There had, at least, been a single smack of success to the day, I reflected. This had ostensibly been my plan, my meeting, my idea . . . and perhaps, stretching it a little, we had even saved the life of old Mrs Fairhurst.

The thought settled, satisfactorily.

It seemed as though, for the first time, I had a claim on the job an assortment of viruses in Douglas's throat had forced me into.

Guilt at the £233-a-month increase flaked and cracked: an old emotion. Today, at least, I had earned the money.

Then Di, the Australian who did so much of the youth work now that Vanessa had scaled down her own efforts, tripped on a square of ice on the lower step of the church while going out to check on uncollected cars and fell on to the pavement ... bruising her face and shattering bone in an arm; and I wondered whether each and every new success I had would always be dismantled, eventually, by an ancient curse.

– 18 –

It had been a good service that Sunday, with the choir singing as loud as they possibly could, and their acting vicar laying as low as any acting vicar possibly could.

I had given out some notices – that was all.

In my mind, on the side bench, I played with a word: *vicaring*. That meant being vicar of a big church, and running it with whatever efficiency came to hand – but without actually believing in anything at all.

Maybe without actually caring very much.

Vicaring was different from being a vicar.

As BBF preached – into the run of the vast series I had beseeched of him – I screened out every word, pulled my eyes off the deeply troubling painting . . . and off Gillian, too.

There: in the choir.

Singing her heart out, as my heart sang out for her.

I was amazed at that moment to watch almost a hundred people proceed to the front of the hall at the end of BBF's sermon.

He had asked them to – to pray with him, was it?

I looked on, goggling, trying to remember what he had been saying.

His voice boomed across the church, over the heads of the hundreds still in their seats, right to the back, blaring regularly now with the name of the man they called the Son of God.

'Let no man here fail to receive these words in his heart,' the Stipendiary Parson's voice boomed.

He was after their hearts – and some were even crying!

Look, I thought, *churches are private places, not places where this sort of thing . . .*

'Do not delay, if you feel God's word on your heart.'

More came up. I felt a mild stomach ache. Some of the church staff on the bench with me moved to talk with them . . .

And what could I do? I had to follow . . .

So I ended up among them, my acting congregation, as it were, chalk faced with discomfort as I heard their prayers; one whooped out the name of the supposed Son of God, a man who had always been a sober type before, loosening a tartan tie and raising his face to the ceiling. Another was quietly saying that name, and I clasped my hands together –

Hypocurate.

– saying 'yes' with her, and suddenly she was weeping, in her own world; and then she jolted forwards to embrace me!

As Francis Bottom waved the band into a scraping melody, just using a hand, people followed a prayer that BBF said from the pulpit . . . and here I was, standing on the floor of the church, among them –

Judas Iscurate

– and, no, I could not bring myself to put arms around anyone's shoulder as the other staff members were doing, but at least said 'Amen' when they had finished praying, BBF prompting them above me, and me keeping on wondering, then, why I had not tried harder to break into accountancy . . . perhaps even corporate accountancy, which was easier to get into, although there was less excitement because you often did not get to travel so much, or see so many of the clients face to face.

– 19 –

I plodded up the concrete stairs to the flat, thinking of Gillian at every step, and reaching the door with a feeling that I could have climbed a thousand steps without pausing in my thoughts of her.

Breathless, hand on door knob, I stopped for a second, contemplating the service.

It was disturbing. Only minutes before, I had quietly left the main body of the church – leaving scores of churchgoers talking animatedly about the sermon behind me.

A sermon I had missed, I thought, turning the door knob, because I was not even able to focus my mind on the words.

And even when I had tuned in, right at the very end there, when they all started coming to the front . . . I had felt as though I was on another planet.

But I had played the part well, I considered, pushing the flat door slowly open. Yes, Gillian would have seen me from the choir – admired the way I moved around the hall, perhaps. Seriously, lugubriously: gliding, almost.

It was worrying, though, to have felt so alien to it.

Perhaps I am more lost than I first thought.

I flicked the switch on the wall, but the light failed to come on. 'Blast,' I said quietly.

The only other light in the place was a lamp in my bedroom. I would have to swap the bulbs.

A feeble glow was diffused from the staircase, and I could just make out the lounge lampshade above my head.

Moving below it, I reached up for the broken bulb.

Groping, my fingers found the outside of the plastic fitment, and then moved in –

'Aaaah!'

I snatched the hand away. There was no bulb there: just live metal prongs which my fingers had missed by an inch.

In the dark, I searched for the bulb on the carpet. It was not there.

I clicked tongue against teeth in frustration.

And then there was another click –

Around the corner, in my room.

The bedroom was illuminated.

Out of sight, the bed creaked. In the crack between door and hinges, I saw a black shape rise from the mattress.

Then it presented itself in the doorway.

'What's happening?' I asked.

'I took your bulb out,' said Ben Jivvard.

'Why?' I asked, painfully.

His response was a rush of movement towards me, a roar of anger or something worse . . . and then a hurricane-hard grabbing action that clamped my shoulders between his giant hands and knocked me backwards, shaking my glasses off and making my head flick like the tail of a whip.

His face was right up against mine. He swore, lividly. I noticed the bristles had grown. I was panting.

Ben Jivvard ranted like a madman. Why had I not rung him or been in my flat? Why had I been out when I was supposed to be in? Why wasn't I up to the job of vicar?

He was almost screaming. My hearing chased the echoes of his voice down the stairs. There was nothing in the world worse then physical violence, or the threat of it, I decided. I felt close to vomiting, and sick at soul.

'I've got guards, you know – ' I said, pathetically. I was clutching at anything. 'The police – on the end of that phone – ' I jabbered. 'I was in the audience at a judo competition once, so watch it.'

He would not even listen. I just wanted a bulb back in the fitment – as though if the room were lit, all danger and swearing would pass away.

Finally, he released me. Putting a handkerchief over my shaking hand, I pulled the hot bulb from the bedroom lamp and took a circuitous path around Ben Jivvard, before pushing the bulb into the light and switching it on.

The circuitous path seemed to register, shaming him.

I breathed heavily, looking down, trying to get my breath and balance back, reflecting that this was so many million miles away from that glorious, cold afternoon when I had touched Gillian's arms and shoulder-blades.

Ben was staring at me, wide eyed.

'Calm down, now,' I said. 'Easy. Take it easy.'

He ignored the advice. 'Who was it? You?'

'Me?'

'Was it you? You know what I mean.'

'Sometimes I don't even know what I mean.'

'Don't be funny,' he said. 'I'm talking about my wife.'

'Her?'

'Yes.'

'I remember you telling me about your suspicions – '

'Oh – listen,' he began, 'I don't have any suspicions any more, that's for sure.'

A look of relief must have spread across my face. 'I'm so glad, Ben, to hear – '

'Glad? Glad?' he shouted. 'You're glad? Happy that she's confessed everything, everything except the name?'

'I'm not glad about that.'

'Don't give me that,' he said.

'I didn't give you anything.' I bent to retrieve my spectacles, and slipped them into my jacket pocket.

For effect, I ventured: 'Would you like to pray?'

'Have you got a voodoo doll?' he asked. 'If you have, then we'll do some praying. If you've got some pins, we might even say "Amen" too.'

'What can I do?' I asked, at last.

Instantly, he replied: 'Stop it.'

'Stop what, Ben?'
'Is it you?'
'I don't understand – me doing what? What have I done?'
'You know,' he said. 'Unvicarlike things.'
A dreadful realisation began to dawn.
Ben levelled his voice at me like a gun. 'Do you deny it's you she's been seeing, then?'
I was stunned. 'I – yes, of course. Of course I do.'
'It's someone on your staff.'
'It can't be.'
'She says it is.'
'Adultery, Ben? No, that can't be possible.'
A list of staff members scrolled up before my dilated pupils like film credits . . . counting voluntary helpers and full time members, there must have been more than twenty.
No. It was not possible. It would require hypocrisy on a scale only certain people were capable of. Most of them acting vicars.
'That can't be possible, Ben.'
'You're saying my wife's a liar, are you?'
There was silence.
Then I asked: 'Did you look in her diary?'
'Yes, I did, though I had to tear it open to do it.'
'What did it say?'
'I prised open the drawer, though the thing clicked up so that didn't show, but when I got the diary I had to tear the binding. I didn't want to fiddle with hairpins. So I looked at all those dates I told you about, you know – '
'Yes – '
'– and there was nothing there.'
'Nothing?'
'Not a sausage. Well, shopping actually. But nothing else.'
'You see!' I said, victory threaded through the words.
'But then she confessed.'
'No.'

'Yes – because she saw I'd opened the diary – '

'And I suppose she wanted to know why, did she – '

' – yes, why, and what was so important I had to tear it, and then she admitted – well, first she admitted paying someone to do her shopping, as it happens. But then she could see – I don't know, I was so on edge. She just seemed to say, you know, "Yes," all of a sudden.'

'Yes?'

'Yes. She just owned up to it. She knew I knew. Then I started crying, and she went all soggy, and she said it was such a relief to be able to tell me.' Ben breathed in. 'And that was when she told me it was – it was someone here.'

'Did you – did you tell Mandy about our conversation?'

'Yes.'

'So she knows I said you could read the diary.'

'She thinks it was your idea. I'm sorry, I had to – '

The sentence fell away. I was disgusted. His wife had every motive to fire grievous accusations off at members of Saint Peter's staff if she had been told its leader had sanctioned her husband's diary-busting.

My fears about newspapers getting the story returned. What a page lead this would make: the Conservative who promised to bring God back into government stands weeping in front of the rector he accuses of stealing his wife.

But I felt pity for Ben, too.

When he had composed himself, he said: 'We're trying to hold it steady. She won't say the name – she says we need to put it behind us. I'm in the spare room for the moment.'

It seemed Mandy had won everything. I wondered what sort of a vixen she was.

There was to have been a healing meeting in the middle of the following week, and I considered telling Ben that he ought to go there and ask for help.

But then I remembered I had cancelled it. The idea of healings in the main body of the church, with people gyrating, appalled me beyond measure. Bingo would have been better. So I took fast action to stop it, ringing Hendon to tell him we now had enough spare money to pay for the refurbishment of the west side wall, as I had suspended donations to unproductive missionaries. 'This is good,' he had said, making the accountant in me swell with pride. 'You're working on your product, and cutting down your outlay. I like it. Do the west side with my blessing.'

I commissioned the workmen with special instructions: 'The wall needs to be refurbished quite thoroughly. There's a painting there, a big picture of a man's face – you'll have to take that down and put it into storage.'

I was killing birds.

Ben left, leaving my soul shaken. Recalling BBF's service, I wondered whether physical violence was the only spiritual experience still available to me.

It seemed everything was falling apart. No sooner had we successfully saved an old woman from the cold, than a church worker broke her arm. Builders had to be brought in to prevent healing meetings. People would keep asking where Douglas was, and I would wonder if they asked because they wanted him back: because I was failing? And failing publicly?

Of course I was failing. I knew I was. This whole business, of being appointed to a curacy by the cloth ears of a church secretary, and then elevated to rector by a group of undiagnosed viruses . . . it was a PhD study in failure.

They only had to look at me in services to know it. To watch me shrinking back, white faced, against the panelled wall, as sermon after sermon whistled over my head . . .

And at the core of all this vicaring was the only hope the world had to offer: my Gillian Mitchell. She had infected every moving muscle in me – had hijacked my dreams like bearded terrorists. All I wanted was to be with her. But I knew she could probably no longer bear the sight of me, and rightly so.

I replaced the missing bulb with one of low wattage. The room became dim and gloomy, and I felt like a spectre in it.

I am the light of the world.

Could I win Gillian Mitchell by preaching the kind of sermon I had watched tonight? By bringing a hundred – *No, a thousand* – people to the front? By emptying every seat?

I contemplated it. Could I discard the usual, downbeat approach they were used to – like a traffic warden caught pasteing a ticket on to a windscreen and forced to explain it? Could I find something razor sharp, lift my voice as actors did, and fling it all at them like throwing-knives?

And how many would have to come forward before I would be able to look across the floor of the church and know that my Gillian loved me? Fifty?

Or seven hundred conversions?

Or would I have to empty every seat, even the seats in the choir?

Will it have to be a thousand?

I wondered if there were consultants who could be hired for such a sermon, and reached, unthinkingly, for the *Yellow Pages* book by the telephone. My hand changed course as it neared the directory, for there it was, still – my Bible.

Some gladhearts opened theirs at random, letting the leaves separate by gravity in the conviction that the verse their eyes alighted on was a direct message from God. None of them, strangely, ever appeared to receive miraculous guidance from anywhere but the middle of the Bible.

Listlessly, I let mine fall open too.

> The Lord has appointed you priest in
> place of Jehoiada to be in charge of the
> house of the Lord; you should put any
> madman who acts like a prophet into the
> stocks and neck-irons.

I smiled sardonically, mumbling the name of the book and the reference numbers on the page. 'Jeremiah, chapter twenty-nine, verse twenty-six.' It meant nothing: nothing meant anything any more. I felt so terribly alone.

Downstairs, I weaved through the crowds in the tea room with just the right speed of foot and angle of body to look unstoppable and busy, and unattacked by Ben Jivvard.

'Hi, John,' I said. 'Hello, Peter. Hi, Shannon.' I nodded. 'Good to see you, Mrs Dibble. That's a nice fox around your neck.' And, moving on: 'Philip – how are you? You're looking well.'

Then: 'Hello, Marion. I hear Mrs Fairhurst is a bit better – that's good, isn't it? Oh – yes – Brinny. I feel we've met already. No, of course I don't mind if you have to dash – oh – hello, Gillian.'

In the noisy room, we were totally alone. Faces whirled around us like a carousel. All I wanted was to soak in her beauty and her radiance for a few seconds.

'Hello, Mark,' she said. The fine curves in her peach face, which lengthened when she smiled, were now quite short.

'So you're in from the wilds. Pinner.'

'I managed to get in, yes. There's no snow now.'

I was abashed for a moment, considering everything.

She was quite curt: 'I expect you want to get on.'

'I had better do.'

I might have been shaking.

Flatly, she said, 'Don't let me keep you.'

I left her, knowing only that I loved her more than anything, more even than my own life, and told myself: *You are a madman.*

I greeted Jane Bull rather too pompously, and then waved to Vanessa, handing out paper to students. Thinking of the tablets months ago, I put added vim into the greeting. Near her, Richard returned it with a warm, if concerned, smile. I realised he must have seen me with Gillian.

Daniel Ogumbaye did not seem to be around. BBF was at the Coppers, talking to people crowding around him. I walked through the big doors into the cold night air.

Just a few yards from the last step, a man lay on the street in a huddle of clothes. He was asleep under the awning of a shoe shop, trunk heaving with icy breaths. I recognised the crescent of face that was visible.

The Limo under the Lemon Tree.

The tramp looked in a far worse state than he had done while washing in the church lavatories, and a mad thought struck me: that I should wake him, bring him back to the flat, and give him Vanessa's old bed.

But then I was hit by an odour like lettuce years past its sell-by date, and abandoned the idea. Having him there would require the installation of a system of airlocks. And it might reach church magazines . . . the newspapers . . .

I made a mental apology to the tramp as I passed him, and walked a long hoop back to Saint Peter's.

Approaching the church in the darkness as the few remaining parishioners drifted out, I saw an intriguing scene played out in one of the side doorways.

Framed there were Daniel and Morag, deep in discussion.

Knowing I would not be visible in the darkness, I moved closer, leaning against a set of railings. I rested both wrists on a horizontal bar, and pressed my face between two of the vertical spikes.

Yes: there they were. The two of them – talking.

The scene would have been unremarkable, but for the deduction I made on seeing it. Something about the way Daniel held his Bible, perhaps, or the intimate posture Morag had struck; something about the angle of his head, or the great seriousness written on her face . . . all that, combined with something else that could not be put into words – perhaps I had subconsciously heard my name – made it clear the two of them were talking about their acting vicar.

I made one, sparrow-swift, conclusion. They were plotting to get rid of me.

Perhaps they were plotting nicely, with geniality and warmth, but one thing was certain. There were no two people in the church more powerful.

I was conscious momentarily of my posture against the railings, leaning forwards with my face between them.

So. I was in a set of stocks, being pelted.

Having initially protested at the elevation to vicar, it was not so obvious now that I should want to relinquish the post. I could not go back to being curate after such public failure. And there could be no return to Straithe, either; the post there had been filled after a lengthy search, which culminated in the appointment of a man converted during a first career in vermin control.

Well, they would be surprised. I would cling. Clinging was worth £233 a month, after all. Clinging was worth the flat. Clinging might not work if the newspapers got hold of Ben Jivvard's story, but . . .

Above all, clinging was worth staying in the same solar system as the brightest star I had ever seen.

Then they turned and walked away, moving deeper into the almost empty church. I wore dark clothes, and it was dark about me. My face was dark with suspicion, and the black bars on my glasses were dark as I pushed them on to my head, dark angered. No, I was not going to be pushed out. The Church of England would not shake me out of its pocket like loose change left over from a foreign holiday.

Perhaps they had shaken out the last curate. Well, they would not shake me out. I had a faith. *All right, a faith in nothing at all, but at least I believe in nothing with some conviction.*

Then Richard, wheezing with the weight of his boxed guitar, invited me to have coffee at his flat.

As we drank it, he posed a question from an armchair in his dining room: 'Are you happy with everything?'

'Yes, very. I think the snow business went well.'

'Mrs Fairhurst is getting better.'

'There's no business like snow business,' I quipped.

We both sipped our coffee, watching images flicker on his mute television: real-life soldiers storming a village, one getting it wrong and being cut down as he ran.

Richard looked away and said: 'All those problems with this – the sermon, I mean, and what BBF was saying, you know, the church – what you were telling me –'

He sniffed.

'Do you still have all those – those doubts, Mark?'

'You haven't told anyone, have you?'

'Of course not,' he shot back. 'I don't have anyone to tell. I just wondered how it was for you, that was all.'

'I feel I can make a contribution, you know.'

'You can,' he said. 'Just maybe not as vicar.'

I was cut to the quick.

'I don't know,' I said, steadying my voice. 'I feel I've got a lot of experience of where people go wrong.'

'Yes.'

'But you don't agree.'

'Not really, Mark – but I do understand. You admit it. You're just not there.' He swept his oily hair back.

'I'll admit it at any time,' I said gravely, 'but only in this room, and only to you.'

'Maybe I'm just upset we never seemed to get that healing service, whyever that was,' Richard said in a flat tone, as though daring me to reply . . . which I did not.

'Things have changed,' he went on. 'Before you –'

The observation tailed off.

'Before me? What was before me?'

He hesitated. 'Oh, the curate before you was rather different, that's all.'

'Brendan Madill?'

'Yes – Brendan.'

He made his nostrils flare with a movement of his mouth, as though none of it mattered.

'Someone told me he'd been dismissed,' I said. Seeing Morag and Daniel had reminded me. 'It matters, you know, Richard. His file's gone from the church office, too. I looked.'

Richard paused. 'A few people told me he was fired.'

'Who told you?'

'It was all rumours. Daniel or Morag would know.'

'What would you have to do to be fired, though?'

'Quite a lot. Plant a bomb somewhere, I suppose.'

It was left there.

Richard turned the television sound up, and we watched it for a while. But suddenly I was tortured with thoughts of Gillian, and my skin crawled with the urge to ring her. It was nearly eleven. I could not get back to the flat in time.

Perhaps I'll try, though. I mumbled the beginning of an excuse . . .

But Richard's eyes were closed, his mouth lolling. Dim purples and greens from the television danced across the sleeping face. His nose piped staccato breaths.

After a moment's hesitation, I tiptoed through to his kitchen and shut the door. Lifting a push-button telephone beside a slice of pizza with one bite missing, I dialled.

I knew Gillian's number, even the square root of it.

There was a tapping on the line, and echoes, as though my love was pot-holing its way to her.

The ringing did not last long.

'Hello?'

That was not Gillian's voice – but Brinny's.

The contents of my stomach were curdled in a second.

Something told me: *Hang up now.*

But my voice had already betrayed me by speaking.

'Hello. It's Mark here.'

'Hello, Mark.'

I paused.

'Sorry, I know it's a bit late – '

'A little bit, but don't worry. I'll get her for you.'

'Thank you,' I whispered, to the sound of her footsteps.

Richard's kitchen was in a terrible mess.

Gillian's voice, when it appeared, was anxious.
'Hello.'
'Oh, hello. It's Mark. I'm in a friend's kitchen.'
'Hello, Mark.'
'Empringham, that is. I'm sorry for calling.'
'That's – ah – that's all right,' she said hesitantly.
I realised I had nothing to say.
'I was checking your phone,' I said.
'Checking it?'
'I mean – I was – to see if you were there.'
'We saw each other earlier.'
'In the church? Yes, and it was wonderful,' I said.
'It was quite short,' she said. 'I can't understand why you're ringing now.'
'I don't know.'
'It seems a bit funny.'
'I love you, Gillian. I want to be with you all the time, and even leaving a few hours between seeing you in the church and ringing you up now – even that's impossible.'
Urgently, she said: 'Please, please don't upset me! It's not right for you to ring me like this, my vicar, and I – I just don't have those sorts of feelings.'
'Not for me?'
'No, I just don't, Mark.'
'Do you think you ever could?' I asked. 'I'm so lonely.'
'No,' she implored. 'No, I couldn't.'
'I just wanted to ring you, that's all.'
'Well, you probably shouldn't have come to my house like that the other day.'
'I didn't have a clue what would happen.'
'What about talking to someone you know on the staff?'
'It's different with you. I've never – I've never had someone like you before.'
'If you want to come and see me and Brinny some time, you can.'
'Can I see you on your own?'

'It's not a good idea.'

'Just on one day next week? Monday, maybe, or – '

'No, Mark!'

'Please!'

'It's not right.'

'But I – I love you, Gilly!'

'It's not right!'

'Can't we at least talk about it, get some of this – '

'No.'

'Even if I beg you?'

'Please, just say goodbye.'

'Oh, Gillian – '

'Goodbye, Mark.'

'Gillian – '

'Goodbye.'

'Gillian, please – '

'Please. Goodbye. Say it, Mark.'

'Gillian – '

'Goodbye.'

'Oh – Gillian – all right, all right. Goodbye.'

'Bye, Mark. Bye.'

There was a sharp click as she rang off.

For a moment, I forgot how to replace the telephone handset in its cradle.

I turned off the light and crept back into the sitting-room. Richard was still motionless in his chair. I shook him. He groaned, flicking his head sharply to the left.

His eyes opened.

'I'd better be off, Richard.'

'Eh? Oh – ah, yes – '

He was standing before I could stop him.

'It's late,' he muttered, shaking my sweaty hand with his podgy one. 'I'm really sorry I nodded off. I'm just so tired with all the council stuff at the moment. Gosh – I'm sorry if you didn't have much entertainment here. The television doesn't look as if it's been up to much.'

'Don't worry,' I said. 'A tragedy's just been on.'

— 20 —

Walt Lee Tubbs
1605 West Poe
Huntsville
Alabama, USA

To: Pastor
Saint Peter's Church
North London, England

Dear Pastor!
I hope you do not mind me writing, I am writing as I am superkeen on spreading the gospel and am coming to England.

I know there is much to do here in Huntsville (e.g. on drugs) but have decided with my parents that England is the place for further study and to learn! As the English say, HOWSZAT!

Are you English yourself? I am American and I come from the 'Deep South' as it is known, but it is not so deep really (e.g. South America). I want to become a missionary preferably married with the support of a church etc. and spread the gospel and I am booked to do a placement for a year at the London College of Biblical Teaching LCBT.

LCBT starts in April and as part of it we must go overseas (that could just mean England) to do practical preaching etc. and street evangelism, I believe my voice is loud enough for this though am worried about my accent e.g. if in France?

And what about denominations? Not currency I mean churches!

Anyway I was hoping to come to your church as I heard it was the biggest in Britain. And of course I have read most of the books of Baron Bryan Fryers, isn't he resident preacher?

A bit about myself I am twenty-seven and my parents run a minicab firm. My mother worries about my driving there. Will I find it difficult to drive in England as all the signs are backwards?

Well that is nearly all I just wanted to ask if you had lists of accommodation though not in dangerous areas of London, e.g. Manchester? Also are we expected to put a certain amount in the collection? (As a student I will not have much to give.) And please tell me your name. Please SIGN IT if you write.

Driving – please also if you have a copy of the highway rules, for example backing down one-way streets is not legal here and what are the signs for when you should NOT go through a level crossing? I am worried about driving!

I am very much looking forward to everything and wonder if we may soon meet and that I might hear from you soon and remain 'in everything, by everything and through everything' as Saint Paul said I can't recall any of Saint Peter's words (!) I am afraid though will look when this letter is finished and maybe include some in my next one yours truly

Walt Lee Tubbs.

I read the letter twice. It was tempting to tell Mr Tubbs that he was best advised to go through level crossings when he saw red lights flash – but before I could start a reply, Morag was at the door, holding something.

'A couple of things,' she said. 'Di's getting better.'

'Excellent, excellent,' I said. I was trying to sound efficient. 'It's amazing how quickly you can go from snow to sun. Only a week ago the place was an ice rink.'

'It broke a record.' Morag squinted at me.

'I've got a very funny letter from an American,' I said. 'I must show it to you.'

'Oh, I don't have time. The workmen are here.'

'How's it looking? I haven't been down yet,' I said.

'They've stripped the panelling about twenty feet from the altar table. So the painting there – of Christ – that's gone into a back room –'

Excellent, excellent.

' – and tomorrow they're bringing in some new teak. But I've already had to tell one of them to stop swearing.'

'Oh. What did he say?'

'Well, I can't tell you the swearword, obviously –'

'No – I mean – when you told him off.'

'That as a Catholic,' Morag smiled, as though putting a brave face on deep inner pain, 'he'd confessed some of his swearwords in advance last Sunday, so he had to let a few off because he was getting behind with them.'

The church secretary laughed, but the man's activities did not strike me as any more silly than confessing sins after they had happened.

Morag said: 'Something for you, by the way.'

I took two envelopes from her, and blanched.

'Thanks.'

I had sent the top letter only days before. It was now being returned with Royal Mail red crayon through the address, and, handwritten above it: 'Not known here.' Stamped in black ink were the words RETURN TO SENDER.

'Ah,' I breezed, 'I had thought I might drop the last curate a line.'

'Yes,' Morag said.

'He's obviously not in Formby any more.'

'No.'

'I thought I might like to meet him.'

'Oh, I wouldn't do that,' she said. 'And – no, I don't know where he is now. He – he left here very quickly.'

'Why was that?' I asked.

A unique answer returned.

'He was dismissed by Douglas.'

'Dismissed?'

'Yes. And there really isn't anything more to say.'

'But dismissed for what?'

'As I said, there's really nothing else to say about it. And I wouldn't write to him. He won't be coming back here.'

She left me barely able to focus on the last letter, which contained scrawled apologies from Ben Jivvard on Conservative Party notepaper. 'Please forgive me, as one of your parishioners,' it said. 'Mandy and I are barely talking. I am trying to hold it all together. Sorry, sorry.'

A memory of our encounter on Sunday made me shiver, but it had been almost forgotten in the wake of the telephone call to Gillian. Sleepless, I had gone over every syllable. Had I been too possessive, assumed too much?

Of course I have! I had mouthed the words into the pillow.

But did I ever imagine my love would be returned? Or had I only ever intended nothing but to cast myself on her mercy, knowing it meant doom . . . but doom, at least, at her hands: a glorious way to go, when there was nothing in the universe to believe in beyond Gillian Mitchell – no reality beyond the fullness of her lips, the Irish tenor of her voice and the slack reprimand in her posture?

It only took two fingers for the count I wanted to make.

Two fingers: a middle and an index.

One, two.

I extended them at the desk. *One, two.*

One finger was the fact that Morag and Daniel were probably plotting to have me turfed out of the church . . . and if not, they would surely consider the secret letter to Brendan Madill as ample justification to start . . .

The second was Gillian's absolute rejection of her acting vicar. Two fingers: two reasons.

I had used my hand to count the reasons that ought to stop me fearing what I now knew had to be done, which was the preaching of the best sermon that had ever been heard in London, let alone in this big church . . . a sermon which would be given without warning by the acting vicar of Saint Peter's, a sermon to be talked about for months, if not years, after the event; a sermon that would be analysed by analysts and interpreted by interpreters, and radiate into church myth before the last lines were even done . . . which would drag hundreds to the front for conversion; and, yes, I would look around the building as they came, red with the effort of it, and catch Gillian's eye – and know, among the prayers and crying, that she loved me at last . . . and then I would sweep a glance over to Daniel and Morag, sitting separately, of course, their faces etched with shock at the ampage of what they had just heard – and I would be assured that it was not just the heart of Gillian Mitchell that was now safe: my flat and extra £233 a month were safe too.

I sat at my desk, tweaking the corners of the envelope that had been returned from Liverpool, breathing deeply.

Then, gathering up some papers and a book, I walked across the church to the empty first-floor committee room.

I took a seat at the table by the window and drew a pen from my jacket, knowing that at any moment the choir practice Francis Bottom was holding would come to an end.

— 21 —

The more the west side of the church filled up with plaster and discarded shards of panelling, the more it seemed to become a magnet for members of the congregation.

At least a dozen gathered on a Saturday afternoon to clear rubble and sweep the floors. Even Di was there, with her bleached hair and arm in a cast; her and a good ten more. One had a flute. The others were singing a chorus Francis Bottom had recently taught the congregation –

> Everyone's full of this brilliant love,
> The love of God, rising high
> Over our heads
> Building bricks, building bricks
> Building bricks of love.

I approached them slowly as they sung and worked. The flute player saw me and lowered her instrument, and I noticed a pink sticker on the case that said, 'He's coming back quite soon.'

'Carry on,' I told them as a few looked up and greeted me. Di straightened her back, groaning in Australian.

'Be careful with that arm, Di,' I said.

'I am,' she told me. She was moderately attractive: Gillian was a googol times more so.

A googol is one with a hundred zeros after it.

The woman started on the flute again. I had left it too late to tell them how grateful I was. Stepping up on to the stage, I looked back for a moment at my parishioners.

My parishioners.

If it were not for Gillian Mitchell, I concluded I would already have been destroyed by the world I inhabited. I walked around Saint Peter's like a vicar now, perhaps . . . but I felt more like stone moving on a trolley, draped in cloths from a rectory wardrobe like some piece of unsold modern art.

The Mark Empringham who had put up a dogfight against belief, drawn up smart rules to excuse himself from all he was supposed to live for . . . that Mark Empringham, under bombardment from something like anti-matter in the external atmosphere, had shrunk within himself like the kernel in a nut; he had shrivelled almost to nothing.

Without my love for Gillian, I would be nothing.

I was right, of course, about them all: all one thousand of them. They were goons. If you were going to follow a fiction, why not choose a Wilbur Smith novel, or something exciting by Spillane? It seemed incredible that they had picked on a dull rag-bag of a book, sixty-six books long in fact, written without regard to grammar or plot and widely available in hotel rooms. I was thoroughly fed up with the Bible and all talk of it. There was no prospect of my ever being or becoming good enough to be counted a real Christian. And while I pretended I was there already, I was dismantling my real self by degrees.

The alternative was to declare my position: *Lost*.

It was no alternative.

My hope was simply that after my sermon Gillian would be mine, and end this half-existence. Mine, she would blow life into me. I would be born again. Suddenly secure in my post and the £233 extra a month, I would delegate everything and spend all my time with her. Then I would cash in the pension rights on my salary and move with my Queen to Poole.

Glancing back at the group at work around the west wall, I walked through the door at the rear of the altar.

I looked into one of the small storage rooms, and caught sight of it immediately: there, draped in a dust-sheet, was the unmistakable outline of the painting that had drifted in and out of my dreams and tormented me during services.

Vicars should never look furtive . . . but I did now.

There was no one outside on the street.

There was no one near the storage room, and the squeaky hinges of the doors which led to it would act as alarms.

Yes, there it is.

It had done no one any favours there on the west wall and, since I had removed this man's words from my thoughts, there should now be nothing to stop the removal of his face from my church.

I was cleaning up my life.

Richard had said the picture did not mean very much to real believers. The face certainly meant a lot to me.

All authority is mine, he had told his disciples.

Well – sorry, chum. *All authority is mine.*

In a swift movement, I lifted a leg and rested a foot on the material, feeling the ridges of the top edge of the frame beneath my shoe.

I took some of the weight off my other leg, pressing the raised foot down hard, my body rising under the low ceiling.

There was a sharp crack, and a loud rip of canvas.

I felt relief that I could not see the picture at the moment its existence was terminated.

Well, it must have broken while the builders moved it, mustn't it?

In the empty room, I practised the words.

'Well, it must have broken while the builders were moving it, mustn't it?'

Oh, dear. We'll just have to have a space there on the wall while we look for another picture.

'Oh, my. Well, we'll just have to have a space . . . '

Perhaps a Brueghel? Or something by La Tour? It's a shame to have lost it, though.

'It's a terrible shame to have lost it. It's a terrible shame for the church,' I whispered in the quiet room.

I'll see if the builders can tell us anything.

'I'll see if the builders can tell us anything about how it might have happened.'

It must have broken while the builders moved it . . .

In fact, I doubted the destruction of the painting would mean very much to anyone. Later in the day, on the touchline of a London league match between two church football teams, I wondered if anyone would even bother reporting it.

If they did, of course, I had the reaction ready: *It must have broken while the builders moved it, mustn't it . . .*

A trace of vapour appeared from between my lips, proof that the words had been more than just thoughts. I supplanted them with a loud cheer for the Saint Peter's side.

'A wonderful shout!' said a voice beside me. 'A dozen more decibels, maybe fifteen, and we may begin to claw back.'

I looked down at BBF, and then over the thinning silver hair at his statuesque wife. Both were braced against the cold in thick, old-fashioned clothes.

The football sailed over the players, looped down and hit one full in the face with a sharp slap.

Someone shouted angrily: 'Control it!'

The Saint Peter's team had scored two own goals. This seemed to cause great anguish to BBF, who had been comforted by his wife. At intervals, in a tortured voice, he would go over the sequence of passes that led to the disasters.

'I don't think Guy had a chance of stopping it,' I contributed.

'Guy?' BBF asked. He could put very few names to the faces of congregation members, even in the football team. It was one of his few failings as a churchman.

I said: 'Stonnet, his surname is. Guy Stonnet. I think he's been very upset since his engagement broke up with a girl called Grace – I noticed when the ball came towards him he didn't really seem to be paying attention.'

'Poor chap,' said the Stipendiary Parson.

'Yes,' said the acting vicar.

'He shouldn't be in goal if he's upset over a girl,' said the wife.

'You've got to struggle on,' BBF murmured. 'I did.'

'That was different,' his wife said, mysteriously.

As the two sides huddled over half-time oranges, BBF shocked me with a sentence.

'Have you seen the papers today?'

Immediately, I thought of Ben Jivvard.

'How did they find out?' I asked.

'I – no, this story – sorry – ' The question threw the Stipendiary Parson into confusion. 'Find out? They always seem to, I suppose – I'm talking about this minister – '

'Oh. I don't think I've heard about this.'

'It's all over the news,' he said. 'The government's Minister for Employment. A believer. But then someone got photographs of him at a fairly spirit-filled service with his hands up in the air, grinning and singing. Waving. The photographer must have been hidden under an altar, because there was part of a curtain hanging across two of the pictures. They were splashed over all the front pages this morning, and we heard on the way here that he resigned at lunchtime. At twelve minutes past one, we heard it. A believing minister, resigned – a tragedy.'

Minister for Fruit and Nut, I thought.

'Oh, dear,' I said.

'Perhaps he came under a number of kilograms of pressure from somewhere. Perhaps the top.'

'I should think it made him look a fool.'

'Christ looked a fool,' BBF said. A whistle sounded on the pitch, and he raised his gaze and tilted his chin up an inch so that I was captured by his eyes in a single, startling moment, as though by a lasso.

'Yes, he did,' I said, keeping my breath even. I was suddenly very frightened of the Stipendiary Parson.

The two sides went at it hammer-and-tongs during the second half, which included a scuffle between both sets of wingers. The fight ended when someone drew their attention to the presence of BBF on the touchline.

Later, knowing they were going to win, the other team began singing: 'We're whopping the biggest church in the world, yes we are . . . ' The title gave me a momentary feeling of great importance, soon crushed by all the old pangs.

Only one person in the universe could save me.

I felt a new religion would be in order. Not the old one of Christianity – a busted flush, clung to by the sad, the silly, and the intellectually retired – but a gleaming new faith that looked to the needs of the modern man and the modern acting vicar: *Gillianity* . . . a belief that salvation from everything in this world, and any other world beyond it, could be released by one small kiss from Gillian Mitchell.

Incredibly, we met that afternoon, only an hour after the end of the football match, and in my flat. Breathless from the heavy-going stairs, she appeared at the door.

Startled, I could only say: 'Oh.'

She stood there in heavenly beauty. Shorter than me, of course; her womanly figure pressing against the insides of a white sailor-style jacket and trousers; lips full, scarlet as ever; those thick curls tumbling over her forehead.

'Can I come in?'

'Please do.' My voice sounded throatier than normal.

'Thank you.' She moved around the lounge, swirling a bit like a ballet dancer, confused about where to sit.

Is she enjoying this? The idea looped overhead.

The official answer came in seconds.

'I'm finding this really difficult,' she said.

'So am I.'

'Not in the same way.'

'Love – is – is what I feel for you, all the time.'

Gillian's response was to sit forward.

'Mark,' she began, nervously, 'I wanted to ask you if we could just not have any contact for a while.'

I tried a desperate evasion. 'You know your father's tattoos – how old was he when he had them done?'

'He only has one. And please don't go off the point.'

'I am so serious about you.' I adjusted my glasses.

'I have terrible fears.'

'About us?'

'No –' she waved a hand impatiently. 'Not about us at all. There's no chance of – between us, I mean. I'm just having terrible fears about – damaging – your – ministry.'

I looked down at my hands. 'I'm struggling on with it.'

'I don't want to stop you winning people for God.'

'Nothing could do that,' I said, incredulous at the words even as they were uttered. But I had been scorched by the dreadful honesty at the New Year party.

'Even me?'

Can I hear disappointment in her voice? I loved that voice. It rang bells everywhere, in every cathedral in my heart, at every door in my head.

Now Gillian was sounding those bells as alarms.

But she had never done anything else with them.

I was lucky just to have her in my flat for a moment.

She knew nothing of the sermon that was going to mount the pavement of her soul.

Casually, as though there was no sermon, I placed the plastic arm of the record player down in the middle of a Presley album. But the honeyed voice came out with words of love, about surrender, and I snatched the needle off with a tearing sound: the sound of picture-canvas ripping.

Gillian was pointing at the floor.

'What are they – ?'

'Down here?' I had my feet on them.

'They look like crisps.'

'Wood shavings,' I said. 'I was going to clear them up.'

'Wood shavings? Has something broken?'

'No. I was making something.'

I went into the spare room, took an object off the bed, and handed it to Gillian as though it meant nothing.

'This?' The block was upside-down, and she placed two corners between thumb and forefinger and twirled it, drawing breath as it span round and she saw the carving on one side.

'Oh – it's quite lovely.'

'It's not finished,' I countered quickly.

She read: '"The king of love my shepherd is, whose goodness faileth."'

'Whose goodness fails "never", it should say. "The king of love my shepherd is, whose goodness faileth never." It's the words of a hymn.'

'I know. What's it for? Your wall?'

'For your wall, Gilly.'

She sighed, as though looking back to the days when she had been untroubled by the affections of acting vicars.

'I can't accept it, Mark.'

'I know. I need to do the last word.'

'Not even then. It would – it would mean too much.'

Gillian was tough, but was that the tiniest crack I had just heard – a hairline crack – in her voice? Had she suddenly been touched, deeply, by a block of wood with deceptive words carved in it?

If so, how much more vulnerable would she be to the most powerful sermon preached in two hundred years, since Wesley?

Earthquakes began as hairline cracks.

— 22 —

Too long afterwards for it to matter, I heard of the peculiar exchange Gillian had with a member of staff on the way from the flat that Saturday afternoon.

She found him on the steps leading up from the tea room to the lobby, standing vacantly.

His reaction to her concern was abrupt.

'I can't talk here,' he said.

'Would you like to talk?' she asked.

He stared out of the Coppers for a moment.

'You live with Brinny, don't you?'

'Yes,' said Gillian.

'I know her, a bit. Please don't tell her any of this.'

Soon they were ordering tea in a hotel down the street.

The staff member asked: 'How real do you think sin is?'

'As real as this tea, I think. And nasty,' Gillian said.

'But have you?'

'Have I what?'

'Sinned? And been forgiven? By God?'

'Yes,' she said. 'God has forgiven me for everything.'

After a pause, the staff member said: 'I can't be.'

'You can. Of course you can.'

'No. I've done too much.'

'It shouldn't – it doesn't matter,' Gillian said.

'It does in this case.'

They drunk tea for a few minutes in silence, like an interval between rounds.

'Is this a long time ago?' Gillian asked.

'Recent.'

'How recent?'
'Now,' the staff member said. After another silence, he added: 'I have had sex with someone's wife.'
Gillian tried to keep her reply steady. 'Are you sure?'
'I don't think it was an optical illusion.'
'I don't know what to say.'
'I don't know what to do,' the staff member said.
'Have you talked to – I don't know, to the vicar about it?' The question had come off the top of her head.
'We don't have a vicar, remember – unless – '
'I meant Mark Empringham.'
' – unless you meant Empringham, I was going to say, but look at him! What good can he do? He walked down the aisle of the church the other day with a piece of masking tape stuck down the back of one trouser leg!'
'I think he had torn his trousers before the service.'
'Oh – you know him, do you? I – well – well, anyway,' the staff member went on, 'he is my boss, in a sense – even if he doesn't behave like one.'
There was a pause.
Then the staff member said, 'It's a member of the congregation, too.'
What could Gillian say? When I finally heard the account, it was that she had offered verses from the Bible.
'Everyone has sinned, it says. You're no different.'
'But adultery – '
'I know.'
'People got vaporised for that in the Old Testament. And with the wife of someone in the church, too.'
'Yes, I know. But remember – "the wages of sin is death, but the gift of God is eternal life." Remember the Bible.'
He ignored her. 'I didn't want it to start. I had to go round and visit her husband about a talk he was doing for the businessmen. I think he makes plugs for boats, or something – anyway, when I arrived she was there on her own.'
'And what happened?'

'He phoned up while I was there to tell her he couldn't make it, and we had sex,' the staff member said bluntly. 'She seemed to be ready. She had the sheets all folded back. I haven't – had – not since I was sixteen.'

'Was that it? Was that all? Just that time? Just then?'

'No. I can't believe it. It kept happening!'

Gregory Runting began crying.

Gillian Mitchell comforted him by placing a hand on his, and prayed a prayer in her head for his riven conscience and his peace of mind.

Through tears, Grunt mumbled: 'One time, I had to hide in a wardrobe – me, a lay assistant in the biggest church in the country – almost – half-naked in a wardrobe – '

'It is awful.'

'I can't be forgiven, can I, really?'

'I think you can. You've got to take responsibility.'

'I am. I was even thinking of ringing the papers, or a radio phone-in – I just feel I ought to be exposed.'

'Don't do anything silly, Gregory.'

'It's too late to say that.'

. . . Naturally, I knew nothing of the exchange when Grunt rang my flat the following day, an hour and a half before the morning service, to say he would not be there.

'You're not ill, I hope?' I said down the telephone.

'I've got a painful stomach ache,' the cold voice came back. Innocently, I joked: 'Perhaps it's a pregnancy.' There was an odd burst of disjointed words and spluttering at the other end. 'That doesn't sound too good either,' I added.

Gillian's positively last appearance at the flat had made me feel buoyant as the new day dawned. But I was weighed down quickly by a visit from Vanessa and Daniel, who arrived without notice, saying they had 'quite an important' matter to discuss, which would 'need to be announced'.

I sat down on an armchair, keen to hear what it was.

When they left, I was holding a piece of paper marked with blotchy biro. My hands were trembling.

During the service, when the moment for notices came, I took the piece of paper into the pulpit. I smoothed out the notice that had been prepared under the supervision of Vanessa and Daniel, and glanced over at the mess left by the builders.

Then I made the following announcement, curling up the toes in my right shoe and pressing the scrap of paper down on the hardwood lecterntop until my thumbs went from red to white.

'You'll all be very sorry to hear, I'm sure, that there's been an act of vandalism on the church premises.'

I heard my voice boom from the speakers.

'Well, we feel we do just need to remind you today of the need for security, of not leaving things lying around, and particularly letting someone know if you see anything or anyone suspicious – doing anything suspicious at all.'

I raised my eyes, and addressed the ocean of intent faces directly.

'Because yesterday – we think it was Saturday – someone went into the back of the church and quite deliberately destroyed the winning entry in our under-sixteens painting competition, a watercolour entitled *The Quietness of the Holy Dove* by Theresa Hooley.'

There was such a widespread intake of breath that I feared it might suck me out of the pulpit.

The parishioners started talking. I raised my voice slightly, shaking my head.

'There's no cause for panic. The police have been informed. I did think it might have been the builders, but I understand they've not been near the picture, which was just sitting there under a sheet. We're obviously all very sorry. It was in a large frame, and one of my colleagues tells me it was going to be put forward as a replacement for the – the – ah – the old painting – of – the – ah – face –'

That face. I looked down at the lectern.

'A replacement, anyway, for the painting that the church has had on the west side there for many years. Clearly, that won't happen now – and we are very, very sorry.'

Then, at my invitation, Theresa Hooley came up to the front. She was crying, of course. The congregation applauded gently as she accepted a consolation copy of the latest church songbook, signed by all members of staff. As she resumed her seat, I moved back to the side bench: arthritic, almost, with the burden of it.

That afternoon, Richard Burts agreed to read the evening notices (I could not ask Daniel: it would be yet more evidence of lack of commitment for him to discuss with Morag), and I excused myself from the second service.

I rolled the Datsun on to the street for the first time in weeks, and then took it coughing over the flyover, feeling a wheel lift off the tarmac at exactly the point where I remembered it rising on the car's first-ever approach to the church.

I'm the sort who'll never marry.

I had an end-of-term feeling. The sense of something terminal.

I mourned my loss of life.

The Datsun – a coffin now – staggered its way around a spaghetti junction, and then the two of us zipped off, west.

In the car speakers, Elvis was singing something gospel.

The King, I thought. *That man truly was the King.*

Elvis.

Aimless, I stopped at a tiny village before Oxford and had a thick sandwich in a pub, with a glass of beer. Sitting in my Birkham scarf by a lock, I watched hardy boatsmen take their vessels past, returning their salutes vaguely.

Soon the sun was the buckle in a red belt, fading fast. If I left in ten minutes, I could make an appearance in the tea room after the service ended; circulate; catch sight of my Queen, perhaps . . .

As I walked back towards the car, moving down a sidestreet, there was the distinct and surprising sound of Christian choruses.

I hesitated, sampling the moment, picking my place in infinity, imagining the street a dark room capped with a fluorescent blue roof, scuffing the sole of a shoe on the gravel for assurance that this was reality, and I was still deeply implicated in it.

In the quietness, the scraping sounded like a chainsaw.

The faint Sunday music continued, holy as the setting sun. The name of the alleged Son of God crept into a verse, but for once it was of no concern. *Let them sing it,* I thought, staring up at the glowing sky. *How can I stop them?*

I reached the front bed of a garden, and found the singers, all outside, warmly wrapped, sitting on a tarpaulin. The guitarist wore fingerless gloves. There were fifteen or so of them. 'Join us if you want,' one called out. 'We're just praising God.'

Praising who?

I would rather have praised my Datsun and left in it, but it was two roads away. Inexplicably, I took a seat with them, and soon they were singing again. The strings of the guitar were only a few inches from my ear.

I did not sing. I ran a finger around my collar.

Thank goodness, no vicar's garb tonight. They don't know who I am. Just an open-necked shirt. That's fine.

The music carried on, and now I felt a queasy peace at heart as they sung the name of the supposed Son of God . . .

And then suddenly I was joining in at intervals, singing from a typed sheet I had been handed, every sung word a surprise; just singing the words around that name as numb facts, like racing results, closing my eyes and barring thoughts of the illogicality of it, sealing off fatal descriptions of religion of the Left or Right; of Fruit and Nut and Pass-the-Port . . .

Sealing off the disastrous turn things had taken at the church; not sealing off Gillian Mitchell, because it was impossible to, but allowing the thought of her to roam positive as I sung, eyes closed . . .

There was a warm tap running in me. When I caught sight of it, the coursing water stemmed and turned to salt. Closing my eyes, I saw views over a vast canyon; I was flying over it with silent wings, gaping down at an ocean of space.

God's love?

A shoeprint left by the last curate?

Or my empty soul?

Whatever was happening, it had to be left exactly where it was, and so I shrugged and left them with a rustle of jacket as they sung on. Getting back to the Datsun, I slammed a heel into one of the wheel arches in frustration.

One of them saw it. Greatcoated, he had followed in a square's glasses.

'Who are you?'

'I'm just from a big city,' I said.

'London?'

'That's it.'

'Why were you singing there with us – why did you leave so fast?'

'I don't know.'

'Why did you kick your car?'

'The wheels need aligning.'

'Do you need help?'

'No.'

'Have you found God? Is that why you're here?'

'I'm not looking. I'm going home.'

– 23 –

As expected, the place was falling apart. No one had been near it over the winter. Weeds and thistles were crawling out of the soil, feeling for spring. Bricks of dried earth and plastic scraps lay strewn across the area we had arrived to inspect. Tufts of hard grass dominated a border.

'It's a mess,' Vanessa said.

The big allotment, four miles east of Saint Peter's, had been left in the will of a parishioner. When it was overgrown, men with rasping rural voices would ring the church and complain by shouting into their telephones.

'I wish we could sell this. Look at it.'

'We can't, of course, with Mrs Dent still in church.' Vanessa's reference was to the wife of the late owner. 'So I think we'll need to get a gardener to clear it. Bother.'

'That means money,' I said. I thought of money. Fifty-pound notes, fluttering. Digits on accountancy calculators.

We hobbled into the centre of the allotment. The plastic scraps cracked underfoot. I bent down, unsteadily, and picked one up. The ground was bumpy.

'It's like sin,' Vanessa said.

'What is?' I was balancing at an angle.

'This mess. Overgrown. The human heart.'

Impressed, I made a mental note; and then followed it with a verbal error.

'Interesting, you saying that. I might use that for a sermon I'm doing.'

'A sermon? You don't usually – '

'I know, I know.' I instantly regretted voicing the thought. 'I know I don't.' The soil was so bumpy that neither of us was able to stand up straight. 'I think I am doing one, though – I've just had Morag put it on the sheets.'

'When's it for?'

Our postures were crooked.

'An evening, in about six weeks.'

Vanessa moved her feet for a more secure stance, but stumbled . . . and then span her head at me.

'Six weeks, Mark? That's a guest service.'

I stared straight ahead at a line of tower blocks.

'Yes – six weeks,' I said, firmly.

'But usually you – you do the more – um – the more theoretical sermons. And the counselling, of course.'

'I have done, yes.'

'The guest service is where we get hundreds of non-Christians coming in, Mark.' She changed her footing. 'You don't really intend to preach in one of them, do you?'

Now I was the one to try for a better posture on the lumpy ground, and ended up staggering forwards, knock-kneed.

'I thought I ought to do one, at least.'

Vanessa persisted. 'Can't BBF manage it?'

I felt humiliated. The point was abundantly clear.

'BBF's doing a series – so – I didn't think – '

Vanessa cut in: 'Okay. No problem. Up to you.'

Working in silence, we set about clearing the allotment.

Vanessa ripped up a clump of plant life with a groan and then a chirrup. 'This happened last year. We came just to look at the place. We ended up on our hands and knees.'

A thought struck like a truncheon.

'That was you and Brendan, was it?'

Vanessa spoke through teeth clenched with the effort of tugging at long-rooted weeds, her back to me.

'Yes, he came too.'

I kicked at a mound of earth, knocking the roof off a six-storey worm dwelling. The bloody, bulbous shapes writhed in the soil, daylight shocking movement out of them.

'It's a shame he ended up being fired,' I said.

Vanessa worked on, but slowly her elbows and arms glued up; now she was looking into the distance, away from me.

'How did you know that?' Her tone of innocent inquiry was so false, it might almost have been weeded itself.

'Does it matter? I just wondered why he'd gone.'

Vanessa rose and faced me, one leg bent like Elvis.

'I remember when you first asked about him – when you first arrived. BBF was there too. You must have thought it was really strange – we didn't say anything.'

'I did think it was very strange indeed.'

'It was strange,' she confirmed. 'The answer to your question – why he was fired – is that he basically –'

She tailed off.

'Yes?'

She gathered herself. 'He basically went mad.'

'Mad?' I asked, dumbfounded. I flung the word back at her, angrily. 'Mad? What sort of mad?'

'A sort of mad that made him do a mad sort of things.'

'What sort of things, then?'

Now the mud and sky and trees were whirling around me.

'Oh – they weren't really mad things at first.' She let out a tugging laugh, and looked downwards at the soil. 'I think – well, Douglas – was just – overtaken by it.'

Mesmerised, I shoved my dirty hands deep into pockets.

'Overwhelmed, I mean. Oh dear, I probably shouldn't be telling you any of this – but he got – Douglas, that is – got a request – for a job reference. That was how it started.'

'A job reference? What, Brendan had applied for a job?'

'Yes. But about the most bizarre job you could imagine. He applied to be a big-wheel operator at a fairground.'

'You're not joking, are you?'

'No. Douglas called him in, and Brendan just said he was too cut off from real people, and he wasn't getting the chance to do what Jesus Christ called him to do, to help – '

'The poor, I suppose – '

' – exactly, the poor, and the sick and so on – and I gather Douglas just suggested that maybe this big-wheel thing wasn't the way to go about it – '

Vanessa took a fumbling step backwards.

'The people from the fairground wanted to know if he had experience on something called a Jensen Pulley System.'

'Did he? I suppose not.'

'Of course not. I just remember the name because Douglas said it showed how completely strange the incident was at the time. None of us knows anything about pulleys. I think Douglas started watching Brendan closely – you know – and he noticed he was telling everyone in the church they ought to be out helping the sick and the poor, and asking why they weren't and so on – '

'I can almost understand that. I've often thought the church is a bit cut off, a bit exclusive.'

'Of course. But it got worse. Once he just walked out of a service in full view, and later said he felt he'd been called away to help someone under a doorway.'

'That is – ah – unusual,' I said. I was tingling with mixed sensations: a cruel urge to despise the last curate's fervour; yet a chill of appreciation at its potency.

Brendan Madill.

'Then there were some – very odd things,' Vanessa went on. 'There was a by-election in the area of the church – in Islington South, I think it was. We were watching one of the candidates being interviewed in the street, you know, on television, and there was the usual crowd behind him – and then suddenly, in the back of the picture, we saw Brendan appear – moving sideways into the frame, as though he wasn't meaning to – with this white banner. A sheet on sticks. It just had the word "Help" painted on it.'

'Really?'

'We talked to him afterwards, and he said he was trying to urge people to do more for the helpless – he admitted he could have given the wording more thought – '

'So why did he start all this, do you think?'

'He told me we were all missing the point.'

'Missing the point?'

'His lower lip trembled when he said it. He thought all this talk – in the pulpit, the coffee bar – I don't know – he thought it was all somehow offensive. It wasn't reality.'

'But that's not enough to get him fired, surely.'

'But he was very visible. And then he started doing other things – sleeping in cardboard boxes, you know, taking petitions round the church for more soup kitchens, or more homes for the elderly, even for The Queen to pay tax – '

'I'm beginning to get the drift – '

' – and even, I don't know – he had this sort of hollow-eyed look after a while – '

'Depression?'

'Maybe. But some people thought he was so high powered – he seemed to be remorseless, you know, with homeless people staying in his flat, making a terrible stink all the time – '

'Did Douglas accept it?'

'He once saw the top of a tramp's head on the windowsill, and then he told Brendan to get them out. But he said Brendan's reaction was to quote something out of the New Testament – verbatim, word for word. As though it justified what he was doing. Chapter eleven of something. I think it was Hebrews. The whole lot of it. Word for word. Three or four minutes of – I don't know, Hebrews eleven.'

'And what did Douglas say?'

'You know what Douglas was like. I think this long passage came to an end, and Douglas just stood there – and then he said, "I see your point." You know what he was like.'

Vanessa continued: 'It was building up into a crisis. He was obsessed that the church had got it wrong. He once sat at the side of the stage in bare feet – no one knew why.'

'So what did Douglas do?'

'I think he started by saying something like, "Well, maybe the job at a fairground wasn't the right thing, so why not try for some others?" And then he'd mention a few.'

'The Salvation Army? That sort of thing?'

'Exactly. And I think there's another group in London called We Are The Ones Who Are Aiding The Poor, as well. "WATOWARATEPO", for short. And the Clippings Trust.'

'Toe clippings, is that?'

'Railway clippings, of course – as in, people who sleep on them. But anyway, Brendan never followed any of them up – I think he almost liked being chief irritant to Douglas.'

'Oh.' I was taken aback.

'And then he produced this huge draft for a sermon, basically telling people to get up and go and take someone into their homes, not even waiting to hear the end of the service, and anyone in a thick coat ought to leave it in the lobby on their way out –'

'I get the drift,' I said. 'It's unbelievable.'

'Oh, but all that was nothing compared to the last thing. I can't remember how they found out. A call from the bank, or something, I think. Anyway, it turned out that more than four months of collection money had gone.'

'No.'

'Yes. Instead of banking it, he'd been ferrying it out to east London and shoving the coins and notes into the pockets of down-and-outs while they were asleep.

There'd even been something in the local papers there about it.'

'Is that why Hendon – '

'Hendon never knew. But yes, that's why he's paranoid about the budget now. He thought he had it under control, and then it suddenly crashed into the red. He called it the "April Surprise". He was literally climbing the walls. He's never really trusted our finances since then.'

We drove back to the church in silence.

At length, I asked: 'Did you sympathise? With him?'

'When he was sacked, of course,' Vanessa replied.

Her next sentence slammed me back in the seat.

'Actually, I think I was probably in love with him.'

Struggling for a reaction, I said: 'Ah – so he was something of a gadabout, was he?'

She seemed upset. 'Not at all.'

Vanessa stared out of the window at a line of trees.

'I suppose I was asking if you had sympathy with his theories, and so on,' I explained.

The student leader turned her face towards mine.

'He just went mad, I think. It really wasn't based on a relationship with Christ – just a kind of mania.'

We turned into Saint Peter's car park, and I wound down the window and typed four digits into a pad on the barrier. But the green-and-white-striped arm did not swing up.

I buzzed Kennett on an intercom.

'Can you come down?'

'No problem,' the hoarse voice barked.

Cold, Vanessa and I shuffled through our own thoughts.

'I shouldn't have told you that,' she said, finally. 'All that stuff about Brendan.'

'Don't worry,' I replied. But then I realised her tone of voice had betrayed something, and asked: 'Why not, anyway? Why do you say that?'

'I can't say.'

The truth sank in. 'Am I leaving too? Is that why?'

'Oh – come on, Mark, it's not like that at all – '

'I know Daniel and Morag want me out.'

'Well – even if they did – it's not the same – they always – all of you – always saw it as a temporary – '

'What's he told you?'

'Oh – only that they're about to advertise for someone.'

The revelation had not taken much prising.

'They need my sanction to fill the post,' I said, stiffly. I fished a tissue from a pocket . . . and found it and the insides of my trousers thick with allotment dirt.

'Mark – there won't be anything awful about it, will there? We all follow Christ, don't we?'

Kennett appeared before my response. Then Vanessa asked: 'You're not really doing that guest service, are you?'

And now the janitor was gargling at me. 'For goodness' sake, sir, was that you throwing tissues out of the driver's side? They drift over the car park! Can't you find a bin?'

But I was too caught up in thoughts of the last curate to answer or mind.

– 24 –

I'm cracking up. Cracking up like the last curate.

Off my rocker. One brick short of a full load.

One verse short of a sermon.

What am I going to do when they kick me out? Or just stick an advert somewhere, trying to find someone else?

They'll get him instantly, of course.

Yes. The world and his fiancée will want to work here.

Anyone with a clean driving licence and a smudged dog collar, and half a dozen grotty talks in a binder . . . they'll all come for interviews if the thing gets advertised.

Every Anglican curate under thirty in the directory.

Because there's profile, for starters. Asteroid-high profile. A bit of broadcasting, public speaking . . .

And audiences unimaginable for most clergy: a thousand at every sermon, twelve hundred in the collection . . .

Wall-mounted cameras, eager volunteers, a choir hitting notes dead-on, floral displays done by committee . . .

I'll lose my Gillian.

Good grief, I'll lose my love – my dearest, darling Gillian – the minute the new man gets ratified on church notepaper or whatever it is they'll use to do it.

The minute the new rat gets ratified . . . the moment the new Pope gets paper-noted . . . the second the new nutter gets rat-churched . . . that instant, I'll lose my darling, darling love . . . the darlingest love, my sweetest love of all . . .

Is it so crazy to think a single sermon could do it?

No.

Public pressure, of course, is what'll make sure.

They won't let me go. Not ever. Parishioners will form a human barrier by the car park, throw a tuna net across the front door, write letters to Morag if she tries to pull a fast one to get me out – or send me things, framed . . . come and take pictures at the flat . . . publish books about the sermon . . .

And there'll be a sheet of something to send all the people who come up to the front after it. There's going to be hundreds of them up there wanting some sort of follow-up.

Of course they could be so overwrought they might not even be able to give their names. The volunteers might be so overwhelmed they won't even be able to hold a pencil.

Now concentrate. Think about the shape of the sermon.

What was it they used to say about shape at Birkham?

That there were 'curves', 'steps', and 'toggles' and 'laps' and 'the dead attention area' . . . and all kinds of other technical terms for how we put The Message across . . .

I never had a message.

Never had a message but one: GET ME OFF THIS PULPIT AND GET ME OFF IT FAST.

GET ME A JOB IN ACCOUNTANCY.

STOP THIS RUDDY CHARADE.

Oh, my . . .

Pull yourself together. Have another cup of coffee.

All right, you made some mistakes . . . but not that many.

Cut out the trembling. And think.

What are you going to preach from?

'Chapter.' That's what Birkham called it.

The problem is not knowing any chapters. Apart from a bit of Genesis one, or whatever that other bit is that talks about judging; or the story of the three sisters –

Perhaps . . .

Perhaps I should . . . oh.

Now – that could be it.

What class that would show! What pazzazz!

To preach from whatever it was the last curate –

What an idea! Hebrews! The thing he screamed at Douglas!

Chapter ten, was it?

No: it was eleven, for sure. Hebrews eleven.

Wouldn't that be rich? Wouldn't that be fabulous?

To take the very same passage ... and preach it to undying fame this time? To thousands coming up to the front, and Gilly there behind the pulpit, loving me at long, long last?

Hebrews, chapter eleven.

Hebrews eleven, the route to heaven.

Eleven Hebrews, to give her loving views.

My Gillian ...

It's – ah – kind of appropriate, as the Americans say.

To take the very chapter – Hebrews eleven!

Whatever it says!

It doesn't matter what the heck the thing says!

Just shooting it at them – great balls of fire!

Great preached balls of fire!

Just whooosh!

Hebrews eleven!

Whooosh!

Whooooooooooooooooooosh!

– 25 –

'I think something's very wrong indeed with him.'

My hand wrapped around the door knob at the very moment that I heard the female voice speak inside the room.

'As I say, there's good reason to – oh – Mark. Hello.'

'Hello, everyone.'

Daniel and Morag smiled with a warmth that undermined all logic crediting them with base intentions. I grinned with the wan grin of a stockbroker forced to dismiss freak results from a company in which he has failed to invest client money. The third person, Derrald Skuse, extended an arm with a cry.

'Reverend Empringham! Terrific to see you!'

'Hello, Derrald.' Skuse was a middle-aged man who played the organ now and then, dressed in clothes that made him look like a sheriff, and lived with his mother.

We shook hands: his jerked as though at an organ-stop.

I pulled out a different sort of stop.

'Please carry on. I know you were all talking about me.'

'Mark – ' Daniel began, thickly.

'It's obvious. You were saying something was very wrong indeed with me.'

'Not at all,' Morag said. 'Honestly, Mark. We weren't.'

Derrald shrank back nervously, as though from a crime.

He mumbled: 'Well, this room could do with a lick of paint and some better wallpaper, that's for sure.'

Daniel caught my eye. 'You haven't been – ah – I don't know how to – Mark, you haven't been drinking, have you?'

'Only a milkshake.'

'But what could make you think like that?' asked Morag. Her voice perplexed me, momentarily. Something in it spoke of genuine concern. 'Since you ought to know, Mark, we were talking about one of the lay assistants. Derrald here wanted to – to pass something on to us.'

The suggestion of drink, or unsteadiness, still smarted.

'It was a banana milkshake, as well. That's all.'

Stepping forward, I slipped on a fold of carpet.

Daniel moved as though to catch me.

'I'm fine, Daniel.'

'Glad to hear it.'

Derrald made for the door, saying: 'I'm playing Mother some Chopin. Tricky. I like to look the score over first.'

He was gone. I stood my square yard of frayed rug.

'Ah – I – ah – don't – ah – I don't mind being – being talked about – but not with people in the congregation.'

'We really weren't, Mark. Neither of us.' Daniel was more relaxed now, taking all this in his stride, no doubt . . . just like the time he had to preach a sermon on Providence at an hour's notice, after the guest speaker's Berkshire home was crushed by a toppled crane. Yes, cravatted Daniel, treacle-smooth to the core, was a man who could think under metric tonnes of pressure – let alone the few feather-measures now being applied by a lame-duck boss.

Morag spoke next. 'Is everything all right, Mark?'

'I don't know.' *I'm lost*. 'Is it?'

'Is what?' Daniel asked.

'Everything all right. That's what you asked.'

'I didn't think I had done,' said Daniel.

'He means me,' Morag said. 'You just seemed so –'

'So suspicious, or something.' Daniel put his hands on his hips and tilted his head like a bird. 'Or just upset.'

'Superstitious? Upset? Me?' I asked.

'Yes.' They spoke in unison.

I paused, rubbing fingers on my chin as Ben Jivvard had done, feeling stubble the morning's razor had missed.

'Perhaps I'm just tired.'

'You have a lot of responsibility,' Morag said.

'More now than you've ever had.' And that was Daniel.

'The refurbishment?' I said. 'Well, that's done now.'

'No – just being in charge at all,' Morag explained.

'You've hardly even been here six months,' Daniel added.

I asked: 'So how much longer am I going to be here?'

Something in the room began to tremble . . .

An acting vicar.

'Pardon?' asked Daniel. Outside, an ambulance careered past the church, sirens howling.

Racing to save my career!

'I'm just wondering how much longer it's going to be possible for me to stay,' I said.

Haltingly, Morag replied: 'Well, curate was a permanent post. We never thought of you leaving it, and –'

'What about vicar?' I persisted.

Daniel and Morag looked at each other again. Then, perhaps on a hidden cue from Daniel, Morag tottered to the desk and pulled a folded sheet from the drawer.

'Come here, Mark, and tell us what you think of this.'

I walked to the desk, and read the typed capitals.

And then read them again . . .

And then straightened up, words buzzing in front of me.

Morag asked: 'Mark – are you all right?'

'You're swaying,' Daniel said.

The words stopped buzzing; started whistling.

'I'm fine. Vertical. Thank you. Dread naught.'

'Obviously, you would need to sanction the form of words,' I heard one of them saying.

So they really did want rid of me, want rid of their acting vicar as sweetly and kindly as anyone had ever wanted rid of anyone else . . . but want rid of me, none the less, exactly as I had suspected; and not just Daniel and Morag. There was no doubt that most of the Parochial Council, who would ratify any appointment, were in on it.

The text Morag slid from her desk drawer invited any clergy interested in the post of 'Rector, Saint Peter's Church, North London' to come for initial meetings with church staff. No salary was mentioned. The bullet-long paragraph of deadly print had not yet been fired off to the Anglican newspapers.

'We were just waiting for you to get a moment to give the thumbs-up to the actual form of words,' Morag said.

Short of breath, I drooped in the armchair in a corner.

Every fear is now real, I told myself.

They came to my side with evident concern: Morag stooping, Daniel towering.

'What's up?' he asked.

The answer was the first phrase that came to mind.

'Rib gout, I think.'

And then, crowding me, the two church workers made it all sound so sensible and pleasant and eminently reasonable and happy and, yes, even wonderful. Mark, you were only acting as the vicar here, the PCC was obviously going to have to start looking for a permanent chap . . .

But I wanted to stay, to win her heart.

And, after all, your original job still needs doing . . .

The one you gave me by accident.

. . . your job as curate, Mark, where some of your work was really very valuable . . .

Some of it?

You're very young, too. It's unheard-of for someone your age to run pretty much the biggest church in the country . . .

If you're good enough, you're old enough.

What Morag and Daniel did not say was that it was simply impossible to hang on as deputy after being demoted as chief.

No career movement of that kind would ever happen in accountancy.

The conversation – a rockfall – echoed for hours after it ended in handshakes and useless smiles.

It was now more obvious than ever that all the things in the world would hang on a single sermon. Although I had successfully suggested the advertisement be kept in a drawer for a while to see if there was any better way of arranging the syntax, that only bought time up to the guest service.

And it made the sermon more last-ditch than ever before.

Failure would see the stage floor opening below me.

If it came, I would lose my heroine.

For a fortnight, there had been no contact between us, unless dreams counted. I carried her around in my soul, heavy as a stacked deep-freeze. Curves in roads were her curves; the first puffy clouds of spring were varying profiles of her face (and blue between them was the stroke-of-something she had once applied to her eyelids); a sports-car purr was the lowest resonating chord in her voice; and the rejection she had meted out, paradoxically, was executed with such silly kindness that it had somehow turned into an historical gesture of hope.

Ironically, the meeting with Morag and Daniel also gave me something to be thankful for. At least the sermon would go ahead. And then – my Scarlet Lipstick would be mine.

Simple. *The sermon lives.*

I began to feel better.

The sermon lives indeed.

I felt much better.

So it was hardly surprising that the handset of the telephone seemed to become a curled finger, and beckon.

Asking its operator to ring his crowned Queen and make sure of her presence at the April guest service.

'Oh – all right,' she said.

'You don't sound certain,' I said.

A little time, just a little while longer . . .

'I just wondered why you called,' Gillian replied.

'I'm preaching.'

'Oh. Fine. I'll try and make it. Okay.'

. . . and she will be mine.

'Please do more than try,' I insisted.

She sighed, Irishly. 'Why is it so important?'

At the twinkle of an eye, at the sound of the trumpet . . .

'It's a guest service.' There was a mad urge to say that plotters had decided it would be the last sermon from their vicar. But – no. That secret was well worth keeping.

'The choir is singing that night, Mark, so –'

'I just wanted to know you'd be coming,' I put in.

'All right, I'll be there.'

. . . Gillian Mitchell shall be mine.

'Promise?' I asked, half-joking.

Wearily, she said: 'Promise.'

Then as though returning from a distance, Gillian said: 'Mark – I think there's something I ought to tell you.'

'What?' I asked her. 'About the guest service?'

'Not about the service. Don't worry – I'll be there.'

I felt a cool chill down the line of my spine.

'What, then?' I asked.

'I don't know if you're interested. But I think I've found someone, and I'm seeing them a bit, and I suppose I feel quite excited, and I thought you ought to know.'

I rang Vicki, of all people.

'That's a sad story,' she said, toughly. 'But whoever she's seeing – I mean – these things never last, probably.'

'What things?'

'Oh – kissing,' she said, rubbing skin off my heart.

'You don't know who it is, do you?' I asked.

'Mark! How could I? I haven't even seen you recently.'

'But I thought Vanessa might have told you.'

'Of course not. I don't even know if she knows Jean – '

'Gillian.'

' – yes, Gillian. Nessie's here now, actually. Want a word with her?'

'Vanessa's there?' Stunned, I replayed Vicki's side of the conversation. 'Did she hear all that, then?'

'She's in the loo.'

There was a distant flushing sound.

'I'd better go,' I said. 'I'm – ah – busy. Preparing a sermon. Hebrews eleven.'

'Can I come?'

'The first Sunday in April,' I told her quickly, saying goodbye and hanging up before she did.

For four or five days, I sank under the weight of what Gillian had told me, and even considered trying to become a Christian to escape the burden of it. Had she gone for ever? It was impossible to say. Who was she seeing? No one knew.

Will the sermon bring her back?

If I ever doubted it, I relived the vivid images of BBF at the pulpit that night, his palms hard down on the struts, leaning into his audience like the prop in a scrum. I returned to the imprint of their faces; to whatever call it was he had made to do with the Bible. Something about it being a good book, probably, and all the people who agreed that God was good should come up to the front . . . whatever, that was the approach: the leaning, the megaphone voice when you least expected it, the soft words and the pointing and then a punchline swung at you like meat from the back of a truck. It could lay an audience low, no matter who they were, thresh them out like wheat. The idea that some part-time eye-fluttering and romance between Gillian and whoever-it-was could get in its way was plain preposterous.

But having taken all those thoughts in their fullest cycle, the memory of Gillian on the telephone would resurface. If this person who had plunged in, muscled in, in this disgraceful way, became bored at the key moment at the beginning of April . . . would he insist they bunked off church and went out for dinner? Or to a zoo? A film?

Will that baboon be kissing her in a half-lit seat in some seedy cinema, while I preach the sermon that explodes in the history of Anglicanism like a thousand-ton bomb?

No recollections of BBF's power in the pulpit were able to quell the anguish at the moment that thought came.

And then all obsessions became one. The sermon was everything. There was no other event or thing on earth which merited interest on any comparable scale. Not foreign wars, not motorway pile-ups, not weather, not Scotland, space, transatlantic yacht teams, Ben Jivvard, Vanessa, Richard –

A pebble struck the window of the flat.

What day is it?

Blinking, I moved across the lounge. Bold spring sunlight was splitting the room into light and dark. I threw up the sash window with a panic of wood on wood.

That face on the pavement . . .

'Hey – Mark! Buddy! How are ya?' He was waving.

'Stewart!' I shouted, recognising the face down below.

'Yes – it's me! What are you doing up there, like Rapunzel in her castle? You idiot!'

Out of sheer embarrassment, I jerked my head back in . . . but then shouted at the lounge ceiling: 'I'm coming down.'

At street level, he hugged me.

'Your hair's not as long as Rapunzel's! Old bud!'

'Where's Ducky?' I asked.

'Stayed in Wales,' he said, 'where the air's clean. And you don't get knocked down trying to cross the road. And – '

'All right, all right. Don't keep reminding me.'

Stewart's exuberance was overpowering. Somehow, my old friend had always been able to draw me out of myself.

'So – come on – '

'Come on what?' I asked, laughing.

'What's the uniform? Let's start with that.'

'I'm an accountant.'

'Well – a joke from Mark! So early on!'

'I'm having fun,' I lied.

'Doing what?'

I told him, in the broadest terms, as we found seats just inside the church. For a moment, he looked puzzled.

'I don't understand.'

'What do you mean?'

'What I mean is, I don't understand where you go from here. For goodness' sake, Mark, you're not even thirty yet, and you've done it.'

'Done it? I haven't done anything. Done what?'

'You've made it,' Stewart said, 'and don't you pretend you haven't! Gosh – to be honest, Mark, I always used to wonder if – if you would. But now I come to see you at what I assume's going to be some two-storey loo backing on to a car park, with a spire the size of a police cone – and I find you top of the tree in this giant place! Must be one of the biggest in the country! And you're the chief cop!'

Stewart put his hands to his mouth, and made a sound like a police car. I smiled, too tired to explain.

'You can't say biggest. It's too hard to measure. Biggest congregation, yes, perhaps. We get about a thousand. But we're not as physically big as cathedrals, for example.'

He laughed raucously. 'And you're running it – don't you see? It's like being chief executive of that big place across the road! Marple & Schwartz! And to think – if you hadn't sent me that Bishop letter thing by accident, who knows what you'd be doing now?'

'Who knows?' I said, airily.

Stewart looked at me, searchingly.

'Mark – I just wonder – if you're missing out on sex.'

I felt an urge to cough up blood.

'Sorry – I didn't mean to be blunt. It's just that we're getting on for thirty – as it happens, I've just turned thirty – ' He waved a hand. 'Forget it. I'm out of order.'

'Don't worry,' I said. 'Sorry I didn't send you a card.'

'You look weary, that's all.'

'The burden of presidential office.' Stewart always seemed to make me mock myself.

Then he exploded a surprise: the thatching had not been going so well, he said – Ducky and he might have to do some boring work in London. When could they visit the church?

'I wouldn't have thought it was your cup of tea, especially this place, Stew.' I was wrinkling my nose.

'So whatever happened to evangelism, then?'

'Well, I do quite a bit of counselling.'

'I think we'll be around in five weeks or so.'

Before I could find the page in my diary, the approach of a colleague distracted us.

It was Grunt, walking past.

'Ah – let me – '

I was about to introduce him to Stewart, but Gregory Runting did not acknowledge the attempt to win his attention . . .

Head on chest, he was gone a moment later.

'Are you sure you work here?' Stewart asked, snorting in amusement. 'Or was that guy the Bishop?'

'I don't know. He must not have heard me.'

'He was a couple of yards away!'

Flipping through diary pages, I found the weekend.

'Just casing the joint,' he said. 'Dipping our toes in.'

'It's the second weekend in April, is it?' I asked.

He produced his own diary.

'No – hold on. I think – ah, here we go.'

'That's wrong, is it? That's five weeks.'

'The week before.'

'The first?'

'Sunday, April the first. The evening, I think.'

I glanced away. 'I don't know if that's possible.'

'Oh – you'll be away, will you?'

'It's too aggressive for you. The church.'

'Ducks and I are only going to get a feel, for heaven's sake, Mark. And it would be great to see you – in your element, so to speak! That's the reason. Are you telling me you're not preaching then, or something?'

'But that's – in a month, that's a guest service. So – '

'No, come on. Don't "but". We're just coming along for a bit of London. We haven't done that well in Wales. We've got to get back with the big wheels for a bit – people like you.'

'It's just that – '

'Why don't you try and preach that Sunday?'

'I think – um – I think I am.'

'Terrific. Now – look, let's have a browse around this massive nave you've got through here – come on, Mark, stop looking so dazed – get a grip – take me through when the walls were built. I want to know everything – and that – look at that ceiling! That's high! And you can tell me about the – look at the size of this place – do you pick the hymnbooks, and so on? Is it like a vicar's manifesto, when you do that? Choose the books? And – down there – what about that? Did you pick the paintings, too? Did you pick that one at the end of the wall – is it supposed to be Christ, that one?'

– 26 –

Walt Lee Tubbs
1605 West Poe
Huntsville
Alabama, USA

To Mark Empringham
Acting Pastor
Saint Peter's Church
Ferndown Highway
North London/England

Dear Pastor Empringham!
Thank you for the letter, I feel I know you already!

The stamps used must have cost how much? Was this a problem and if so please tell me when I arrive at the church which I will do, I will tell you the exact date but the plans for LCBT are still up in the air, I think it is April or May.

My plans will take me to Scotland, is the kilt compelled there by law or just an option for those that visit?

Looking for your guidance on that. PRAISE.

Also thank you for the directions to the church and full address of it, amazing how long the address is in such a small country, you need more than just surnames!

Driving is still worrying me! You gave no advice except on the railroad crossings – yes, I will avoid them as you suggest. But I am still wondering about driving, because in Scotland I will not have a car. Only when I get to London will I get a car for the first time, and we all know about London traffic. I am nervous! Yes, LEFT is the side, is that just for small vehicles though? Anyway I only have an automatic licence, not gears, so PRAY ON THIS ONE.

Which side is the seat? First thing I will do Pastor on getting the car will be see you, I can't wait. I am staying in Kent, where is it?

Yes and also by the way, we heard about the government minister who resigned there for his joy in God, he was photographed singing with enthusiasm. Very, very bad. We saw *Newsday Live* and then a well-known Bishop commented, etc.

As I said LCBT is an early summer course, what do you think of it? I expect much as it has been praised here, especially by Dug Krugenheit do you know of him, the preacher?

Any more on the English roads or driving the car when I pick it up (scary), then my telex no. in Huntsville — 414 354 55610 for urgency (it is a fear)

Walt Lee Tubbs.

Three Weeks Later

– 27 –

I rewound Dug Krugenheit.

The television screen showed a snowstorm as the film whirred back in the machine. I ejected the cassette and placed it at the top of a pile of tapes.

Dug Krugenheit – *No Room For Blackness* (Mex. City).

Steve & Glad Grimney – Church of Redeemer, S. Dakota.

Rev. Oei Z. Akamuturo – Milan Stadium, w. translators.

Ted Walsh – *How Long Have You Looked?* (Amsterdam).

Dug Krugenheit – *The Heat of Krugenheit* (Oslo/Moscow).

Prof. G. P. Lampin – *Academic Searching* TV show.

Jerry and Gwyn Theoman-Timm – Vancouver Gospel Hall.

I had watched the recordings of the Dug Krugenheit missions at least half a dozen times, often freezing the frame to study postures struck on and off the podium, and scribbling down the best lines: 'Mister, this is better than Vegas! It's better than Atlantic City! It's better than a jackpot on a one-armed bandit!'

I froze the picture, too, as Jerry Theoman-Timm jabbed his finger at the Canadians, noting angle and facial position as the finger blurred and stopped on the screen . . .

And slowed the film when, at the climax of his sermon, the Japanese Mr Akamuturo clasped hands tight to his thighs and jumped up and down in the pulpit as though on a pogo, pebble-lensed wire spectacles jiggling on the bridge of his nose; or watched again and again the way Ted Walsh, after a twenty-minute monotone, would suddenly bellow a string of words at the gallery spotlights – as though raising the alarm for a forest fire in hell!

And then I practised them.

'You –'

Jab.

' – must be –'

Jab-jab.

' – saved.'

Jab-jab-jab.

And then, pushing folded newspaper pages around the window frames of the flat for insulation, I tried the Walsh Shout: reading quietly for five minutes, and then bellowing a sentence into the air, arms shooting out . . .

The Akamuturo Pogo was next: suddenly clamping hands on legs and jumping up and down, spectacles bouncing . . .

It had taken a lot of time, all this.

Dismayed, I had discovered that chapter eleven of the Bible book was not exactly the stuff of podiums:

> Now faith is being sure of what we hope for and certain of what we do not see. This is what the ancients were commended for.
>
> By faith we understand that the universe was formed at God's command, so that what is seen was not made out of what was visible.
>
> And without faith it is not possible to please God, because anyone who comes to him must believe that he exists and that he rewards those who earnestly seek him.

'Well – that's – that's not exactly worth stopping the presses for,' I had mumbled on a first reading.

But I learnt it, none the less. Familiar with every phrase of the chapter, I went back to work on the delivery.

'Mister, that's better than Vegas!'

'That's better than a jackpot on a one-armed bandit!'

Dug Krugenheit did his sermons on the move, using all the available space. The preacher would pace forward, hectoring – and then stalk away from his audience, his back to them. Last, he would spring up the steps of the pulpit and cry out from the summit in a loud voice.

Camera shots of congregations showed many in tears; some calling out and waving. It was exactly the kind of response I would need. Nothing less could win Gillian Mitchell; nothing less could be expected to. There had been no occasion in the history of the planet which offered more to play for. And, with the stopwatch already ticking on my tenure of employment at the church, no scenario imaginable which left less to lose. Nothing would be gained by doing things in halves.

So alone, I struck Krugenheit poses across the flat, switching some of the Americanisms: 'Sir, this is better than Blackpool! It's better than Brighton! Better than winning a lot of money on a fruit machine!' I borrowed a large mirror and watched myself move in it – bending a leg like Glad Grimney where the motion underlined a verse; sighting on a fingernail to jab home strong paragraph endings; checking the angle of an eyebrow against a freeze-frame of Professor Lampin; rehearsing control on the landing after a jump.

And in the middle of one of these lengthy daily sessions – there was a sound close to the door.

Just before it, I had been practising the sole moment of extravagance in an address a preacher called Monty Roberts had given to the Warwick Round Table.

I read from the script: 'In the eleventh chapter of Hebrews, Paul describes faith. "All these people were still living by faith when they died," he says.'

And then the movement –

Snap to the right.

Heel-of-the-hand slap on forehead.

Same arm flung out.

Turn head slowly back (right to left).

'By faith when they died!' I repeated. 'They were still living by faith when they died!'

And then, using a line from a pamphlet issued by Good Word Press: 'Most people have faith in something – be it that their car will get them to work, or that their partner loves them, or just that they will live to their next birthday –'

The Theoman-Timm Treble-jab –

– alongside a yelled question and exclamation borrowed from Dug Krugenheit's Mexico City address: 'Will you save your life by belief? Please!'

Jab-jab- . . .

I was about to segueway into an Akamuturo Pogo, when a rustle at the door of the flat cut short the movement.

'Who is it?' I asked.

Did they hear me doing all that?

The reply was silence. Not even more rustling.

I froze, catching my reflection in the mirror.

Tilting forwards a bit too much: straighten up a bit. Watch the left leg. Must keep it straight on the lean, or it bends inwards and makes the whole thing look weak.

The thought was interrupted by the sound of footsteps.

I cocked an ear for a moment. No. Whoever it was had been and gone. The steps were fading on the stairs.

Did they hear me doing all that? Whoever it was?

I went to the door and opened it, seeing no one. Had it just been BBF, perhaps, coming down from the fourth? If so, what was the rustling?

The question was answered by a glance left of the flat door. Something shoe-sized had been left there, bundled in creased brown paper, shoved up against the wall.

Taped to it was a square of card with a name on.

My name.

Unwrapping the object in the flat, I recognised it the instant a first corner became visible. The lettering on the block of planed wood I had posted to Gillian after completing the inscription was uneven, but not messy:

'The King of Love My Shepherd Is, Whose Goodness Faileth Never.' The last word was slightly shallower in the wood. There was no note.

I examined the thing again, feeling a moment's appreciation. Then I walked through to the kitchen, brusquely toed the lever on the pedal-bin, and threw it in. Not so long ago, the same bin had held the swept-up curls shaved off when the final word was carved, painstakingly, into the wood.

And what had that last word been?

Never, I reminded myself. *Never, Never, Never.*

Well, we'll see about that.

No one ever says never and means it.

I was feeling ebullient; bullish.

You don't have words like 'never' and sermons like this.

I had all the movements.

Reviewing the sermon, limbering up, I sensed raw identity with the last curate in every nerve. He had suffered at the hands of this awful thing, Christianity. So had I. He had suffered at the hands of this awful church, and so had I. He might have gone down the tubes – among the sequels to Vanessa's account had been two allegations of propositioning women worshippers – but at least I could still wave his rebel banner from the pulpit summit.

I will bring a thousand to the front, on their knees.

Yes. The last curate and I were bound together now, bound as invaluable proof of the one fact that made the Christian faith, and the claims of God – or whichever mass hoaxer had set the whole thing up – quite impossible.

The fact was that we had both existed snug within its framework, bowed our heads with its people, sung the songs, prayed the prayers, talked the talk, drunk the coffee . . . and gained nothing from it all but hurt and damage.

And, in my case, quite possibly a broken heart as well.

We were as important in testifying to all this as the Dead Sea Scrolls. What they spoke for, we spoke against, for we were at the hub, right at the centre of it all – and right at the place where the spokes were supposed to lock in, there we were, calling: 'Look, you idiots! We're closest here, and we've seen it all – and there's nothing to see, nothing but Mandy Jivvard's adultery and Vanessa's epilepsy, and whatever bug it was that robbed Douglas of his rectory, and all these lying eyes which warm you up when they're about to take your job away, and cancer, and fudge cake, and Marple & Schwartz making buckets for themselves across the road like face-slaps in perpetual motion – and yes, some of us are friendly, sure, but you got friendship in the Third Reich, and Namibia, and it's all unreal here, utterly unreal, because no one here realises life is like accountancy, do they, and that's one of the signs it's not real, they don't realise you add up blood vessels and feelings and bones and teeth and veins and that's a life, it's not this wispy thing that glides around like heather, this God business we're in, this glass flag that curates are supposed to fly and acting vicars are supposed to live by and real vicars are supposed to die by; and here you come all the same, all of you, you keep coming in here and coming in here and coming and coming and coming and you don't understand, you don't understand that we've seen it all, that we're right at the centre, that we've been right at the head of the biggest church in the country and there's nothing here at all, unless you count wrist-watches bleeping at bad moments.'

I was staring at a man lying flat on his face.

Goodness knows what time of day it was. Just after lunch, probably. But there he was. His toes pointed in at the cold tiled floor.

It was nine days before the guest service.

Not much more than a week, and she is mine.

I had walked into the main body of the church, and seen him there – lying at the front.

Dead?

I raced to him: then jarred to a halt.

The man's back was swelling slightly, almost imperceptibly, with regular breaths.

Not dead. He was murmuring too.

I coughed, but the man did not seem to hear.

Something in the way he was lying suggested he had sunk to his knees, and then spread out – quite deliberately.

So what was he doing here? Splayed out, distracting me when I could be checking the script and reviewing films, looking at photographs and practising delivery?

Or when I could just be dreaming of my Scarlet?

Like a cannonball, it shot through my mind: *How dare he?*

I gritted teeth behind him. The man, apparently unaware, kept on with his prostrate murmuring.

Quietly, I said: 'Excuse me. This is a church.'

And then, a bit louder: 'This is a place of worship. Not a bedroom.'

No response.

Moving closer, leaning over him, I saw his eyes were closed. I vaguely recognised the features. He had once congratulated me on the way I read out notices.

The murmuring became a word.

'Unworthy . . .'

I jumped.

Is he talking about me?

I leant closer.

'Not worthy to be called your son . . .'

He must be.

I listened, petrified.

How much does he know?

'Save me . . . forgive me . . . forgive . . . unworthy . . . me . . .'

He was referring to himself! And was so engrossed in this spreadeagled act of self-abasement and self-embarrassment at the front of my empty church that he did not even know he had company.

A faint glistening streak, where a tear might have been, marked an area to the right of the bridge of his nose.

Then I heard the man name the alleged Son of God.

That did it.

This is just too much – asking for forgiveness like this, on a weekday. Why can't he wait? Why can't he wait nine days, just nine, and then collapse at the front at the end of my sermon?

I felt sworn at, and left quickly. But somehow I could not wipe the glistening smear on the man's face out of my mind. *Is that truth? A tear, drying on a face?*

Shockingly, amid so much certainty . . . the certainty of a pile of tapes, a script, a sense of vision and purpose at last, photographs of preachers in inspirational poses, chunks lifted word-for-word from the countless commentaries stacked in the flat . . . the certainty of my utter and eternal love for Gillian Mitchell, with her scarlet lips and immaculate hips . . . shockingly, amid all that certainty I was conscious – as I had been conscious when, guitars playing, one of the singers in the garden by the river had reached out to touch my shoulder – that there were some things in the world of which I simply had no understanding whatsoever.

– 28 –

Five days to go.

The tensions in my head and arms and legs and neck were at fever pitch. Richard Burts and I bumped into each other in the tea room.

'How's it going?' He was clearing chairs.

'What?'

'The sermon, Mark. Last time we met you said you were deeply into it. It's for Sunday, isn't it?'

'Oh, that. No – I haven't really been doing much on that. Leave it till the last moment, I always think.'

Let him get a shock.

'I thought you'd dropped out of it when I saw the sermon schedule. Your name didn't seem to be there.'

'That was Morag's mistake, I think. She put "Preacher to be announced". She forgot. But never mind.'

Richard sighed deeply, placing hands on hips.

'I really haven't seen you – doing much,' he said. 'Are you still taking care of the counselling?'

'The last few weeks – no. I've passed some names on to Hugh. I was beginning to feel I'd heard almost every problem there is. Everyone seemed to know someone in an iron lung.'

'You haven't been lying low, then?'

'What makes you say that?' I was guarded.

Well – like – the embassy dinner, I mean. It was a bit strange to have thirty high commissioners here, and all those seconds-in-command, and then slides – but no vicar.'

I remembered. I was deep in a paper on animal imagery in Hebrews; a largely useless exercise, as it turned out.

'What were the slides of?'

'I wasn't really looking,' he said. 'It seemed to be lots of mountains from overhead, then a close-up of a Bible.'

'I'm sorry I missed it. I think I got in a dates mix.'

'But a lot of people noticed, Mark.'

I shrugged. 'Oh, well.' It couldn't matter now.

Across the room, two elderly ladies raised their voices in discussion. I took off my glasses to polish a lens.

'Someone was asking after you, too,' Richard said.

'From which embassy?' I asked.

'Not a diplomat. It was the wife of someone in the church who was helping to host it. The Conservative – you know, fairly high-profile sort of bloke – big guy –'

'Ben Jivvard?'

'Yes. His wife came up to me.'

'But I don't really know her.'

'She asked me to send you her and her husband's regards. That was it. I'm afraid I didn't quite get the significance.'

'How strange.'

'She gave me a note, too – but I've left it at home.'

'For me?'

'Yes – in an envelope. She thought you'd be around.'

Standing there in the tea room, I had a sudden jolting shock at the thought of what the next days held.

'Are you okay?' Richard wheezed.

'Just a bit out of breath,' I wheezed back. I reached out a hand and placed it at the top of a pile of chairs.

'We haven't been out since that Chinese,' he said.

'I'm still digesting it,' I joked.

'I used to enjoy seeing a bit of Grunt, but he's been on terrible form lately.'

'I think I heard that. I've not seen him at all.'

'He just doesn't seem to be interested in anything any more. Still – well,' Richard went on, 'I suppose you would have told me, wouldn't you, if there was any major –'

I smiled, and gave his arm a tap.

'Don't worry. No major problems with staff or vicar.'

He looked at me, gently.
'You're quite a loner, sort of thing, aren't you?'
'Not really,' I said.
'No one here would say they knew you, though.'
'I thought I got quite close to – to Douglas, perhaps.'
'This church can be lonely. It's so big. It's amazing how many people you get here on a Sunday – '
'How many I get here?'
'Oh – come on, Mark – I don't mean you personally. And you've made some – ah – some great decisions – like the one to – um – get the – ah – builders in, to do the west side – '
'I got some complaints about that, considering all the money came out of the budget for missionaries.'
'Well. It was a decision, at least. And I think Sonya and Martin Cook, and the Byfords, have found other jobs now. But I mean – if you look at the church, for example – it's as packed as ever. No one's been leaving.'
'That's because I've got BBF to do so much preaching.'
'But we might have even had an increase in numbers.'
'That's people back from winters abroad.'
'And Daniel feels his side of things is going well – the business lunches, and so on and so forth – '
'He's always saying that. I haven't seen the figures.'
'What figures?'
'The conversion figures.'
'What? The – what figures?'
I marched the answer out. 'The figures for the number of businessmen and other people who have been converted as a result of all this entertaining at the church's expense.'
Richard frowned, deeply. 'I – I – don't – '
I shoved my hands in my pockets, and looked down at the carpet: 'I just think we need results, Richard.'
'I never thought I'd hear you say that.'
'Conversions,' I said.
'Yes. I know.'
'I trained as an accountant. The preliminary training.'

'And you're right.' Richard grasped the thought like a hot towel, without flinching. 'We do. We need results. We need people committing their lives, every bit of them, to – '

'Yes,' I interrupted, not wanting to hear the name. 'That's my policy – as vicar.' I ignored his quizzical stare. I would need Richard's backing if there was pitched fighting to get me out of the job. And he needed to be ready for what was going to happen on Sunday. Afterwards, I did not want him thinking it was a fluke. He had to think it was policy.

Walking towards the concrete staircase, I felt a twinge in my side. The small but deep wound inflicted several months earlier – when a punk rocker at a club in South London had taken a comment about his hair in the wrong spirit and stabbed me with a snooker cue – bit from time to time.

The twinge made me feel professional, in some way.

It grated out a welcome thought: *I am a real vicar. Wounded in action.*

The tug of pain reasserted itself.

Not just an acting vicar.

The world, I considered, had made its mark on me. Now I was about to make my mark on it.

In five days, she will be mine.

A few hours later, Mandy Jivvard's sealed letter was handed to me by Daniel, sporting a new cravat.

'Left on Morag's desk, Mark.'

'By Richard Burts, probably.' I directed the words at Daniel with as much coldness as I dared.

'One piece of business, Mark – I know you're busy with lots of things, but – '

'Carry on,' I said. We were on the landing outside my flat. Inside, the lounge was strewn with every imaginable accessory for the sermon. Daniel had to be kept out.

'Shall I come in?'

'Could we talk out here?' I said. 'I'm just a bit sensitive about my private space.'

His look verged on anger. 'Fine. We'll talk out here, where it's chilly. I just wanted to show you this again – '

Putting a hand inside his jacket, Daniel Ogumbaye whipped out a copy of the hated draft advertisement and held it in the air in front of me, top and bottom edges taut.

'Remember this, Mark? Morag and I just thought – '

'I remember.' I was grim. 'What do you want me to do?'

'We must just – obviously we have to – get a formal word from you to publish this, since you're currently in Douglas's position. That's just the way the Church of England works.'

I felt blood climb to my face.

'I won't give the approval just yet, if that's all right.'

If Daniel was stunned, he showed only a tenth of his reaction. But ten per cent was enough. Narrowing his eyes, he said: 'You won't give your permission?'

'I don't think I want to give it just yet.'

No. After reflection, I simply did not want the advertisement published. Not before the sermon, not after it, not ever. And I was in a position to say so. Sunday would mark a point in English church history. The moment I climbed down from the pulpit, unsackable, Daniel, Morag, Francis Bottom, and anyone else in the plot to oust me would realise their error. My refusal now would spare their blushes later.

'You don't want it published?'

'Not yet – no, I don't. No.'

'When?' Daniel asked, a rare tremor in his voice. 'I mean, you've stalled and stalled – you said you were going to think about the wording for a couple of weeks – and then, when you didn't come back on it and we pressed you, you made some crazy complaint about a "disguised subjunctive" in it, and told us it had to be taken out – and now you're saying, what, you're going to try to stop us releasing it at all?'

'I think you may want me to. I can't say any more.'

He ignored the comment, chopping the air with a hand.

'Well – look, Mark, to be quite blunt – there really is nothing to stop us publishing this thing, whether or not you agree. If you really want to get theoretical and legal about it, there's got to be at least two votes – two votes – on the PCC to stop it going ahead, including yours. And with respect, having talked to the PCC members – well, there's not much point in the two of us falling out over something that's going to happen anyway. Definitely.'

'Two votes?'

'Two votes,' Daniel repeated.

'Wait a second,' I said.

I turned on the ball of a foot, and half-opened the door of my flat. Hugging the edge of it, I walked in.

After a moment searching, I found the object and grabbed it off a shelf. Hugging the flat door again, I confronted Daniel on the landing: the pot cupped in a raised hand.

'As you well know, this cactus is technically a member of the PCC. It was on Douglas's windowsill downstairs, and I now have it. I understand it was put up for election as a joke, under the name of Andrew Prickles. Vanessa's youth group did it. So it's technically in the Parochial Council.'

I revolved the plant-pot in the air, and both of our gazes locked on the cactus as it moved.

'This votes for me. It is now in my possession, so it votes for me. That's two votes. You and Morag can't place the advertisement, Daniel.'

We stared at each other for a few moments, with expressions of the most concentrated seriousness conceivable. The mouth of my colleague was so tense that his lips had thinned almost to nothing. My lower lip was vibrating.

'Don't do this, Mark. You don't know what you're doing.'

I replied: 'I do. Trust me. I genuinely do.'

Twisting unnaturally where he stood, he turned his back on me and left . . . jogging down the staircase.

I waited until I was sure Daniel had gone – and was out of earshot – and then shouted after him: 'You're fired!'

The words echoed down the concrete stairs.

Trembling, closing the flat door behind me, I read the note from Mrs Jivvard.

> Mr Empringham – I was sorry to hear you decided to involve yourself in what was strictly private,

it read. It was written in pencil, on a smallish sheet.

> I may not be the best-bred of women, as I am often acutely aware, but I do understand the meaning of privacy. A church is surely *not* the place for issues of morals, ethics, etc., to be aired like this – is it?
>
> I am writing to let you know that my husband and I shall require no further help from yourself. I understand that at your instigation he gave you a story that I 'confessed' to an 'affair' with a 'member' of church 'staff'. My husband knows the name of this person now and is perfectly satisfied there was no such affair, there was a friendship and nothing more. It was all said in a rash moment, and of no concern to you.
>
> I am also deeply upset at your suggestions to my husband to open my diary and to generally 'pump' him for information.
>
> I am extremely upset that you have now introduced this element of moral intrusion into what used to be a great institution here in North London. Believe me, despite yourself, my husband and I do not intend to stop coming to Saint Peter's.
>
> M.S.J.

•

The letter gave me a thick headache.

Sleeping lightly that night, I dreamed again of stealing the painting from the west side wall; of being chased from the church, and then staying out in the cold with it.

But this time I made sure I carried the picture into a back alley in the dream. And, starting a small fire there with old newspapers, I reduced the face to a pile of ashes.

– 29 –

The thick headache came and went in waves, and was still coming and going in waves on Thursday.

Three days to go.

Shopping for fruit and vegetables, fumbling among a stack of leeks, I was swept, momentarily, with a terrible coldness. Distracted, I hugged my black jacket.

But the coldness was within me. The spring sun and wool jacket proved it. It felt as if the Mark Empringham at the heart of my being had done a bunk, and now what I feared had come about: I was nothing but stone ... stone on a trolley ... an office building caving inwards, exterior intact. My soul had shrunk to a pin-head. Surely, the only way to resurrect it would be to climb those pulpit steps, and shout the truth over the lectern: *lost*.

It was the last doubt I could afford to feel before the sermon. For reassurance, I visualised the final script lying in the flat. All the videos were cleared away. I knew every frame by heart. The commentaries were stacked, waist high, with card fins poking out between plundered pages.

I guessed all truly great ventures were struck by moments of doubt – perhaps, as in my case, outside a grocery.

The doubt had fully surrendered by the time I arrived at a hospice the vicar of Saint Peter's was required to visit promptly every Thursday, bang on two o'clock. I was welcomed by the middle-aged Scottish matron, Rosamond Lanes.

If only she knew the breadth and deadly sharpness of the

sword hanging over my head, I reflected, as we shook hands.

'Good afternoon, Reverend.'

If only she knew that my name is about to take its seat in the cockpit of Anglican history.

'Would you like some tea, Reverend Empringham?'

If only she knew that in seventy-two hours, I will be in the arms of the most beautiful woman in the world.

'Shall we pray, Reverend, while the tea is made?'

If only she knew that by Sunday night, there will never be a whining call for me to pray again. I will be above it.

We took seats in the front room. A young man grinned at us, rose from his armchair, and excused himself.

Miss Lanes began her prayers, and I cringed internally: desperately, vacantly, trying to formulate my own.

'We pray for Des, who we've just seen leave this room, in his struggle with a brain illness.' Miss Lanes leaned forward at a slightly more intense angle. 'I pray for the cooks. And we thank you, God, that you took Myrna to her home last week without pain at the end. I thank you for her faith in you, which shone through her. I thank you for the way it reflected on the others here. I pray many of them will find you, and I pray for the work of Reverend Empringham as he talks to them. I thank you for your glorious love – and the incredible salvation you have given to those of us who believe, through your son, Jesus Christ, whose sacrifice on the cross was enough to cover all our sins, now and for ever.'

Miss Lanes moved slightly in her chair. 'Amen.'

I repeated: 'Amen.'

She was still bowed, clearly expecting me to continue.

I cleared my throat.

'God – ' I began.

I cleared my throat again. 'Er – God – '

I breathed in.

'I – ah – I thank you for chips.'

I paused.

'Amen.'

There was a further pause, and then Miss Lanes repeated the closing word in her Scottish accent.

'Amen.'

If she had any feelings about the briefness of the prayer, which was inspired by the lunch I had eaten an hour earlier, the matron did not show them as we got to our feet.

We were about to begin the customary tour, when one of the hospice staff rushed into the room.

Two words in her first sentence made my jaw drop.

'Mr – oh, sorry, Reverend – ah – Empringham – I beg your pardon, I've just – Gillian Mitchell – I didn't – '

'Calm down, Susan,' Miss Lanes said, firmly.

'Beg your pardon, Miss Lanes. There's a call for you, Reverend. A Gillian Mitchell. I'm sorry – I didn't know you were here.'

I was aghast.

In seconds, I was at the phone.

'Mark, I'm sorry to call you there – I rang the church, and they gave me the number. I just wanted to catch you.'

'That's fine,' I said. 'How are you?'

'I'm well. We – um – haven't really – well, we haven't seen much of each other, except just saying hello – '

'It's a shame.'

She seemed to pull herself up short.

'Right. Well, I was just ringing because I felt I had to say I – I – feel pretty bad about giving back that thing.'

'The carving?'

'Yes – the carving.'

'Don't worry about that. The inscription was uneven.'

My Gillian's voice was full of her wonderful Irish, as she insisted the object was beautiful – 'but just not the sort of thing that should pass between the two of us.'

'I think I knew, really,' I said.

'I still feel bad about it. I want to apologise.'

'Well – I took a close look at it before I threw it away, and I decided it wasn't up to much anyway.'

'You threw it away? You didn't, Mark.'

'I didn't think anyone would like it as much as you.'

The line went quiet for a full twenty seconds.

I was next to speak. 'Are you still coming on Sunday?'

'Sunday? What's that?'

My hands went cold. Everything went cold.

She's forgotten.

'I'm preaching.'

For a second, the whole of history and the whole of the future was balanced on the edge of a one-pence piece.

'Can't you come?' I asked. The desperation was tangible.

'I'm just looking at my diary,' she said.

A distant page flicked.

'I'm – yes, I'm coming anyway,' she said. 'It's a guest service that evening, isn't it? The choir always sings at them.'

'Thank you for ringing,' I said.

She dallied.

'I was really upset about the carving – especially since I just shoved it there against the wall.'

But my thoughts had moved from the carving.

'Last time we spoke properly – you said you were seeing someone, Gillian. Romantically.'

She sighed. 'I said I was because I was, that's why.'

'Are you still?'

'Mark – I thought when I called, now, you know – I thought we'd gone far enough for it not to matter as –'

'It will always matter.'

'Well – okay – I'm not with him any more – but I don't want to feel, every time I see you, you know, I have to –'

'Sorry.'

' – to answer some sort of Spanish Suspicion.'

'Spanish Inquisition, Gilly. What happened to him?'

'He just – he wasn't right. He didn't really believe in Christ, if you want the honest answer. He never spoke about it at all. He only went to church about once a month.'

'I go every Sunday – twice, sometimes.'

'Mark – '

And there we left it. The torrent of adrenalin I experienced as the impact of the conversation sank in unleashed a surge of energy that took me all round the hospice, through every private room, past every patient, without stopping. Leaving the building, the sharp spring air was like glorious confirmation that everything I wanted would soon be mine. The headache was gone.

On the way to the Datsun, parked on a corner, the line of a familiar song piped around my head . . .

I'm getting married in the morning.

I unlocked the door and threw my scarf on to the passenger seat. The car started in one, with a rattle and a roar.

The course between here and now and there and then, from hospice drive to pulpit steps, was now free of obstacles. I had the sermon: I knew what I had to do with it.

I am the captain of my soul.

The Datsun wound slowly into a one-way system north-east of the church. It came to a halt at a set of three red traffic lights, suspended where the road widened.

In the twinkle of an eye, at the sound of the trumpet, we shall all be changed.

The lights went green.

Three Days Later

– 30 –

'The sermon tonight comes from Hebrews, chapter eleven. Please, if you will, turn to that chapter in your Bibles.'

I shifted an inch on the reinforced pulpit floor.

Earlier in the day, at my request, Kennett had dragged the pulpit to the centre of the stage.

Now a line of staff sat on the bench at the edge of it.

In the corner of my right eye, I could see them.

Daniel.

Vanessa – looking composed, for once.

Grunt.

Jimmy Lyle, a visiting vicar from Cumbria.

His curate, Simon Sckuelph, also visiting.

BBF.

Margaret Millstrom, Associate Director of Pastoring.

Jane Bull.

I glanced over at them.

A shiver went up my leg. Then down again.

In front of the pulpit, worshippers were packed together as closely as I had ever seen them packed. A fault in the closed-circuit relay system, which was causing it to pick up bursts of children's television, had prevented the tea room being used as an overspill area. So latecomers and their guests had overflowed back into the main separate body of the church.

Overflowed into the tiered benches on the balconies, into the wings.

On to scores of extra plastic chairs.

Here and there, a few even sat on the windowsills.

And now –

Now, as one, they turned crinkling New Testament pages.

And what are you thinking now, Daniel? Do you like it? Do you like the choice, Morag? Hebrews eleven? You weren't expecting it, were you? The last curate's exit line!

I adjusted my script on the lectern.

The choir were amassed behind me: a squadron.

My Gillian was dead-centre. Right behind me.

My darling love, I love you.

I had seen already how she looked, as beautiful as she had ever looked. Black skirt, white shirt, a turquoise ribbon tied humbly in her hair, lips puffed, legs crossed firmly in grey stockings. How I loved her.

At no point in the service so far had she looked over at me on the staff bench – but then I had never expected her to.

Now she must be looking, though. Where else is there to look? Only straight ahead. At me.

Halfway down the left-hand balcony, Ben and Mandy Jivvard were clearly visible.

Morag was twenty seats back, left of the pulpit.

Vicki had not let me down. She was a row behind Morag.

The man I had seen flat out in front of the altar was now making a good job of sitting upright in an aisle seat.

I picked his face out among hundreds.

Frenetically conducted by Francis Bottom, Richard Burts had been strumming his guitar with four or five musicians.

Now they sat attentive, instruments on legs.

They are looking at me.

Right in the front row were Stewart and Ducky. They had ignored even the heaviest hints about not coming. So the last thing I wanted was what I now had: Stewart in the front row, beaming up at me as if we had a private joke in common.

This is much more important than you, Stew, I thought.

Later, looking back, I could remember every detail of that first moment.

I remembered the dead hush.

I remembered my eye catching Vicki, leaning forward.

I remembered the hundreds of faces bent upwards and downwards at me; many regulars, many guests.

I remembered a sudden throaty cough from a side seat.

I remembered my first movement: a careful flowering of the palm and fingers, borrowed from Steve Grimney.

And, above all, I remembered the tiny, anonymous snigger that greeted it . . . a snigger that should have been a warning.

It was harder to remember what happened next.

Certainly, after announcing the text, I read from it.

And certainly, not far in, I executed a Walsh Shout.

Later I remembered becoming aware of a peculiarly stony quality to a silence during one of my carefully timed pauses.

And how, sighting down the line of a finger for a Theoman-Timm Treble-jab, my eyes fell on a man and woman doing something with their coats.

Nor was it hard to remember strangely cold expressions when, as Dug Krugenheit had, I climbed out of the pulpit and waved my Bible from the floor of the jet-black stage; or a cackling laugh that came, from who-knows-where, at a moment when I had expected to hear wails of repentance . . .

But although I remembered going from the beginning to the end of my script, I could not remember the middle.

And although there were extensive head and leg movements in there, for sure, and Greek dotted about for authority, and arms thrown wide at least twice, and single sentences in the style of television news . . .

'I once fell down. On some stairs. But hell, ladies and gentlemen, is further down than any stairs. Do not look down! Look at Hebrews. It tells us: "Enoch was taken from this life, so that he could not experience death." Be sure –'

The Akamuturo Pogo –

'Be sure that you will not fall down! Will you save your life by belief? Please!'

. . . I remembered acute, strained silences.

I remembered restlessness on the balconies, as though a huge, private joke was going on in complete silence.

And after twenty-five minutes, I realised.

The truth came on me like a small wasp, evaded the hand flung out to swat it, and stung like a killer bee.

It was obvious.

I had made of myself the biggest fool any man had made of himself: the biggest fool ever made of anyone.

I have become the biggest fool in the country, in the biggest church in the country.

After weeks of writing and practising; of longing to crown myself a King, one yard from my Queen . . . it had taken a half-hour of reality for everything to collapse.

I had shouted; they had laughed. A man with an eyepatch just kept grinning.

I was so sure of it. So sure of what would happen.

Up there, baffled, I snatched at the thought.

How big a fool have I become?

I measured my foolishness against the Eiffel Tower and Mars; against the vast front of Marple & Schwartz.

I measured it beside Texas.

But there was no comparison.

Sizing it under the vast, sloping roof, I realised it could not even be sheltered by vast, sloping roofs.

I was so sure of it all.

But I had been wrong. And, approaching the end of the sermon, I knew it. It was the worst place for the realisation to come, for it came at the precise moment I had planned to escalate my delivery to mountain-heights at which no man or woman among the crowded thousand in front of me would be able to resist the call typed at the top of the last page of script.

'Come up, now, everyone. Come up to the front.'

I read it like a robot, hearing it leave the pulpit as the thick wires and big speakers sent it running off walls, off heads, under seats, around handbags; along the centre of the ceiling, up balconies, past doors, down pillars . . .

'Every one of you. Come up, if this is on your heart.'

I swallowed.

'Come on.'

Am I whining?

No one was moving. I read on.

'Don't worry about your coats. They won't be taken. Just think about the need to repent, all of you – '

I paused, unable to believe what I had written next.

' – whether your sin be fare-dodging on trains – or arrogance in a post of leadership – or gluttony with puddings and cakes – whatever it is, you need to clear it off your soul, and you need to do it now. Tomorrow may be too late. Come up, all of you. Think of faith, and Enoch. Come up.'

Is it shock? Is that what's written on those hundreds of faces below me? Shock?

I began to shake in the pulpit. I wished the floor would open up for me, as it had once done for Douglas, an aeon ago.

Not one single, solitary person is moving a muscle.

Where there had been rustling, there was now silence.

People were frozen in their seats.

Where there had been craning necks, there were now bowing heads. Where Vicki's hand had covered a cheek, it now covered the whole of her thin face. And the face was angled down, in despair.

I did not dare look at Stewart and Ducky.

To fill time, I pulled a handkerchief from my pocket.

'Do excuse me.'

I put it to my nose, and blew it into the tense silence.

The blow sounded like a foghorn.

'I beg your pardon,' I said.

Flailing, I read from lines at the foot of the page: lines meant for hundreds of tearful worshippers moving towards the front – moving, as Gillian was to have been moved at last in her heart for me . . .

'Just come up slowly,' I read, vacantly. 'Come up to the microphone we've put at the front here, below the pulpit. It is turned on, and you can speak into it. Say a small prayer, if you like. Don't worry if you feel the need to cry. You may want to ignore the microphone. That's it. Come up in an orderly way. No scrum, no pushing.'

I looked up from the script, and over the lectern.

Everyone was seated.

And then something happened.

There was a rustle on the staff bench.

Carefully, so that I did not catch the eye of Daniel, or Vanessa, or BBF, or anyone else on it . . . I looked over.

Pale faced, Grunt was rising to his feet.

He adjusted his jacket, and shot his cuffs.

I glanced forward again, not sure what to do.

But the rows and rows of worshippers were not looking at me now. Their heads, too, had turned towards the staff bench.

Grunt was walking towards the centre of the stage.

Walking towards me.

I wondered for a moment whether Gregory Runting, joint lay assistant, was going to try to physically pull his vicar out of the pulpit. I tightened my grip on a strut.

But he veered. He veered off the stage. He stepped off the edge. And it was instantly obvious where he was going.

It was as though each parishioner and every guest in the church had signed an agreement not to breathe.

Even the faint sound of traffic on the highway outside seemed eliminated as Grunt reached the front of the church.

Slap bang in front of the entire congregation.

Slap bang in front of me.

Right there at the end of the centre aisle, directly below me, Gregory Runting raised his right hand and laid it across the top of the microphone.

'I want to confess,' he began.

My mind scrambled thoughts like eggs. Suddenly, images came together in jigsaw form – the door handle of Morag's office, as she had spoken inside it: 'I think something's very wrong with him' . . . the disturbed behaviour of the lay assistant . . . the accusations shot randomly by Ben Jivvard . . .

One second too late, the jigsaw fell into place.

'I want to confess adulterous behaviour. It is time for me to do so. I will not name anyone, but I have been guilty of behaving in a disgraceful, sexual – '

I stood, helpless, in the pulpit.

What can I do?

' – sleeping with a woman, someone who is married – '

I could do the only thing that could be done – speak across Grunt, stop him . . .

'Thank you, Gregory,' I said, voice as loud as possible without making it sound like panic; but Grunt went on, and so I had to go on, too – 'Gregory, thank you – thank you – and I – I also want to confess,' I said, grabbing everything that jumped up in my mind and throwing it out of my mouth like compost – 'I think I should – I should also confess that while I was – '

Grunt was still going . . .

' – that while I was in my last job, as a curate in the West Midlands – '

I was raising my voice to cancel his –

' – in my last job, at a church in a village called Straithe, I was convicted – '

Keep going, keep going, keep going –

' – convicted of not having a television licence – which makes me, too, a criminal in a sense, and so it's for everyone here to search themselves, to find – '

Grunt was . . . no, Grunt had stopped.

' – to find – '

Grunt had stopped.

Now he was looking over his shoulder, up at me.

Everyone was looking at me.

I glanced around.

From the staff bench, I heard Daniel hiss: 'Francis! Francis! Last hymn! Last hymn!'

And then Francis must have waved a baton or a hand, for the musicians started playing . . . just at the moment that I, for whatever good reason, said: 'Let us bow our heads, and pray where we sit – '

But in ones and twos, and then dozens and scores, the members of the congregation rose to their feet . . . not to pray, but to sing . . . defying the leader of their church . . .

And I was aware of something happening halfway down the left-hand balcony – yes, roughly where Ben and Mandy Jivvard had been sitting – no, exactly where they were sitting, in fact – they had started screaming at each other. For a few seconds the sound of the screaming competed with the sound of the congregation's ragged and distracted singing of the opening lines –

> Great is your faithfulness
> Oh God my Father
> You have fulfilled
> All your promise to me
> You never fail
> And your love is unchanging
> All you have been
> You for ever will be
>
> Pardon for sin
> And a peace everlasting
> Your loving presence
> To cheer and to guide
> Strength for today
> And –

Shaking, I dithered on the pulpit.

I did not know the words to the hymn.

I could not go back to the staff bench.

I could not stay in the pulpit. I had no hymnbook.

But to leave the pulpit, I would have to turn my back on the congregation. I could not do that: I would see Gillian.

Fortunately, it was customary for the vicar to walk down the west side aisle during the last line of the final hymn.

How many verses does this song have?

It did not matter.

Departing from custom, I descended the steps of the pulpit ladder-style – facing the worshippers, not the choir.

The last object I caught sight of, before clamping my gaze firmly on the carpet underfoot, was hanging on the refurbished west wall.

The painting of Jesus Christ.

As I walked the length of the aisle, eyes down, I heard singing stop either side of me. My acting parishioners, I presumed, were turning from their songbooks to stare.

I did not look up as someone pulled open the white door at the back of the main body of the church, letting me into the domed lobby . . .

Nor did I stay in the lobby to shake hands as the last hymn ended, or raise my eyes as I walked through the Coppers into a thick mist that had gathered outside . . . heading for the outside door to the concrete staircase that lead to my flat . . .

To my flat, where I now had an appointment with a pair of brown suitcases.

– 31 –

My senses leapt to life.

The hardman, the stone, the trolley –

All bust to bits.

It was as though, after months of frostbite, every cubic inch of bone and soul in me retrieved feeling: and suddenly.

In the mist outside the church, I smarted with agony and shame. A flight of stairs later, yanking suitcases from a shelf, I wanted to cry out.

I am destroyed. I have destroyed myself.

I moved clothes and belongings, cast a swift, wry glance over a third letter from Walt Lee Tubbs, and gingerly picked up the Bible from a low table near the television. Feeling unworthy of contact with the book, I put it down again.

That was one thing that would not be coming with me.

The lower floors were silent.

Were Daniel and Morag standing at the exit of the church, formally apologising for the most mammoth disgrace of a sermon their church walls had ever encompassed?

Telling the stricken faces, perhaps, that they had always thought something was amiss with me; that I had never really got the point of any of it, had kept going on about accountancy? Saying that the similarities between Mark Empringham and the last curate should have been spotted earlier – and we suppose it was partly our fault, of course, but then he did get so very argumentative towards the end . . . and it just got so difficult to bring things up with him . . . and then he did something to the missionary budget . . .

What else are they saying down there?

' – and frankly, he was taken on by accident – '

Strangely, the thoughts did not prompt malice. All of my anger pointed at me, like spears in a circle. They had been unlucky, not evil; I had been evil.

And now, like the last curate, I am destroyed.

At that moment, there was a knock at the door.

A double-knock.

I jumped. It was a sudden jump. There was rather more of Mark Empringham to it than the jumps in the pulpit.

Here they come. To kick me out. But at least they'll see the suitcases and clothes, and know I'm going anyway.

'Come in,' I sighed. 'I expect you have a key.'

The door opened slowly, with a creak.

My visitor was –

My visitor was Gillian Mitchell.

She walked in carefully, and pushed the door shut.

'Hello, Gillian.'

The words were paper thin. I was instantly numbed. *Is this a mirage? A holograph?* As if in support of the theory, the flawless image in the lounge did not reply.

'All well?' I asked, stupidly, through blank shock.

The reply came slowly, in Araldite Irish.

'Not too good, no.'

Gillian stood gravely in the centre of the room. There was a darkness around her eyes. Something tiny twitched in her forehead, once.

A vest was dangling from my right hand.

Hearing a voice as grave as I had ever used, I asked: 'How bad was it? How bad was it, really?'

Instead of answering, my Scarlet Lipstick began to cry.

I watched as her face folded, eyes spilling full tears across her round, light cheeks . . .

One tear stumbling on a puffed-up red lip . . .

Tears flowing past knuckles raised to stem them . . .

And then Gillian moved towards me as I stood there,

motionless, vest in hand, and put her arms around me, sobbing violently. Her chest heaved against my front.

'There are so many angry people down there.'

A profound grief washed through me. I dropped the vest, raised my arms, and put them around her, gently.

The lucky right side of my jaw moved in Gillian's hair. Buried in my cheek, the top of her head dislodged my glasses.

I looked past her, touched by an infinite sadness.

'So was it that bad?' I said, quietly.

'It was worse.' She was sobbing.

'I'm sorry, Gillian. I let you down.'

After a minute, the crying stopped. She pulled back.

'I thought I was doing it for you,' I said.

My vision was cut by the rims of the crooked glasses.

Wordlessly, staring down, she shook her head.

'I'm sorry, Gillian. I'm completely unworthy – of – '

Unworthy. The words petered into nothing.

She cut in: 'I realised while you were up there – I knew what the point was of what you said at the party.'

'The party?'

'At New Year.'

'Yes. That was true. I regretted saying it.'

'How on earth did you manage to go on for so long here?'

'I don't really know. By not preaching, I suppose.'

I looked out into the mist, towards Marple & Schwartz.

'You don't believe in God at all, do you, Mark?'

I bit my lip for a second.

'No.'

After a pause, I added: 'I don't even know if I believe the sun will come up over that building tomorrow.'

Something about the sentence caught Gillian full on.

I saw her eyes brim with tears again, her lips trembling.

'Gilly – why are you here?'

'I asked you that, once.'

'I remember,' I said. 'At your home. In the snow.'

'And you never came back.'

'I wasn't invited back, Gillian. I wanted to, so much.'
'I scared you off.'
'I scared myself off.'
'I meant to.'
A tear made a line down her cheek. 'I don't really know why I'm here, Mark, if that's what you're asking.'
'Nothing can save me, Gillian.'
She misunderstood.
'Of course He can. No one is out of God's – '
'I didn't really mean that,' I interrupted. 'I was talking about my job here. That's gone.'
'Is it? I suppose so. But – '
'Don't say it doesn't matter, Gillian. I could have been an accountant if it wasn't for a couple of bad interviewers. I did this instead – this – and now this has gone – '
I gestured at our surroundings. 'There's nothing left.'
'Your glasses are wonky,' she said.
There was silence as I adjusted them.
There is no point in continuing this conversation.
Then, in a flash, an image of the man flat out in front of the altar came to me –
Unworthy
– and, not rehearsing the sentence before it came from my mouth, I blurted out a truth that had lodged thoughtlessly in me, like a strawberry seed between wisdom teeth.
'I would do anything to get hold of Jesus Christ.'
Gillian narrowed her dark eyes.
'Do you mean that?'
I said: 'I don't know what I mean. If only – ' I wheeled half-round, pointing at the telephone – 'If only I could ring him on that. I could ask him about all this chaos.'
'He could save you, Mark.'
'I've gone too far for that. That television licence thing – the local papers got hold of it. I never should have said it today. I'd put it behind me. I'm past saving.'
'You know, I spoke to Grunt – to Gregory – before tonight,' Gillian said. 'He said the same thing.'

Speaking quickly, as though it hardly mattered now, she described their meeting on the staircase.

Aghast, I said: 'He could have been counselled by me.'

'He said he couldn't.'

Another dream died.

'It's such a mess. Not just me. Everything.'

'Forget the mess,' she said.

'I can't. Not while you're here. I'm not worthy of you. You're so – so pure, and so kind – you were so kind to me –'

'I wanted to help. I didn't know how.'

'Help?'

Something in me shuddered, and broke up.

'Please, Gilly, don't talk about help if it's just a lie. They're all coming to grab me – and everything's broken, Gilly, so don't just waffle – they're going to chuck me collar-first into the fog out there –'

I might have expected her to say something, but offence seemed to freeze into Gillian's features.

She took three short paces to the door, reached out for the handle and opened it, turning to me as she did.

'Goodbye, Mark.'

I was at her side in a fraction of a second.

'Gillian – forget what I said. Forget the love stuff, too. I need it. Help me. I want to get a hold of that – that man – Christ. Whoever he is.'

Her hand fell to her side. Free, the door swung an inch.

'You're kidding me.'

'I know I can't ring him. But for the first time, going down that aisle – I can't explain – the picture, I don't know if you've looked at it like me – for the first time, looking at it on the way out – the picture of Christ – I knew I'd been running away. Have you seen it?'

'Of course I have.'

'Yes, but you haven't noticed it like me. It's like it's been moving eyes, or something – prodding me, prodding,

prodding, popping up in my dreams, and meanwhile, here I am, chasing here and there with all this – this drivel –'

The smallest of small smiles flickered on Gillian's face.

'Gillian – I can't explain. I keep comparing myself to the last curate, and I deliberately took the sermon from one of his favourite passages, and I've been trying to find out about him – and it's like, I don't know, uncovering a cancer or something – like that guy is my soul, or all my wrongdoing totalled up in a till, and suddenly I realise what I'm doing, but it turns round and destroys me – and tonight – for the first time, tonight, I feel really ashamed. I want to be saved.'

She was looking at me.

'I wish I could understand you.'

I said: 'I want to be saved. I don't care if I have to leave the church tomorrow. What do I have to do?'

'What do you want to be saved from?' Gillian asked. 'From that lot in the tea room, and what you think they're going to do to you? Is that it? Saved from them?'

I drew breath. 'I want to be saved from – from me.'

'Do you actually know who Christ was? Do you know?'

'Jesus Christ? Probably not,' I said. 'Is he involved? I don't even know his middle name. He was a nice chap. That's all I know. That's all the information I've been given.'

And then we heard footsteps coming up the stairs.

– 32 –

We sprinted out of the flat and up the staircase.

The steps arrived on the landing below. There was a loud knock, and then Jane Bull's throaty voice, calling down: 'No. I thought so. He's not here.'

Stock still, Gillian and I glanced at each other.

'I just hope BBF doesn't come up,' I breathed.

'Or come out,' Gillian whispered, gesturing at the Stipendiary Parson's door.

'Are you sure?' Someone was shouting up the stairs.

'His door's open. There's no one in there,' Jane called.

'I can't bear this – I can't bear it.' That was Gillian.

'I know,' I whispered. 'It's been like this the whole time I've been here. Completely ludicrous.'

Other voices echoed, up and down the staircase. I recognised one of them: Stewart Weeks.

But he did not call up again.

Then Jane Bull could be heard bounding off . . .

And Gillian and I clattered down the staircase in a whoosh of thoughts and Sunday clothes, saying nothing, racing down the dark passageway behind the tea room, me blocking my ears to the outraged hubbub inside it, rushing up the spiral stairs over the kitchens . . .

We reached the student alcove and dashed in. It was empty. A pile of cushions was lit orange by a streetlamp in the mist outside. Slowly, I closed the door.

'Listen, Mark. He wasn't just a nice chap.'

Gillian caught her breath.

'I don't know what to tell you,' she said, finally.

'I thought this was going to be easy. Just tell me what I have to do.'

She breathed in. 'Obey God.'
'By doing what?'
Gillian paused. 'It's more than that – I would – '
'I know about Christ, I know about his teachings – be nice to people, don't kill anyone, don't watch blue films – '
Gillian cut in. 'Is a teacher all you think he was?'
'The best man on the planet, ever. Am I getting warmer?'
'Colder.'
'Colder?'
'You're as cold as Mars, Mark. Because if all he did – '
Our voices crossed each other, both raised.
'Look, Gillian, this is urgent. You know I'm a preacher myself. I've done all of this from the pulpit. So, okay, if necessary, I'll believe he rose from the cross as well – '
'Rose from the dead – '
'Yes, okay – wherever it was – I'll believe that too, if I have to – he died on the cross, rose from the dead – '
'Right, so – '
'From the tomb – '
'Yes – '
'But – hold on – where does that get me?'
'What do you mean?'
'Where am I now that I wasn't ten minutes ago?'
Gillian frowned. 'I don't know. There's more to it.'
'Am I saved yet?'
'Not if you have to ask that.'
'I want it, Gillian. Show me it. Just show me. Help me.'
'Can you believe that Christ is alive?'
'Of course. Why not? I'll start now. He's alive.'
I stared at her, intently, waiting for what came next.
'If all that matters is what you believe, Gilly – '
'No – Mark – you've got to change, too.'
'Change?'
'Your behaviour.'
'But – I don't mug old women – all right, the television

licence, yes – but everything was out of joint then –'
'Come on, Mark, you've preached a dozen sermons on –'
'The licence was an idiotic lapse, a stupid –'
'It's nothing to do with the licence!'
'I'm trying, I'm trying,' I said. 'I'm trying to see what you mean. And there isn't that much time.'
Firmly, Gillian said: 'We're not getting anywhere.'
'Look,' I began, 'he was more than a nice chap. He rose again. Fine. And I'll change my behaviour – be kinder –'
'He's alive.'
'All right – he's alive as well,' I agreed.
'But it's more. It's more than just believing it, Mark.'
She breathed in, as though loading up.
'You've got to – you've got to know it.'
Looking at my shoes, I said: 'I want to know it.'
'Not it. Him. You've got to know him.'
I laughed. 'It's like asking a beggar for his last twenty quid. I can't pay.'
'You've said all this in your sermons, haven't you?'
'No, I haven't. I missed it out.'
Gillian looked as though she might walk out of the alcove. There would have been no words to stop her with if she had done. But then, rather than turning towards the closed door, she said: 'He is alive, you know. Christ.'
'I wish you could prove it.'
'It's true. Don't you understand, Mark? It's what you preached from tonight – it's Hebrews eleven. It's what you were going on about from the pulpit – faith. Faith, faith, faith. "Being sure of what you cannot see." It's like wind.'
'You can feel wind.'
'Electricity, then.'
I chewed on the inside of my mouth. 'You can feel that, too. In our flat, there used to be a toaster –'
'The disciples saw him, walking and talking.'
'I didn't see the disciples.'

'Don't make it harder than it is, Mark. He's here.'
'I know, and I know I need – '
'Don't cry!'
'I can't help it.'
'Please, Mark – come on – you're not alone – '
'I'm sorry. I don't have the faith, Gillian.'
'You need to pray.'
'I've ruined everything.'
'Pray, then.'
'I can't pray – or at least, I haven't since – I don't know, ages ago, when I first arrived here – and I prayed for Vanessa, too. But it's like talking into a biscuit tin.'
'You can't tell that until you try properly.'
'This is the worst kind of evangelism,' I said. 'The kind where you make the person feel like waste paper.'
Her reply came in a flat tone. 'That's not true.'
'It's a bit harsh on waste paper, in my case,' I said.
'Do you know what salvation is?'
'I don't know. A fire escape. The ladder down the side of the church, two suitcases – a train ticket – no – '
Gillian was solemn. The deep darkness of her Irish hair made her face look angry. 'This is not the time for jokes.'
A crossbow bolt of a pang hit my heart.
We stood in silence. I stared at the carpet. The noise in the tea room rose through the rotten floorboards.
What are they saying down there?
'I don't want to leave it like this,' said Gillian.
'Nor do I.'
'The biscuit tin, Mark – of course it's like that. That's almost the point – it's like a dead telephone until you make that connection. And you make it by – by – '
'Don't say "by repenting" – '
' – by, yes, by repenting – repenting of – '
' – of my sins, yes, yes – that's exactly what I've been preaching! And not a word of it ever got through to me!'
After a while, Gillian said: 'Look, I was supposed to be

meeting Brinny downstairs. She'll be wondering where I am.'

'Leave me here, then,' I said. 'I need to think.'

'Why don't you pray?'

'Maybe I will.'

'Ask for forgiveness for your – for your sins.'

'I'll be here all night.'

'There wouldn't be anything wrong with that.'

Gillian left.

Alone, I turned to the window, and looked out.

'Help me, God.'

There was no answer. 'Help me. Forgive me, I beg you.'

But nothing seemed to change in that instant.

Coldly, I sank to my knees on the floor.

'Christ, please, help me.'

I squeezed my eyes shut.

'Please do something. I'm sorry about what I've done. Please, urgently, do something. Appear, or something.'

Silence.

'You're alive,' I said. 'I believe you're alive. So go on, help me. I'm sorry about everything.'

My watch ticked. That was all.

Opening my eyes, I whispered: 'What did I do wrong?'

There was no answer.

I leant forward, placed my palms on the carpet . . . and, eyes closed again, prayed: 'Please don't break your promises, God, wherever you are. Anything – whatever you want me to do – '

But nothing happened: nothing at all.

– 33 –

I saw no one for the rest of the night.

Locking the flat door, I spread clothes and books across the carpet.

I took ornaments off shelves, peeled a dog-eared postcard from the wall, and began putting everything into the suitcases.

Three people came up the concrete stairs, one at a time, as the evening went on. When their footsteps got within range, I switched off the flat light.

They knocked, each of them, several times.

I stood motionless in the darkness.

Richard Burts was the only one who spoke.

'Mark – are you in there? Have you gone to bed?'

No reply.

'Mark? Are you there? It's Richard. I've just come from my flat, through the fog. I was hoping to see you.'

He heard nothing inside the flat, and saw no strip of light at the foot of the door.

'Obviously not,' he muttered.

At eleven-thirty, I put on my pyjamas and yanked the straps tight shut on one of the cases.

In a pointless gesture, I tried to shove the Bible into the waste-paper bin. A pile of cartons and papers screwed into balls made the book stick out, menacingly.

So I walked to the bedroom with it in my hand, angling it left and right like an outsized fan, looking blankly ahead at the tired wallpaper over the bed.

Sitting up against the headboard, I opened the book, blithely.

> Now a man named Lazarus was sick. He was from Bethany, the village of Mary and her sister Martha. This Mary, whose brother Lazarus now was sick, was the same one who poured perfume on the Lord and wiped his feet with her hair. So the sisters sent word to Jesus, 'Lord, the one you love is sick.'
>
> When he heard this, Jesus said, 'This sickness will not end in death. No, it is for God's glory so that God's Son may be glorified through it.'

Changing position in the bed, I cleared my throat and skipped a page.

> Jesus said to her, 'Your brother will rise again.'
>
> Martha answered, 'I know he will rise again in the resurrection at the last day.'
>
> Jesus said to her, 'I am the resurrection and the life. He who believes in me will live, even though he dies; and whoever lives and believes in me will never die. Do you believe this?'

'I wanted to,' I told the printed page lying in my lap.

> When Jesus saw her weeping, and the Jews who had come along with her also weeping, he was deeply moved and troubled. 'Where have you laid him?' he asked.
>
> 'Come and see, Lord,' they replied.
>
> Jesus wept.

It was a quarter to twelve. I looked at the bedside clock:

when I left the church, it would have to come too. Lifting if off the table, I dropped it gently on to the floor.

> Jesus, once more deeply moved, came to the tomb. It was a cave with a stone laid across the entrance. 'Take away the stone,' he said.
>
> 'But Lord,' said Martha, the sister of the dead man, 'by this time there is a bad odour, for he has been there four days.'
>
> Then Jesus said, 'Did I not tell you that if you believed, you would see the glory of God?'

'No, you didn't,' I told the page. 'You never said anything like that to me at all.'

> So they took away the stone.

In the darkness of the dining room, the telephone rang.

I froze for a moment in bed, then swung my legs out from between the sheets, stood up, and walked out of the bedroom, grimacing.

'Hello?'

'It's Gillian.'

'Oh. Hi.' I could not identify my feelings.

'I'm sorry I deserted you earlier on.'

'That's okay.'

'I always seem to be apologising for things,' she said.

'Not at all.'

'What did you do?'

'Nothing. Prayed, I suppose.'

'You – oh, Mark, that's fantastic! You prayed! At long last! So you've done it, at last!'

'What? What have I done?'

'You've prayed, that's what you've done.'

'I can't even remember what I was praying for.'

'I'll tell you what it was, Mark. It was for – '

There was a swathe of crackling on the line. Someone else would have to oversee the repair of the switchboard.

At the telephone in her hallway, Gillian heard the voice break through the interference. 'Anyway, I'm resigning tomorrow. I'll probably go and live with my parents for a while.'

'No, don't resign.'

'I have to.'

'But what about what happened tonight?'

'Well, I don't think it's enough.'

'Enough for what? For your – salvation?'

'Enough to keep me here, I suppose I mean.'

'What are you doing at the moment?'

'Reading.'

'The Bible?' She was guessing.

'I suppose so – yes, I suppose so.'

'Which bit?'

'Oh, the bit about Lazarus,' I said, indifferently.

When we hung up, resolving nothing, Gillian opened her Bible at the same chapter, and read it from beginning to end.

> Then Jesus called in a loud voice,
> 'Lazarus, come out!'
> The dead man came out, his hands and feet wrapped with strips of linen, and a cloth around his face.
> Jesus said to them, 'Take off the grave clothes and let him go.'

By the time she came to the final lines, I was flat out in bed, mouth open, on the edge of sleep . . . sheets pulled up to my chin, book dumped next to the clock on the bedside rug.

Gillian wore a frown when she turned off her bedroom light.

Three Hours Later

– 34 –

I woke with a start.

Up on an elbow, I looked at the glowing dial that ought to have been there on the bedside table, but was not; and then, groping for the clock on the floor, raised its luminous face to my sleep-soaked one.

Three in the morning. The clock face said three.

Why did I wake like that?

I had no idea.

My last night in this bed.

The memories of the sermon, of Gillian, of Grunt, of Richard's voice on the stairs – they all came back, hard as fists. I turned my head, groggy in the pitch darkness, like a boxer slugged to the canvas. There was no sound, not even a stray car on the street. The room was as silent as a tomb.

I had woken as though shocked by something, but could remember no dream. A breeze was coming from the lounge.

I groaned. The sash window must have been left open.

Wobbly as a hospital patient, I climbed out of bed and shuffled from the room in the blackness.

At the lounge window, I separated the curtains an inch.

But the sash was locked tight.

I stood there for a full five minutes, a forearm on the exposed window frame for support, staring down at the floor.

Then, clearing my throat with a dry cough, I spoke into the silence.

'Is there someone in here?'

I noted the huskiness in my voice. A flash-frame of Ben Jivvard shot across my mind.

No reply.

'Elvis? Elvis Presley? Is that you? Hound Dog?'

There was a breeze, but there was no breeze. There was something warm in the room, something breathing, perhaps.

'Who is it?'

But there was nothing in the room. There was movement, but there was stillness. There was something and nothing.

I turned, just a few inches from the window frame, and threw the curtains apart.

My eyes bulged in their sockets.

'My – my – my –' I began, but no other word came. I shrank back from the window, eyes locked on the thing in the mist outside . . .

'My – my –'

There, hanging in mid-air, distant as if on a hill.

As clear as day, in the darkest fog of night . . .

A cross was suspended above the road outside, fixed in a bright aura, hanging in the night mist . . .

'My – my – my – God –'

I screwed up my eyes, peering at the image and the light around it. Was it moving now?

Moving towards me?

'God,' I murmured, 'God – forgive me –'

Instantly, I remembered the dream that had spun me into sudden consciousness.

Without warning, while attending a church raffle, I had been struck down critically ill beside the tombola.

Deathly pale and gasping, I was whisked over the heads of a staggered crowd.

I saw Vicki down there, and Stewart, and Douglas; Morag, Francis, Margaret Millstrom, Vanessa – all of them, all looking up, eyes popping as I flew over, whizzed over them in the blurred grey colours of dreams, sick as any man could be, flying on a huge stretcher, spluttering, choking out final breaths, white as a sheet . . .

And then I had taken the final breath.

It was a choking cough that became a lung-deep rasp.

A scrum of doctors had pulled out stethoscopes.

Heads shaking, they pocketed them again.

My socks and shoes were pulled off.

A grave opened, the stretcher tipped, and I was in it.

There was a delay.

And then, out of nowhere, there had been a yell.

I recognised the voice outside the tomb as the voice of a close friend . . .

'Come on!'

And I had risen from the slab; moved towards the great stone door that stood between me and my dear friend; had given it the kind of kick that would have converted rugby balls from the wrong end of a stadium; and next, moving back a yard, prepared to put my shoulder to it . . .

I raced towards the big tomb door, unable to wait a moment, shoulder down –

Smashed into the thing with a sepulchre-shaking crunch of stone on bone . . .

And had woken with a jump.

Now I bit my lip in the dark, replaying the vivid images. Frightened to look back at the cross, I looked back none the less. There it was still, framed in a square of light, hanging in the dark fog as another cross must have hung over that black hill, long ago . . .

I was definitely alone in the room; that was obvious. And yet I was definitely not alone.

There is someone in here with me.

Wondering if I had finally gone mad, I spoke into the darkness.

'I agree with everything you ever said.'

At that moment, something seemed to arrive inside my pyjamas. It might not have done, but it seemed to. It could have been jacket pocket warmers, or a crop sprayer, or shredded candy, or flapping racetrack tickets. It felt like all four, and more, and at the same time did not feel like anything other than what it was: a kind of radiant calm . . . a rinsing, sweetness, and the opposite of boredom.

I stood there, still as the night, listening in darkness to no sound at all. Concentrating.

Then I connected Lazarus and the dream, and was struck by the awesome glamour of the Crucifixion.

Two tears welled up. One in each eye.

Outside, the cross blurred in its box of light.

I breathed deeply, raising my head, and felt freedom stream into it above the hairline.

'Either I'm going off my rocker, or –'

Exhaling long and slow, I failed to complete the muttered sentence. I looked from window to carpet, from carpet to bedroom, and back to window; wanted the last curate to help, or even Kennett with his spanners . . . but they were suddenly less important than the drains under the church.

The only car of the deepest hour of night chose that moment to career past, down below, exhaust rattling.

And then I realised.

I was having a spiritual experience.

The Next Day

– 35 –

After trying for half the morning from the telephone beside the pine kitchenware shelves, Gillian finally got through to a human being at the church.

'This is Morag,' the telephone voice said.

'Oh – I don't think we've met, but I'm Gillian Mitch— '

'I know you from the choir,' Morag cut in. 'I've seen your name on the lists for weekends in Woburn. I didn't realise you were Scottish.'

Gillian did not attempt to correct her. 'I'm ringing from work,' she said, raising her voice to make herself heard above the noise of three Japanese men who were rapidly opening and then slamming the most expensive breadbins. 'I've been trying for ages. I've just been getting the machine.'

'The switchboard is fairly sophisticated,' Morag said, in a superior tone. 'When we have full PCC meetings, it automatically – '

Her voice was suddenly drowned out in a hiss that sounded like a steam train coming down the telephone line, followed by two whizzing sounds like fireworks.

Gillian frowned. 'Hello? Morag? Are you still there?'

There were noises, but no distinguishable words.

'Hello? Morag?'

'Yes – hello.'

'Ah. I can hear you again.'

'I could hear you all the time. It must have been something at your end.' Morag's voice, as always, was faintly remote. 'I was just saying – during important meetings, the answering machine comes on.'

'I was trying to get through to one of the staff.'

'Who?'

'Mark Empringham.'

There was a pause, and the line stayed silent for it.

'Mark is in the meeting too.'

'How long will he be in there?' Gillian asked.

'It's a long meeting,' Morag said. 'I've only just popped out. I need to go back in.'

'Can I ring at lunchtime?'

'Ring after two,' Morag said. 'If you're sure you want to speak to him.'

Gillian found it hard to concentrate that morning, seconded to the tills for a day. She served her customers, but struggled to look them in the eye. She made a mistake on the till and had to go through a roll of receipts to clear it up. Wrapping a block of wood with half a dozen razor-sharp kitchen blades in, she found herself thinking about the carving that had been made for her . . . and accidentally tipped the block so that a knife slipped out, embedding itself in the carpet beside a shopper's foot.

In the washrooms, she applied lipstick and then used fingers to straighten her hair.

'I love that colour,' a colleague said.

'What – the shirt?'

'Your lipstick.'

'Oh – that. My mother used to wear it. I used to like it, but I'm wondering if I might try something else. Seems to me I've always got this on.'

'Are you okay?'

'Not really,' Gillian said. 'Does it show?'

'You look a bit frazzled. I thought it might be the weather. It's getting muggy.'

'It's not the weather.'

'Can I do anything? What is it – Herbert?' Herbert was the manager of Gillian's section.

'For once, no.' She smiled weakly. 'Not Herbert.'

'Another man? Men trouble?'

'Well – yes, maybe so. In a way.'

'Say no more.'

'I don't think there's any more to say.'
'Why don't we have lunch together?'
'I can't. I've got to make a phone call.'
'Gillian – are you in love, or something?'
'I doubt it.'
'Summer's coming. You ought to be.'
At two, prompt, Gillian rang the church from a pizza restaurant and asked to be put through to Mark Empringham. To her relief, someone else was on the switchboard. To her surprise, she was put through to the flat without a murmur. The phone was picked up after two rings.

– 36 –

'Mark – what's happened? I'm on my lunch break.'

I replied dully, speaking into the telephone as if I was speaking across the counter of a bank. 'I've just come out of a four-hour meeting. They had half the PCC there – you know, the church's ruling body. Anyone who could take the time off work came. The others sent messages.'

'Messages? About what? Mark, what was the meeting for?'

'Can't you guess, Gillian? After last night?'

She searched for words at the other end of the line.

Then she said: 'It was about you.'

'Yes. I was formally sacked about two hours ago. If you'd like the technical description, Morag will know – it was something to do with gross ineptitude, unanimous votes of a quorate PCC, and making serious theological errors.'

In fact, the only member of staff who had come to my rescue, as I sat there in front of them all, had been BBF.

One after another, they had pointed out areas of the sermon at which they had taken offence.

'You were jumping around! You jumped off the pulpit!'

I sat there, listening.

'You said hell was "further down the stairs". What on earth did you mean?'

'I think I even heard you say that if you believed in something enough, it would start to exist! You said the Greek economy was an example!'

'You claimed the Psalms were written by Saul!'

'Oh, now –' And that was BBF, brimming with decency. A respectful silence fell on my accusers. 'I think all of these are probably easy mistakes to make – in what is, after all, an exegetic jungle.'

But their minds were made up. BBF, in any case, was not on the PCC. Note was made of the slashing of missionary funds, of large legal claims currently in process against the church after I had 'naïvely' admitted formal liability for damage to a school in Hove during a visit by youth groups, of repeated absences, the lacklustre preaching leading up to yesterday's disaster, vacant looks allegedly worn around the church, two pages of a faxed letter from 'a Mrs M. Jivvard' in which serious allegations of clerical malpractice were made. They even said BBF might have been caused to break down emotionally by my relentless commissioning of sermons – a charge he waved away, but without quite enough conviction.

There was a vote, something was written down, and then I was sacked. It was as simple as that. Then Daniel, silent for most of the meeting, argued that I should be allowed to offer my resignation formally. Around the table, there was a moment of nodding so spasmodic that for a second it appeared as though the PCC members were trying to do a Mexican Wave with their heads. I said: 'I'll offer it, then – freely,' and one or two faces jerked in my direction to check there had been no sarcasm in the words. But there was none, and they could tell by looking at me.

I had two weeks to leave, I was told.

It was possible to appeal to the Bishop of London, the Right Reverend Tristran Stuart (the name made me flinch); or to the highest court in the Church of England, the Arches . . . but they did not advise it. 'You can't win, Mark,' one said, leaning forward confidentially, with a tenderness that somehow underlined the gravity of the offences.

'Would you like to speak now? Is there anything you want to tell us?' The question came from the back of the room, from someone whose head was obscured by a plant.

I thought it over, and stood up.

'Only that you've conducted this quite fairly, and I'm sorry to be going.' I swallowed. 'It was – it was – um – a shame, what happened last night.'

'It was more than a shame,' someone muttered.

'I was ashamed,' I said, and caught Daniel's eye for an instant. He was staring with a forehead creased in something like puzzlement, a finger laid pensively across his lips.

After a moment, I added: 'Thank you for everything.'

I sat down again.

'That's all,' I said quietly, addressing the tabletop.

There was no point in asking whether they would give me back my old job as curate.

When it was over, I walked up the stairs to the flat.

My mind ought to have been in turmoil, but it was not. I tried counting up to forty, and the sequence was immaculate. Raising a hand to the knot in my tie, I discovered it straight and neat already.

I found myself thinking: *Surely, this is not how things ought to be?*

When I had finally climbed back into bed in the early hours of the morning, I slept peacefully. There were no more vivid images, no more dreams, so far as I could tell.

Later, on waking, I had searched my stomach for the panic and grief of the day before, expecting them to return – banging at brain and body, bailiffs at a debtor's door. But I seemed to have been invaded by an uninvited serenity.

I knew what it was, but did not want to know. The guess kept coming into my mind . . . and I kept sweeping it back, like stray hairs combed away without a mirror. My heart was testifying to something my head did not want evidence of, was not equipped for.

The call summoning me to the PCC meeting had come a minute after the alarm on the bedside clock, and I had rushed out, leaving bedsheets strewn everywhere.

Returning, I found the flat as I had left it: dim, curtains drawn, lights on.

I kicked a suitcase to the wall, sat on the edge of the bed and flicked through the newspaper delivered to my door.

Several lines of print on an inside page caught my eye.

> A senior London banker quit his desk after 'throwing a wobbly', colleagues have disclosed.
>
> They said the man smashed coffee flasks, hurled a computer at a secretary and broke a window on his way out of the key Financial Luring Department of fund managers Marple & Schwartz.
>
> Workmen were taping up the window at the weekend as a high-level internal inquiry began.
>
> It's not known what position the banker – said to be 'stressed' after a divorce – held. Last night one colleague called him 'very senior, quite unpopular, and now completely stuffed'. He was only prepared to identify the man as Matthew.
>
> The 'wobbly' came after a crash in Yen sheet issues, high-risk holdings the man is said to have bought in large numbers against the advice of external –

Putting down the newspaper, I raised myself from the bed and drew the curtains.

The mist had cleared. Monday morning lights were burning as brightly as they ever had across the front of Marple & Schwartz, and there – *Yes, there, among them . . .*

Two lengths of tape crossed on the window I had once seen Matthew moving in.

So that was it. They had left the light on, burning through the fog of the previous night.

A sacred cross, glowing on a misty, distant hill . . .

Had been no more than emergency masking tape, stuck on a cracked pane by workmen too lazy to switch off lights.

I felt the desire to meditate.

Am I mad? Have I gone stark, staring mad?

But suddenly thoughts of the PCC, of sackings and television licences – and even Emily – were as fleeting as snowflakes on the hot hob of an oven. I knelt on sheer inspiration, confessing my whole life a hideous act of treachery, and felt the hand of . . . well, it had to be God, or Christ . . . a real hand, anyway – no masking tape in sight – on my heart, in response . . . a touch in which I had never previously believed, had brushed off as Fruit and Nut whenever it had crossed my path, seen as nothing but a fifth-rate substitute for the warm aura of accountancy . . .

I prayed in uncut rushes, kneeling by the bed.

Then Richard Burts rang, wheezing commiserations.

'I'm incredibly sorry, Mark. I'm at work. I sent a note supporting you, but they put it down as an abstention.'

'I'm sad, too.' I could not tell him. What was there to tell that would not sound like fraud – a desperate, last-ditch attempt to avoid eviction from a cushy curate's flat?

'When are you going?'

'Tomorrow, or the day after.'

'I'm shocked,' he said. 'But then again – '

'I know, Richard. You don't have to remind me.' The service, the day before, now felt a light year away. 'I had a rather too – ah – complicated agenda last night, I think.'

'I suppose hearing about the Needle has upset you, too.'

'Who?'

'Oh.' Richard's voice rose a semiquaver in anguish at having to explain. 'Well – you know – that bloke who writes in one of the Anglican magazines. Reviewing the preachers.'

'Which magazine?'

'Um – the – I think it's called *Magevangelism* now.'

'What – the "Eye of the Needle" column? What about it?'

'Oh, dear. Well – it's probably not true, Mark, but someone said they recognised him in church last night.'

'At my sermon?'

'Um – yes. The – er – Needle.' He coughed.

'How easy is it to recognise him, though?'

'Apparently it's not that hard. He wears an eyepatch.'

My stomach flipped. In less than a fortnight, I would be publicly savaged.

Conscious of his gaffe, Richard added: 'Sally Halewood told me she enjoyed it, though. She said it was about time there was – I can't remember what she said – "more Hollywood" in the services, I think it was. She commented that – '

'Don't bother, Richard. Don't even try. Don't worry.'

'I wish you'd taken my advice, and just stayed curate.'

'You were right.'

'I didn't mean to bring it up. Sorry.'

'It doesn't matter. You've been a good mate, Richard.'

'Do you need anything?'

'Only two suitcases. And I have them already.'

In truth, I could have gone that afternoon. There was no one else to say goodbye to. No one, that is, bar one . . . whose telephone call from a pizza restaurant at exactly two o'clock put the formal, tragic seal on my period of employment at Saint Peter's church.

– 37 –

'So that's it, is it?' she asked.

Gillian was desperately trying to read the voice at the other end. 'You're not going to protest? Or appeal?'

'You know how bad it was. You were there, Gillian.'

She hesitated at the telephone, which was bolted to a panelled wall beside a line of customers.

'Can I do anything?'

'No.'

'Nothing?'

'Where are you?'

'At a payphone – in a pizza house,' she replied, and added: 'You sound so sad.'

'I just had a visit from Daniel and Morag.'

'Really?'

'That was sad. They brought me a present – a black washbag with some soap in.'

'What did they say?'

'They said they remembered me telling them at the beginning, when I went on a visit up north somewhere, that I didn't have a proper washbag. So they bought me one.'

'They just talked about the bag? That was all?'

'Well, Morag might have said something about the zip. But there wasn't anything else. That's the British for you.'

'The English, Mark.'

'Yes, the English. Not you.'

A spike-haired man began waving his bill angrily at the cashier, shouting out the names of different pizza toppings.

Distracted, Gillian asked, 'Can I come and see you?'
'Oh, Gilly – why? You can't stop it, you know.'
'I want to, that's why.'
'To stop it?'
'To come.'
'And I'd like you to. But I don't want you to be upset. The packing is done.'
'I don't mind if I am upset,' she said, realising instantaneously that she was unlocking the secret of her heart . . . just as a former acting vicar had opened up the secret of his, for her, on a snow-driven day months before: and she had brushed it aside, like paste pearls.
She fed another coin into the telephone.
'Gillian – ' the voice in the earpiece began – 'I just don't want you to get – to get drawn into it all. I want – '
'Mark,' she cut in. 'Something's changed. Something's happened with you. You told me you loved me, and now – '
The spike-haired man had still not been allowed to pay. Suddenly, he jumped on to the counter, yelling at the top of his voice. Three aproned waitresses appeared from nowhere to haul him down.
'I can't hear you, Gillian.'
'Someone's shouting his head off next to me.'
'Why don't we meet, then?'
'When?'
'Would it be all right – for you to come over here?'
'Just say when,' she said.
'Whenever.'
'I'll try and get out of work early.'
'But listen – please, not here. Not the flat, Gillian.'
'Where, then?'
'Do you know the burger bar down Clemence Road?'
'I'll find it.'
'On the corner of – um – Clemence Road and Hook Close. Just follow the smell and the sound of the hotplate.'
'I know where you mean.'

'Gillian – you know, you don't have to –'
'I do.'
She hung up the phone.
I glanced around the room, and my eyes found the Bible.

– 38 –

The painting looked very different, tilted and moving. Seeing it, I jarred to a halt. 'Where are you taking that?'

The overalled men holding it stopped too.

'Who's asking?' one said.

'I'm the – ah – I'm – the – '

But I was not at all sure what I was any more.

They looked impatient, squinting with the weight of the painting and the sunlight streaming in through the Coppers.

'Hurry up, mate.'

'I've been acting vicar,' I said briskly. 'It's just that – well, that picture's been on the west wall since – '

'To the rectory,' interrupted the man at the back.

'Oh.'

The slanted face in oils seemed dramatically altered.

Before, the picture had been all moving eyes and judgement. But now, scrutinising it for signs of the naked threat that had kept me skulking away for months, all I saw was a faded face in inappropriate yellows, held at an undignified tilt.

This was no icon, I reflected. *This is an eyesore.*

'Why the rectory?' I thought the flat once used by the Tredres had been let to a group of visiting Arab businessmen.

'New man there, I think,' said the workman at the back.

'A new man?'

'They asked us to move some stuff around.'

'Does he look – does he look Arabic, at all?'

The man at the front laughed. 'No one's asked us to

put a drilling station in, put it like that.'
'And I haven't seen any curved swords,' the other laughed.
I persisted: 'But someone's definitely moving in?'
The man at the back suddenly spluttered, 'Oh – er – this is – here's – ah – the man to ask,' flicking his head to indicate someone on the other side of the painting.
As they loped off, down towards the pavement, shuffling and groaning and adjusting the position of the picture of Christ with each new church step, I found myself with Daniel.
'I didn't see you there.'
'It's a big painting,' he said, in yet another cravat.
There was a pause as uncomfortable as a shard of broken glass in a glove.
'Thanks again for the washbag,' I tried.
Blankly, he explained. 'We had to find someone else. Quite quickly. We rang him today. We knew the guy, so – '
'A new rector – already? Can you say who he is yet?'
'Oh, he's a vicar in South London at the moment.' He said the name. 'He was very forceful on women priests. He's not Arabian, by the way.'
He breathed in, deeply.
'We're just moving a few extra things into the flat. He's single, so we want to fill some of the space Douglas's wife would have taken up. It's a good moment, anyway, for . . . '
The explanation curled on, like smoke from a fag-end. I did not listen: to listen was to die slowly.
'Good, good,' I heard myself saying.
Then Daniel stopped, and looked at me more keenly.
'What does that say about it?'
That?
He was pointing at my right arm.
What does my arm say about it?
I dropped my gaze. I was carrying a black plastic bag with odds and ends from the flat in it: a battery charger,

spare kitchen rolls, a one-cup water boiler, a Swiss pipe, an Elvis Presley cassette with mangled tape during the chorus of 'I'm Left, You're Right, She's Gone', a small chisel.

A haversack stuffed with shirts hung from my shoulder.

But Daniel was pointing elsewhere. 'Under your arm.' He added: 'The Bible, I mean. What does that say about this?'

I paused. Good grief. I was taking belongings out to the Datsun, on the way to meeting Gillian. It seemed so unfair to bring the Bible into it.

'Sorry, Mark. I suppose I was hoping you would have – '

Outside, an ice-cream van started playing a melody of ear-splitting pings and pongs, interrupting him.

Say nothing. He doesn't have to know.

The sun on my head made me feel like a minor saint.

I suddenly wanted to tell him. I wanted to say yes, I had woken in the night and felt the mist from God's breath – and when I had got up the next morning, expecting to write the whole thing off as trauma, it was still there.

I wanted to say that the Christ of Christianity was probably exactly the man he said he was, not just a nutter with a few good lines . . . a fact that made nearly everyone wrong about nearly everything.

There was even an answer to his question: a Bible paragraph I had found after speaking to Gillian, which had sucked in my eyes with a whoosh like the nozzle on a vacuum cleaner.

I had copied the verses on to the last piece of headed church paper in the flat. They spoke to me. That was all.

'Has anything spoken to you? That's all I mean.'

'Not – no, not really, Daniel.'

'It's – I know how you must be feeling, Mark.'

'Don't worry,' I said. There were huge walls between us.

'Gregory is going on a retreat.'

He made it sound military.
'Oh.'
'So – I don't know – but I just wondered if anything from the – ah –' and now he was pointing again – 'if anything from there had, you know, helped make sense of it.'
'Nothing, really.'
How many more times?
Daniel, too, was bound to see any explanation as a cynical attempt to cling to a cherished flat and salary. To say anything at all would be a disaster, I told myself.
'So do you see all this as totally senseless, Mark?'
'I suppose I feel like the two sides of the Grand Canyon have been moved together by someone using dynamite, and it was done on my head,' I told him. 'I'm leaving tomorrow.'
The ice-cream music stopped, abruptly.
'What about – well, saying goodbye to people?' Daniel's brow creased.
'Like who?'
'Well, ah –' I could see him struggling for the name of anyone who cared a fig. 'What about Vanessa?'
'She dropped me a nice line, and I wrote her a note.'
'Vicki? Her sister? You know her, don't you?'
'I suppose –'
'I'm sure she'd like to see you. I'm meeting her for lunch tomorrow, a late lunch, if you'd like to join –'
'Maybe I will,' I said. 'I'd like to see her.' It sounded right, somehow. Perhaps Daniel would leave early, and I could tell Vicki what had happened. I would use a few short, sharp sentences – the kind she liked. And she would take it in her stride, accept it unflinchingly, without seeing it all as a bid to stay vicar. Then, I guessed, she would mention that she had given up following New Thinking and started classes on Balkan history: 'But what was that,' she would add, 'about Christ being alive, and God loving me?'
And I would tell her – tell her it was nothing to do with

being good or kneeling. We would pray there at the restaurant table, and she would find out and be staggered.

'All right,' I said. 'I'll be there. Tomorrow. Lunch.'

Daniel turned and looked out to the road.

'Is that your car? On the corner? The yellow one?'

'The Datsun Cherry? Yes. I moved it so I could load up.'

'I'd be a bit careful, leaving it there like that.'

'Well, if anyone stole it, I'd be grateful. The whole wing section on the right side, under the bonnet, is – '

'I don't mean stealing. I mean clamps. Wardens.'

'Oh – thanks,' I said. 'I'll move it as soon as I can.'

I had forgotten the Datsun by the time I walked into the burger bar. Gillian was already there, and I was late.

'I'm sorry, Gillian. I was talking to Daniel.'

She got up instantly, walked over and touched my arm.

'Are you okay?'

'Yes,' I said. I had the urge to wail, and hug her. Now I could find no reason for the gap I had opened between us.

We sat down at a table.

'Gillian, I don't – '

'No, Mark. Don't say – don't say "don't" anything. I've just come over here to see you. That's all. Don't tell me you don't think it's a good idea, or I'll only be hurt, or any rubbish like that. Just order something.'

I chose chips, a bun, and a sliver of grilled chicken.

'How are you feeling?' she asked.

'I don't really know, Gilly.'

She reflected. 'I feel sick.'

'Why? You must have known something like this would – '

'It just seems so unfair, though. To you, Mark.'

'Is it, though?'

She shrugged. 'I suppose – I don't really know. I just – I don't want you to go. I don't care how stupid that sounds.'

'I don't know. You remember last night – the two of us in the alcove, you explaining it all to me, and me not getting any of it? That was supposed to be my profession.'

A feeling of desolation swept over me.

Is this how life will be, for ever? These dense, coded conversations? Can I not tell her I believe that God is love, because he showed me some of it? Can I not tell her that?

Gillian threw away her reply. 'I thought it was so important. But you said it made you feel like waste paper, and I was sorry afterwards that I said everything I said.'

'Don't be.'

'But I went into some sort of overdrive. I like you for you, Mark. I didn't want you to feel there were only a few minutes left, or something.'

'There's lots left.' I wondered what on earth I was talking about.

'I think I love you, Mark,' Gillian said.

Far more shocking than being sacked, the observation came totally without warning. Nothing in anything Gillian had ever said had suggested it. My teeth froze on the warm bun.

'I do,' she added.

I looked down at the table, then up. I put down the bun, a chunk of it still clamped between my jaws.

I swallowed. 'I didn't know that,' I said.

Then we looked at each other. Now it was her turn to avert eyes. She picked up a glass of juice, flicked a black curl off her forehead, and raised the drink to her mouth.

'Shall we go for a walk?' She put the glass down in a definite movement. 'Otherwise the smoke from the grill over there is going to make us both smell like quarterpounders.'

'With cheese,' I added, nervously.

On the mile of common at the back of the close, I praised early Presley, talked about the spring weather, and complained that accountancy had been unfairly maligned.

'It's the attraction of columns, you see – of a whole life

there, from top to bottom – and of a total – of totalling everything to the nearest decimal –'

I fell silent. I was not sure what I was saying made sense any longer. Besides, as I had spoken the words, Gillian's hand had found mine and wrapped around it.

The breeze picked up, then dropped again. It was going to be a still, mild evening.

'Gillian – is this – are we being wise, do you think?'

'I'm really sorry for the way I treated you, Mark.'

'You interrupted me. I was going to go on and mention solar-powered calculators and the audit gross box.'

We both laughed. It was my first successful joke.

'I don't want you to go.'

'I don't want to go away from you, Gillian. I've watched you for so long, you know, and then I fell in love with you when I met you, even more deeply. For ages I didn't think about anyone but you.'

'Why didn't you just tell me?'

'Gilly – don't you remember?'

I smiled . . . but the smile must have faded quickly, because she asked what was wrong.

'I'm not sure if anything is,' I said. 'I just had a memory of something – except I don't know what it was.'

'Well, you've had an awful day.' Her gentle, Irish voice somehow masked the naïvety of the understatement. 'I do love you, Mark. And for me – this, here – being with you – like this – it's a kind of heaven.'

As if at a private joke, I chuckled. 'Oh, Gilly – for a moment, if you can, forget heaven,' I said. 'Just kiss me.'

I had not meant it seriously. But on the gravel path, under cotton wool clouds, we faced each other without words.

There seemed to be very little more that anyone could say. In my heart was a warm, well-kept secret about the salvation of the entire world. In my hand was Gillian's, from knuckles to fingertips. We looked into each other's eyes. There was no shame.

Then, for the first time in my life, I bent towards a woman.

Her eyes slid softly shut.

The breeze brushed her cheeks.

Cluelessly, I shut my eyes ... and then realised I could not see, and opened them again. I was fearful of missing her lips with mine. I moved my head towards her face, stooping, and found them.

Our mouths touched, and then pressed hard on each other. We were kissing, and she was definitely permitting it. There was the sound of fabric scraping in stone as Gillian twisted her toes in the gravel, moving closer towards me. I opened my eyes, saw her cheeks slanting away from mine, her eyes closed, mascara in close-up. She put an arm gently around my back, clasping me tightly with it. I rested one of my arms along the line of her hip in a neutral action, afraid she might ask me to remove it.

Then I put another arm around Gillian, and she put another arm around me.

I thought of the scarlet lip gloss now being pressed against my lips – doubtless coming off on them. The thought induced a wave of the most pungent, sizzling fondness for her. We kissed, and I heard her breathe in slowly through her nose. There was a tiny click in her throat. The movement of her lips on mine brought back a flood of memories, all flashes, of moments when I had not been able even to think of telling her what was in my heart. Closing my eyes again, I felt the breeze on both our faces, soldering our cheeks at the thin line where they met. We kissed for what seemed like the length of a dull sermon, her shoes scratching in the gravel as she adjusted her position against me.

We were not interrupted. After a while, we simply moved apart, opening a corridor of cool air. I could not even recall who had stopped first. Gillian's right hand was flattened on the outside breast pocket of my jacket, and as she moved back she lengthened her arm as if she wanted to keep the hand pressed there. She nipped the centre of her bottom lip with her front teeth. Glancing away from her self-consciously, I saw the sun had tumbled in the sky and decked the high-built clouds with pennants of pink and orange.

In the twinkle of an eye, at the sound of the trumpet, we shall all be changed.

'What are you thinking?' Gillian asked.

'Too much,' I said. 'I think I think about too much.'

'Just then, I mean.' So soft, her voice might have been used to stuff pillowcases. 'Your face went dark.'

'I really don't know, Gilly. Change, I suppose. I just get too wound up with things. A verse from – I don't even know where – has been rattling around in my head for ages. About eyes and trumpets. Looking into yours made me think of it.' My voice was cracking slightly, and I cleared my throat. 'But I know one thing for sure. I'm so happy to be here with you.'

I wanted to tell her I loved her, as she had told me . . . and as I had told myself so many times before. But, for no reason I could understand, I was not able to. I wondered how much she noticed or minded.

'This is so strange,' she said.

'You know, Gilly, so much of what has happened here has been strange. I've narrowed it down – I now know that either London is strange, or I am.'

She chuckled.

'Brinny told me not to get involved,' said Gillian.

'Why not?'

'With you. She said you were confused.'

'I'm not,' I said. Her hand found mine again, and we turned back towards the church. 'At least, I don't think so.'

Now we were laughing together.

'You know, Mark, it's brilliant that you see a bright side to what's happened. I don't know if I could – I think it's what I like about you.'

'I think I've got a future.'

'You have.'

'There are worse things than being sacked, especially from there.' I was suddenly feeling buoyant – a king. I gestured majestically at a distant pyramid of church roof.

'Don't you feel, Mark – don't you feel worried about what'll happen next? In your career, I mean.'

The two of us were walking back towards the close: a couple, if anyone had to guess.

'I don't know what I feel. I saw a magazine recently where a woman who was head of something – I'm not sure exactly what it was, but I think it was a shoe business – she said in an interview there was no way anyone could know what they wanted to do in life until they were twenty-nine.'

'I like that.'

'She was in charge of something.'

'I think I like her.'

'And at least I know why I was asked to leave Saint Peter's. It's not as though someone sent me a black spot, or something.'

'But why don't you put in an appeal against it?'

'To who, though?'

She hesitated. 'The Queen?'

In the road ahead of us, a car backfired. I thought of assassinations. Whatever murmured answer I gave to Gillian's suggestion was drowned out by the beating of wings, as a score of birds fled the branches above us.

We were nearly at the overgrown path leading back to the road, when Gillian asked: 'Do you think it's possible to get something for nothing?'

'What do you mean?'

'I just wondered. I used to believe life was full of free things. The better the prize, the more free it was.'

I thought of Straithe, suddenly: of the television detector van, of the suppressed mirth of the inspectors, young lads, who found my crumpled licence, long expired . . .

of the local newspaper article which had cut my stomach from me in a few bald lines of print.

'It's probably dangerous to think you can,' I said.

'Can what?'

'Get things free. You always get found out, and then you have to pay.'

'Always, do you think?'

A fleck of something blew into my eye. Blinking it out, I caught the silhouette of a cross: Christ hanging there, the sky aglow behind him, listening for the answer.

'Someone has to,' I said.

'Because I was just thinking, Mark – about us – and that, you know – for us to see more of each other – would – I don't know, I suppose it would need a sacrifice.'

'Yes.'

'Do we feel enough to make it, do you think?'

'We don't know what the sacrifice would be, Gilly. If I moved away –'

'Are you going to?'

She had raised her voice because we were on Clemence Road and cars were passing us now, but it sounded as though she had raised it in panic. We came to a halt on the pavement, and I turned to her.

'Where are you heading?'

'Oh, Mark – I don't know – I just don't want –'

'Listen – we can carry on talking in my flat,' I said. 'Don't worry. I'll give you the keys. Hold on.'

I fished inside my trouser pocket, and found them in the folds of a handkerchief.

'Here.'

I prayed: *God, forgive my stupid silence.*

'Why are you giving me these?' she asked.

'I've got to run over and move the car. I forgot to do it – I was so excited about seeing you. It's in a bad place. You go on up.'

The yellow Datsun came into view at that moment, parked on a corner of pavement, radiator grill pointing at the church steps from the other side of the road.

'Are you sure?' she said.

'We can't leave it all like this, Gillian,' I told her.

That's better, I told myself. *Take charge.*

'Have you got any more to pack?'

'I think it's nearly all in the car.'

'So – you're – you're really going, Mark.'

'Gilly – I don't – I don't know for sure what's happening. You head on upstairs and we can talk about it all night, if you want.'

And then I blushed, correcting myself: 'All through the early part of the evening, I mean.'

'Don't be too long.'

'No. I promise I won't.'

She went into the church through the side door which opened on to the foot of the concrete staircase. I looked left and right, and crossed the busy road.

Reaching the passenger side of the car, I felt in my pocket for the keys . . . and realised, in the instant my hand touched the handkerchief for the second time in as many minutes, that I no longer had them.

'Oh, no.' I was exasperated.

I wondered if the driver's door might have been left unlocked, and walked around the rear of the car to find out.

It was then that I saw the triangle of yellow on the back wheel, matching the bodywork of the Datsun almost perfectly: the yellow triangle that was a plate, rivets, curled rods, bolts and a padlock.

The car had been clamped.

'I don't believe it,' I said aloud.

I sensed the amused glances of the pedestrians passing behind me as I straightened up, hands on hips, moving my stare from the clamp to the church. It was now in shadow. I directed my gaze first at the steps and the open Coppers, and into the darkened lobby: and then, wondering if Gillian might have reached the flat and could telephone for help from it, raised my eyes.

Is she there?

If not, I would have to follow her up the stairs and use the telephone myself.

As though panning a camera, I swept my gaze slowly away from the big dome, over the vast front of the building and up towards the flat. Up, past the small windows in the towering curved column of wall around the spiral staircase, up and up, towards the giant, sloping, football-pitch-sized brown roof that had been my first sight of the place . . . moving my eyes right, then, into the hulk of main wall high above the road, making out the window of BBF's flat by the stripe of the curtains, one floor above the window of mine.

But then, rather than lowering my gaze to the flat underneath, I raised it . . . to the sky.

– 39 –

Gillian found the flat as barren as a prison cell.

Looking down on the street from the lounge window did not occur to her. Instead, she scanned the empty shelves and floor as if searching for a clue to something ages old.

A sheet of headed church notepaper, askew on the desk, caught her eye. Gillian walked across the room, and read it. 'They surrounded me on every side, But in the name of the Lord I cut them off.'

A quizzical look passed over her brow. She lifted the piece of paper from the desk.

> I will not die but live,
> And proclaim what the Lord has done.
> He has chastened me severely,
> But he has not given me over to death.

The verses echoed somewhere. They might have been from the middle of the Bible: maybe from a Psalm. Or an ancient prophet, perhaps.

The handwriting was easier to identify – and the author was obvious, anyway. She was standing in his flat.

And then Gillian Mitchell shut her eyes, thinking of the moment another mouth had been laid on hers, and feeling the same cool breeze play in her fringe . . . this time, a draught through six inches of open lounge window. From the road below, there was a sound amid the traffic: some squealing of tyres, a distant shout. Gillian paid no attention. Slowly the long-furrowed frown vanished. The thin crescents around her mouth thickened by a hair's breadth, and a most private of smiles dithered on her lips. She opened her mouth and filled her lungs with air, as if trying to capture the moment in a single breath. Wholly relaxed, Gillian walked over to the window to close it.

As she leant forwards to pull at the window, she glanced down at the street and gasped. She pressed her face to the pane.

Her short breaths became clouds on the glass. Panting, moving her head, she tried to make out the shapes below.

'No, no – '

Gillian yanked at the window, pulling it wide open with a bang. She put her foot on the sofa and jumped up, leaning out, shouting at the top of her voice: 'Mark! Mark! Mark!'

The answer was a siren, coming down the road.

'Mark! Mark!' Gillian shouted. 'Mark Empringham!'

Below her, a brown car was slewed across the pavement. It looked as though its bonnet had been welded to the bonnet of the Datsun, which was pushed back over the kerb as though to make way for the growing crowd of people in front of it.

The door of the flat crashed back into a shelf as Gillian threw it open and rushed through.

She flew down the staircase.

Outside the church, Gillian put a hand to her head, and wavered.

An ambulance jerked its way towards the scene. Its siren was sounding in bursts as it weaved in and out of the traffic.

She ran across to the central reservation.

'Who is he?' someone asked. A car horn sounded.

Gillian heard herself repeat the question. She could not see further than a line of backs.

Next to her, someone was whispering – 'I think he's alive, but I'm not sure.'

The furthest of two elderly women in hats replied: 'Never. He went about fifteen feet through the air. Fifteen! It was horrific.'

Her friend said: 'You didn't see it. It was worse. He was on the pavement, looking up – and then this brown thing came round the corner, and did a sort of squiggle into him.'

There was a shout from the other side of the crowd.

'Move away from him! Come on! You're preventing the emergency services getting through! This is a blackspot!'

The siren wailed again.

Then there was a great deal of movement. The ambulance lurched up, a van at the head of the jam rolled forwards, the wedge of people huddled in front of Gillian split to let it through – and she saw.

A man lay on the tarmac, one arm thrown out to his side.

'Mark,' she said, and ran forward.

A second car, also trying to squeeze between the accident and the throng around it, screeched to a halt.

'You idiot!' the driver shouted.

In a second, a policeman had Gillian by the wrist.

'You stupid idiot!' the car driver shouted again.

'Madam – come on – '

'Please let me through. I have to go through.'

Her eye caught the policeman's, and he understood.

'Do you know him, madam? All right – follow me.'

'I've got to see him.'

'Just a minute. The lads over here have to go to work.'

The ambulance door slammed. Its crew were suddenly all over the figure. A sheet went up on twig-thick metal struts; a red case rattled on to the paving stones; a driver ordered people out of the way. Some seemed suddenly ashamed.

The policeman held Gillian's arm with a grip that meant she had to wait. In an instant, other officers had arrived. One marched straight to a young-looking man with a peculiar, high-stacked hairstyle, standing shakily against the wall of a building. Snatches of the conversation drifted over.

'Is this your licence? American?'

'Yes.'
'Issued in – what, Huntsville? Is that what it says?'
'Yes.'
'Where's that, sir? West coast? Surfing area, is it?'
'Alabama.'
'So what happened here?'
'I just don't know, I think I –'
'Lee Tubbs? Is that your name? Is that what this means?'
'Just Tubbs.'
'Just Tubbs? What's that – short for Justin, is it? So why is Lee typed down here, sir, if you don't mind me asking?'
'That's the full name.'
'So why does it say Walt as well then, Mr Lee?'
'That's my first name. Walt Lee Tubbs is the full name.'
'Was he in the car when you hit it, Mr Tubb? Was he in it? What was he doing – was he pulling out?'
'I – can't – I don't –'
'Where were you heading?'
'Towards the church – right there.'
'Do you know how to steer an English car, Mr Tubb?'
Hearing the words but not taking them in, Gillian stood, staring. An ambulanceman pulled tubing from an oxygen mask in a flurry of hands, and pressed it on to the white face.
'Don't worry,' the policeman said, into her ear.
But Gillian had noticed that the front of the bonnet of the brown car was spattered with blood.
'Is he –'
Out of the corner of her eye, she saw the policeman's face turn towards hers.
'They're doing everything for him, madam. Absolutely everything,' he said. 'Just wait a few minutes. Be patient.'
But she suddenly cried out – and, in the moment that his fingers loosened in shock at the noise, Gillian pulled away from the policeman and rushed forward, skidding to a halt beside one of the ambulance crew.

'We're going to have to get him out of here,' he was saying. 'He's only wheezing it in. If we hadn't seen it, I don't think anyone could have – '

'He took a hell of a knock,' his colleague said. 'The front of the thing tipped when it hit the kerb, so – '

'Mark, Mark,' Gillian cried.

The policeman walked up behind her. Unsure of what to do, he stopped in his tracks.

Close enough to see the pores, Gillian placed a hand on the cheek. She was astonished at its coldness.

'He's in shock,' someone said quickly. 'He's grey. You do that. You carry on. Just talk to him.'

'Mark – Mark, I love you – I love you – please don't go away from me.'

The eyes were closed.

'Internal injuries,' someone said.

A woman put her head on the chest, and frowned.

'It's weak.'

'Please – ' an ambulanceman began, touching the woman's shoulder. 'We've got proper equipment to do that.' She stood up, and moved back to the edge of the crowd.

Too grim even to go on crying, Gillian heard the tin chiming of metal stretcher tubes slid from the back of the ambulance. Moving her hand to the other cheek, she lowered her face . . . and pressed it again on the skin that had touched hers only an hour before, placing her lips on the pale ear.

'Mark, Mark – darling Mark,' she whispered into it. 'Mark – I was up in your flat, and I saw the piece of paper. Don't you remember, my dear, dear acting vicar?'

Gillian reached down to take hold of a hand, and found it wet with blood. She squeezed it.

'Mark – the thing you wrote – you must remember. Go on, tell me you remember, my dearest.' No one could hear what she was whispering. The crowd had grown bigger again, and a gloomy silence had descended on it.

Tears welled in her eyes, and dropped on to the pavement.

And now they were getting the stretcher ready. After a moment threading toggles through eyes in metal poles, the ambulancemen kneeled down, two feet from Gillian.

'Slide it,' one said.

Another caught his finger on something, and swore.

Pressing her face harder against the cold cheek, Gillian whispered: 'Mark – my darling, darling, darling. Don't go, my love. Come on, remember, what did it say? "I will not die." Mark – my great, great friend – my best friend – "I will not die, I'll live" – oh, Mark – remember, Mark – it's me, Gillian, Gilly, you remember me – please, don't go – don't go, Mark, don't leave me here on my own –'

Then, just as the men had the stretcher under the body, Gillian felt movement in the limp fingers she was clasping.

'Oh, Mark –'

Her hand was suddenly squeezed by the bloodied hand it was holding. For a moment she was not holding anything, but being held; Gillian gasped, and looked up and around her, but as she began to form words, the stretcher was loaded with a shunt and a shout and a push, and then one of the drivers called for the ambulance to be started quickly.

'Let me come with you,' she said.

'We can't, young lady, we –'

'Please, let me sit at his side – please –'

'Are you a relative? Wife?'

'No, I –'

'Fiancée?'

'I – no – I –'

The motor roared to life. Suddenly, Gillian's arm was clamped again by the policeman: 'Wait here for a second, my dear, and we'll go behind the ambulance in the patrol car.'

There were a lot of policemen now. Three or four were

talking to the driver of the brown car; several more were guiding the traffic past in slow columns.

The heavy stretcher was lifted on to a trolley in the back of the ambulance, and Gillian could not help calling: 'Please! Please let me come! He squeezed my hand!'

No one heard her, but the ambulance driver must have caught her eye and guessed what she had shouted, for he called back through the cabin window: 'It's a five-minute run, love. Only five minutes. Casualty wing. He knows where.' He pointed at the policeman. 'We need space in the back.'

The ambulance span round with a screech, and instantly the traffic was thrown into chaos: cars bounced up on to the kerb, or swerved over the centre lines to let it through. Stunned, Gillian watched the rapid progress of the vehicle as it shunted everything else off the road, racing for its destination, sirens howling wildly.

But then, a hundred yards away and still locked in dense traffic, the distant white shape seemed to lose all urgency. The driver appeared to be making no further efforts to overtake; the siren suddenly died; the spinning blue light on the roof slowed, and then stopped rotating altogether.

The ambulance crawled up to a long queue at a set of lights along with everything else, and Gillian took one easy guess at what had happened inside it.

– 40 –

Vanessa picked up the telephone after one ring.

'Hello? Is that the curate's flat?' a voice asked.

'Yes,' she said. 'Though I'm not the curate.'

The male voice coming out of the earpiece was strangely familiar to her.

'Who is that?' it asked.

'This is Vanessa Spicer. The head of youth work.'

'Ah – Vanessa – ' A touch of nervousness seemed to creep into the voice at the other end. 'This is – um – Brendan.'

Vanessa felt slightly out of breath on hearing the name, and fought to control her voice. 'Oh. Brendan – how are you?'

'Fine, thank you. How about you?'

'I'm all right, thanks. I'm still – well, as you can tell, I'm still doing what I was doing when you were here.'

'How about your health?'

'Good, at the moment.'

'You've moved flats.'

'Yes,' she said. And then she added: 'How did you know?'

'I've got a note from – I think it's your current curate,' he said. 'It's signed "Mark Empringham", and it gave this flat as his address. So I asked to be put through. Was that still old Morag on the switchboard?'

'Probably.'

'She didn't recognise me. The card says to ring this flat, that's all. Here, I've got it in my hand. It says – oh, I don't know, that he's been trying to get in touch, and hasn't ever managed it. It seems to have got to me via about a dozen different addresses. It was sent ages ago.'

'I'm afraid you won't be able to get hold of Mark.'

'Well – could you give him a message? I've been moving around a lot since I left Saint Peter's, so if you could tell him I'm now in London, in Docklands, quite near the –'

'I won't be seeing him, actually.'

'Oh? Is he –'

'Not here, Brendan. That's right.'

'But he was there?'

'Yes – yes, of course, he was here – he used to be in this flat, actually – until two months ago –'

'But he's not there now?'

'He's – he's gone now, Brendan.'

There was a pause.

'Gone?'

'Gone for good.'

'For good?'

And then Vanessa told him about the accident.

Finally, she said: 'It was terrible.'

'It sounds it,' he agreed. 'It sounds awful.'

'The whole business – of this car just knocking him down where he stood on the pavement –'

The line went quiet. There was a low-pitched whistle from the other end, but nothing else for several seconds.

Then Brendan said: 'But he's all right now, you say?'

'I gather he's very well indeed – I heard that from, oh, I can't remember who –'

'It sounds like he was lucky.'

'Blessed, Brendan.'

'But I mean – when you've got someone critically ill in the back of an ambulance, and then all the electrics go and the thing breaks down on the way to hospital –'

'You wouldn't call that lucky.'

'No – I suppose not,' he agreed. 'Blessed, then.'

'What nearly killed him was a rib breaking and going into his stomach. He was out cold because of the pain. But once they'd fixed it, he was all right. It took him a while to get better, though. He had a lot of bruising and cuts.'

'What – gosh, I don't even know what to ask.'

'Yes, it was terrible for all of us, seeing him go.'

'A rising star, cut short.'

'He hasn't worked in the church since then.'

'You don't know what he might have been writing to me about, do you, Vanessa?'

'I – no – no, I don't.'

'Sure?'

'I don't think so.' She hesitated, and then added: 'I think he wanted to get some tips about taking a job here.'

Brendan Madill laughed, grimly.

'I could have given him a tip not to,' he said. 'Since I left the church – and I really have left – I've begun to see that most of what goes on in them is complete and utter – '

Whatever he was saying was overwhelmed by a moment of heavy crackling on the line.

' – and I see you haven't even managed to fix that rotten telephone exchange yet,' he added.

'No, not yet. But don't be so fierce with me, Brendan. You sounded so much calmer a minute ago.'

'I'm sorry,' he said. 'It just infuriates me, that's all. You can't even organise a miracle with a switchboard. How's your sister?'

'She's – well, you won't like this,' Vanessa began. 'She was – it's a funny thing, really, but she was very attached to Mark Empringham.'

'Really?'

'She's started coming to church, actually – ever since his last sermon here.'

'So you wave to her in the front row, do you?'

'A different church.'

'Ah.'

Vanessa glanced out of the window. The sky was grey.

'So what are you doing now, Brendan? Now that you've left the Church of England?'

'I've retrained,' Brendan Madill replied. 'I'm now doing something that helps society. In fact, my office is about six or seven miles south-east of where you are now.'

'I never knew,' said Vanessa. 'What are you up to?'

'I suppose you'll have a theological problem with it. As it happens, I'm a tax inspector with the Inland Revenue.'

Quietly, Vanessa ground her teeth. 'Really?'

'Yes. Really.'

'That's a bit of a coincidence. Because Mark's – I think this is right – he's doing something along the same lines.'

'Accountancy?'

'Some sort of book-keeping, for a charity of some kind.'

'What sort – do you know?' Brendan asked.

'Missionaries, I think.'

'Really?' Something had crept into his voice.

'I'm not sure.'

'Missionaries, though?'

'Inner-city ones. Nothing Continental, I don't think.'

There was a silence at the other end.

'Yes,' Vanessa went on, 'the girl he's just got engaged to – he's engaged, I forgot to mention – she works in a supermarket, I think, quite high up – poultry – so she'll do most of the breadwinning for both of them.'

'Poultry-winning, you mean.' Brendan added: 'That's nice.' Then his voice changed a gear. 'And you don't know why Mr Empringham would have written?'

'I don't,' Vanessa said. 'He was someone who – he kept a lot to himself. He doesn't come back here to visit, either.'

'It seems strange – writing to ask about working there, when I'd left ages ago. Why couldn't he ask any of you?'

'As I say, I don't know. He should have done.'

'Yes, he should.'

There was a peal of summer thunder outside, and the skies began to spit, flecking the windowpane in places.

Vanessa watched as the view through the window blurred.

Then the spitting turned to downpour, and, as rain spread across the glass, she saw the front of the huge Marple & Schwartz building on the other side of the road drain of all detail, and become a simple slab in white stone.